# Reviews for Denise Hunter's Past Novels

". . . a romantic adventure about unconditional love and forgiveness."
—*Library Journal* review of *Surrender Bay*

"Hunter's characters are well drawn and familiar. [W]ill appeal to all women readers with the taste for a good love story."
—*Foreword* magazine review of *Surrender Bay*

"[In *Surrender Bay*], Denise has turned the spotlight on the depth of God's love for His children in a story that will remain with you long after the last page is read."

—RelzReviewz

"No one can write a story that grips the heart like Denise Hunter. If you like Karen Kingsbury or Nicholas Sparks, this is an author you'll love."

—Colleen Coble, author of *Abomination* and *Anathema*

"In *Finding Faith* Denise Hunter once again brings me to tears with her thought-provoking story. For depth and emotion, this author always hits her mark."

—Kristin Billerbeck, author of *Split Ends*

"*Saving Grace* kept me turning pages from the minute I opened the cover and kept me up way past my bedtime . . . A story of triumph over heartache."

—Deborah Raney, author of *A Nest of Sparrows*

"You absolutely have to read *Mending Places . . .*"

—*Dancing Word*

"[*Finding Faith*] kept me in tears as the characters struggled to find truth. A captivating story that will touch every woman's heart."

—Diann Mills, Writing Coach and author of sixteen books

**Other novels by Denise Hunter include**

*Sweetwater Gap*

*Surrender Bay*

*Finding Faith*

*Saving Grace*

*Mending Places*

# The Convenient Groom

Denise Hunter

**THOMAS NELSON**
*Since 1798*

NASHVILLE   DALLAS   MEXICO CITY   RIO DE JANEIRO   BEIJING

Published in Nashville, Tennessee, by Thomas Nelson. Thomas Nelson is a registered trademark of Thomas Nelson, Inc.

Thomas Nelson, Inc. titles may be purchased in bulk for educational, business, fund-raising, or sales promotional use. For information, please e-mail SpecialMarkets@ThomasNelson.com.

Scripture taken from the HOLY BIBLE, NEW INTERNATIONAL VERSION®. © 1973, 1978, 1984 International Bible Society. Used by permission of Zondervan. All rights reserved.

Publisher's Note: This novel is a work of fiction. Names, characters, places and incidents are either products of the author's imagination or used fictitiously. All characters are fictional, and any similarity to people living or dead is purely coincidental.

**Library of Congress Cataloging-in-Publication Data**

Hunter, Denise, 1968–
    The convenient groom / by Denise Hunter.
      p. cm.
    ISBN 978-1-59554-258-8
      1. Women authors—Fiction. 2. Marriage counselors—Fiction . 3. Radio personalities—Fiction.
    4. Advice columnists—Fiction. 5. Weddings—Fiction. 6. Temporary marriage—Fiction.
    7. Nantucket Island (Mass.)—Fiction. I. Title.
    PS3608.U5925C66 2008
    813'.6—dc22

                2008003380

*Printed in the United States of America*
09 10 11 12 RRD 12 11 10 9 8 7

For Jesus, my tower of strength,
my shelter in the storm

*Dear friend,*

I'm so glad you chose to embark on this journey to Nantucket. I hope you'll enjoy your brief visit to the quaint New England island and the characters who inhabit this story.

While this series was still in its conception stage, God laid a very meaningful scripture on my heart: Zephaniah 3:17.

> *The Lord your God is with you,*
> *he is mighty to save.*
> *He will take great delight in you,*
> *he will quiet you with his love,*
> *he will rejoice over you with singing.*

As I breathed in the comfort and peace the verse offers, I couldn't help but notice that these characteristics of God's are some of the qualities a woman looks for in a man. As that thought jelled, it struck me that a love story between a man and a woman could be a beautiful allegory, showing the depths of God's love. At that moment, this series was born.

One of the things I love about Jesus' parables is the way those stories, subtle as they are, allow us to see a familiar truth with fresh perspective. My goal with this series is to show aspects of God's character through the relationship of the hero and heroine and to trust you, the reader, to make those connections yourself.

Zephaniah 3:17 is so rich I decided to break up the verse and show one characteristic of God in each book. *The Convenient Groom* takes the second line: *He is mighty to save.* What if you had a God that would push through all obstacles for you, his beloved? This story plays out that theme through the characters of Kate and Lucas.

After you've read the story, I hope you'll take the time to read through the discussion questions as a way of digging a little deeper into the story's layers. Most of all, I hope this simple love story will enable you to see Christ's love in a new and exciting way.

Yours in Christ,
Denise

*"The LORD your God is with you,*
*he is mighty to save.*
*He will take great delight in you,*
*he will quiet you with his love,*
*he will rejoice over you with singing."*

Zephaniah 3:17

*Let your face shine on your servant;*
*save me in your unfailing love.*

Psalm 31:16

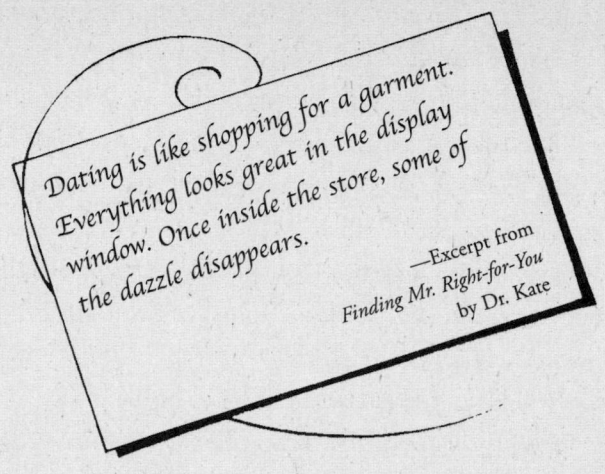

*Dating is like shopping for a garment. Everything looks great in the display window. Once inside the store, some of the dazzle disappears.*

—Excerpt from
*Finding Mr. Right-for-You*
by Dr. Kate

# Chapter One

The red light on Kate Lawrence's cell phone blinked a staccato warning. But before she could retrieve the message, her maid of honor, Anna Doherty, waved her pale arms from the beach, stealing her attention.

Anna's smooth voice sounded in her headset. "Kate, can you come here? We've got a few glitches."

"Be right there." Kate tucked her clipboard in the crook of her elbow, took the steps down Jetty Pavilion's porch, and crossed the heel-sinking sand of the Nantucket shoreline. In six hours, thirty-four guests would be seated there in the rows of white chairs, watching Kate pledge her life to Bryan Montgomery under a beautiful hand-carved gazebo.

Where was the gazebo anyway? She checked her watch, then

glanced toward the Pavilion, where workers scurried in white uniforms. No sign of Lucas.

She approached Anna, who wore worry lines as naturally as she wore her Anne Klein pantsuit. Anna was the best receptionist Kate could ask for. Her capable presence reassured the troubled couples she ushered through Kate's office.

Right now, Anna's long brown hair whipped across her face like a flag gone awry, and she batted it from her eyes with her freckled hand. "Soiree's just called. Their delivery truck is in for service, and the flowers will be a little late. Half an hour at the most."

Kate jotted the note on her schedule. "That's okay." She'd factored in cushion time.

"Murray's called, and the tuxes haven't been picked up except for your dad's."

Bryan and his best man had been due at Murray's at nine thirty. An hour ago. "I'll check on that. What else?"

Anna's frown lines deepened, and her eyes blinked against the wind. "The carriage driver is sick, but they're trying to find a replacement. The Weatherbys called and asked if they could attend last minute—they were supposed to go out of town, but their plans changed."

Kate nodded. "Fine, fine. Call and tell her they're welcome. I'll notify the caterer."

"Your publicist—Pam?—has been trying to reach you. Did you check your cell? She said she got voice mail. Anyway, your book copies did arrive this morning. She dropped this off." Anna pulled a hardback book from under her clipboard. "Ta-da!"

"My book!" Kate stared at the cover, where the title, *Finding Mr. Right-for-You*, floated above a cartoon couple. The man was on his knee, proposing. Below them, a colorful box housed the bold letters of Kate's name. She ran her fingers over the glossy book jacket, feeling the raised bumps of the letters, savoring the moment.

"Pam wants a quick photo shoot before the guests arrive. You holding the book, that kind of thing. You should probably call her."

Kate jotted the note. While it was on her mind, she reached down and turned on her cell.

"Ready for more great news?" Anna asked. Her blue eyes glittered like diamonds. The news had to be good.

"What?"

"The *New York Times* is sending a reporter and a photographer. They want to do a feature story on your wedding and your book."

Fresh air caught and held in Kate's lungs. Rosewood Press was probably turning cartwheels. "That's fabulous. They'll want an interview." She scanned her schedule, looking for an open slot. After the reception? She hated to do it, but Bryan would understand. The *New York Times*. It would give Kate's initial sales the boost it needed. Maybe enough to make the bestseller list.

"Here's the number." Anna handed her a yellow Post-It. "That tabloid guy has been hanging around all morning, trying to figure out who the groom is. I told him he'd find out in six hours like everyone else. The rest of the media is scheduled to arrive an hour before the wedding, and Pam's having an area set up over there for them." Anna gestured behind the rows of chairs to a square blocked off with white ribbon.

"Good. I want them to be as inconspicuous as possible. This is my wedding, and a girl only gets married once, after all."

"One would hope." Anna said. "Is there anything else I can do?"

Kate gave her a sideways hug, as close to an embrace as she'd ever given her assistant, her fingers pressing into Anna's fleshy shoulder. "You're a godsend. I don't know what I'd do without you."

"Oh! I know what I forgot to tell you. The gazebo. It should have been here by now. I tried to call Lucas, but I got the machine, and I don't have his cell number."

"His shop's closed today, and he doesn't have a cell." The man didn't wear a watch, much less carry a phone. She should've known better than to put something this crucial in his hands. Kate checked her watch. "I'll run over and check on it."

The drive to town was quick and effortless, but Kate's mind swam with a hundred details. She jotted reminders on her clipboard when she stopped for pedestrians, occasionally admiring the cover of her book. She called Pam for a quick recap about the *New York Times* reporter, and by the time she hung up, she was pulling into a parallel slot on Main Street, in front of Lucas's storefront.

The sign above the picture window read "Cottage House Furniture." On the second floor of the Shaker building, the wooden shingle for her own business dangled from a metal pole: "Kate Lawrence, Marriage Counseling Services." She needed to remind Lucas to remove it; otherwise he'd leave it hanging for another year or until someone else rented the space.

Kate exited her car and slid her key into the rusty lock of the shop's door. Once inside, she passed the stairs leading to her office and walked through the darkened maze of furniture to the back, where she hoped to find Lucas. She bumped an end table with her shin. *Ow!* That would leave a mark.

The high-pitched buzz of a power tool pierced the darkness, a good sign. "Lucas?" She rapped loudly on the metal door with her knuckles. The noise stopped.

"Come in."

She opened the door. Lucas Wright looked up from his spot on the cement floor at the base of the gazebo, his too-long hair hanging over one eye. He looked her over, then turned back to the spindle and ran his thick hand over it as if testing the curves.

"Aren't you supposed to be at the beach?" he asked.

Kate crossed her arms. "I could ask you the same thing."

He stood, agile for his size, and backed away from the gazebo. Sawdust from the floor clung to his faded jeans and black T-shirt. "I was just finishing."

"You were supposed to be there an hour ago. The gazebo needs to be put in place before the sound system, and the florist has to decorate it, and there are people waiting to do their jobs."

He faced her, looking into her in that way of his that made her feel like he could see clean through her. "Today's the big day, huh?" Putting his tool on his workhorse, he dusted off his hands, moving in slow motion as though he'd decided tonight wouldn't arrive until next week.

Kate checked her watch. "Do you think you can get this down to the beach sometime today?"

Walking around the piece, he studied it, hands on his hips, head cocked. "You like it?"

For the first time since the week before, Kate looked at the gazebo—the white lattice top, the hand-carved spindles, the gentle arch of the entry. At the top of the arch, a piece of wood curved gracefully, etched with clusters of daisies. The gazebo's simple lines were characteristic of Lucas's work, but she'd never known him to use such exquisite detail. The piece had an elegance that surpassed her expectations. He did beautiful work; she'd give him that.

"I do. I love the etching." She sighed. Just when he irritated the snot out of her, he did something like this, caught her off guard. She always felt like she was tripping down the stairs when she was with him.

*Focus!* "It needs to find its way to the beach. Pronto."

"Yes ma'am." His salute was unhurried.

Before she could offer a retort, her cell phone pealed and buzzed simultaneously, and she pulled it from her capri pocket.

"Hello?"

"Kate?"

"Bryan." Turning away from Lucas and toward the door, she eyed a crude desk with a metal folding chair that bore countless rusty scratches. "Good morning." A smile crept into her voice. It was their wedding day. The day they'd planned for nearly two years. "Did you sleep well?" She hadn't. She'd rumpled the sheets until nearly two o'clock, but that was to be expected.

The silence on the other end, however, was not. "Bryan?" Had she lost the signal?

"Um, Kate, did you get my message?"

There'd been a blinking red light this morning. She'd assumed it was Pam's voice mail and hadn't checked. Suddenly, she wished she had.

"No. What's wrong?"

"Are you sitting down?"

"No, I'm not sitting down. Just tell me." An ugly dread snaked down her spine and settled there, coiled and waiting.

"I'm on my way back to Boston," he said. "I left a message this morning. You must've had your phone off."

Kate's stomach stirred. She stared at the wall in front of her—a pegboard with a zillion holes, metal prongs poking from it, tools and cords everywhere. "What happened?" Some emergency, maybe?

*What emergency could trump our wedding?*

"I can't marry you, Kate."

The words dropped, each one crumbling under its own weight. The stirring in her stomach intensified. "That's not funny, Bryan." It was a terrible joke. He'd never been good with jokes. His punch lines left you leaning forward, waiting for the rest.

"I'm in love with someone else."

Pain. A huge wooden spoon, tossing the contents of her stomach. Her legs wobbled, trembling on the wedge heels of her sandals, and she clutched the cold metal of the folding chair. "What?" Was that her voice, weak and thready? Someone had vacuumed all the moisture from her mouth, sucked the air from her lungs.

"I'm so sorry," Bryan was saying. "I know this is awful. You don't deserve this, but I can't marry you. It happened slowly, and I didn't realize what was going on until recently. I tried to put it out of my mind, but I just can't. And I can't marry you knowing how I feel. I'm so sorry, Kate."

"What?" It was the only word her mind could form at the moment.

"I know there's no excuse. I should have told you before now, but I thought it would go away. I thought I was just having cold feet or something, but it's more than that."

"We've been together for two years, Bryan."

It was a stupid thing to say, but it was all she could think of. Memories played across the screen of her mind in fast-forward. The day they'd met in line at Starbucks in downtown Boston when Kate had gone there for a conference. Their first date at the Colonial Theatre. The long-distance courting and weekend visits. The e-mails, the phone calls, the engagement, the book. It all whizzed by, coming to a screeching halt here, at this moment. Here, in Lucas's dusty workshop. Here, in front of the special gazebo they were to be married in.

"I've already called my family and told them. I know there's a lot to do, and I'll help any way you want me to. And then there's your book . . . I'm so sorry."

*Sorry. You're sorry?* She pictured the precise rows of white chairs, the tent being erected as they spoke, the photographers.

The *New York Times*.

She closed her burning eyes. Everything would have to be cancelled.

At that thought, humiliation arrived on the scene, sinking in past the pain of betrayal. The weight of it pushed at her shoulders, and she grabbed the hair at her nape. *Think, Kate! This is no time to lose it.*

"Stop, Bryan. Just stop and think about what you're doing. Maybe you're letting your issues with your parents' divorce affect your decisions. This kind of fear is perfectly natural before a wedding, and maybe—"

"No, it's not that—"

"How do you know?" She forced reason into her tone. Used her soothing voice—the one she put on when things got heated between one of her couples. "We love each other. We're perfect for each other. You've said it a hundred times."

"There's something missing, Kate."

She wobbled again and steadied herself with a hand on the chair. "Something missing"? What was that supposed to mean?

As her mind grappled with that seemingly unanswerable question, she felt a hand at her back, leading her into the chair. She was sitting, her head as fuzzy as a cotton-candy machine, her emerald-cut engagement ring blurring before her eyes.

"What do you mean there's something missing? The only thing missing is the groom. For our wedding that starts in five hours. Five hours, Bryan." Now she felt the hysteria building and took a full breath, nearly choking on the way the oxygen stretched her lungs.

"I'll help in any way I can."

"You can help by showing up for our wedding!"

Her mind ran through the list of people she'd have to call. Her dad, the guests, her publisher. She thought of the money Rosewood Press had spent on this elaborate beach wedding. They'd flown in friends and family from all over the country, paid for the photographer, flowers, caterer, the wedding attire. Kate had only wanted a simple wedding, but with the release of the book, the marketing department had other ideas. "An elegant wedding and a surprise groom just as the book releases. Think of the publicity, Kate!"

A knot started in her throat and burned its way to her heart.

"I'll always care about you," Bryan said.

The words fell, as empty as a discarded soda bottle on a deserted beach.

*Enough.*

The adrenaline coursing through her veins drained suddenly, leaving her once again weak and shaky. She couldn't talk to him anymore. She wasn't going to break down on the phone, wasn't going to beg him to come back. It wouldn't accomplish a thing anyway. She'd heard this tone of Bryan's voice before. He was a man who knew what he wanted. And what he didn't want.

And he didn't want Kate. She suddenly knew that fact as surely as she knew tomorrow would be more impossible to face than today.

She cleared her throat. "I have to go."

"Kate, tell me what I can do. My family will pitch in too. I want to help fix things."

She wanted to tell him there was no fixing this. There was no fixing her heart or the impending collision of her life and her career. Instead, numb, she closed the phone, staring straight ahead at the holes on the pegboard until they blended together in a blurry haze.

He was leaving her. The man she loved was walking away. This wasn't supposed to be happening. Not to her. She'd been so careful, and for what? A hollow spot opened up in her stomach, wide and gaping.

Instead of the headlines reading "Marriage Expert Finds Her Mr. Right," they would read "Marriage Expert Jilted at the Altar."

Kate had never considered herself prideful, but the thought of facing the next twenty-four hours made cyanide seem reasonable. How could this be happening? To her, of all people? She'd written a book on the subject of finding the right mate and had managed to find the wrong one instead. By tomorrow the whole world would know.

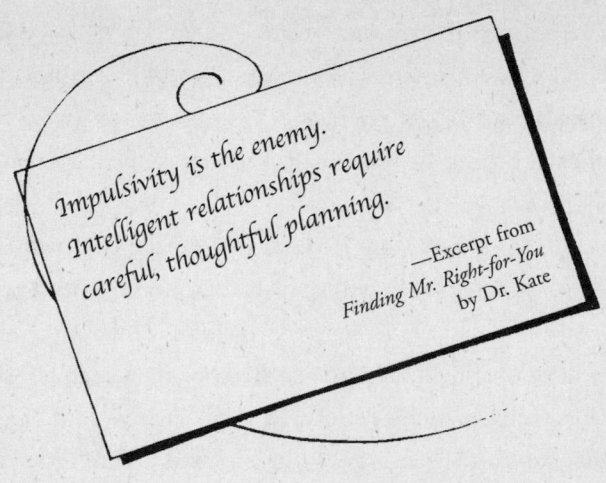

*Impulsivity is the enemy. Intelligent relationships require careful, thoughtful planning.*

—Excerpt from
*Finding Mr. Right-for-You*
by Dr. Kate

# Chapter Two

Lucas watched Kate snap her phone shut. Maybe he should've left when he heard the gravity in her voice, but he couldn't. Like a pedestrian gawking at a car accident, he'd watched Kate receive the news. When he realized what Bryan was saying, he'd wanted to hunt the man down and pummel him until he felt the same pain as Kate. Instead he'd ushered Kate to the chair, wishing he could pull her into his arms and tell her it was going to be okay.

But that was the last thing she wanted.

Now she faced the wall, unmoving. Her glossy black hair hung straight, almost to her wilted shoulders. He'd never seen her so motionless. She was always on the go, steady as a clock; he'd been mesmerized by that the first time they'd met. Now, her stillness seemed unnatural.

He took a step toward her. "Kate?"

She must have forgotten about him, because she jumped slightly, then ran her hand across her face before turning partway. Her hair, always tucked behind her ears, had come loose. Her eyes only made it to his knees.

"Lucas." She studied the floor as if the paint and varnish stains were one of those abstract paintings to be interpreted. "I guess you heard."

Her voice was small. But he watched her straighten her back and turn to look fully at him. A scared little girl in a woman's body. Her eyes went past him to the gazebo for a second before flittering back.

"I . . . I guess I won't be needing that. I'll pay you for it, though. It's really beautiful." Her voice choked on the last word.

"I'm not worried about that."

He half expected her to cave in then, but instead she shot to her feet and began to pace, her heels clicking across the floor. "I have to think," she muttered. "I have to think."

*Ka-clack, ka-clack, ka-clack,* spin. *Ka-clack, ka-clack, ka-clack,* spin.

Lucas wasn't sure what she meant. Was she trying to figure out how to win Bryan back? Or giving up—making a mental list of everyone to be notified. He couldn't imagine the mess.

But if anyone could wrap her hands around the task, Kate could. He'd watched her patch up marriages that were dangling by a thread, juggle her syndicated column with her counseling service, and write a book in her spare time. Kate was an incredible woman. Bryan was an idiot if he couldn't see what he had.

Kate jerked to a stop and pressed her fingertips to her forehead. "He left me. I have no groom. The newspapers, the media, my publisher. My career. It's over."

She looked fragile and out of place in his expansive and dusty workshop, her short pants and white blouse immaculate, her black belt encircling her tiny waist. But then Kate always looked as if she'd been snapped straight from an ironing board.

"I thought he loved me," she whispered, her words wavering.

Lucas took a step toward her, then stopped, anchoring his hands in his pockets. "It's going to be okay." It felt lame but it was what he always told his baby sister, and it made Jamie feel better. Kate, however, was not Jamie.

"It is not going to be okay." She leveled a look at him. "I've been dumped five hours before my wedding. Everything is riding on this wedding, both personally and professionally. My Mr. Right left me. Do you not understand the irony?"

*Maybe he wasn't your Mr. Right.* It was on the tip of his tongue, but he caught it in time. He watched Kate's hand tremble against the side of her face. He hadn't known Kate was capable of trembling.

"I'm supposed to be an expert. Not just in relationships, but in finding the right mate. People write me for advice and trust me to give them answers. I wrote a book to help people make good matches, and I can't even make one myself." She looked away and dragged in a shaky breath. "I'm a failure."

"You're not a failure. Your fiancé made an idiot decision; that's not your fault."

The metal chair creaked as she sank into it, the sound echoing in the quietness of the room. "That's not how everyone's going to see it."

He reckoned she might be right about that. People could be judgmental, especially if the media put a nasty spin on it.

"I've got to do something," she mumbled through her fingers. "How can I fix this?"

Lucas didn't think it was possible. She had guests, a slew of media, and all the wedding fixings. Everything but the groom, and that was most important.

*Everything but the groom.*

The words ricocheted around his head until, one by one, they fell into place like tiles in a Scrabble game.

*Everything . . . but . . . the groom . . .*

He rubbed the back of his neck, walking toward his work station. It was crazy. Crazier than crazy. It was insane. She'd laugh if he said it out loud. That thought tightened his gut.

Her phone clattered, vibrating on the metal desk. He watched it do the jitterbug.

"I can't answer," she said. "I can't deal with it right now. I don't know what to say." She crossed her arms, and her shoulders scrunched up as though she wished she could cover her ears with them.

Together they watched the phone. *Ring-bzzzzzzzz . . . Ring-bzzzzzzz . . .* When the noise stopped, there was a palpable relief.

Kate drummed her fingers on her lips, quickly at first, then slowing. Her lips loosened, turned down. Her stubborn chin softened. "It's hopeless."

The phone rang again, chittering across the desktop. Kate glared at it, looking as though she might throw it across the room.

"I'll answer." He reached for it.

Kate stopped him with a hand on his arm. Her grip was surprisingly strong. "What'll you say?"

He met her gaze: wide, olive-brown eyes too vulnerable for words. "I'll just take a message."

After a moment, she released his arm, and he picked up the phone, snapping it open.

"Hello?"

A pause. "Is Kate there?" A woman's voice, out of breath.

"She can't come to the phone right now. Can I take a message?"

"Is this Bryan? Don't tell me she's letting you see her before the wedding."

"No. This is a—a friend." That was stretching it. He turned and leaned against the desk.

"Okay, well, tell her to call Pam. No, wait, she won't be able to reach me for a while. Tell her I have good news. This is really important, so be sure and tell her right away. The *Dr. Phil* show called, and they want her to make a guest appearance next month."

Great. Lucas met Kate's eyes, glanced away. Just what she needed.

"Did you get that?" Pam asked.

"Got it. I'll let her know." He closed the phone and set it on the desk. He could feel Kate watching him. Maybe he didn't have to tell her just now.

"Who was it?" Was that hope lilting her voice? Did she think Bryan had changed his mind?

"It was Pam."

She stared at her manicured fingers, clenched in her lap. "Oh."

She'd actually gotten on the *Dr. Phil* show. He'd known her popularity had grown nationwide with the column and book and all. But *Dr. Phil.* That was a whole new ball game.

"What did she want?"

Her knee brushed his leg as she shifted. He crossed his feet at the ankles and gripped the ledge of the desk. "It's nothing that can't wait. She wants you to call her back."

Her upturned face and searching eyes melted him. Have mercy, she was beautiful. He looked away.

"She said something, didn't she? Something you don't want me to know."

Restless energy pushed him away from the desk. He should've known she wouldn't let it go. He shouldn't have answered the phone. Her type A personality required her to know, even when she already had more than she could handle.

"Excuse me, but my life is hanging in the balance right now. Could you please just spit it out?"

Kate had straightened in the chair, her hand grasping the rounded edge of the back. Her left hand. Lucas watched the diamond engagement ring twinkle under the work lights. "She just wanted to let you know about an interview she set up, is all. You can call her later when you—"

"Who's it with?" Her tone demanded an answer.

He exhaled deeply. She was like a ravenous dog with his last meaty bone.

"I know it must be big. She wouldn't have called me today if it wasn't. And stop looking at me like that."

"Like what?"

"Like you feel sorry for me. Who's it with?"

*Fine, Kate, fine. You win.* "Dr. Phil."

He watched her mouth slacken, watched her blink and swallow, watched her eyes change, deaden. He hated it. Hated he'd had any part in bringing that look to her face.

She was still again, and he hated that too. Maybe it wasn't too late to chase Bryan down and knock him flat on his face. He should be here picking up the pieces, making things right. But he wasn't. Lucas was there, and what could he do?

*Everything but the groom.*

The words flashed in his mind like a lighthouse beacon, teasing him. *It's crazy.* And even if it wasn't, it was self-serving.

*You could save Kate's wedding. Her reputation. Her career. It's an honorable thing.*

*But I would also be getting what I wanted. Is that selfish?*

*You were willing to let her go, because you thought that was right. Was that selfish? She needs you now. And you're in a position to help her.*

"What am I going to do?" Kate asked

She turned her doe eyes on him, looking at him, needing him. It was heady. He wanted to protect her, to gather her close, the way a hen gathers her chicks under her wings.

"How am I going to face everyone? What am I going to tell the media? My publisher?" For the first time, her lip trembled, and she caught it between her teeth. "They paid for everything; did you know that?"

Should he say it? Should he offer himself? Could it even work? "Maybe it could."

"What?"

He didn't know he'd said it aloud until he heard Kate's response. Well, he was in just deep enough, he figured he might as well dive in headfirst. "I have an idea. It's a little crazy."

Surprisingly, she breathed a wry chuckle. "My whole life's a little crazy at the moment."

He studied her. She was actually looking at him with something like hope in her eyes. "Way I see it, the only thing missing is a groom."

Her laugh was sharp. "A necessary ingredient, I think you'll agree."

He nodded once, hoping she'd put two and two together so he wouldn't have to say it. "What if there was a different groom?"

Now she reared back slightly, blinking. *Great. She thinks I'm nuts.*

"I don't exactly have a waiting list, Lucas."

He shuffled his feet, then leaned against the workhorse, not sure if he was ready for what came next. *Just say it. The worst she can do is laugh in my face.* "What if I stood in for Bryan?"

He scuffed at the white paint on the tip of his right tennis shoe as silence closed in around him. A long silence. An uncomfortable silence. If he could've caught the words and pulled them back, he would've. Instead, he glanced at Kate. The expression on her face reinforced his wish.

"Why would—" She cleared her throat. "Why would you do that?"

*Why would I do it? Because I love you.* But he couldn't say that. Why hadn't he thought this out before he'd opened his big mouth?

He lifted his shoulder. "To help you," he said.

Her brows pulled together. "We're talking marriage here, not some little favor."

Favor. What if he made a bargain with her? What if she could do something for him in return? "I'd want something in return." *What? What do I want in return?*

At that, her eyebrows slackened as her lips took up the tension, pressing together. Her glare was direct and meaningful, and he immediately knew what she was thinking.

"Don't flatter yourself," he said.

She shook her head as if dislodging a distasteful picture. "It doesn't matter. It wouldn't work. Even if the rest of the world doesn't know who I was marrying, my dad does. And so does Chloe, my editor, and Pam and Anna. Not to mention Bryan's family."

A definite glitch, but was there a way around it? Now that the idea had settled a bit, it was growing on him. He shrugged. "Would they keep quiet?"

She gave him a double take. "Keep quiet?" Her fingers found the high collar of her blouse. "You're actually serious."

His heart was a jackhammer gone wild under his rib cage. He scratched at the dried paint on his thumbnail. "Would they?"

She turned away, her black hair swinging saucily. "You can't— you can't just marry me. Marriage is permanent. At least to me it is. You don't just make a willy-nilly decision to marry someone. People don't do that." She faced him again. "I don't do that."

No, Kate didn't do that. She planned every step days in advance, every detail in order, everything in its place.

At least she hadn't laughed at him. He straightened and shrugged as casually as he could, given that he felt like a man whose date had turned her head when he tried to kiss her. "Suit yourself."

He began wrapping the cord around the sander. It was a stupid idea anyway. He could only imagine his mom's reaction if his parents returned from their trip to find their son not only married, but married to Kate Lawrence. He'd never hear the end of it. And neither would his dad.

Nonetheless, it didn't do much for his ego to know Kate would rather see the death of her career than marry him. He stuffed the ache further down and set the sander on the shelf next to his favorite drill, waiting to hear the click of her heels as she left the shop.

Instead, Kate's voice broke the silence. "The people who know Bryan was the groom . . . what if one of them leaked it? Besides, there's the marriage license and the tuxes. Something could go wrong, and if everyone found out, it would be a bigger disaster than what I have now—if that's possible."

*Okay, already, I get it.* "It was a stupid idea." She'd made that plain enough. "You should get out your little notepad and make a list of things to cancel."

"Wait. Just wait a minute; I have to think." Apparently she did her best thinking while pacing.

*Whatever.* He turned back to his tools. He didn't see what there was to think about. At this point it was just a matter of facing the music. He didn't envy her that. But if Bryan was loser enough to jilt her at the altar, he wasn't good enough for her.

He kept silent while she pondered her situation. By the time she spoke again, every tool was put away—something that hadn't happened since he'd installed the shelving unit.

"I think I could arrange to keep everyone quiet. My editor and Pam certainly wouldn't say anything. I can trust Anna and my dad implicitly. I have a couple of distant relatives here, but they'd keep it to themselves."

She was thinking out loud, not even looking at Lucas. "Bryan's family is small, and they're mostly from the Boston area. There were eight relatives here, plus his best man. He could surely convince them to keep quiet. He owes me that at least." Her eyes softened for a moment as if the thought of him made her ache.

Kate was actually considering it. He'd never known her to do a spontaneous thing, and here she was, thinking about marrying him at the last minute. *She must be desperate.*

Kate looked Lucas over from head to toe; he squirmed, feeling he'd somehow failed the examination. "The tux won't fit. You're taller; your shoulders are broader. We'd have to get you fitted quickly. Mr. Lavitz is a good friend of yours, isn't he?"

"Well, yeah . . ."

"The marriage license might be a problem." She tapped her foot and chewed on the side of her lip, her eyes searching the buzzing fluorescent fixtures for answers. "And we'd need an exit strategy. Maybe a year? Give my book time to succeed and give me time to get another book going. We could get a quiet divorce . . ."

Her eyes closed. "I can't believe I'm talking about marriage like this. Like it's a cheap business arrangement."

Lucas watched her face as she wrestled with her principles. "He backed you into a corner. It's not like you have so many appealing options."

She looked at him suddenly, her brows pulling together. "Why are you doing this again?"

*Why? Why?* How could she help him? She was a marriage counselor, but he wasn't married—yet. His parents' marriage was solid enough, though they loved to fuss at each other. Everyone knew it was just who they were, but an outsider might think . . .

"Lucas? I'm running out of time here."

"My parents' marriage. If you could help them."

Her eyes brightened. Ah, he'd hit the bull's-eye.

"It's in jeopardy?" she asked.

He cleared his throat. Stuffed his hands in his jeans pockets. "They fight a lot lately." He needed more, but he didn't want to lie. "My mom left for a few days last month." On a girl's weekend trip, but Kate didn't have to know that. "Jamie—she's my little sister— said Dad enjoyed her absence." He'd actually said he enjoyed having Jamie all to himself. But that was close enough, wasn't it?

"And you want me to counsel them?"

"No." The word came out a little sharp. "They're both leery of all that psychobabble stuff." Her eyebrows rose, and he rephrased. "You'd have to be sly about it. Get to know them. Get them to open up. You can handle it."

"That's it? That's all you want?"

He wanted much more, but it was a start. "It's my parents' marriage."

"Of course. I didn't mean to make it sound trite." Kate steepled her fingers and tapped the tips together. "I don't even know if this is possible. I think there's a waiting period on the marriage license."

He hadn't thought of that. Maybe the plan was dead in the water. But hadn't his friend Ethan gotten married at the last minute? "I think it can be waived. Nancy Rallings is the town clerk, and I furnished her house. I'll see what I can find out."

He couldn't believe she was considering it. He could be marrying Kate in a matter of hours. In front of friends, family, and media. His legs suddenly quaked as he remembered the article in the paper spelling out the details. The wedding was going to be a media circus. They might want to interview him.

His mouth felt like it was stuffed with sawdust. "No interviews," he said.

It took Kate a moment to hear him, lost in thought as she probably was. "What?"

"I'll let the media snap all the photos they want, but I won't give interviews."

She shrugged, eyeing him. "I agree—we don't need to complicate things. What about your family? How are they going to feel?"

That gave him pause. His mom had been urging him to move on since Emily died five years ago. Kate, however, was the last person his mom would want him moving on with. If he told his mom the marriage was temporary, she would be rude, scare Kate off for good. But if she knew he loved Kate, she'd have to make an effort, wouldn't she?

"My parents are out of town right now, but my brother and sister are here. I'll call my parents afterward and tell them we got married. And I don't want them to know the particulars. As far as they're concerned, it's the real thing." Besides, if it worked the way he hoped, there'd be no exit strategy needed. He held out his hand. "Deal?"

His breath caught and hung below the mass in his throat.

Kate stared at him, her eyes a mixture of fear and resolve. Then she put her hand in his. "Deal."

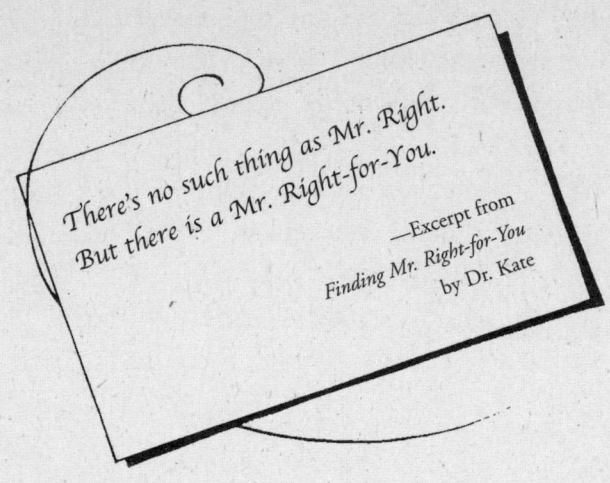

*There's no such thing as Mr. Right. But there is a Mr. Right-for-You.*

—Excerpt from
*Finding Mr. Right-for-You*
by Dr. Kate

# Chapter Three

If Kate had to explain the change one more time, she was going to pull every last hair from her head. The horror etched into the eyes of Anna, Chloe, and Pam had been enough to start the second-guessing. They'd run over the pros and cons, quickly, more for their benefit than anyone's. Kate had covered that ground a dozen times already.

Her dad had listened silently, with shoulders squared and back straight, his only parental concession the lone worry line stretching across his squeaky-clean forehead.

*It'll be okay, Dad. I know what I'm doing.*

He'd taught Kate to think independently, and he never questioned her decisions. Even now, the most he'd said was, "Kate . . ."

When she'd called Bryan with her announcement and demands, she'd been met with a long silence. She'd almost enjoyed his obvious shock and unspoken, *You're what?* Just when she thought he might have gone unconscious behind the wheel of his car, he asked her to repeat what she'd said. She'd ended up going through it three times, until he eventually assured her his family would keep it quiet. She supposed he wasn't eager for word to get out that he'd jilted Dr. Kate at the altar.

At least one group hadn't needed explanations. Lucas had introduced her to his brother and sister, Brody and Jamie. Brody, a lanky, curly-headed version of Lucas, was home from college on summer break, and Jamie was a teenager with dark hair and braces. They accepted the news of their brother's impending matrimony with friendly smiles before exchanging a silent glance Kate didn't have time to decipher.

Now, four hours, one wedding license, and countless moments of stark terror later, Kate stood in her white gown, feet poised at the foot of the aisle. The media cameras clicked in machine-gun fashion, capturing a three-quarter view. She curved her lips upward and forced a twinkle into her eyes.

Thirty feet down the aisle, waiting in the gazebo, was Anna; Lucas's best man, Ethan; the justice of the peace; and Lucas.

*Lucas. Is this really happening?*

The musicians started the wedding march. Kate curled her arm around the stiff material on her dad's arm and took the first step. A gentle breeze blew off the ocean, ruffling her hair and veil and feathering her strapless A-line gown against her legs. She'd finally found the satin dress at a boutique in Boston after scouring numerous magazines and shops. Now what did it matter that the gown was perfect or that the hem hit the floor precisely?

How had it come to this? Bryan was supposed to be waiting at the end of the aisle. They matched. They were a fit according to everything she knew about personalities and relationships. They had so much in common—their love of exercise . . . organization . . . punctuality . . . loyalty . . .

Well. She supposed she'd have to rethink the loyalty part.

She passed her Aunt Virginia in the second row, wearing her trademark cherry-red lipstick. Her brown hair coiled above her puffy white face like thick chocolate shavings on a pile of whipped cream.

The groom's side was half-empty, but what did she expect with last-minute invitations? Jamie sat on the first row beside Brody, her brown hair caught up in barrette. Two part-time employees from Lucas's shop sat on the next row, straining to see around a tall, spindly man she recognized from someplace.

She imagined how upset Lucas's parents would be at missing the ceremony. And at finding out about the wedding after it was over . . . But it was what Lucas wanted, and it was his decision. They'd have to smooth things over later.

*They* . . .

She was going to be joining another family. The thought struck her hard and quick. She didn't even know these people—she barely knew the groom!

*What am I doing?*

She didn't meet Lucas's eyes until she nearly reached the gazebo and then realized her mistake. A bride would be gazing adoringly at her groom. Was she smiling widely enough? Her dry lips stuck to her teeth.

Lucas had cleaned up well, even shaved his perpetual five o'clock shadow. His long hair was combed back from his face. The hairstyle, combined with the formal suit, gave him the look of a nineteenth-century nobleman. His eyes met hers, pulling her in—a solid lifeline in what felt like a turbulent storm.

They reached the foot of the gazebo, and her dad stopped and kissed her cheek, then took a seat on the first row.

She was on her own now.

*What am I doing? . . . What am I doing? . . .*

She stepped into the gazebo as the last strains of the wedding march rang out and drew to a halt between Anna and Lucas. Her bare arm brushed his. In the distance, whirring clicks of cameras captured every second of the event, and she knew the best photos would grace the pages of tomorrow's newspapers. But as the justice began talking, all Kate could think about was the way the heat from Lucas's arm seeped clean through his tux and settled against her skin like a thick fog.

"Marriage is commended to be honorable among all men," the justice began. "And therefore is not by any to be entered into unadvisedly or lightly—but reverently, discreetly, advisedly, and solemnly." He emphasized each word, his bushy gray eyebrows inching upward disapprovingly. When Kate had told him Lucas was taking Bryan's place, she'd been half-afraid he'd refuse to perform the ceremony. But he'd only pressed his lips together and nodded formally.

Now he continued. "Into this holy estate these two persons present now come to be joined for life."

*Joined for life.* She turned her head a fraction of an inch toward Lucas as the ugly scent of fear filled her nostrils, mingling with the tangy, salt-laden air. Life? She hardly knew him!

*What am I doing?*

She dragged in a breath and slowly released it, careful to keep her expression neutral. *There's no going back now. Focus. Just get through the ceremony.*

Was Lucas afraid too? Was he asking himself what he'd gotten into, wishing he were back in his shop, sitting in a thin layer of sawdust? Was that his arm trembling against hers? He had every right to panic. He was giving up a year of his life. He was being thrust into the public eye.

*What if he backs out? Right here in front of everybody?* Jilted twice in one day. Had it ever happened before? She imagined the headline. *"Dr. Kate Jilted at Altar by Two Grooms."*

The justice stopped talking, and the moment's silence sent alarm scuttling through Kate. Instinctively, she slid her right hand from her bouquet and reached out, searching for an anchor. When her fingers touched Lucas's hand, his encircled hers. It was warm and strong, and—oddly—confident. *It's going to be okay,* his grip said.

Mrs. Petrie began her solo, her warbly, butterfly soprano wafting on the breeze, and Kate's mind wandered. The song had seemed perfect for her and Bryan. How could she have been so wrong? Who was it who had stolen his heart? Just the night before, he'd held her close and kissed her good night at her apartment door. What was it he'd said? *"I guess I'll see you soon."*

Had there been something in his tone? In his expression? Some warning she'd missed? She'd been too flushed with excitement to notice. And just like that he was gone.

And now she was marrying Lucas. Committing a year of her life to a man she didn't love. Good grief, most of the time she didn't even like him. Not that he was a bad person. He was just so . . . irritating sometimes. Vexing. The way he was late and careless and so laid-back she wished she had a remote control so she could push the fast-forward button.

She couldn't think of a man less suited for her.

Mrs. Petrie finished the song and returned to her seat. The justice began talking about the seriousness of the vows they were about to take. Kate wanted to plug her ears. She was a proponent of life-long marriages. It was her life's work to help couples stay married. And now she was making a mockery of the process.

*I'm a hypocrite. A fraud. What would my readers think if they knew?*

The justice turned toward her, and Kate focused her attention on him as he announced the reading of the vows. She was supposed to face Lucas. She handed her bouquet to Anna and turned toward Lucas. She wasn't sure if she was capable of breathing, much less speaking.

Then she saw the corner of Lucas's lip tilt up ever so slightly, his eyes soften. Instinctively, she relaxed.

*I can do this.*

The justice read the vows, and Kate repeated them. "I, Kate Lawrence, take you, Lucas Wright, to be my husband, to have and to hold from this day forward, for better or for worse, for richer, for poorer, in sickness and in health, to love and to cherish, from this day forward." Kate swallowed hard. "Until death do us part."

The last words were rushed, but she'd done it. Now the justice prompted Lucas.

He repeated the vows, and he did it well. His eyes said as much as his voice. The way he looked at her . . . It was the way every bride yearned to be looked at. Like she was precious. Like she was his chosen one. His voice was low, as if rumbling up from the deepest part of the ocean. It was more than credible. It was convincing.

The justice said a prayer and ended it with an amen. "It is tradition to exchange rings as a symbol of the love between a man and a wife."

Rings! Kate felt something akin to a tidal wave inside her. Bryan's best man had her ring. Lucas wouldn't have a ring to put on her finger. She turned a desperate look toward the justice, but he was looking at Lucas as he spoke. ". . . representing the unending love of your union." He cleared his throat as if the words had left a foul taste.

Kate stared hard at the justice, hoping mental telepathy would work just this once. *There are no rings!*

But then Lucas turned to Ethan. When he faced Kate again, he held a ring in the hollow of his palm. He'd taken care of it. Relief washed over her, and she smiled her gratitude.

He took her left hand in his and slid the ring onto her finger until it rested beside the glittering diamond. "With this ring, I thee wed." The look in his eyes burned the words into her heart.

The band was white gold, elegant in its simplicity. When had he had time to buy a ring? And how had he known her size?

The justice was prompting her to get Lucas's ring. She turned to take the ring from Anna. There was no way Bryan's ring would fit Lucas. She hoped it would at least slide over his knuckle. Maybe no one would notice.

She took the ring from Anna's palm . . . but it wasn't Bryan's white-gold band with diamond-shaped cuts. This one matched the one Lucas had put on her finger. She turned toward him and took his hand in hers. The ring slid easily onto his wide, tapered finger and looked bright against the darkness of his skin. "With this ring, I thee wed," she said.

Lucas caught hold of her hands, and the justice gave his closing thoughts. Kate was aware of nothing except Lucas's hands holding hers, his fingers rough and calloused against hers. She noticed that he was almost a head taller than her five-foot-five frame. One strand of his hair had come loose and fallen over his forehead, rogue-style. Her gaze fell to his eyes. He looked straight at her, into her, anchoring her.

The justice was making his closing statements. "By the power vested in me by the State of Massachusetts, I now pronounce you husband and wife."

The relief she felt brought a smile to her face. *It's done. I made it through.*

"You may now kiss the bride."

Her eyes flew back to Lucas. In all the commotion of last-minute changes, she hadn't even thought about the kiss. Had he?

One of his eyebrows quirked as if challenging her.

She leaned toward him and felt his hands go to her waist. She brought her fingers to his jaw just as their lips met. His mouth was soft against hers. His lips moved slowly, deliberately, as he pulled her closer until their bodies nearly met . . .

*Oh my . . . goodness . . .*

It was over in seconds, but it left her rattled. Good grief, he was a great kisser. Who would have thought?

He was watching her, most likely noting her newly flushed cheeks. His eyes twinkled as if he could tell the kiss had left her shaken. She drew her shoulders back and tilted her chin as the justice said his final words.

"I now present to you Mr. and Mrs. Lucas Wright."

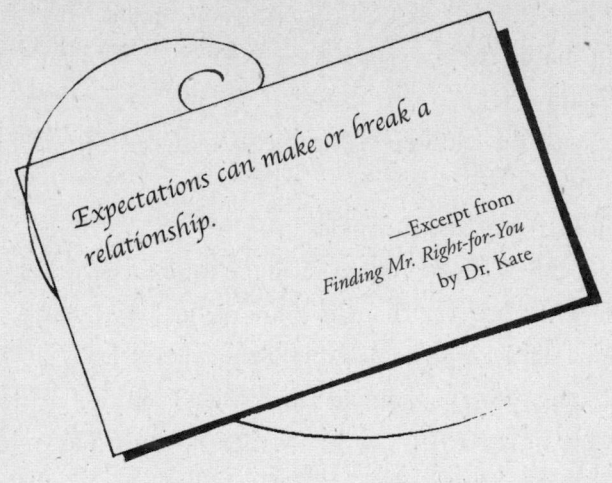

*Expectations can make or break a relationship.*

—Excerpt from
*Finding Mr. Right-for-You*
by Dr. Kate

# Chapter Four

"In honor of the first man in her life," the DJ announced from the makeshift stage, "The bride would like to have the first dance of the evening with her father."

Kate disengaged herself from Lucas's friends and wound her way through the circular tables to the parquet dance floor, where her dad waited with extended hand. She went into his arms with the first notes of "Unforgettable" playing behind her. It was the only part of the day going according to plan. Everything else had been turned on end, but sharing this dance with her dad was exactly the way it was supposed to be. Kate closed her eyes and relished the normality of it, unwilling—unable—to think past this moment.

"You're holding up well."

She looked up at her father. His face had aged the last couple years, and Kate realized she hadn't visited him in Maryland enough. Phone calls and letters didn't allow the same connection, and she'd spent most of her spare weekends with Bryan in Boston. And for what?

"Really?" She felt as transparent as Saran Wrap and just as fragile. Making rounds with Lucas had been hard. Everyone wanted to know how they'd met and how they'd kept it a secret. Lucas's eyes had said it all. *We didn't.* The two of them had a million details to work out. She didn't know how they'd remember everything they'd come up with on the fly tonight.

"What do you know about this guy?" Her dad shuffled stiffly, leading more like a boot-camp drill sergeant than a dancer. His hair—what was left of it—was combed neatly to the side in a part not quite deep enough to be a comb-over.

What did she know about Lucas? Not even enough to fill a pen cap. "He makes furniture, and his shop is right below my place on Main Street. In fact, he owns the building. I was renting my office space and apartment from him. He did the renovations."

She'd let Lucas know months ago that she was moving out this month. Little had she known she'd be moving into his home. She realized she didn't know where he lived.

"What else?" A benign smile hid his concern.

"He's a nice man, Daddy. Harmless."

She glanced over her dad's shoulder at Lucas. He stood with Ethan, hands resting in his vest pockets, his jacket long since discarded. His white shirt was crisp and fitted, tapering from broad shoulders down to narrow hips. Maybe "harmless" was overstating it.

"I'm not leaving until morning, so if you need anything tonight, call me."

Kate laughed. "Not the words most fathers say to their daughters on their wedding night."

"This isn't most wedding nights."

Kate sobered. No, it wasn't. She didn't know how she was going to survive the honeymoon at the White Elephant, much less the next year.

"If anyone can do this, you can." Her father squeezed her hand in a rare gesture of affection. Behind him, the vocalists belted out the chorus, the lead singer's face reddened from the strain.

"Thanks, Dad."

They danced quietly for a few moments before her dad broke the silence. "I know your mom and I had our disagreements, but I wish she could be here tonight."

Kate didn't want to think about her mom, tonight of all nights. "You're here. That's all that matters." They took one last turn as the band wound down the song and the crowd applauded.

Lucas approached as her dad stepped away. "May I cut in, sir?"

Kate knew he'd scored brownie points for the honorific title. Her dad smiled cordially, but the look in his eyes warned that the points wouldn't carry far.

The band struck up the song she'd selected for the bride and groom's "first dance," and her heart stuttered. "When a Man Loves a Woman" had been their song. It had played on the radio the first time Bryan kissed her. A constricting knot lodged in her throat as Lucas's hands came to her waist. She felt his eyes on her, and she worked to steady her smile. There were people watching. Always people watching. She had to hold it together.

As if sensing her need to hide, he pulled her close. She laid her cheek against his chest, away from all the faces. Above the swelling music and chatter, she could hear the waves swooshing the shoreline with rhythmic certainty. The consistency of the sound soothed her.

"It's gonna be okay, Kate," Lucas's voice rumbled next to her ear. "You'll see."

Her eyes burned, threatening to spill, and she blinked. *Breathe, just breathe.* She needed to think about something else, anything else, but the thoughts wouldn't budge: *"I'm in love with someone else."* Were harsher words ever spoken?

"I'm glad we have a minute alone," Lucas said. "Because I have a question for you."

She swallowed. "What's that?"

"Are we going on a honeymoon?"

Her laugh was feeble. "I'm sorry." She pulled back enough to look at him. "We have reservations at the White Elephant for the week. Is that okay?" He had his work, after all. But if they didn't take a honeymoon, people would wonder.

"I have a couple jobs to finish up this week, but I'll get them pushed back." He pulled her closer. "The White Elephant, huh? Your publisher went all out."

She moved her hand down his shoulder. "The hotel offered an unbelievable rate. They'll get a lot of publicity."

"Surprised you didn't want to go to Hawaii or something."

She shrugged. "Nantucket's done so much for me. I wanted to do something to help the community. The publicity is good for the island." She smoothed the stiff lapels of his jacket. He'd put it back on for the dance. For the photos that were being snapped.

He'd been a perfect gentleman all evening. She was beginning to wonder why he'd gotten on her nerves before. "Thanks for not shoving the cake in my face," she said.

His lips tilted. "Wouldn't dream of it."

The singer crooned the chorus, but Kate kept her eyes on Lucas. They were supposed to be the "happy couple." It was harder than she'd imagined; the pretending was wearing her out.

"So when does this shindig end?"

*Not soon enough.* "The band has to stop at nine thirty."

Lucas started to look at Kate's watch, but she grabbed his hand and kissed it. The hairs on the back of his hand tickled her lips. "You're dancing with your bride. Time is meaningless."

His eyes clouded, and he settled his hand at her waist, looking away.

"When the band winds down, we'll make our exit," she said. "There's a carriage scheduled to take us to the White Elephant."

It hit her how deceiving appearances could be. For all that this looked like a fairy-tale wedding, a true marriage, it was a farce. Empty and fake, it was an elaborate mansion, gutted on the inside.

"I haven't packed." He spun them around, surprisingly graceful.

"That's taken care of."

The flash of a bulb flared just off the dance floor. She gave Lucas her "adoring bride" smile, letting her eyes rove lovingly over the planes of his face even though she was seeing black spots, as the photographer snapped half a dozen more photos. When he stepped away, she continued. "Anna is going to grab some things for you tonight. That is, if you don't mind her riffling through your stuff. You can pick up the rest of your things tomorrow."

"Not sure how I feel about a stranger riffling through my underwear drawer."

She could tell by his tone that there'd been a shift in Lucas's mood, though she had no idea what had caused it. Of all the things to fuss about. He'd married her at the last moment, but the underwear drawer stopped him cold? What else could they do? They couldn't send his family after his things and have them knowing he hadn't planned for his honeymoon. Even Lucas wasn't that disorganized.

"Do you have a better idea?" she asked.

He looked over her head now, wearing an insipid smile. "Fine. Just send Anna."

Kate opened her mouth to respond, then changed her mind. The last thing she needed was an argument on the dance floor.

~

Kate faced the mirror in the bathroom of the White Elephant's Shoreline suite. Her dark hair, caught up on the sides, disappeared beneath the triple-layered veil. Her makeup still looked fresh, her dress stunning. Her shoulders, carefully tanned over the past month, looked every bit as lovely as she'd hoped.

Only none of it mattered now. Bryan loved someone else, and she was married to a man she barely tolerated.

*Ah, but my career is salvaged. At least I have that.*

She set her heavy bag on the marble counter and opened it, resting the floppy lid against the beveled mirror. The zipper clanged against the glass.

The carriage ride to the hotel had seemed to take forever even though it couldn't have been more than ten minutes. She was tired of pretending. Which didn't bode well—the entire next year would consist of nothing but pretense, and just one night of it had worn her to the bone. Her feet hurt, her head ached, and all she wanted was to slide between the sheets and pull them over her head.

Maybe it wouldn't feel so awful in the morning. The sun would come up, it would glitter off the harbor, and the fresh air would remind her it was a new day.

At least she wouldn't have to move from Nantucket. It had been the one thing she'd dreaded. She pictured Bryan's apartment in downtown Boston and sighed at the thought. She'd never go there again. Never sit on his couch and eat popcorn while they watched CNN.

She turned her attention to her suitcase. Her clothing, carefully rolled to avoid creases, was packed in colorful bins all lined up in rows. She scanned the pieces and realized the satin and lace article she'd planned for tonight would hardly suffice. Instead, she pulled out a shirt with a mock turtleneck and a pair of knee-length shorts. It would have to do.

She looked in the mirror, noting her drawn expression, and willed herself not to cry. Then, with a sigh, she began the tug-of-war of releasing herself from her gown.

Lucas was sitting in the armchair when she reentered the room, his elbows braced on his knees. His gaze flickered over her, and she realized he must be eager to change.

"Anna should be here soon with your things."

He nodded.

"Sorry she couldn't get them over sooner."

He nodded again.

*Well, don't go getting all chatty on me.*

Giving up, Kate began hanging up her clothing, one item at a time, trying to ignore the fact Lucas was probably staring at her backside. They steadfastly held on to their silence until a few minutes later when a tap sounded on the door. Kate practically leapt across the room to let Anna in.

"Is everything okay?" Anna whispered with a hug.

"Sure." Kate summoned up one last smile. She would've offered more, but Lucas was hovering, obviously wanting to change.

"Here you go," Anna said to him.

He took a paper bag and a noisy cluster of keys from her.

"I couldn't find a suitcase or duffel bag."

"That's okay. Thanks for going to the trouble."

Anna looked at Kate. "Well . . ."

"Well . . ." Kate's brain raced, trying to think of a reason for Anna to stay. *Perhaps she'll notice the slightly manic look in my eyes and take pity.* But with a wave and a quirk of her eyebrows, Anna was gone.

*Traitor.*

Rather than run screaming after her assistant, Kate continued unpacking, stashing her socks and underclothes in one of the armoire drawers while Lucas disappeared into the bathroom. He returned in record time.

Wearing only a pair of shorts.

*Oh* . . . Kate's gaze skittered away. As if things weren't awkward enough already.

She was acutely aware of his appraisal as he sat in the armchair. What was he thinking? More specifically, what did he expect from this marriage? If it were Bryan, she'd ask—or likely, she'd already know. How many conversations she and Bryan had had about their expectations. They'd been as prepared as an engaged couple could be.

Feeling him watching her, knowing she was procrastinating, Kate placed her alarm clock and Day-Timer on the nightstand, then stowed her suitcase in the closet. When she could delay no longer, she returned to the bed and pulled the covers down, glancing at the pillow on the other side.

*Just what does Lucas expect tonight?*

*Does he think . . . ?*

She sat on the edge of the bed, facing the wall and a framed print of a lighthouse, back rigid, heart racing. She wasn't naive. Men expected sex on the honeymoon.

She and Lucas were married now, and, technically, it was his right to expect it. But . . . it seemed wrong. Theirs wasn't the typical marriage. There was nothing typical about this honeymoon. And there was no way she was offering her body like some . . . some ancient temple priestess.

Still, this was a conversation they should've had before the wedding.

She didn't want to fret over it all night either. She glanced at him, still sitting in the chair. He was leaning back, his head turned toward her. The room was big, and he seemed far away. A good, safe distance. But she could hardly yell across the room.

Kate forced her tired legs to support her weight and walked toward him.

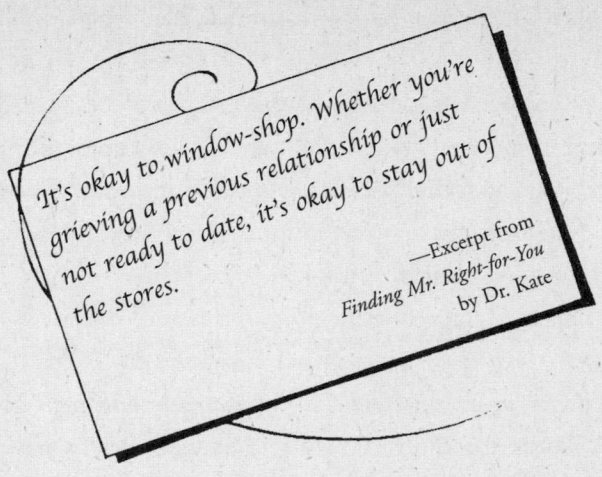

*It's okay to window-shop. Whether you're grieving a previous relationship or just not ready to date, it's okay to stay out of the stores.*

—Excerpt from
*Finding Mr. Right-for-You*
by Dr. Kate

# Chapter Five

Lucas watched Kate sit on the edge of the couch, perching like a robin on the rim of its nest, alert for the first sign of danger. He wanted to put her at ease, let her know she was safe with him. He wanted to protect her. He would never hurt her. *You are so precious to me, Kate.*

*My bride.* He savored the word on his tongue.

Kate wrapped her arms around her stomach. "It occurs to me there are some issues we haven't addressed. Perhaps we can discuss the most imminent one now."

So formal. He half-expected her to produce a twenty-page document, spelling out the lay of the land for the next 365 days, and insist he sign it.

"What's on your mind?" He folded his hands on his bare stomach.

She licked her lips, her eyes flashing down to his bare chest for the briefest of moments before she stared at her tanned knees.

"Sleeping arrangements." She cleared her throat. "I appreciate what you did today by stepping in for Bryan. I don't know what you expected from me tonight, but—"

Her cheeks bloomed with color.

*I don't know what you expected from me tonight, but I have no desire to sleep—or do anything else—in that bed with you.* He imagined the words she didn't say. Was that what was worrying her? Making her clutch at the nun-high collar of her shirt, making her face turn a dozen shades of pink?

What kind of jerk did she think he was, expecting to be compensated after she'd just been jilted at the altar by the man she loved? As if he'd want her like that—still pining for someone else. After the tenderness of his previous thoughts, the idea sickened him.

"Believe it or not, Kate, sleeping with you is the last thing on my mind." It came out sharper than he'd intended, but blast it all if it didn't tick him off that she thought so lowly of him.

"I was planning to take the couch," he said. "The bed's all yours."

Her gaze bounced off him, and she stood, nodding once. He watched her go without a reply, long legs extending from knee-length beige shorts. She flicked out the bedside lamp before slipping into bed.

He turned out the other lights and settled on the sofa. Grabbing one of the puffy throw pillows, he turned on his side and drew up his knees so he'd fit.

*Does she really think so little of me?*

His thoughts returned to the first time he'd met her, when he'd shown her the space above the shop. She'd worn white slacks, a blazer, and fancy heels that made him wonder how she climbed the stairs without falling flat on her face.

"It's a large space," she'd said. "I didn't realize it would be wide open."

He looked around at the scuffed white walls and wood floor, dulled by a layer of dust. Except for the small office and restroom at the back of the building, it was an open space. "Used to be a photographer's gallery. You said something on the phone about making it a living space and an office of some kind?"

She walked the room, her skinny heels clacking on the floor. "I'm a marriage counselor. I'd need a small lobby area and a private room for counseling. I was hoping to make my living space up here too. It's big enough, I think."

With rent so high on Nantucket, it made sense to combine the two. She moved toward the back of the building, jotting something on a clipboard, and he walked to the front of the room, giving her time to look around undisturbed. Outside the front windows, dead leaves sailed on a gust of wind. A handful of tourists walked the brick sidewalks.

"What's your policy on renovations?" Kate was making her way toward him, her silky black hair swinging. She was all business, straight to the point. He wondered if she was good at what she did. She didn't seem warm enough to be a therapist. Then again, what did he know about it? Or about her?

"How long were you planning to stay?" He didn't mind renovations so long as she'd be there a while.

"It depends on the terms of the contract."

The space had been empty for two months. The summer people

were gone for the season, and with winter coming he'd have a hard time renting it to a merchant. "If you cover cost of materials, I'll see to it the renovations are done."

She nodded, glancing around at the space as if she was trying to envision it completed.

Now that the season was over, he'd have extra time. Too bad Brody was back at college or he'd ask his brother to help.

"How soon would you need it done?" he asked.

Kate wrote something on her paper while he noted that she had a tiny mole on one side of her pointed chin and lips full enough to beg a man's attention. "I'd like to get my business up and running as soon as possible. The living portion is less urgent. I can sleep in the office back there or even in my new office until it's finished."

It was an awkward time of year to open a business. She seemed a little citified, and he wondered if she'd ever wintered on the island before. Oh, well. Wasn't any of his business.

"Give me a day or so to think it over, and I'll get back with you," she said, extending her hand and shaking his.

The next day she signed the contract and moved her luggage into the old office at the back of the building. They agreed to meet that afternoon to go over renovation plans. She was waiting for him when he arrived, and he realized he was probably a tad late. She checked her watch before sitting at a padded card table she must've brought.

"The builder's coming, isn't he?" She set a manila file on the table and folded her long, slender fingers on top of it.

Did she think he was hiring a crew or something? "I'm the builder." He took a seat opposite her.

Her eyes widened, and she blinked twice, her black lashes fluttering. "But—but I thought you built furniture."

Her eyes were a bewitching mix of green and brown. He wondered what color her driver's license said they were. "I do build furniture. But I've done plenty of carpentry and plumbing and wiring. I built my house, and I've done room additions."

"Do you—Are you a *licensed* builder?"

He found her tight little smile amusing. Did she think his walls were going to collapse or his wiring was going to burn the building down? "I'm licensed. If you want to check out my work, I did all the renovations downstairs. It was an open space like this when I bought it."

"Oh. Well, your shop is very nicely done. I just didn't realize you'd be doing the work, that's all."

Ever since that first meeting, ruffling her feathers had served as a cheap form of entertainment. He knew she'd been pleased with his work, though his pace seemed to aggravate her. She even tried to put him on a schedule at one point, telling him when he should have the drywall completed, when he should have the bathroom and kitchen plumbed. The woman lived and breathed by the agenda she had with her at all times.

Still, there was something about her.

Now, as he lay staring toward the shadowed fireplace in the darkened room, he realized all her plans had blown up in her face. He wondered what she would've thought if he told her that first day that she'd marry him three years later. She probably would've laughed in his face.

And yet here they were, on their honeymoon.

*Yeah, I'm on the couch. She made it real clear she wants nothing to do with me.*

And he'd made it just as clear he wasn't interested. Too clear, maybe. He hadn't exactly been the picture of loving-kindness.

He heard a sound coming from the general direction of the bed and lifted his head. A sniff, muffled by a pillow or the bedspread. A quiet hiccup, then another sniffle.

With a sigh, he lay his head back down and closed his eyes. He was a dog. Why had he snapped at her like that? She was grieving. She hadn't had time to recover from the shock of being dumped before she'd found herself married to another man for the next twelve months.

His hands fisted, clenching the pillow until his fingers ached. He wished he could put his arms around her and tell her it was going to be okay.

He wished it was him she loved so much.

⟨∽⟩

Kate felt another sob rising and muffled it with the pillow. Two years with Bryan. Two years spent getting to know him, investing in the relationship, coming to love him. How could he leave her so suddenly, so cruelly? The betrayal was almost too much to bear.

Had his lack of commitment been present all along? Is that why he'd never come to the island, except once, early on in their relationship? She'd made the trip to Boston out of respect for his job. Her hours were more flexible than his, and they were able to spend more time together when she traveled to see him. If it had been up to him, maybe he wouldn't have made the long trips.

Their weekends together had been special to her. They holed themselves up in his apartment, talking and just being together. Bryan turned down invitations to events and get-togethers so they could have time to reconnect. He'd seemed committed.

She was so confused! Kate reached out into the vacant space of the bed where Bryan was supposed to be, her fingers sliding across the cool, empty sheets. Her heart felt as empty.

She pulled the other pillow into her stomach and remembered all the grieving women she'd counseled. Women who'd poured their life into a relationship only to have it jerked from under them at a moment's notice. She hadn't known it felt like this. Seeing others endure it and suffering through it yourself were two different things.

A memory flashed in her mind. It had been shortly after her mom kicked her dad from the house. Her mom's reddened eyes and baggy clothing had become part of her identity, and Kate couldn't remember the last time she'd seen her smile, much less laugh.

Kate entered the tiny living room where her mom sat curled on the couch, staring at the TV, though Kate didn't think she was watching. Kate picked up the remote and flipped through channels. If only she could find something to cheer her mom up. Something to make her forget. Something to make her smile again.

When Kate flipped to *Roseanne*, she turned up the volume. Her mom always laughed at that show. Sitting beside her, she pulled her knees to her chest and yanked her nightgown over them, stretching the thin pink material to its limits.

The show's audience laughed at something Dan said, but a glance at her mom dampened Kate's spirits. Her face was blank, the light from the TV glazing her deadened eyes. Why was she so sad? If she missed Daddy, why didn't she ask him to come back?

Kate felt her own eyes burning, watched Roseanne's living room blur. She missed her dad, and her mom obviously missed him too. Why wouldn't she let him come back?

Her mom popped to her feet. "I'm going to bed, pumpkin." Her words sounded squeezed from her throat, as if a scarf was wrapped too tightly around her neck.

"Good night," Kate answered, but her mom was already down the hall, closing her door. The light in the room flickered as the scenes on TV changed. Kate watched the room glow white, then blue, then white again.

From down the hall the sound of her mom's muffled weeping reached her ears. Kate had grown to hate the sound that escorted her to sleep each night. She turned up the volume and lay on the itchy tweed couch, then pulled a pillow to her ear . . .

Now, Kate turned over and dried her face with the sheet. She hadn't thought about that night in years. Not until now, when her own life seemed to have taken over exactly where her mother's had left off.

A sound reached her ears, and she lifted her head from the pillow, listening. A second later, she heard it again—a long, loud snort coming from the direction of the couch. *Great. Just my luck.*

Her new husband snored.

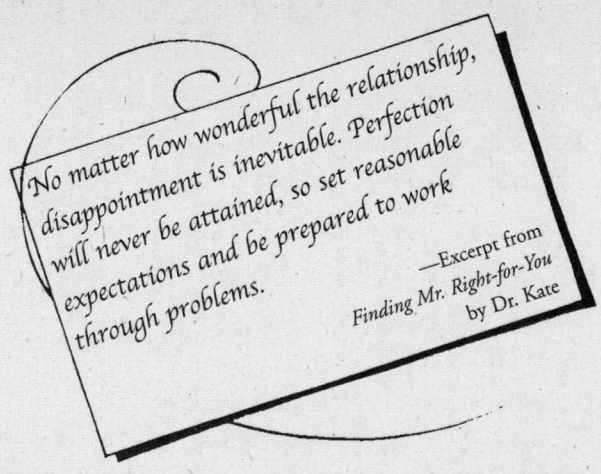

*No matter how wonderful the relationship, disappointment is inevitable. Perfection will never be attained, so set reasonable expectations and be prepared to work through problems.*

—Excerpt from
*Finding Mr. Right-for-You*
by Dr. Kate

# Chapter Six

A distant clattering woke Kate. She stirred, stretching her limbs, before opening her eyes. The room was dark, and she tried to get her bearings as the events of the day before emerged, rising like a tsunami out of a still sea.

She'd married Lucas.

She was on her honeymoon.

Kate closed her eyes, wishing for the oblivion of slumber again. Maybe she could fall back asleep. For a year.

Another noise, a quiet clinking, disrupted her efforts. Apparently Lucas woke before the break of dawn. She rolled over and tugged the duvet over her head, but moments later the rich aroma of brewing coffee beckoned her. *Aaahhhh . . .* She pushed the cover down and sat up against the heap of pillows, untangling her legs from the sheets.

"Sorry," Lucas whispered from the wet bar. "Didn't mean to wake you."

Kate rubbed her eyes. Her lids felt heavy and swollen. "You're forgiven. Especially if you made enough for me." She needed it right now just to keep her eyes open.

He turned on a light over the bar. "How do you take yours?"

"Cream and sugar." What she'd really like was some good espresso, but the coffee should be decent in a fancy hotel like this. "Do you always rise so early?"

She heard the splash of coffee into the cup. "Yep."

Great. She hoped he didn't expect her to talk in the morning.

Before she could make her legs work, he brought her a mug. "Thanks."

He'd apparently already showered and dressed. His wet hair hung in strings beside his face. The five o'clock shadow was back.

She took a sip. It was good for regular coffee. Strong enough to wake her at least. For the rest, they had cappuccino and lattes at the restaurant. She'd made certain of that before she'd made the reservation.

As she sipped the brew, her mind kicked into gear. She thought about the wedding and Lucas's family. She thought about the media and the articles coming out in today's papers. What would they say?

Then she thought about Bryan. Was he planning to marry this other woman? Why hadn't she asked who it was? Maybe he'd realize he made a mistake and break up with the mystery woman. Why hadn't Kate told him this marriage with Lucas was temporary? Maybe she and Bryan could still be together someday.

"What's on the agenda today?" Lucas's voice startled her.

She sipped her coffee. "What makes you think there's an agenda?"

He gave her that lazy half smile. "Because you're Kate Lawrence." The smile faltered. "Well. Guess you're not anymore."

She was supposed to be Kate Montgomery. She remembered the way she used to jot her name with her boyfriends' last names when she was a teenager. She'd say the name out loud, testing it on her tongue. She hadn't even thought of her married name with Lucas until the justice pronounced them man and wife. *Kate Wright.* It sounded strange.

Lucas studied her from across the room, and she remembered he'd asked a question. The itinerary. She had it memorized. "We were supposed to go to the beach today, surfside. Bryan wanted to—" Why was she rambling about Bryan? "Anyway, it would give us time to make plans, if you're up for it." He didn't seem like a beach person, but she could be wrong.

He shrugged. "Sure. I'll need to swing by my house and pick up my things first."

He'd need to know what she had planned in order to pack accordingly. She rattled off the agenda, noting the whaling museum, the day trip to Martha's Vineyard, and the other points of interest she'd planned to take Bryan to.

The more things she listed, the higher Lucas's brows went.

"What?" Kate asked.

"There any room for spontaneity on that list?"

"Spontan—what in the world for?"

His crooked smile was slow. "Tell you what. I'll do everything on your agenda if you'll allow one day of spontaneity."

Kate frowned. What was the point? She'd included everything a person could want from one week on Nantucket. She studied Lucas skeptically. "What would we do?"

His head cocked. "Planning kind of ruins the point."

She sighed. She supposed it was his vacation too. "Oh, all right. One day." Her hollow stomach let out a growl. "I'm starving." She hadn't taken more than two bites at the reception.

"Room service?"

She was ready to sit down to a big, hot breakfast. "I was thinking the restaurant."

He leaned against the back of the sofa, hands in his shorts pockets. "Won't that seem odd?"

*Odd? Oh.* Newlyweds would still be in bed at this hour. For several more hours, at least. She felt her cheeks grow warm. "Maybe you're right. Will you order something while I grab a shower?"

He gave a mock bow. "Your wish is my command."

Kate refrained from rolling her eyes.

⌘

While Kate showered, Lucas called room service and placed their order, then puttered around the room awhile, procrastinating.

He couldn't put it off any longer. The last thing he wanted was for his parents to read about the wedding in the paper before he told them. As it was, it wasn't going to be much fun.

He picked up the phone and dialed his mom's cell. "Hi, honey," his mom greeted him. "Hang on a second. I need to plug in the phone."

A moment later she returned. "Ah, there we go. My battery was about to go, and I didn't want to lose you. Everything okay there?"

"Everything's fine. I just called with some news." He gulped, ambled across the room, and leaned on the armoire. "It might be a little, uh, surprising. Are you sitting down?" It didn't matter if she was. When she heard the news, all the miles between them wouldn't seem like enough.

"I'm in the car, Lucas. What's wrong?"

"Well, you won't believe it, but I—" *Just say it.* "I got married last night."

The silence betrayed her shock. Three seconds dragged by. He heard the clock on the wall ticking them off. Then . . .

"Mar-ried!" His dad said something in the background before his mom spoke again. "Who in the world to? I didn't even know you were dating."

Neither had he. "Well. We kind of kept it under wraps. Low-key." Nonexistent key. *I have to tell her; there's no way to soften the blow.* "It's Kate, Mom. Kate Lawrence."

It sounded like his mom sucked the air from the hotel room through the phone line. But he didn't have to wait long for her to recover. "Kate Lawrence. Kate Lawrence?" She jabbed each syllable at him. "Lucas, how could you?"

"I know. I know, Mom. I knew you'd be upset. That's why I didn't tell you until now."

"You mean until it was too late to do anything about it!"

"There's nothing you could've done about it anyway. I'm a grown man, and I make my own decisions. Especially about whom I marry."

"You didn't even invite us to the wedding." She sucked in another breath. "The wedding! She was supposed to have some big production with the media!" His dad mumbled in the background again. "For heaven's sakes, how did it look that we weren't there? The whole country is going to know we missed our son's wedding!"

"It was actually a small, intimate affair, Mom, and I'm sure—"

"This is awful!"

"I know you're shocked, and I don't expect you to be happy about Kate. But I want you to remember one thing." He waited until she stopped huffing. Then waited two beats beyond that. He needed her to hear what he said, take it to heart.

"I love her, Mom. Regardless of the past—which, incidentally, she's not responsible for—Kate makes me happy."

He could almost hear his mom's frustration, her emotions torn between her unresolved anger and her son's happiness.

The shower in the bathroom kicked off. He wanted to be off the phone before Kate returned.

"Were Brody and Jamie there, at least?" His mom's words sounded as though they'd been squeezed from a lemon.

"They were there. My identity was kept a secret from the media, you know. Nobody knew it was me until last night."

"Well, you could have told us."

His dad's words were muffled. "Let it go, Susan. What's done is done."

Sage advice, but easier said than done, and probably not welcome coming from the man she blamed.

&#x262C;

Kate left the foggy bathroom, feeling somewhat refreshed, though still sleepy. She should have asked Lucas to order a latte. She walked into the room, where the breakfast food was set out on the coffee table. Lucas sat in the armchair, waiting to dig into his home fries, over-easy eggs, toast, and stack of crispy bacon. In front of Kate's seat was a plate of fresh melon, granola, and yogurt. Her stomach protested.

She put her dirty clothes in a plastic laundry bag, settled on the couch, and stabbed a berry with her fork, sliding it into her mouth.

"What's wrong?" Lucas loaded his fork with potatoes and took a bite of bacon.

"Nothing." The berries were good. Sweet and juicy. Healthy.

"I didn't know what you liked."

Of course he didn't. It wasn't like they'd dated. He didn't even know how she took her coffee or that she liked to sleep in. "This is fine. It's good." She took a bite of granola to prove it. It was homemade, crunchy and sweet. Just not what she'd been in the mood for.

"Here." Lucas scraped an egg and half his potatoes and bacon onto the plate his toast had been on.

Her mouth watered. "I'm fine, Lucas."

He slid the fruit to the side and pushed the plate in front of her. "Eat up."

They ate quietly, and by the time Kate set her fork down, she'd made up for the meal she'd skipped the day before.

"I went out and got the paper while you were getting ready."

"Which one?"

"The *Mirror* and the *New York Times*." He produced sections of the papers from the coffee table's shelf.

Her insides were an ocean buoy in the wake of a speedboat. "Did you read them? What did they say?"

*Oh, please, please.*

She grabbed the *Times* first. There they were, her and Lucas, on the cover of the "Style" section. A photo of them dancing. They were looking into each other's eyes, and the photographer had captured Lucas's smile.

"See for yourself," he said.

Her eyes flitted to the article. Its heading read "*Dr. Kate Marries Mr. Wright.*" She smiled. "Clever."

"Thought you'd like that," Lucas said.

She read aloud. "'Syndicated columnist Kate Lawrence, known to audiences as Dr. Kate, married Nantucket native Lucas Wright in a ceremony last evening on Jetties Beach in Nantucket. The wedding was scheduled to coincide with the release of Dr. Kate's book *Finding Mr. Right-for-You.*

"'The identity of the groom was kept secret until the ceremony—part of the publicity campaign surrounding the book's release.

"'Lawrence said she met her Mr. Wright when she rented the space above his furniture shop in Nantucket Town. "He renovated my apartment and my office. Then I guess he renovated my heart."'"

Kate glanced at Lucas, her face warming.

His lip quirked. "I had no idea," he said.

"Dream on." Kate went back to the article.

"'Lucas Wright is a furniture maker, known locally by wealthy vacationers who summer on the island. When asked about their future plans, Lawrence said, "We plan to stay in Nantucket, of course. It's our home."

"'*Finding Mr. Right-for-You* is Dr. Kate's first book. She will appear on the *Dr. Phil* show later this summer, and she plans to continue her column while she works on her second book.'"

Kate put the paper down. "It's all good," she said in wonder. *We did it.* They'd pulled it off—at least, if the *Times* was any indication. "What does the *Mirror* say?" She picked up the next section. The photograph was a close-up of them in the carriage, waving good-bye, the tulle of her veil blowing to the side. It had much of the same information as the *Times*, though presented with a more local approach.

When she was finished, she picked up the *Times* again, noticing the way the paper trembled in her fingers. "Rosewood will be thrilled. I can't believe how relieved I am." Relieved wasn't the word. If she'd gone through with the wedding only to be found out, it would've done more damage than being jilted.

"Did we cover all our bases?" she asked. "We have to be sure those who know aren't going to say anything."

"I told Mr. Lavitz when he fitted me for the tux about the need for discretion. He's an old friend—I know he won't say anything. And you know Nancy and the justice will keep quiet. They're town officers. They know how to be discreet."

"Pam and Chloe and Anna won't say anything. My dad's a given. Who else knows?"

"Bryan's family," he said.

It was the biggest risk of a leak. Had Bryan told them? Kate chewed on her lip. What if one of them read an article and told a friend or two the wedding was a farce? What if they contacted the media?

"Maybe you should call him and make sure." Lucas leaned forward, planting his elbows on his knees, bracing his coffee cup between his palms.

Kate had been thinking it herself, but dreading it all at the same time. It hurt to think about Bryan. She'd been up half the night thinking about him, about how he was supposed to be in bed beside her. *This was supposed to be the beginning of our life together.*

*Suck it up, Kate, and move on. You've done it before, and you can do it again.* She'd made a lot of sacrifices along the way, and she wasn't giving up now.

"You're right." Her watch said it was just after eight. Late enough to call. *What, am I worried about waking the man?* She should have called him in the middle of the night. He'd kept her awake, after all. It would've served him right.

"Why don't I go home and get my things while you make the call?"

Kate nodded, wondering what to say to Bryan. "What about your parents? You need to call them before they see the papers."

Lucas folded the paper and stood. "Already did, while you were in the shower."

"What did they say?"

Lucas shrugged. "They were shocked, naturally. I told them we'd kept it low-key because of the media."

"Weren't they angry they weren't here for the wedding?"

"Disappointed. They were glad Brody and Jamie were there."

Kate tucked her damp hair behind her ears. "Oh, good. Well, I guess we'll have to make it up to them when they return."

Lucas left, and Kate retrieved her cell phone. She dialed Bryan's number, her heart drumming a syncopated beat.

The phone rang twice before a woman answered. "Hello?"

Kate's words clogged her throat. She was there? In his apartment? In the apartment that was supposed to be *theirs*?

"Hello?" the woman repeated.

Kate took the phone from her ear and started to hang up.

But she had to talk to Bryan, had to make sure he'd spoken with his family. She put the phone back to her ear and heard shuffling sounds, then Bryan's voice.

"Hello?" His voice was morning scratched.

Kate clamped her teeth together. Were they in bed together? What had happened to their agreement to save themselves for marriage? Apparently it had only been Kate's conviction.

"Kate?"

"Yes, it's Kate. I can't believe she's there with you. For heaven's sake, Bryan, we were supposed to get married yesterday."

She heard a rustling noise—sheets? "Excuse me if I'm wrong, but didn't you just spend the night with your new husband?"

His comment made her skin tingle, made the flesh under her arms go hot. "After you deserted me on our wedding day!"

"What do you even know about him, Kate?"

"What do you care?" She stood and paced the length of the room. What was she doing? She had to settle down. It would accomplish nothing to have Bryan angry at her. "I didn't call to argue. I called to make sure you'd talked to your family. Did you make them understand how important it is that they keep their mouths shut?" She could've worded it more nicely, but he wasn't exactly on her favorite-people list right now.

"I talked to them. I told you I would." His voice was tight.

What did he have to be angry about when he had another woman there in bed with him? While she'd been crying over him in their honeymoon bed, he'd been—She closed her eyes and shook her head to dislodge the image. She couldn't bear the thought of it right now.

"My career is riding on this, you know," she said. "Do they understand the magnitude of—"

"Yes, yes, they understand. Do you think I want to be in the spotlight as the jerk who jilted Dr. Kate at the altar?"

"Well said."

The silence was deafening. She should hold her tongue; she really should. She was a counselor, for crying out loud. Where was her control?

"I'll let you go." Perhaps he'd get the double meaning. "I just wanted to be sure things were taken care of."

She hung up before she said something she'd regret later. When she set the phone on the coffee table, she realized her hand was shaking.

Bryan was in bed with her. Kate's Mr. Right in bed with someone else on what was supposed to have been their wedding night. Could life be more unfair?

At least he'd made his family understand the importance of keeping quiet. That was the main thing. And the articles were positive.

*Look on the bright side. I'm going to live through this and come out stronger.* The year with Lucas would pass quickly, and then she could get on with her life and career.

She realized she hadn't told Bryan the marriage was temporary, but given the situation, she didn't want to give him the satisfaction. Let him think she would be bound to Lucas for the rest of her life. Maybe it would make him squirm just a little.

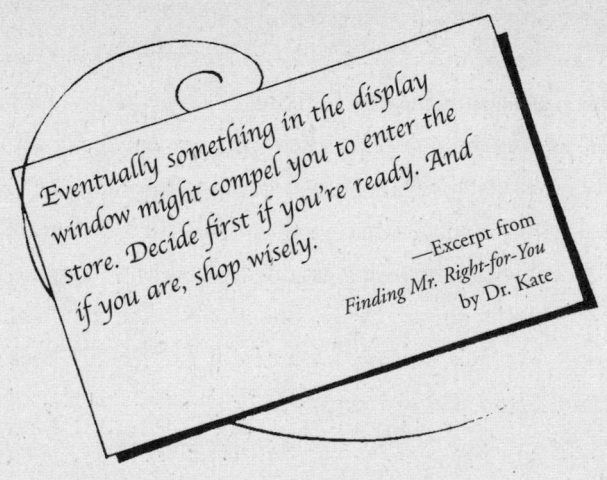

*Eventually something in the display window might compel you to enter the store. Decide first if you're ready. And if you are, shop wisely.*

—Excerpt from
*Finding Mr. Right-for-You*
by Dr. Kate

# Chapter Seven

Kate shrugged off her cover-up, took her list from the tote, and lay belly down on the beach towel beside Lucas. She squinted against the sun's reflection on the bright white paper.

"Okay, we need a story. We already told people how we met, but I think we need more details to make it realistic. Your family will probably want to know what we do together. They'll expect us to know things about each other."

"I know you take your coffee with cream and sugar." Lucas leaned back on his elbows a foot away from her. The wind blew his hair away from his face.

"But you don't know that I drink a triple-shot latte every day before work. Or that I prefer showers to baths. Or that I'm allergic to cats."

"Hope you're not allergic to dogs."

"Do you have one?"

He lay back against the towel, folding his arms behind his head, his eyes closed against the sun. "A sheepdog named Bo. You'll love him."

She wasn't much of an animal person, but she supposed she could deal with one dog. Wasn't a sheepdog like a miniature Lassie? She could deal with a little dog as long as he was well trained.

"Found him alongside Milestone Road when he was a pup," Lucas said. "He was missing a bunch of fur on his neck, and I couldn't find his owner, so I kept him."

She jotted down the information. *Sheepdog, Bo.*

"What else should I know about you?" she asked.

She watched his chest rise and fall, glistening under the glare of the sun. His skin was dark, his chest well defined. She wondered if he worked out or if the muscles came from his work.

*Stop staring!* She sneaked a glance at his face to be sure she hadn't been caught looking. He'd probably think she was checking him out. Which she hadn't been.

Well, not too much.

"I like to sail, watch documentaries on TV, and fix anything broken."

Kate scribbled more notes. "Anything else?"

A muscle twitched in his jaw. "I was married before. I guess you need to know that."

How had she not known? "What happened?"

His eyelids fluttered, and he swallowed, then shifted, clasping his hands together on his flat abdomen.

"Sorry if I'm prying, but—" His family would expect her to know. She wondered if his ex-wife lived on the island. Maybe Kate knew her.

"Her name was Emily. She died five years ago."

*Oh.*

She studied him. His tone was so soft, it obviously still affected him. Did he still love her? Maybe that's why she hadn't seen him with another woman.

"I'm sorry," she said.

"Her family used to summer here. I met her when she came to the shop for a rocking chair. The business was getting off the ground, and we started dating. The rest was history."

Kate waited for him to finish. The only sounds were that of the waves crashing the shoreline and the laughter of children playing in the shallows. "Is that when you built your house?"

He crossed his ankles. His legs were long and thick, covered in wiry black hair. "No. We lived in a cottage in Cisco after we married. I didn't build my house until . . . until after."

She didn't have to ask "After what?" It was still painful for him to talk about. Kate wondered why he'd married her. Given the way he obviously still felt about Emily, he had to care a great deal about his parents to be willing to sacrifice a year of his life to save their marriage.

She hated to grill him, but she'd be expected to know. She set the pen on the towel and propped her head on her palm. "How did she . . . die?"

She didn't think he was going to answer. She wasn't even sure he'd heard her softly spoken question over the seagulls' cries. But after a moment he sighed.

"It was my fault. Guess that's why it's still hard to talk about."

What did he mean? She wanted to ask, wanted to know the details. Even though Lucas irritated her, he wasn't the type to harm anyone. In fact, he was always helping people. In his own time, but helping them nonetheless.

"She had allergies—lots of them. The environmental ones like pollens were easily controlled with medication, so it wasn't a big deal." He shifted. "She'd tested allergic to peanuts as a teenager, but she'd never had a reaction. She avoided them, though, because her doctor told her to."

Two teenagers behind them tossed a Frisbee, and it sailed over them and landed a few feet away, flicking up the sand. Lucas waited while they retrieved it.

"The week she died, I'd done the grocery shopping. I bought a bag of chips that were fried in peanut oil." He shook his head. "Didn't even think about checking the ingredients. I used to tease her about being overly cautious."

Kate's heart went out to him. Couldn't he see it was an accident?

"I'd been at the shop working on an order I was running behind on, and when I came home . . . it was too late."

She watched his face, the way his jaw clenched, the way his lips tightened. She wished she could console him somehow. "I'm so sorry."

His chest rose and fell. "It was a long time ago."

Five years wasn't that long. He'd been married to the love of his life and now he was sitting on the beach with his counterfeit bride. She wondered how he felt about that.

He turned and opened his eyes, squinting against the glare of the sun. "So that's my story. What's yours?"

She appreciated his desire to change the subject. "What do you want to know?"

Lucas watched Kate turn her head until her cheek rested in her hand. She looked like a little girl, her sun-flushed cheeks bunched up against her palm. He already knew more about her than she was aware. She was twenty-eight, her favorite flowers were daisies, her birthday was November 26, and she color-coded her Day-Timer.

He went for the unknown. "How did you become an advice columnist?"

She smiled. "Friends in high school always came to me for advice, and I was good at giving it." Kate shrugged. "I started on my life plan my junior year in high—"

"Life plan?"

"A plan detailing my short- and long-term goals." She said it as if everyone had one. "Anyway, I realized I had a knack for helping people with relationship decisions. Then I took a fabulous writing class in high school and started my first manuscript." She cocked her head. "It was bad, but I didn't know it at the time. However, I realized I wanted to combine my love for helping people with my love of writing."

"You had all this planned out before high school graduation?"

She flipped onto her side. "Sure. I knew I wanted to get a psych degree from Cornell and go into counseling so I could support myself and gain experience while getting my writing career started."

"You were born on Nantucket, right? Is that why you're here now?"

"My parents grew up here, and, yes, I was born here. We moved to Maryland when I was five because my dad got relocated. Then, when I was in college, a friend invited me here for a week to stay in her parents' cottage in 'Sconset. What can I say? It felt like coming back home."

"So you added Nantucket to your life plan?"

"Are you making fun of me?"

How could he criticize when she'd met all her goals? Except he was sure marrying him hadn't been on that list of hers. "What about the column?"

She stuck her knee out to the side, and he worked to keep his eyes away from the smooth curve of her hips. "I started it at Cornell for the school newspaper. At first I wrote my own questions; then students began writing me, and it all took off from there."

Apparently she set her mind to something and made it happen by sheer will. "Ambitious one, aren't you?"

A wind tousled her fringed bangs. "I like helping people. Initially in my practice I focused on couples with marriage problems."

"You seemed to build up a decent clientele." He was in his shop enough to see clients passing up and down the stairs on the hour.

"The more I counseled married people, the more I began to see that people were making poor choices in the spouses they selected. They'd come to me, polar opposites, wanting different things out of life, and wonder why they couldn't get along. I started putting together a plan to help people make better choices about who they marry."

She made it sound like it could be boiled down to cold, hard facts. "What about love?"

"Well, of course, there has to be love. But by choosing to date the right people, you limit yourself to those who are best suited to you."

He turned on his side, mirroring her position. "How do you know if they're suited to you until you know them? And once you know them that well, aren't you likely to have fallen in love with them already?"

Her breath huffed out. "What is this, an inquisition?" She rolled onto her back, propping her head on her bag, and closed her eyes. "My plan is detailed and well thought out. If you want to know more, read the stinking book."

She'd gotten snippy in a hurry. Maybe she felt defensive since her fail-proof plan hadn't turned out to be so fail proof.

Which reminded him of her ex-fiancé. Lucas wanted to ask if she'd called him, but judging by her set little chin, maybe now wasn't the time.

Something at the corner of his vision caught his attention. A man in dress clothes sat on the sand down the shore, holding a camera with a zoom lens. He looked as out of place as a diamond in a toolbox.

Lucas looked at Kate. "I think we have company."

She didn't bother opening her eyes. "Who?"

"One of the photographers from the wedding. Down the shore a ways."

She opened her eyes.

"Don't look."

Kate looked at Lucas instead. "Is he looking this way? Does he have a camera?"

"Yes and yes."

"Which one is he?"

"I don't remember. He was at the wedding, though. The one with spiky hair and artsy glasses."

She sighed. "He's from *Cosmo*. I guess they wanted some honeymoon shots for the article."

"They could've asked instead of sneaking around like the paparazzi."

"They can't. I made it clear to my agent the honeymoon was off limits. Did he see you looking?"

"No. But he has a zoom lens that can probably see the amber flecks in your eyes from a hundred feet."

She tucked her hair behind her ears. "Great. I guess we haven't exactly looked like newlyweds, have we?"

He rolled on his stomach next to her, their sides brushing. Her skin was warm, and the feel of her smooth skin against his leg stoked a fire in his belly. "We could consider that our first fight."

"Wasn't much of one." She smiled.

She was probably thinking they made a much better photo now, lying so close and gazing into each other's eyes. But all Lucas could think about was what her sun-warmed lips would taste like. The wedding kiss seemed like a distant memory and Kate had been shell-shocked. What would a slow, lingering kiss feel like here on the beach, under the sun with the salted breeze stroking their skin?

"Why are you looking at me like that?"

*Because I want to pull you in my arms and give that man a lensful.* "We're honeymooners, remember?"

She pulled her lip between her teeth. "Oh. Right. And we just had our first tiff. Maybe we should kiss and make up."

With the sun shining into her face, her eyes ran more toward rich brown than olive. Like melted caramel. "It's a thought," he said.

"Okay, go ahead." She tilted toward him. Her eyes skimmed his face and fell on his lips.

He grinned, leaning over her until his shadow blocked the sun from her face. "I have permission now, huh?"

She touched his jaw. "What?"

"Are you sure it's on the list for today?" he teased.

She twitched her eyebrow. "You sure know how to ruin the mood." Was her voice a little breathy?

"There was a mood?" Before she could answer, he closed the space between them and kissed her slowly, reveling in the way she reciprocated. His hand settled on her side where her silky bathing suit clung to the curve of her waist.

For a moment he let himself forget she was only responding for the camera. He remembered every time he'd seen her leaving her office, every time he watched her walk down the sidewalk, hair swishing with each step. Every time she knocked on his shop door late at night to complain about the noise.

*All those times I wanted to grab her and kiss the living daylights out of her.*

Kate pulled away from him, breaking his thoughts. "There. He should've gotten plenty of good photos."

The cold wave of her words doused the mood. Trying for nonchalance, he turned onto his back and closed his eyes, hoping she couldn't see his heart thundering against his chest wall. He'd wanted the kiss to be more than show. He wanted it to be real.

*You got yourself into this, man.*

"Is he still there?" she asked.

They'd only started playing the game, and already he'd tired of it. "I don't know." And he wasn't going to look.

"I guess we shouldn't look."

He felt her hand, delicate against his own.

*She's just pretending. Don't forget that.*

"Let's talk about your parents. I need to know anything that will help me understand their problems."

Lucas was tired of the whole thing. Right now he wanted to blurt out that his parents didn't have a problem, that he'd married her because he loved her. But that would only scare her away.

He swallowed. "I'm not sure what's wrong between them. They just fuss a lot."

"You said your mom left for a while. Did they have a fight?"

This was going to be harder than he thought. "I don't know. I really don't know what the problem is. That's why I need your help."

Her fingers intertwined with his, and he felt the wedding band.

"Don't you feel you can talk openly with your parents?"

He cringed. He was getting himself in deeper and deeper. "I'm not a talker—you know that much about me." The seagulls cried out, and another wave hit the shore. "I'm just not good with words, and I don't think they'd want me interfering anyway."

He needed to make sure Kate was subtle with his mom. Otherwise Kate would find out it was all a ruse. "You'll need to get to know my mom before expecting her to open up." *Good luck with that.* He couldn't imagine anyone his mom would be less likely open up to.

An instant later panic struck. What if his mom confronted Kate about her mom? No. As soon as the panic hit, it evaporated. His mom didn't confront people. She killed silently with subtle digs and innuendos, God love her.

"That goes without saying."

"And leave Jamie and Brody out of it. I don't want them stressing about our parents." Or setting Kate straight about their fussing.

"If they live with your parents, they know what's going on. Even young children pick up on conflict. It affects them more deeply than you realize."

Her voice held a tone of sadness. He looked at her, but she turned onto her back, withdrawing her hand, and closed her own eyes. Lucas had a feeling there was a load of hurt backing up that statement, and he wondered if Kate would ever trust him enough to share it.

❧

Lucas took Kate's hand as they climbed the steps of the White Elephant. The week had passed quickly. It was hard to believe tomorrow it would be over. His Spontaneity Day with Kate had proved to be a challenge. She seemed unacquainted with the idea of letting things happen and had spent most of the day trying to figure out what they were doing next.

Now, she looked tired and sun drained, her cheeks reddened from their walk through 'Sconset. Maybe he'd order room service so she wouldn't have to go back out for dinner.

They entered the lobby floor and passed the registration desk. Kate stopped suddenly by a woman at the desk, withdrawing her hand from his.

"Mrs. Hornsby?" Kate touched the woman on the shoulder, and she turned. The woman might have been attractive if not for her puffy eyes and tight, bronzed lips.

"Dr. Kate." Mrs. Hornsby straightened and turned her lips into a semblance of a smile.

"Are you okay?" Kate asked.

Lucas stepped away to give them privacy, inspecting some literature on the desk. He couldn't help but hear their conversation.

"I'm fine." The woman said, but her words crumbled like a soggy cookie.

Kate took her arm and pulled her away from the desk. "What are you doing here? Did something happen?"

Lucas heard the woman restrain a sob. "Earl is having an affair. I have proof this time. I just—just couldn't stay there."

"I'm so sorry." Kate's tone softened. She rubbed the woman's arm. "Do you want to talk?"

Mrs. Hornsby laughed feebly, wiping her eyes. "Oh, honey, no. It's your honeymoon. Besides, you're not even counseling anymore." She withdrew a tissue from her beige purse and dabbed her eyes. "I'll be fine."

"Don't be silly," Kate said. "Are you finished checking in?"

The other woman held up a key card. "Yes."

Kate squeezed her rounded shoulder. "I'll be right back."

She approached Lucas, and he put the brochure for a whaling tour back into the holder.

"Would you mind having dinner alone?" Kate asked, then lowered her tone. "She's a former client, and she could use someone to talk to."

"Of course not," Lucas said. "Want me to order you something from room service?"

"Thanks, but I'm not sure how long I'll be."

A moment later, Lucas was alone.

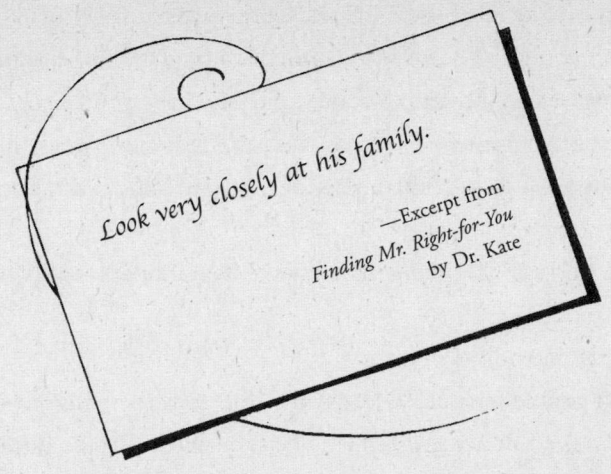

*Look very closely at his family.*

—Excerpt from
*Finding Mr. Right-for-You*
by Dr. Kate

# Chapter Eight

"Start slowing down," Lucas said. "That's it. The one with the truck out front."

Kate navigated her car down the street. It ran parallel to the shore and was lined on both sides by cottages, generously separated by wide grassy lots.

Kate braked and eased into the drive, the tires slurping through the thick layer of gravel. Lucas's house sat off the road about a hundred yards, and behind it, the ocean provided a deep blue backdrop. The nearest house on his side of the street was a couple hundred yards away, the second story barely visible above a rise in the ground.

Kate stopped behind a beater Ford in the drive. *I married a pickup man.*

That thought was barely out before she surveyed the cottage.

Instinctively she liked its character. Gray, weathered shingles covered the small cottage. The trim and porch railing sported bright white paint, and orange flowers of some kind lined the front beds.

She put her car into Park and slid out. "It's nice." Small, but new. There appeared to be a main part of the house and a small addition of some sort.

She popped the trunk and had just grabbed a bag when she heard a shout.

"Welcome home!"

Four people scampered down the hill from the house next door. She recognized Brody and Jamie. The other two must be Lucas's parents. A huge, hairy dog led the pack, and Mrs. Wright trailed the others by several yards, her slender body stiff, her arms stagnant at her sides.

Kate waved and smiled for their benefit. "What is your family doing here?" She wanted to get settled in the house. She was tired of being on public display. The photographer had left them alone after that first day at the beach, but even eating out they'd encountered stares and whispers.

"They live next door," Lucas said. "Didn't I tell you?"

*Next door?* Maintaining her smile was no easy feat. "You neglected to mention that detail." He was going to get an earful later.

"Hey, guys," Lucas called as his family approached.

The dog leaped on Lucas. It was the size of a bear.

"Hey, Bo." He ruffled the animal's floppy ears.

*That is not Bo.* She considered the size of the house and the size of the dog. What was he thinking? She nearly expressed her thoughts, then remembered his family would find it odd she hadn't seen Bo before. They probably wondered how they hadn't seen her there before, living right next door like they did.

Roy Wright approached first, wearing jeans, a Nantucket polo, and a genuine smile. "Welcome, welcome." He hugged Kate first, patting her shoulder as if to burp her. He had a thick head of gray hair and a tan that leathered his skin. His clear green eyes angled downward at the sides.

"Thank you," Kate said. Her eyes met Susan Wright's as the woman came to a stop at the edge of the gravel driveway. "Hello."

Susan nodded, her rose-colored lips pulled back into what didn't quite pass as a smile. "Kate." Her mushroom-shaped hairstyle framed her narrow face and high cheekbones.

"I wanted to get some pictures." Jamie held up the camera that was around her neck. Her smile revealed braces with purple and pink bands. "Did you have a wonderful week?"

Kate felt like she was trapped in a *Raymond* episode. In real life the situation wasn't so amusing.

"It was perfect," she said as Lucas embraced his mom. Brody shook her hand, an apology in his eyes, if not on his lips.

What kind of man built a house next door to his parents? Apparently she'd not only married a pickup man, but a momma's boy as well.

Lucas and his parents caught up briefly before Lucas asked them inside.

"No, we're not staying," Susan said pointedly. "Are we, Roy?" She set a fine-boned hand on her husband's arm.

"Of course not; we just wanted to welcome you home, welcome Kate to the family."

"And take a picture of Lucas carrying Kate over the threshold," Jamie said.

Kate had forgotten about the tradition. A stupid tradition. She didn't want to be cast into the helpless maiden role. "How thoughtful."

She was tired of smiling. She didn't want to smile for the next week.

"Don't pressure them, Jamie." Susan eyed Kate up and down. "Besides, Lucas might not be up to it."

*Score one for the mother-in-law.* Kate smiled through clenched teeth.

"No doubt," Brody whispered to Lucas, wearing a sly smile. "Bet you're exhausted."

Lucas elbowed his brother. "Far be it from me to deny tradition."

"Pick her up, Lucas!" Jamie said. "This is so romantic." She clapped her hands.

"Scrubbing the floor would be romantic to you," Brody said.

"Shut up." Jamie whacked him in the gut with the back of her hand while Bo barked loudly and circled around them as if sensing the excitement.

"I'll get your bags," Brody said, walking toward the trunk.

Before Kate could move, Lucas swept her off her feet. She grabbed him around the neck, latching onto his shoulders as he walked toward the cottage and up the three steps. The camera clicked several times.

"You could have warned me," Kate whispered in his ear. First the next-door in-laws, then the big hairy dog, and now another photo op? Who'd started this dumb tradition anyway? She felt like a worthless sack of beans in his arms.

"Just sit back and enjoy, Mrs. Wright." His breath hit her cheek.

Another photo snapped. "Don't call me that."

He shifted her and pulled open the screen door, then twisted the knob on the wooden door. She should probably help, but wasn't in the mood. She heard yet another click as Bo brushed by, squeezing his enormous mass past them.

Kate clenched her jaw. *Please let this end!*

"That's enough, Jamie," Susan said. "For heaven's sake."

Once inside, Lucas set Kate down and she stepped away, relieved to be on her own feet again. Brody had followed and now handed Lucas their luggage. They stood awkwardly for a moment, Brody looking from one to the other with a grin.

"Well, guess you two love birds want to be alone."

Lucas looked at Kate. "Guess so." Kate refrained from responding.

Brody hugged Lucas exuberantly and, after a slight hesitation, did the same for Kate. He clattered down the steps to his waiting family.

"'Bye, kids!" Roy waved.

"I'll print these out soon and bring them by," Jamie said, holding up the camera.

Susan merely nodded and turned back toward her house.

"Thanks," Kate called.

She stood watching her new in-laws through the screen door as they made their way back up the hill, Brody and Jamie arguing the whole time. Then she turned and narrowed her eyes at Lucas. "You are so dead."

Before he could respond something caught her eye. Her gaze left him to scan the room. "What in the world . . . is all this . . . stuff!"

She stared in horrified amazement at piles and stacks and layers of stuff. Clothes, boxes, magazines . . . The phrase "Early-American Junkyard" came to mind. Was that a shovel leaning against the TV? And what was that smell?

And through it all, Bo wove in and out, his enormous backside wagging. The dog hit a leaning tower of newspapers, and it toppled.

*Lucas is a messie.* She'd married a messie.

"Sorry about that." Lucas kicked a sack aside and closed the front door. "Didn't have time to clean up before the ceremony."

There had been clues on the honeymoon. Socks balled up and left lying on the floor, toiletries spread across the marble counter, wet towels left on the couch.

But this . . .

She felt trapped, and she wasn't even a claustrophobic. What was the floor even made of? She could hardly see it through the stuff. Anna could have warned her, for heaven's sake.

Bo bumped up against her, knocking her sideways. Lucas steadied her. "No, Bo. Come here." He rubbed the dog's head and Bo sat. "Settle down, boy."

Kate picked up her bag. Maybe the whole house wasn't like this. "Where can I put my things?"

Lucas grabbed a few articles of clothing from the back of the sofa and draped them over his shoulder. "Let me show you around."

Bo was up again, circling them, panting happily. Kate glared at him and then at Lucas. Lucas appeared to get the idea.

"Come on, buddy." He let Bo out the front door, where the dog sat facing the screen and barking. "He's just a little excited."

Scooping up a Pepsi can and an empty bowl with a sticky-looking spoon, Lucas led the way down a short hall.

"This is the bedroom."

Bed unmade, clothes heaped on the dresser.

"Yours?"

He opened a dresser drawer, shoved the clothes from the living room inside, and pushed it closed. "Uh, yeah. You can put your bag here." He pushed the heap of clothes to the other side of the dresser, having the grace to look sheepish. "I'll make room in the drawers and closet for your things."

"I was planning on taking another bedroom." *Hopefully a cleaner one.*

He set down the can and bowl and took her suitcase, setting it on the dresser. "I'm afraid this is it."

Kate let this sink in as she watched him attempt to make the bed. He pulled the blue quilt up over the pillows, leaving the sheets in a wad underneath. "'This is it'? What do you mean?"

He pocketed his hands. "There is no other bedroom."

This was getting worse by the minute. "You built a house with one bedroom?"

He lifted his shoulders. "There's only one of me."

How could he be so casual? So indifferent? Wasn't he at all concerned about his space? "Well, now there's two of us, in case you haven't noticed."

One side of his mouth turned up. "I noticed."

"Who builds a home with one bedroom?" And who was going to sleep on the couch? For a whole year.

"I was planning to add on later."

Well, there you go. The answer to their dilemma. How long could it take to build a bedroom? He could add a room on the other side of the house by the living room.

"Uh-uh," he said, watching her face. "Do you know what my family will think if I add another bedroom?"

That they were sleeping separately? Or no—that they were planning to start a family. Why else would they need another bedroom? Jamie would probably start knitting baby blankets and booties. Strike that idea.

"Look. We're grown adults," Lucas said. "The bed's a double, plenty big enough for both of us."

She looked him over. He was easily six feet, maybe an inch or two more, and he was broad. He'd make the bed feel like a twin. The thought of sleeping so close to him left her feeling hot and itchy.

She cleared her throat. "I'll just take the couch." She took the handle of her luggage.

He set his palm flat on the suitcase. "Don't be ridiculous. You can't sleep on the couch for twelve months."

"Sure I can." Especially if he wasn't going to offer. She pulled at the suitcase, but it went nowhere under his grip. "Let go."

"What'll my family think?"

"They won't think anything. They won't even know." She would put her blanket and pillow away first thing every morning. She supposed she'd have to keep her clothing in the bedroom, though.

"You turn in early, Kate. I'm a night owl."

She hadn't thought of that. How could she fall asleep on the sofa if he was watching TV until midnight? She checked the bed out, wavering.

Lucas leaned against the dresser and crossed his arms over his chest, looking smug. "You afraid or something?"

Kate crossed her own arms. "Don't be ridiculous."

"I'm not the one getting all hot and bothered about sharing a bed."

"I'm not—" She ground her teeth and smothered a growl. Why did he have to say things like that? It was like he took pleasure in getting under her skin.

*It's just a sleeping arrangement, nothing more. What am I so afraid of? It'll be like sharing a bed with a friend on a girls' outing.* Her eyes swept over Lucas's solid frame, down to his hairy legs and sandal-clad feet. She swallowed hard. *Okay, not quite like that.*

*I don't have to . . . do anything in that bed except sleep. In fact, I'll be asleep by the time he comes to bed anyway. And he rises before me. I'll hardly notice he's there.*

Resolved, she met his eyes square on. "Fine. We'll share the room."

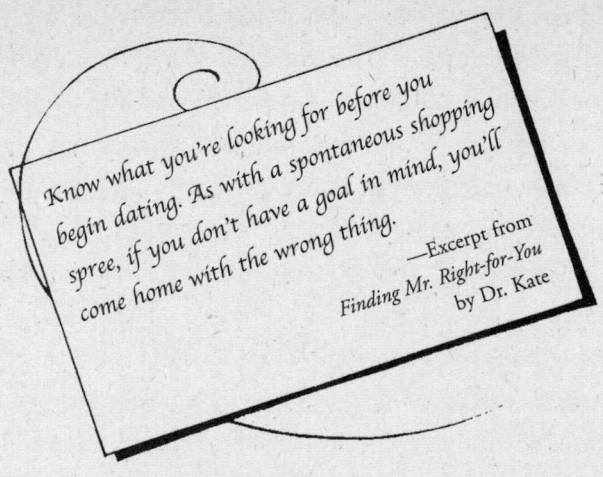

Know what you're looking for before you begin dating. As with a spontaneous shopping spree, if you don't have a goal in mind, you'll come home with the wrong thing.

—Excerpt from *Finding Mr. Right-for-You* by Dr. Kate

# Chapter Nine

It was dark by the time they unloaded Kate's belongings in the cottage. She plugged in her treadmill, which they'd squeezed into a corner of the living room. From here she had a good view out the front window and could watch the news too.

As she contemplated her surroundings, Bo brushed against Kate's legs as if trying to guide her toward the sofa.

"He wants you to sit down and pet him," Lucas said.

"Why is his fur discolored under his mouth?"

Lucas rubbed Bo behind the ears. "Drool yellows the fur." He disappeared into the kitchen, Bo plodding behind him.

Kate grimaced. *I had to ask.*

She turned on the treadmill, making sure it worked, then straightened the square pillows on the couch. She'd tried to tidy up a bit, and now that the floor was clutter free, she saw the nice rug that covered the oak floors. Too bad it was covered in dog hair.

Bo ambled back and plopped down by the fireplace, watching her, his huge, shaggy head cocked. His white hair hung like a dirty mop over his eyes. At least he didn't smell.

"You didn't tell me Bo was so big," Kate called.

"He's a sheepdog," Lucas called from the kitchen, as if that explained it.

"I thought that was like a miniature Lassie. I wasn't expecting a" —there was no call to be rude—"a large dog." Kate stepped past Bo and surveyed the room. Even clean, it felt tiny. The treadmill looked mammoth against the sand-colored wall.

"That's a Shetland sheepdog. He's an Old English sheepdog." Lucas was in the kitchen doorway, two steps away. He extended a cut-glass vase filled with white daisies. "These are for you."

Kate didn't know what to say. "What for?"

He rubbed the back of his neck. "Our one-week anniversary." Was that a flush climbing his cheeks? "It's silly."

The gesture took her aback. "No, it's very . . . sweet." The petals were satin smooth, the stems and leaves clean and groomed. She wondered where he'd gotten them. And when; they'd been together most of the day. "Daisies are my favorite."

"I know."

Kate was sure she hadn't mentioned it on their honeymoon. Even Bryan had always sent orchids for special occasions just because they were most expensive.

Lucas gestured toward the flowers. "You always have them on your desk at work."

She stopped at Flowers on Chestnut for a fresh bouquet every Monday morning after getting her latte. Having fresh daisies perked up the office and inspired her. Strange that he'd noticed. She remembered the daisies he'd etched on the gazebo. She'd thought it a coincidence.

"Well, thank you," she said. "I'll set them on the kitchen table between the salt and pepper shakers."

"I'll do it."

As he returned, Kate yawned. It was getting late, and there was no delaying bedtime. Besides, if she hoped to be asleep when Lucas retired, she needed an early start.

"I think I'll turn in now," she said.

Lucas sank into the recliner and flipped on the TV. Bo curled up at his feet. "'Night. Let me know if you need anything."

Kate stood awkwardly for a moment, but it looked as if Lucas was engrossed in what he was watching. *Well, okay then.*

After completing her beauty regimen and brushing and flossing, Kate changed into her pajamas. She surveyed the bed and felt something cold wedge between her ribs.

*I can do this. I can. No big deal.* She snorted at the thought. *Yeah, right. I'm about to climb into the bed of a man I barely know. And he's going to climb in later.*

Her eyes fell on a worn quilt crumpled between the bed and wall. She retrieved it, spread it across the bed, then rolled it like a giant burrito. Next, she laid it down the center of the bed as a barrier between the two sides. *There, that should do it.*

Kate clicked off Lucas's lamp and rounded the bed, settling on her side. The sheets were soft and cool against her skin, the mattress giving slightly to her weight.

She turned her face into the pillow and immediately regretted it. It smelled faintly of Lucas, all musk and woodsy. Even here, she couldn't escape him.

She thought of the daisies and chided herself for thinking ill of him. He was trying. It wasn't his fault they were so different. Or even that they were stuck together for a year. In fact, he'd saved her life, and she should be grateful. He'd salvaged her book and her career.

She'd called Pam twice from the White Elephant, and Rosewood was thrilled with the wedding publicity. Several cable network shows wanted Kate to make an appearance. Rosewood was talking about a possible book tour, and Pam had scheduled numerous phone interviews with radio shows and newspapers. Kate wondered how she'd keep up with her articles and find time to write another book.

No matter, though. If the publicity sold book one, it would be worth it. And at least she would still have her office space to work in since Lucas hadn't rented it out yet.

She thought of Lucas's family and wondered how she was going to find time to help his parents' marriage. She'd sensed the tension between Susan and Roy. Maybe she could find an activity to do with Susan. It would give them time to talk.

Kate turned and pulled the quilt over her chilled shoulder. It was quieter here than in town. If she listened closely, she could hear the water hitting the shore, and a clock ticking somewhere. The TV program Lucas was watching barely filtered into the room, and a slit of light from the living room underlined the door.

What time would he retire? She hoped he kept to his own side of the bed. Judging by the rumpled sheets she'd found upon her arrival, she had her doubts. He was used to having the whole bed.

Kate was too, but she planned on hugging the edge all night.

*If I ever fall asleep.* She rolled over again and resituated the pillow. She'd already made a to-do list for tomorrow, which usually freed her mind to sleep. She was tired, so that wasn't the issue.

As it had all week during quiet moments, her thoughts turned to Bryan. Kate hadn't called him again, nor had he called. She supposed there was no reason to expect him to. She shouldn't even want him to.

But feelings didn't flip off like a light switch. She wondered if he'd seen the photo and article in the *New York Times*. Part of her regretted not telling him her marriage was temporary. The other part hoped it sowed seeds of jealousy.

*He's not jealous; he's with another woman. I'm the one who's jealous.*

She didn't want to dwell on it anymore. The sound of the woman's voice when she'd answered the phone, the rustling of covers before Bryan spoke. It was torturous.

*Think about something else.*

Kate turned her thoughts to her book and upcoming *Dr. Phil* appearance. Ten seconds later, she was thinking of the daisies on the kitchen table. *Ah, we've come full circle.*

*And I'm still awake.*

Kate was about to shift when the door opened. She lay still, not daring to open her eyes. She heard the whoosh of something dropping to the floor. Then another whoosh.

He was *not* undressing!

Seconds later, the mattress sagged under his weight. The force of it nearly pulled her to the center, but she braced herself on the edge. The bed shimmied, and the covers shifted as he slid under them. His foot brushed hers, and she fought the urge to pull away. How had it gotten past the barrier?

*Breathe deeply. I'm asleep.*

When he finally stilled, the only sound was the ticking clock and the waves. And her own breath. She could even hear her heart. Her arm, pushed under her pillow, ached, but she didn't move. How awkward would it be if he realized she was awake and started a conversation? What was he wearing over there, anyway? She was afraid to know.

Kate opened her eyes and stared at the big lump beside her. He was facing the other way, and already his breathing had evened out. Not fair. How long would she lie awake? Why couldn't she go to sleep?

She tried to think about her book, about next week's article, about anything other than the very male body inches away. Her skin prickled with heat, and she wished she could throw off the covers.

A few minutes later, a quick snort pierced the silence. Three seconds later a long grating snore sounded.

*And he's off to the races.*

Kate closed her eyes on a sigh.

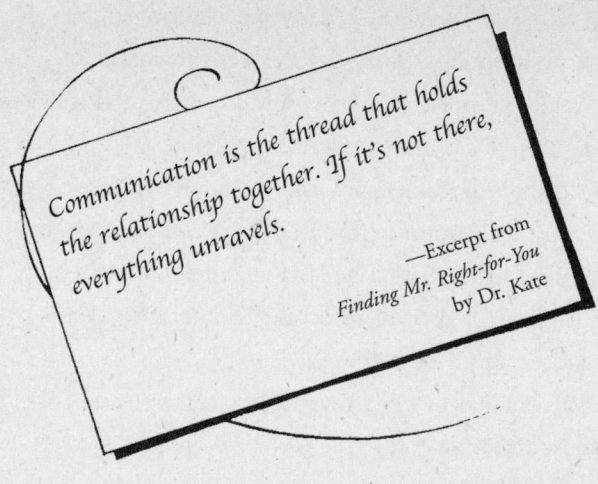

Communication is the thread that holds the relationship together. If it's not there, everything unravels.

—Excerpt from
*Finding Mr. Right-for-You*
by Dr. Kate

# Chapter Ten

Lucas pushed open his parents' door, and Kate entered the bright two-story cottage. She could only hope his family didn't enter his house as freely. They were seventeen minutes late—a fact that didn't seem to bother Lucas at all. How a man could be late when he'd done nothing but piddle around all morning, Kate had no clue.

Inside the door, an oval braided rug covered aged wooden planks, and daylight poured in from the transom over the door. Voices and clattering pans sounded from the back of the house, and the smell of fried chicken beckoned.

"We're here," Lucas called, shutting the door.

Jamie scurried into the cozy foyer and hugged Kate first. "Hi, Kate. Hi, Lucas."

They followed Jamie into the cheery yellow kitchen where Roy drained skinless potatoes in a strainer over the porcelain sink. Susan, her tiny frame wrapped in a lavender apron, turned from the stove long enough to give a brisk nod and say hello.

Jamie disappeared, and for the next few minutes Lucas made small talk with his parents before Roy shooed them from the kitchen. "Go on up and get settled. The kids are already up there."

"What should I get you to drink?" Susan asked Kate.

"Whatever you have is fine . . ."

Susan's penciled-in eyebrows hiked, clearly indicating she was waiting for a better answer.

"She likes tea, Mom, sweetened." Lucas stared pointedly at his mom, giving Kate a moment's gratification. He was actually taking up for her. Strangely, the notion lifted her spirits.

He took her hand, and Kate followed him through the foyer and up the stairs. The banister was thick and swirled at the end. "Why are we going upstairs?" Kate asked halfway up the flight.

He made the turn at the landing and continued. "We eat on the widow's walk."

A mental picture of the two-story house formed. Kate vaguely remembered a large widow's walk on the top, an historical feature of many Nantucket homes dating back to the whaling days.

Her legs wobbled, not from exertion, and her fingers tightened on the banister. "You eat on the roof?"

They reached the second floor and he took another flight of stairs, this one narrow and steep. Their feet thudded on the hollow wooden steps.

"It's tradition."

Tradition. That explained it all. He could have mentioned that little detail earlier. Didn't he know she was—

The dark stairwell opened to bright blue sky. And vast views of the island. High, vast views. Kate stepped to the side, keeping to the brick chimney chase.

Jamie and Brody greeted them from a round table, set for six, and centered on the square wooden platform. A spindled railing encompassed the perch. Lucas pulled out a chair for her on the other side of the table.

"I think I'll sit over here if you don't mind." Kate smiled at Lucas's sister. "By Jamie." As if that was her sole reason.

Lucas sat beside her. "Good idea. This is where the view's at."

For the first time, Kate looked outward. Her only thought had been keeping the solid brick of the chimney at her back, but now that she looked up, all she saw was open sky and the ocean spread out far below, disappearing into the horizon. She put her hands on the table and twisted the rings on her finger.

"Can I see?" Jamie asked, gesturing toward her wedding set. Okay, not a set exactly since Bryan had purchased one and Lucas the other. Luckily they were both white gold.

Jamie touched the emerald-cut diamond with her index finger. "Pretty. I didn't know Luc had such good taste."

"Or that he would part with that kind of cash," Brody said.

Kate and Lucas traded a look. "She's worth it," Lucas said.

"I read all your columns," Jamie said. "I can't believe you married Luc."

Lucas's chair creaked as he shifted. "Thanks a heap, sis." He tugged at his sister's high ponytail.

"You know what I mean," Jamie said.

Kate leaned back until her hair snagged on the brick behind her. "Shouldn't we help your parents? I feel bad just sitting here." Actually she felt bad about sitting up here period, and helping downstairs would get her off this bird perch. *And put you in the ring with your new mother-in-law.*

"Mom likes to wait on everyone," Jamie said.

"If you go down, Dad'll just shoo you away." Brody shook his curls out of his eyes.

"How did school finish up this year?" Lucas asked.

"He's thinking of switching majors again." Jamie snickered.

"Shut up, squirt." Brody elbowed her. "Mom and Dad don't know yet," he warned them.

The wind blew across the roof, ruffling the red plastic tablecloth, and Kate grasped the arms of the lawn chair. What kind of family ate on the roof?

"What do you want to switch to?" Lucas asked.

Brody planted his elbows on the table. "Architecture."

The sound of approaching footsteps halted the conversation. Susan entered, balancing a tray that held a pitcher of iced tea and six glasses. Lucas took the tray and set it down for Susan to pour the drinks. The ice cubes crackled as the tea splashed over them.

Susan set Kate's glass down. "Thanks." Kate let go of the wooden arm long enough to take a sip.

When Roy brought up the food, everyone passed the dishes, helping themselves. Kate couldn't believe the trouble they'd gone to. Fried chicken, mashed potatoes and gravy, buttered noodles, and coleslaw that looked homemade.

She picked up a drumstick and bit into the crispy breading. *Heaven.* "This is delicious."

"Thanks," Roy said.

"I wish you wouldn't fry it." Across from Kate, Susan picked the breading from a wing with a fork. "I keep telling him to bake it skinless. I swear when you get to be our age, the very smell of food causes weight gain."

Kate didn't see a spare ounce on Susan's petite frame.

"You'll walk it off this week." Roy spooned a heap of mashed potatoes onto his plate and covered them with a ladling of gravy.

"Your arteries are clogging as we speak," Susan said. She took a tiny portion of potatoes and set the bowl on the side table.

"I'll die a happy man." The look Roy sent Susan didn't seem happy.

"Suit yourself," Susan said. "But for heaven's sake, could you at least wipe the grease off your chin so we don't have to look at it?"

Lucas gave Kate a pointed look. Yes, there was tension between the Wrights.

"Would you like the pepper, Kate?" Roy asked.

Kate slid her fork into the slaw. "No, thank you. Everything is perfect. You're a walker, Susan?" She hoped to ease the tension between them.

"I have to be if I want to stay slender. You should try it."

Kate felt her temperature soar as heat singed her cheeks. Maybe she wasn't as small-boned as Susan, but she kept her weight well under control.

"She does," Lucas said. He looked at Kate. "Mom walks every day too. Maybe you could walk together."

Kate's eyes narrowed, but she refrained from outright glaring at the man. Besides, she had to spend time with Susan if she was going to keep her end of the bargain. She just wasn't sure every day was necessary.

Lucas scooted his chair closer to the table and Kate could have sworn the whole platform shook. Her hand tightened on the metal fork.

"Actually, I use a treadmill," she said.

Susan poured Brody a second glass of tea. "Well, that's certainly easier."

Kate chewed a bite of food, then swallowed the dry lump. "On second thought, walking outdoors might be a nice change of pace from my incline training."

She wasn't willing to give up her treadmill time, but walking with Susan would give Kate time to figure out how to help their marriage. If she could stand being with the woman that long.

"It's settled, then," Susan said.

"Look, the Porters have their boat out."

Kate followed the line of Jamie's finger and saw a bright yellow sail on the water. The view made her dizzy and she focused on her slaw.

Roy was addressing her. "What did you and Luc do on your honeymoon?"

"Roy, for heaven's sake." Susan took a bite of white chicken meat.

"Well, I'm not asking for juicy details. I'm just making conversation."

Kate wanted to crawl under the table.

"We went to the beach." Lucas smoothed things over. "And to the whaling museum. Kate had never actually gone."

"We took a boat to the Vineyard and went shopping," Kate added.

"*You* went shopping?" Jamie asked Lucas.

Roy set his chicken thigh down and wiped the grease from his fingers with a paper napkin. "It's amazing the things a man in love will do."

He said it as if to get a dig in on Susan, though Kate wasn't sure what it meant.

"Well, I wasn't surprised Lucas was in love with you," Jamie said. "The way he spent all that time renovating your apartment and refurbishing your floors. I knew he was falling for you."

Kate tried to catch Lucas's eyes, but he seemed intent on his food.

"And all the time he spent on the gazebo," Jamie continued. "We should have known there was more to it. He worked on it forever."

Kate wondered about the mottled blush that climbed Lucas's cheeks. She hadn't known he was so easily embarrassed. Well, Jamie could think whatever she wanted so long as she bought their story.

⟨⟨⟩⟩

Tourists and locals alike clogged the cobblestone surface of Main Street. Lucas took Kate's hand and led her through the Fourth of July throng. They'd watched the watermelon- and pie-eating contests and gotten soaked during the water fight between the fire departments. Now it was time to find a spot on the beach for the fireworks.

When they neared Jetties Beach, Lucas adjusted the blanket and picnic basket in his arms and ushered Kate through the Pavilion. The place looked different than the night of their wedding. Had it only been two weeks? He wondered if she was remembering too.

All day they'd run into friends and acquaintances. Kate had constantly had her hand in his or her arm wrapped around his waist. Having her at his side made him stand taller. At one point, they found themselves standing by Selma Bennett, an editor at the *Mirror*. Lucas had leaned down and pecked Kate on the lips. Her eyes widened before she leaned into him for the briefest moment.

Now they exited through the back of the building and crossed the sand where people were spread out across the beach, lounging on blankets and beach chairs. When they found an empty spot, Lucas shook out the piecework quilt, and they ate their turkey sandwiches and Doritos, then snacked on fresh strawberries.

Lucas popped one in his mouth and leaned back on his hands, his legs stretched out to the edge of the quilt. Smoke from firecrackers and salt from the ocean blended together in a unique concoction that reminded him of Independence Days long past. Laughter and chatter filled the darkness, punctuated by the sharp pop of firecrackers, as the crowd waited for the public display to begin.

"Nantucket knows how put on a Fourth of July shindig," Kate said.

"Can't believe you've been here three years and haven't come."

She shrugged. "I've always been out of town." She didn't have to say she'd been visiting Bryan.

Two blankets over, Bryce Webber, who ran an online community and discussion forum, saw them and waved. They returned the greeting, Kate leaning into Lucas's side as if suddenly realizing they were still on display. He sat up, draping his arm across her shoulders. He could get used to this.

When Kate plucked a strawberry from the Rubbermaid container and looked into his eyes, he wanted to claim her mouth then and there. But she touched the strawberry to his lips instead. Lucas opened his mouth, accepting the offer, and her fingertips brushed his lips. *Have mercy*. The tang of the fruit didn't compare to the sweet taste of her lips.

The first firework exploded, drawing Kate's attention to the sky over the barge where the fireworks were shot from. A red glow, a reflection of the firework, blossomed over her face. Lucas already had fireworks going off inside. The big booms were only an echo of his heart.

With Kate nestled into his side, they watched the display. He could've lain there the rest of the night, her fingers tucked inside his. But all too soon, the fireworks ended, and they were packing their things and heading to his truck.

Lucas felt a disconnect between them as soon as they left the traffic and turned toward home. The ride was quiet. Kate sighed deeply and crossed her arms against the coolness of the night as the truck bumped along the street, jangling his keys. He itched to reach across the expanse and warm her hands in his.

"Quite a day, huh?" he asked.

Kate leaned her head against the passenger window. "Mmm."

Lucas turned off the air and adjusted the temperature. "What'd you think of the fireworks?" They might not compare to Boston's, but he'd always thought Nantucket put on a pretty good display.

"They were good."

Lucas felt his spirits deflating like a punctured inner tube. They'd been close all day. Kate seemed to enjoy his company, even his touch. Her eyes lit when she laughed at the things he'd said. Somehow he'd let himself believe it was real.

But it wasn't real. Her affection was for appearances. And now, feeling Kate disengage from him was . . . hurtful. He wanted it back, the way they'd interacted, the way she'd looked at him, touched him. How could she turn it off like a spigot?

How had he not realized how difficult this was going to be?

⦿

Lucas shut the door hard behind Kate. She set her purse on the sofa table as he brushed by her and disappeared into the bathroom. Ten seconds later, the shower kicked on.

Was it her imagination, or was something bothering him? Kate took the picnic basket into the kitchen and tossed the trash. It had been a good day, but tiring. She'd seen everyone she knew, it seemed, at some point. With everyone congratulating them, she felt obligated to play the happy honeymooners, and it had worn on her.

Not that Lucas was hard to be affectionate with; he'd played along beautifully. But she was tired of being on display. By the time the fireworks ended, she was ready to hole up at the house where she didn't have to pretend.

As Kate finished putting away the picnic supplies, the shower went off. Good. She could use a rinsing herself. Though the weather had cooled after dusk, the sun had been hot and bright overhead all day. Besides, she wanted to wash the sand out of her hair.

Kate gathered her things from the bedroom and headed for the bathroom, her mind on her plans for the next day. When Lucas rounded the corner, she nearly smacked into his bare chest. He wore a blue towel that barely closed around his waist.

Kate stepped aside, averting her eyes. "Do you mind?" She pulled her own bundle of clothing into her chest as she passed.

"Nope." His tone was uncharacteristically sharp.

Kate stopped, ready to return and ask him what was wrong. But when she heard the unmistakable whoosh of the towel dropping to the rug, she darted into the bathroom and shut the door behind her.

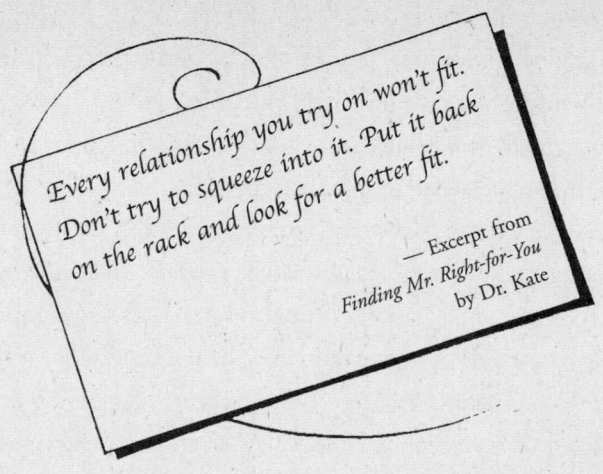

# Chapter Eleven

Lucas watched his mom and Kate cut across the beach, their bare feet kicking up sand, their evening shadows stretching behind them. He hoped his mom behaved herself.

The warm breeze ruffled the corners of the newspaper in his lap as he thought over the past two weeks. He'd enjoyed having Kate around, grown used to it. It felt good seeing evidence of her presence in his house. Her robe on a hook behind the door. Her toiletries a neat row in the medicine cabinet. Her shoes lined up by color inside the closet. He didn't see the point in that one, but whatever.

There'd been a learning curve too. Earlier that week, she'd exited the bathroom, a look of strained patience lining her lips. "I appreciate that you shaved, but would you mind rinsing out the sink since we only have the one?"

He shrugged. "Sure."

She hadn't mentioned the wet towels until the third morning and by then they were a knee-high blue pile in the corner.

What was it with Kate and order? It was like a god she worshipped. Why did everything have to be perfect?

Lucas opened the *Mirror* and shook his head. It did tickle him to watch confusion shadow her face when he cooked. He'd thought everyone dumped the whole package of bacon into the frying pan until he'd seen the way she'd done it, one tedious strip at a time, all neat and tidy.

The woman kept a record of her workouts, for crying out loud. He'd looked at the clipboard one day after she'd exercised, made notes, and disappeared into the shower. She marked the miles, the speed, the incline, and the time she'd walked, down to the minute.

But as much as her librarian ways amused him, he wondered what had her so tightly wound. She lived as if life could be boiled down to one big list. As if by keeping everything in order, somehow she could control things.

You'd think she'd have learned by now that some things were beyond control. If Lucas hadn't known that before Emily's death, he knew it now.

"Hey, Luc." Jamie stepped onto the covered deck and sat in the Adirondack chair beside him. Her lanky legs, already summer brown, extended from a frayed pair of denim shorts.

"Hey, sis. How's summer going?" He gave up on the paper, folding it and dropping it onto the deck.

"Okay, I guess." Jamie twirled a purple flower in her fingers. "Mom and Kate went for a walk?"

He closed his eyes and let his weight sag into the chair. "Yep."

"The gazebo looks good there," Jamie said.

Ethan had helped Lucas move the piece to his backyard overlooking the beach. It was as though it had been built for the spot.

For a while they sat in silence, listening to the sound of the water licking the shoreline. Lucas wondered what Kate was saying to his mom. More important, he wondered what his mom was saying to Kate. What if Kate figured out his parents were fine? He felt bad she was spending so much time on a fictional problem, but he'd had to use some excuse. He could hardly have told her the real reason he'd married her.

"How do you know when you're in love?" Jamie's voice cut through his thoughts.

Lucas looked at his sister, only fourteen, still in braces, and wanted to tell her she shouldn't be thinking about love at her age. But he'd been fourteen once, although it seemed a lifetime ago. Emotions had felt bigger than life then.

"Who is he?"

Jamie wrapped the flower's threadlike stem around her index finger. "His name is Aaron Brinkley, and he goes to my school. I've liked him forever, but he was going out with a girl named Liz." She rolled her eyes.

"Don't like her much?"

"She's a snot. I don't know what he saw in her. But he's been at the beach all week, and Meredith said he broke up with Liz. He asked me to play volleyball today."

Lucas propped his ankle on his knee and clasped his hands on his stomach. "Did you?"

Jamie flicked sand off her shorts. "Yeah, but I beat him."

Lucas laughed. Jamie was a starter on her team and the best player, if he did say so.

Jamie slugged his arm, and the flower went flying. "It's not funny. I think he's mad at me."

Lucas stifled the laugh. "What makes you say that?"

"He didn't talk to me after that." She wrinkled her little nose.

"Were his friends around?"

Jamie's face fell. "I should have let him win." She crossed her arms and chewed on her lip.

"He'll get over it. Trust me."

"What do I say when I see him tomorrow? I really like him."

"*You're* worried about finding something to say?"

She shrugged. "I get tongue-tied with him. I'm afraid I'll say something dumb."

"Be yourself. If he likes you, he'll like you for who you are."

She rolled her eyes. "You sound like Mom."

Maybe he wasn't helping. But given his own love life, he wasn't sure he was qualified to give advice. "What are his interests? People like to talk about themselves. Especially teenage boys."

Her face brightened. "He likes the Red Sox, and I know he's into sailing, so we can talk about that. What else?"

"What do you mean?"

"Duh. I mean, do you have any other advice?"

If only he could condense everything he'd learned about relationships and pass it like a baton. Unfortunately, life didn't work that way. "Just don't be afraid to let him know you like him. He asked you to play volleyball, so it sounds like he's interested. Guys have a lot of pressure to initiate things. It'll make it easier if he knows he's not going to get rejected."

"You think he's nervous too?"

Lucas clasped his hands behind his head. "Trust me, the nerves go both ways."

Jamie was gone by the time Kate returned. The back door fell closed with a smack, and she cornered him in the living room.

"*What* is the deal with your mom?" Her damp bangs clung to her forehead, and her ponytail swung like a pendulum.

Lucas folded the paper again and set it on the table. "What do you mean?"

"I mean she can't talk to me for two minutes without getting in a dig. There's all this subtext going on, and I think it's more than that she missed our wedding. You want to fill me in?"

It was only fair. He should have already. "It's not you. There's some history you don't know about." Maybe her mom had told her the story, and she didn't realize who Susan was. "Your mom was my mom's best friend years ago. They went to high school together. Did your mom ever talk about that?"

Kate shook her head. "What happened?"

It was all ancient history, but to his mom it was the unpardonable sin. A woman scorned, and all that, he supposed. "When my mom and dad were engaged, your mom was supposed to be her maid of honor, only—" How to put it delicately?

"What?"

He sighed. "I guess your mom had a thing for my dad. Something happened the week before the wedding. I don't know the details, but your mom slept with my dad. My mom cut her out of the wedding and refused to talk to her again."

Kate's eyes widened slowly, her jaw following suit. Then she pressed her lips together and jabbed her hands onto her hips. "Why didn't you tell me?"

"I didn't think it mattered."

"It matters to your mom." Kate walked to the window and turned. "How am I supposed to help your parents when your mom hates me?"

"She doesn't hate you. She doesn't even know you."

"She'll never trust me now."

He supposed Kate was right, but he'd been hoping his mom would come around. It wasn't Kate's fault, and it had been more than thirty years ago. "I'm sorry. I should have told you, but I was hoping she'd get to know you and realize you're not to blame."

That seemed to quench the fire in her eyes. "She probably thinks I'm just like my mom. Not only am I guilty by association, she's probably worried I'll betray you just like my mom did her. She's worried I'll hurt her son."

Funny, he was worried about the same thing. But he hadn't considered his mom might be worried for him. "Being a therapist must come in handy."

Kate gave him a wry smile. "I have a feeling I'm going to need all the expertise I can get."

⚬⚬⚬

Two days later, Lucas was remembering his conversation with Kate when a knock sounded on his shop door.

Ethan, his friend and his best salesperson, opened the door. Lucas turned off the sander.

"There's a lady here who's interested in a few custom pieces." Ethan pushed up his wire glasses with his middle finger.

Lucas set the sander on the plywood table. "Be right there."

He removed his goggles and brushed the sawdust from his skin and clothing before entering the showroom. He found Ethan and the customer by his collection of Shaker-style bedroom furniture. The woman had auburn hair that fell in waves past bare, slender shoulders.

"Miss Delaney, this is the owner, Lucas Wright. Lucas, this is Sydney Delaney. She recently purchased a home on Madaket Harbor."

Lucas shook her hand. "Pleased to meet you. That's a nice area."

Though she was tall enough to intimidate most men, her movements were fluid. "I love your work." Her fingers caressed the footboard of a queen-sized sleigh bed made of maple and finished with a caramel stain.

"Thanks. Ethan said you're interested in some custom work."

Another couple entered the store, and Ethan excused himself.

"I love the Shaker style. It's simple but elegant."

It was Lucas's favorite as well. There was something about the old-fashioned simplicity of the lines that drew attention to the beauty of the wood.

"I see a lot of things I like." Sydney gave Lucas a coy look. "But I have some specific pieces in mind for the living room that would need to be custom-made."

"I'd be happy to come and take a look at the space. You could show me what you have in mind."

She cocked her head and smiled slowly.

Lucas realized she'd read too much into his words. He crossed his arms, making sure his left hand showed. "I'll need to take measurements; then I can give you an estimate, and we'll go from there. How does tomorrow at ten a.m. sound?"

"Perfect." She gave him her address and phone number, then hitched her tiny purse on her shoulder. "I can't wait to see what you come up with."

He walked her to the door, but she stopped on the threshold.

"Oh, I hate to be a bother, but I'm looking for a fudge shop I've heard about. Aunt something . . . I have a terrible sweet tooth." Her smile flirted.

"Aunt Leah's Fudge—down on Straight Wharf." He followed her out the door and pointed east. "If you follow Main Street, you'll find yourself on the wharf. It's on the left. You can't miss it."

His brother entered his line of vision, walking up Main Street, his stride slow and loose.

"Hey, Lucas."

Lucas was about to introduce Sydney, but Brody stepped around him and opened the door. "Is Kate upstairs?"

The question caught Lucas off guard. "Sure." He wondered what Brody wanted with Kate.

Lucas watched his brother until Sydney placed a hand on his arm.

⁂

The sound of feet thudding up the wood steps of her office pulled Kate's attention from the letter. A glance at her watch told her it was too early for Lucas. They'd begun eating lunch together on Mondays, Wednesdays, and Fridays. Strictly for appearances' sake.

Sun-blond curls appeared first, followed by the lean frame of her new brother-in-law. He wore a pair of bright orange and blue Hawaiian-print trunks and a white T-shirt.

"Brody." Kate folded the "Dear Dr. Kate" letter and set it on the desk next to the other letters she'd waded through. "This is a pleasant surprise."

He stopped at the top of the stairs and stuffed his hands in his pockets, a move that reminded her of Lucas. "I should've called."

"No, come in. Have a seat. I'm just reading through some letters."

Brody surveyed her desk. "That's a lot of letters." He glanced around the room—what used to be the lobby of her practice. She'd moved her desk to the front so she could take advantage of the natural daylight that streamed though the windows.

"I haven't been up here since Lucas renovated," Brody said.

Kate appraised the room with fresh eyes. The shiny wood floor, the soothing green walls that set off the maple color of the wood trim. She'd found an area rug in shades of green, navy, and beige that tied the colors of the room together.

"He did a nice job," she said. "He's quite the carpenter, your brother." Never mind that it had taken forever to get it done.

Brody sank into the waiting-room chair with a sigh. "I know."

Kate wondered what had brought him here. She set her elbows on the swivel chair's wooden arms and leaned back against the plush leather. Brody crossed his legs, propping his right ankle on his hairy knee. Gravity pulled at the heel of his worn flip-flop.

"So, to what do I owe the pleasure of your visit?" Kate teased.

"I was wondering if you'd help me with something." His eyes darted around the room, settling nowhere.

"I'd be happy to help in any way I can." Kate felt sorry for him in his awkwardness. "Is it a girl problem?" That she was accustomed to. People often sought her advice—not just in letters, but on the street sometimes.

"No, not girls. I got a handle on that." His cocky smile lasted a short second. "It's . . . school." The word dropped like a fifty-pound bag of sand.

"Ah," Kate said. "The switch in majors?"

"Yeah." He shook the bangs from his eyes. "I can't decide what I want to do. I mean, I'm three years into college and I still don't know what I want to be when I grow up." He tucked in the corner of his mouth at his joke.

He was still young at twenty-one, but Kate understood his frustration. "What was your major when you entered college? University of Massachusetts, right?"

"Yeah. I started as an education major. That lasted for a year and a semester."

"What made you decide on education?"

"I thought I could come back here and teach high school. Maybe middle school. I don't know. I did well in school and I thought it would be fun to teach."

"What did you change to?"

"Art." He rolled his eyes. "I know—it's like, what am I going to do with a career in art?"

"Are you good at it?" Kate watched his face, looking for some sign of passion.

"Sure, I guess. My professors thought I was."

Outside the front window a truck braked, the squeal piercing the wall. "What made you change?"

"Does the term 'starving artist' mean anything to you? After a couple semesters, I realized how hard it would be to support a family with an art degree. Megan—she was my girlfriend at the time— thought I should switch to computer science."

"Is that what your major is now?"

"Yeah. I like computers and everything. I get good grades, and I know it would be a good career, but . . ." He punctuated the sentence with a sigh.

Kate waited. She had yet to see him talk about anything that ignited a fire in his eyes.

"So now you're thinking of architecture?"

Brody looked out the window. "It's kind of in the art field, but I could make a decent living."

"Let's talk about things you like to do. Lucas said you play baseball for UMass?"

"I'm shortstop. But I'm not pro material, if that's what you're thinking."

"I'm just trying to get a feel for the things you enjoy. What else? What do you do in your spare time?"

"I spend a lot of spare time at the beach. I surf a little. I wait tables at the Even Keel in the summer to supplement the money my parents give toward college. I've helped Lucas with construction, but I don't have a knack for it like he does."

Kate's legs ached from sitting. She stood and crossed the room. "Any other jobs you've held or volunteer positions you've enjoyed?"

"I enjoy working, so I've liked all my jobs. I was a lifeguard at Cisco beach for a couple summers. When school is in session, I tutor a couple local middle schoolers for extra money. That's rewarding. One of my students is a boy with a learning disability. His parents were really frazzled about his schoolwork. I tutored him last year starting after Christmas break, and his grades went from, like, Ds and Fs to Bs and Cs."

"You must be quite the tutor."

"Nah, Jared just needed some encouragement and help getting organized. He's a bright kid—he just had trouble remembering his homework and focusing." Brody lifted a shoulder. "He's a huge Giants fan and I found ways of relating that to his schoolwork."

"Have you considered changing back to education?"

Brody tucked his chin, and his eyebrows hiked up. "Not really."

"Why not?"

He looked away. "I don't know."

"You seem to like kids and know how to motivate them."

"There's not much money involved in teaching."

"You get summers off . . ."

Lucas grinned. His even white teeth reminded her of Lucas's. "Good point."

The bright sunlight from the window beckoned Kate. "Well, it's something to consider. I wouldn't fret about changing gears with your major. This is the rest of your life you're talking about, so it's important to follow your passion. The main thing is finding out where your passions lie."

"Too bad I can't major in girls."

Kate looked out over the street where tourists meandered down the brick sidewalks. A movement below caught her eye. Lucas stood in front of the shop with an auburn-haired woman. She wore a sleeveless ivory sweater and ivory slacks. The woman placed her hand on Lucas's arm, letting it linger. Her head tilted toward Lucas like she would live or die by his next words.

". . . give it some thought," Brody was saying.

Kate peered though the old, wavy pane. "Who's the woman outside? The one talking to Lucas?"

She heard Brody stand. "The leggy redhead? I don't know her. They were talking when I got here."

Kate felt a twinge of something unpleasant. It struck her as odd at first. She tried to rationalize it as common sense. After all, Lucas was wearing a wedding band, and the way Red was hanging on his arm was hardly appropriate. She glared down at the woman. *Boundaries, lady. Have you heard of them?*

Before she could help herself, Kate took a step toward the stairs with the thought of putting the woman in her place. Then she stopped. She imagined Lucas's amused brow, quirking upward, his crooked smile as Kate staked her claim. She wouldn't give him the pleasure. Besides, what did it matter if Red flirted with Lucas? It wasn't as if Kate had feelings for him.

She was *not* jealous, and there was no way on earth she was going to let Lucas think she was.

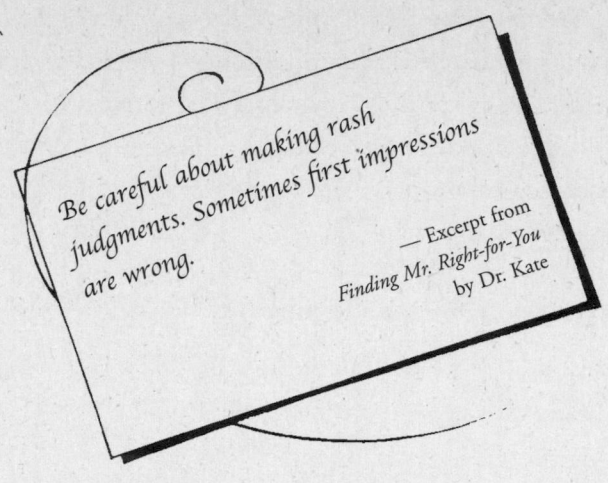

*Be careful about making rash judgments. Sometimes first impressions are wrong.*

— Excerpt from
*Finding Mr. Right-for-You*
by Dr. Kate

# Chapter Twelve

Kate slipped from the bed shortly after four o'clock and felt her way across the floor. From the floor on Lucas's side of the bed, Bo shifted. As she pulled her thin robe from the hook and tiptoed from the room, she heard his toenails clicking across the wood floor. Kate saw no way of making him return without disturbing Lucas.

The house was dark and quiet, except for the living room clock ticking off time. In the darkness she made her way to the back door and opened it quietly, keeping Bo inside. A warm breeze tugged at her cotton robe, and she gathered the belt, tightening it around her waist before sitting.

The dream that had awakened her surrounded her like a thick wet fog. In it, Bryan had come to her office, climbing the stairs with purposeful steps like Brody had. But Bryan wasn't there for advice.

He took her in his arms and proposed to her. When they left the building, they weren't on Main Street, but at Jetties Beach for their wedding. As Kate approached the altar, he turned. But it wasn't Bryan. It was Lucas.

Now, Kate watched the moonlight flickering on the surface of the shadowed water. She closed her eyes and leaned against the wooden back. The oscillating sound of the waves washing the shoreline didn't soothe her. Inside she felt as jolted as she had in the dream when she realized Lucas had replaced Bryan.

*It happened for real too.* Kate sighed. She wished she could fast-forward through the year and get her life back on track. How had she gotten so far off course? What was she doing in this house with a man she barely knew and hardly liked?

*That's not true,* her conscience corrected. *He might grate on the nerves sometimes, but Lucas has his good qualities.* And the last few weeks had been better than she expected in terms of getting along with him. It was just that her life was careening out of control like it hadn't since she was a child. She felt shaken and vulnerable.

A vision of her mom surfaced from the dusty corridors of her mind. Kate had been eleven and had just returned from her best friend's house. She often went to Mackenzie's house just to escape her own. But Mackenzie was mad because Kate never invited her over, and Kate had run out of excuses.

Kate closed and locked the front door before removing her snow boots and wiggling her numb toes. "Mom?" she called, not knowing whether or not to expect an answer. Sometimes she found her mom doing laundry and humming game-show tunes, and other times Kate wished she hadn't returned at all. It was the uncertainty she hated most. Even at eleven she knew it was true.

There was no answer on this night, so Kate set her heavy book bag on the rocking chair, flipped off the lights, and climbed the creaky stairs. Maybe her mom was asleep. She crossed her fingers on the banister as she ascended.

The bathroom light glowed in the darkness. She opened the door and found her mom on the green shag carpet next to a mystery stain they'd inherited with the house. One of her mom's sweater-clad arms draped over the tub ledge, and the other hugged a clear bottle of alcohol. The room smelled sour, and Kate turned on the fan.

"Mom," Kate whispered. She shoved aside the fuzzy pink slippers her dad had sent for her birthday and knelt on the carpet. "Mom."

Her mother stirred as Kate slipped the empty bottle, still warm from her mother's hand, out of her grasp. "Katie, baby." She licked cracked lips and opened her eyes to glassy slits, reaching toward Kate with her delicate white hand. It didn't quite make it and instead thumped on the carpet beside her leg.

"Come on, Mom. Let's get you to bed." Kate helped her mom stand, wrapped an arm around her gaunt waist. Propping her mom's arm around her own shoulders, Kate led her next door to the bedroom. Her mom wobbled and staggered, bumping her bony hip into Kate's and stepping on her cold toes.

When they reached the bed, Kate helped her mom out of her sweater and black slacks. She tugged a nightgown over her head, turned back the covers, and guided her mom into the bed, then pulled the woolly blanket over her. Her breath reeked of vodka.

"Katie . . ." If her mom wanted to say more, it was swallowed by oblivion.

"'Night, Momma," Kate whispered before extinguishing the bedside lamp and leaving the room.

It hadn't been the first time Kate put her mom to bed and it wasn't the last. If her dad had known how bad things had gotten for her mother, he would've gotten custody of Kate. But Kate couldn't stand the thought of leaving her mother all alone, so she kept their secret and spent her childhood feeling anxious and ashamed.

Now, as Kate curled her leg under her, she realized life felt as out of control as it had during those days. And just like then, there was nothing she could do but wait and hope things improved.

Only they never had. Her mother had died an alcoholic.

She tried a pep talk. *You made a better life for yourself. Look how far you've come from that cold house on Stinton Street. You have a successful career, a promising book, and you get to help people for a living. Help people that otherwise might be swallowed whole by their problems, like your mom.*

*But regardless of all my planning, I lost Bryan to another woman, and I'm married to a man I don't love.*

*Only for a year, Kate. Bryan will come to his senses when he realizes his mistake. This other woman is just an outlet for his fear of commitment. Once he realizes that, he'll be back.*

*What am I saying? I can't believe I still want him back after what he did.*

Beside her, the door clicked open, and Bo barreled through, with Lucas following. In the dark, his silhouette revealed tousled hair and a shirt that hung open at the front. Kate looked away.

"You okay?" Lucas whispered.

Bo licked the back of her hand, leaving a warm, wet film on her skin. Kate wiped her hand on her robe and crossed her arms.

"I'm fine. I didn't mean to wake you."

Lucas sank into the chair next to hers and silence settled around them. His presence changed the atmosphere. The masculine scent, the warmth of his large frame only inches away, the sound of his quiet breaths. Before it had felt empty. Now it felt . . . alive.

Kate shifted in her chair. Why had he come out here? He was an early riser, but not this early. Even the birds still slept and there was no light yet on the horizon.

"My family treating you all right? My mom didn't say something to hurt your feelings?"

"Your family's fine." Strange but fine. She hadn't gotten far with Susan, but it was early. First Susan had to like and trust Kate. Then maybe she would open up. And given the history between Susan and Kate's mom, that was going to take time.

"Mom can be tactless sometimes."

Tactless she could handle. It was the crazy that unnerved her. Lucas was probably wondering when Kate was going to keep her end of the bargain. Maybe he didn't understand that subtlety took time. "We're getting to know each other. I'm hoping in the next month or so I can introduce the subject of marriage. I'll let you know how it goes and keep you up-to-date on any progress."

The chair creaked as Lucas shifted. A cricket chirped from some-place under the deck. "Not worried about that."

Kate wondered why he brought it up. Oh, well. She was too tired to figure Lucas out.

She wondered if Bryan was still in bed. She wondered if he was alone. There were things she missed about him—mannerisms. Did Bryan set his hand in the small of the woman's back when he escorted her to the car? Did he hold her pinky on the console as he drove?

A yawn started, and she stifled it. The dream that had chased her from bed kept her from returning for fear that it would resume. Her only hope of escaping it was to stay awake. And even that wasn't working.

Lucas felt Kate move in the darkness. The smell of her hair, a blend of sunshine and citrus, wafted over on a breeze. Did she know how maddening it was to be so close, so *married*, and yet have none of the normal privileges?

No, of course she didn't. From her perspective this was a business deal. Lucas's presence was a means to a goal. She had no idea how much he craved her. How he loved her slightly pointed chin and her almond-shaped eyes, loved the way she brushed her hair behind her ears when she was intent on something.

His advice to Jamie replayed in his mind: "*Don't be afraid to let him know you like him.*" What a hypocrite he was.

Bo rubbed against his leg, and Lucas set a hand on his furry head. His situation was different from Jamie's. Kate didn't have feelings for him. She was still in love with Bryan. Was probably thinking about him right now. Maybe that's why she wasn't sleeping.

He remembered the nights after Emily had died. Lying awake until his eyes ached. Turning a dozen different ways on the bed. Feeling for her empty pillow and pulling it to his chest. If Kate was going through anything close to that, he needed to give her space. And time to get to know him.

"Go for a walk?" he asked. Bo perked up at the word, but Kate only looked his way.

"I'm in my robe."

He scooted to the edge of his seat. "Come on. We'll be back before light."

"But what about—"

"Who cares?" he said. "It'll clear your head." He extended his hand, wondering if she could see it in the moonlight.

She was going to say no anyway. What was he thinking? Kate wouldn't go for a walk unless she'd penciled it in a week ago.

"I guess I can go. I'll have to change first, though." She was inside before he could reply.

When she returned, they stepped off the deck and into the grass. Somewhere in the distance a dog barked, and Bo stopped to listen, his bulk a shadow in the dim light. Then, satisfied the other was of no importance, he led the way down the path toward the water.

When they reached the beach, they turned away from town. The wet, packed sand was cool and spongy under his feet. Lucas wondered what Kate was thinking. He remembered his advice to Jamie and started there.

"How's your column going?"

A wave washed up under their feet. Kate sucked in her breath at the coldness of the foamy water and scampered a few feet up the beach. "I've decided on the letter for my column. The woman wrote a four-page saga, so tomorrow I'll boil it all down to a one-hundred-word question."

He had no idea what went into an advice column, and he started to ask how she'd become syndicated, then thought again. Maybe she didn't want to talk about work at four thirty in the morning.

Bo ran ahead of them, trotting through the intermittent waves that washed ashore, then turned toward them, a still, shaggy silhouette. The moonlight offered enough light to see by. It washed gently over Kate's features, highlighting the bridge of her nose, the bow of her lip. Lucas looked away.

A wind blew across the water, and Kate shivered. "I didn't expect it to be so cool."

Lucas shrugged out of his shirt and placed it over her shoulders.

"Thanks." She put her arms through the sleeves, and he thought her eyes lingered on his bare chest for a moment.

Kate pulled Lucas's shirt tight, overlapping it like a robe. The material was still warm from his skin and smelled like him. The gesture had surprised her, but he'd done many small things that surprised her. Pulling out her chair at dinner, pouring her coffee every morning . . . And she had to admit he was trying to mend his messy ways. He'd even been hanging up his wet towels.

She wondered how Emily had coped with his disorganization. But maybe Emily had been like Lucas. Or maybe she'd considered Lucas's homemade meals and good manners a fair trade-off. Kate wanted to ask, but he never mentioned Emily. Bringing up his late wife would feel as if she was trespassing on sacred ground.

She wondered how Lucas felt about their pretend marriage after having had the real thing. It must feel hollow. Kate could hardly believe even now that he'd done it. That he'd stepped in at the last moment and rescued her.

Then again, he was getting something in return.

"Tell me about your dad," Kate said. Susan was guarded, but maybe Kate could get a fuller picture by learning about Roy.

They caught up with Bo, and he ran ahead of them down the shore, a giant lumbering fur ball.

"He's a man's man. Always liked to work with his hands. His dad was a criminal lawyer, and from what I understand, was disappointed when Dad didn't follow in his footsteps."

"Your dad held his ground?"

"Yep. Dad got a job working for a builder on the island. He framed houses and eventually started his own company."

"Is that how you got involved with wood?" Another wave washed over Kate's feet, tickling her with foam.

"Dad had me using tools by the time I was four."

"But you didn't want to build houses?"

He shook his head. "I like the detailed work. Knew it the first time I made a mantel for a house we built."

"When did your dad retire? And what happened to his business?"

Lucas picked up a shell, examined it, then tossed it into the water before answering. "A few years ago he started having some trembling in his hands. A while later he was diagnosed with Parkinson's disease."

Kate's stomach knotted. How come she hadn't known this before? Neither Lucas nor Susan had mentioned it, and she hadn't noticed any trembling. "I didn't know."

"He decided to sell the business. He was set for retirement anyway, and the work wasn't good for him in the long run.

"What's his prognosis?" She knew a little about Parkinson's, but how quickly did it progress?

"It's a degenerative disease, but its rate of progression varies. Eventually he'll be completely incapacitated, but he's only stage one. There are five stages, and he's progressing slowly."

"Do you think the diagnosis played a role in their marriage problems? It must cause a lot of stress." Why would Lucas worry about them divorcing when his father was ill? Surely Susan wouldn't leave him now. But then, how well did she know Susan?

"They were devastated when they found out. We all were."

No wonder she hadn't known about the disease. Maybe the family was in denial. How would they cope as his condition worsened? "It's lucky you live so close. Your mom will need help." Eventually Roy would be bedridden, and Susan wouldn't be able to handle his weight.

"That's why I built next door."

Kate met Lucas's gaze in the darkness. A glimmer of moonlight shone in his shadowed eyes. "Oh. I thought—" Kate looked away, embarrassed. She'd thought he was a momma's boy. There was no kind way to say it. It hadn't been kind to think it. Especially when his real reason was so unselfish.

"After Emily died, I couldn't live in that house anymore." He seemed about to say more, but stopped.

Kate wanted to know more, but what right did she have to pry? After finding Emily dead in the house, Lucas probably couldn't put the image from his mind. Who could blame him for moving on, starting over? But instead of choosing his own place to live, he'd built beside his parents, to be available for them, and instead of starting over with a new love, he'd stepped in and rescued her. The more she learned about Lucas, the more she realized she hadn't known him at all.

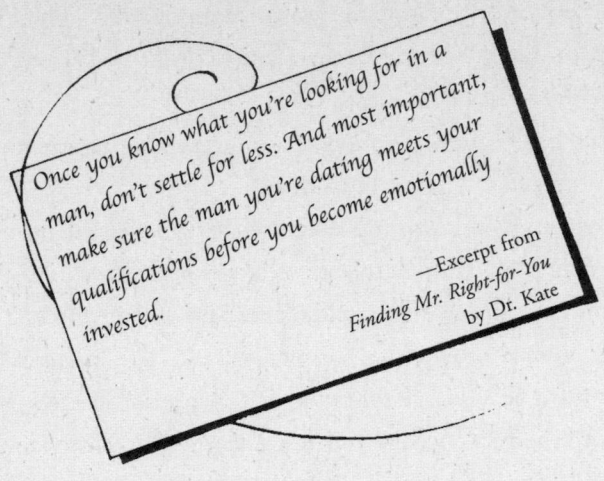

*Once you know what you're looking for in a man, don't settle for less. And most important, make sure the man you're dating meets your qualifications before you become emotionally invested.*

—Excerpt from
*Finding Mr. Right-for-You*
by Dr. Kate

# Chapter Thirteen

"Let's go sailing," Lucas said as Kate stepped off the treadmill the following Saturday, toweling the sweat from her forehead.

He'd just returned from walking Bo, and the dog trotted over to Kate and nudged her toward the bathroom as if to escort her to the shower. Like she needed help deciding where she was going. She stopped at the doorway and pushed Bo with her knee, glaring at the dog.

"I can't," she said. "I need to clean and catch up on laundry and prepare for a phone interview. Plus we need groceries, and I need to run to the bank."

"I saw your list." Lucas filled a glass with tap water. "We can do those things tomorrow. I'll help." He gulped down the water.

"The bank is closed tomorrow."

"We can run by the bank on our way to the harbor."

"My phone interview—"

"Can wait until tomorrow." He set the glass on the countertop. At her look, he opened the dishwasher and set it inside. "Any more excuses?"

They weren't excuses. Well, not exactly. She just wanted to get her list done. But she'd never seen Lucas's eyes lit like they were now, and he'd done so much for her lately in return for so little.

"Come on. It's seventy-five degrees, the sky is clear blue, and there's a good steady breeze."

"I've never been sailing," she said lamely, hoping he'd rescind the offer.

"Doesn't matter." His Colgate smile illuminated his face. "Get your shower, and I'll gather supplies."

Two hours later, Kate watched Lucas from a bench seat on the boat. He hadn't stopped since they'd left the harbor, pulling on this line and that, tying them off on their cleats.

"Can I do anything?" She tightened the strap on her bulky orange life vest.

He pulled up a sail, his muscles straining under his red tank. "Nope," he called over the wind. As he turned the boat with the tiller, the sails fluttered like gulls' wings, and he adjusted them with one hand. He continued doing what seemed like three things at a time, handling the jobs with the ease and dexterity of a man who'd done it a thousand times.

Soon, he turned the boat slightly into the wind and pulled the white sails tight. Kate dug in her satchel for sunglasses and joined Lucas where he steered the vessel. The deck felt unsteady under her feet, and she grappled for a hold.

"Having fun yet?" he asked. His eyes hid behind his own sunglasses, and she saw herself reflected in them.

"I had no idea there was so much involved in sailing."

He smiled, clearly in his element. "It's a blast. I sail a couple times a month at least. More, if I have time."

"Who taught you?" Kate thought it'd take her years to learn everything he'd just done, but then she wasn't a mechanical person. And she could tell already sailing wasn't going to become her favorite pastime. Being at the mercy of the wind was unsettling. What happened when it changed directions? How did you go back where you came from if the wind was blowing the other way?

"Mom. Dad knows how, too, but Mom's the expert. Want to take a stab at it?" He moved to the side, offering her steering privileges.

Her legs shook at the thought. "No, you go ahead."

He shrugged. "Suit yourself. There's soda in the cabin if you get thirsty. Otherwise, just relax and enjoy."

Kate took the bench nearby and grabbed the railing. The hot sun beat down on her face, and she was glad she'd applied sunscreen before they left. Lucas hadn't applied any and she wondered if he'd burn. His sandal-clad feet were braced a shoulder width apart, and his dark hair and T-shirt fluttered behind. He seemed unconcerned about the lack of sunscreen and life vest.

In the distance, other sailboats dotted the ocean. She looked down at the water rushing by and wondered how deep it was. Just then the boat tilted. She gasped and gripped the metal rail. A glance at Lucas hinted nothing was awry, but her nerves jangled just the same. What if they tipped over? The idea of floating in the middle of the ocean made her palms clammy. Maybe she'd feel better below deck, where she didn't have to see the wide expanse of water.

She stood, steadying herself with whatever she could grab. "I think I'll get a soda," she said.

Lucas nodded, lost in apparent nirvana, oblivious to her discomfort.

"Okay, then."

Rolling her eyes, she took the steps down to the galley. Below, the room was dark and cool after the brightness of the sun. Sliding her glasses up, she noted the tiny galley and a booth; beyond that a bed consumed an entire room. The cabin was pleasantly tidy, but she supposed it had to be; otherwise things would bump around.

As if reading her thoughts, the boat turned, and Kate sank onto the soft blue cushions of the booth. A fake plant was anchored to ivory Formica, and Kate smoothed her hands over the surface, appreciating the solid coolness against her palms.

She hadn't known sailing would disconcert her. She hoped she didn't get motion sickness. *Just my luck I'll be hurling over the side of this thing while Lucas laughs at me. Gee, how fun.*

Was her stomach feeling unsettled now, or was she imagining it? She swallowed compulsively as the boat turned again. Was he zigzagging? *For heaven's sake, can't he just point the thing in one direction?*

She remembered the soda Lucas had mentioned and walked carefully across the galley, grabbing a Sprite from the fridge before falling onto the bench as the boat heeled once again.

How long would Lucas want to be on the water? Was this an all-day thing, or would a couple of hours suffice? She checked her watch and wondered if she'd have time to finish her list once they got home. She didn't want to spoil his fun, but there was nothing to do down here, and she hadn't brought a book to read or writing materials to work. What did people do on boats? She didn't see anything in the small cabin to occupy herself, but the thought of going up on deck was enough to weaken her legs.

Suddenly, the boat slowed, its change in momentum bottoming out her stomach. Had something gone wrong? She wanted to go see but couldn't make herself leave the booth's security. Instead she sipped her Sprite, then realized her stomach felt worse. *Please don't let me puke!*

Footsteps sounded, and Lucas entered the cabin, ducking under the header.

"Is something wrong?" Kate asked.

He grabbed a soda from the fridge, then a brown bag, which he dangled in front of her. "Thought you might be getting hungry."

"You packed food?" He intended to be out here awhile. Her spirits sank.

"Just sandwiches. You hungry?"

Kate's stomach protested, but the sooner they ate, the sooner they could return. "Sure."

He put the food on paper plates with sides of potato salad and chips and headed up the steps. "Coming?"

She wanted to eat there in the enclosed cabin where she could almost pretend she was on dry land. But Lucas was already on deck. The last thing she needed was to give him one more reason to tease her. She stood and followed. The next time he suggested sailing, the answer would be a flat no.

Outside the sun was too bright. Kate pulled down her sunglasses and followed Lucas to the bench she'd vacated earlier. The wind drove the boat, and it rocked gently in the waves.

Lucas handed her a plate. "Beautiful day," he said around a bite of sandwich.

The heat of the sun made her skin prickle, and its glare on the water hurt her eyes. "That it is."

She started on the turkey and bacon sandwich. Would they head back after they ate? She could only hope. She scanned the horizon. Land was nowhere to be seen. With that knowledge, a sudden dizziness overtook her, and she focused on her plate. Did Lucas know where they were, how to get back?

"Love the sounds out here, don't you?"

The water splashed against the boat's side, and the wind billowed the sails. A seagull, on its way somewhere, called out. Maybe she was just a city girl, but she liked the sound of people, vehicles splashing through puddles, and the scrape of sandals on the sidewalk.

*Ugh.* Her stomach stirred uncomfortably. Maybe she shouldn't eat. The boat dipped. *Be still!* she thought, as if she could stop it. She set her sandwich on her plate and sipped her Sprite.

"You okay?" Lucas cocked his head, but she couldn't see his eyes past the sunglasses.

"I'm fine." She smiled to prove it and bit into a salty chip.

When the wind gusted and the boat dipped again, she steadied herself with the first thing she could reach: Lucas's leg. "Sorry." She removed her hand as quickly as she'd placed it.

The second chip went down. On the third, she stopped. There was no getting around it: her stomach was definitely threatening to expel her lunch. Kate couldn't take another bite. Her head spun, exacerbated by the boat's movement, and she grasped her plate with both hands.

"Kate." Lucas took her plate, tugging it from her tightened grasp. He set it on his other side. "What's wrong?"

She closed her eyes, but that made her head and stomach feel worse. "I'm not—feeling so well." She swallowed, reminding her stomach that things were supposed to go down, not up.

"Oh, honey, why didn't you say something?" He helped her up. "Come over here."

She pulled toward the cabin. "I just want to lie down. I'm sure I'll be fine." *If I don't die first.* She hadn't felt this bad since she had the stomach flu in the seventh grade and vomited all over Miss Heinschneider's white leather Reeboks in gym.

"Lying down is the worst thing you can do." He guided her to the center of the boat and turned her toward the ocean. She didn't want to look at the water. And there was no place to sit. She was willing to sink to the floor, but there wasn't room. Instead she grabbed the railing and leaned over it. She was beyond pretending she was fine. Pride had fled, leaving desperation it its wake.

Lucas put an arm around her middle and pulled her against him. "Look at the horizon. It'll help."

Kate had read something about that, but given the condition of her stomach, she was skeptical. She followed his directions anyway.

"I don't think we have any medications aboard," Lucas said.

Her head fell against his chest, and she smothered a moan. How had she lived this long and not known the body could feel so bad? At this point, she wished she could just get it over with, Lucas's presence notwithstanding.

"Are you watching the horizon?"

His stubbly chin rubbed against her temple, a welcome distraction. She nodded. The horizon was a fuzzy line against the blue sky. She focused on that line like her life depended on it.

"I'm sorry, Katie." His hand moved up and down against her side. His stomach was like a solid wall against her back. "I should point us toward shore. The sooner you're on dry land, the better you'll feel." His arms loosened, but she clutched them, fearing dizziness would overtake her.

"Wait," she said. If only she could sit down.

He tightened his arms, supporting her, and she stared at the horizon. Was the dizziness improving?

"I shouldn't have let you go down to the cabin earlier. You probably would've been fine."

She hadn't been feeling right before she'd gone down, but she didn't have the strength to say so.

"There are saltines and Coke in the cabin. Will you be all right for a minute if I get them?"

Kate wasn't sure she'd ever feel all right again. She wanted to say no, hesitant to stand without the strength of his support, but she nodded anyway and realized she must have a shred of pride left. She leaned forward on the railing, wishing she'd vomit while he was gone and get it over with.

No such luck. He returned a quick minute later and handed her a cracker. "This'll help."

Kate bit into it and followed the cracker with a sip of the Coke he'd brought while he rubbed her shoulders. It seemed her infirmity had granted him touching rights, but it was a welcome distraction. So welcome, she leaned against him moments later and his arms came around her again.

The saltines were working a little magic, and for the first time since she'd eaten, Kate began to believe lunch might stay put. Relief flowed through her and she relaxed against Lucas's chest. She became aware of his breath at her temple, the heat of his arms against hers. Gradually, relief morphed into self-consciousness. She felt silly and vulnerable. She wanted her strength, her dignity back. Yet, the security of his embrace comforted her.

"Feeling better?" The closeness of his voice startled her.

"I am, actually." Her stomach still rebelled; her head still swam. *But at least I'm not wishing I was dead.* It was an improvement.

"Good." He squeezed her and let go. "I'll get us back to shore as quick as I can."

He left, and the wind brushed the heat of her back where he'd been, chilling her skin. She watched him walk away, his long, steady legs navigating the deck. The wind tousled his hair as he adjusted one of the sails.

For some reason it was harder than she expected to look away. She rested her forearms on the railing and turned toward the horizon.

Later that night, Kate lay in bed alone, grateful to feel human again. Dry land was a wonderful thing. She didn't plan on leaving it anytime soon. After they'd docked, Lucas had brought her straight home, even though she felt better. He'd left with her grocery list and returned with a half dozen bags of food, then scolded her for cleaning while he'd been gone.

She smiled against the feather pillow. She hadn't figured on him being a mother hen. Then she remembered the feel of his solid arms around her and the roughness of his jaw at her temple, and something inside her stirred. Had he called her "honey" earlier?

*What is wrong with me? I love Bryan. This isn't a real marriage, but a business arrangement.*

*And good thing. You couldn't find a more polar-opposite husband. Lucas is everything you need to avoid in a permanent relationship.*

If she were to receive a Dear Dr. Kate letter spelling out her own circumstances, her advice would be to run. *"Don't get involved with someone ill suited to you; it's an invitation for disaster,"* she'd write.

But moments later, when the bed sank behind her with Lucas's weight, she couldn't stop her heart from speeding or her breath from catching. The covers shifted, and she felt the mattress dip down, felt his body almost touching hers.

Then she felt something else. A kiss pressed to the crown of her head.

Everything stilled for a moment as she waited . . . hopeful? Fearful? She wasn't sure what emotion made her heart stutter.

The bed quivered again as Lucas settled on his side, and her heart's pace slowly returned to normal as her eyes searched the darkness.

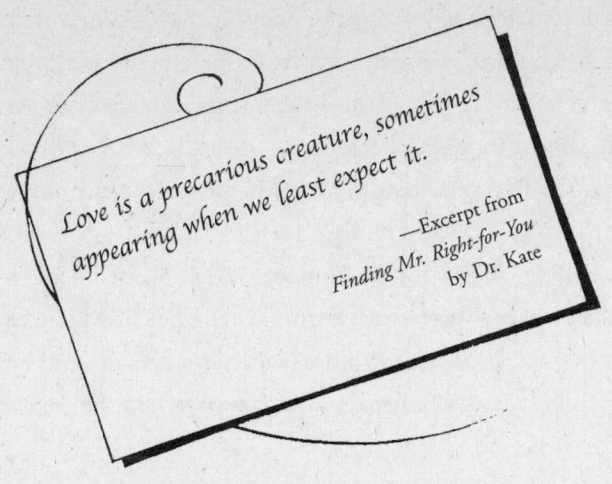

Love is a precarious creature, sometimes appearing when we least expect it.

—Excerpt from
*Finding Mr. Right-for-You*
by Dr. Kate

# Chapter Fourteen

Kate's feet pounded the pavement beside Susan's as they turned the corner and headed toward their homes. She'd decided she would bring up Susan and Roy's marriage today, but if she didn't hurry, Susan would be giving her a curt good-bye and striding up the grassy hill to her house.

Kate checked her watch. She had a scheduled meeting with Mr. and Mrs. Hornsby in an hour. Mr. Hornsby had broken it off with the other woman and they were trying to put their marriage back together. Even though Kate wasn't officially counseling them, she knew they were counting on her help.

She would need a shower before the meeting, so there was no extending the walk.

Their breaths slowed as their strides shortened. Kate tried to find the words. She had to be subtle so she didn't come across like a know-it-all counselor interfering in her in-laws' relationship.

Silence had settled between them; now would be the perfect opportunity to say something.

"Susan, can I ask you something?"

Her mother-in-law stepped over a crack in the pavement. "All right."

"Well," Kate took a few breaths. "I've been thinking lately about conflict in marriage. Well, really, conflict resolution. When you and Roy have a disagreement, how do you handle it? How do you resolve it?"

She stopped, afraid she'd put her foot in her mouth if she continued. Truthfully she wondered if the couple even employed conflict resolution the way they picked at one another.

Susan quirked a brow. "I'm surprised you're asking."

Kate stiffened. "Why do you say that?"

Susan flipped her hair from her face. "Well. You're the expert."

Why did the woman have to rub her the wrong way? "I know. It's just—" *Just what? Tell her I'm taking a poll or something?*

"I suppose studying relationships and actually being in one are two different things," Susan said.

Kate wasn't sure where Susan was going, but she nodded.

"Marriage isn't easy. Conflict is a normal part of it, though. You're lucky Lucas is so easygoing."

*Susan must think—Oh, great.* She thought Kate and Lucas were having problems. She'd probably made the woman's day.

A yappy little dog scurried down a gravel driveway but stopped short of reaching them.

"Roy used to give me the silent treatment for days when he was upset. Sometimes I didn't even know why he was mad and by the time we talked about it, he'd blown it all out of proportion." Susan shook her head. "I used to get so mad when we argued that I'd storm out of the room or even take off in the car."

"Really?"

Susan launched into a story, and Kate realized she'd hit pay dirt: Susan thought Kate needed advice, and she certainly had no trouble offering it. Finally, Kate had a way to get Susan to open up. Of course, Susan was coming at it from the wrong angle, but still . . . Maybe now Kate could finally get some real insights into Susan and Roy's marriage. And finally begin fulfilling her promise to help Lucas.

That evening Lucas was fixing a broken lamp when a knock sounded at the back door. Kate, who was in the kitchen loading the dishwasher, opened the door. Lucas heard his sister's voice. "Is Lucas home?"

"Of course," Kate said.

Jamie entered the living room, and Lucas saw tears sparkling in her eyes. He set the lamp on the table. "Hey, what's wrong, sis?"

Jamie plopped beside him and crossed her arms over her T-shirt. "I just got back from Meredith's house and she said—" Jamie sniffed as a tear escaped. "She said Aaron said I was a loser."

"Now why would she say that?"

Jamie flicked the tear off her cheek. "When we were at the beach last week, you know, after I talked to you, I went up to Aaron and sat with him. We talked and I tried to, like, show him I was interested like you said."

Lucas's stomach sank. He hoped he hadn't given her bad advice. The last thing he'd do was hurt her.

"I thought things went pretty well, but he didn't come to the beach anymore that week, and I haven't seen him since."

"And then you went to Meredith's today?"

"Yeah. We were having a good time and everything, and then she just brings up Aaron and says that he called her a few days ago after I sat with him on the beach, and that he called me a loser!" Jamie wept into her hands. "I made such a fool of myself!"

"Oh, honey, come here." Lucas wrapped his arm around Jamie, and she turned in to his shirt.

"I flirted with him and everything." Her hands muffled her voice. "I practically threw myself at him."

Lucas rubbed Jamie's shoulder. Across the room, Kate loaded a plate in the dishwasher and met his glance, a sympathetic smile on her face.

Lucas returned his attention to Jamie. "Now, hang on. Why did Aaron call Meredith?"

"What?"

"You said Aaron called Meredith and he said you were a loser. Why was he calling her?"

She uncovered her mottled face. "I don't know."

"How do you know she's telling the truth?"

Jamie sniffled. "Why would she lie?" Her eyes widened.

"Well," Lucas said. "Relationships can be complicated. For instance, what if Meredith likes Aaron? What if she's jealous?"

Jamie straightened a bit and wiped her face with the back of her hand. "I guess that could happen. But if Aaron called her, he might like her and not me."

"That's possible too. I'm just saying you should think it through and not necessarily believe everything you're told."

Jamie tilted her head and stared at the stone fireplace. "He did seem interested at the beach." Jamie ran her finger along the couch's trim. "He even said I have pretty hair."

Lucas smiled. "That doesn't sound like a boy who thinks you're a loser."

"I know. I thought he'd call, but it's been almost a week, and he hasn't been at the beach either."

Lucas squeezed her shoulder. "Give it time. Maybe he doesn't want to appear too anxious."

"I guess."

Jamie and Lucas talked until she felt better, and when his sister left, she hugged him before sliding out the back door.

❧

Kate changed into pajamas and opened the closet door, peeking at the suit she'd bought for her appearance with Dr. Phil. It was a dove-gray Ann Taylor with a structured jacket and streamlined pants. The classic white oxford under the jacket was a good contrast for her skin tone and black hair.

She ran her fingers down the soft material of the suit coat, feeling anxiety work into her fingers. She'd been invited on the show to advise an engaged couple who was having difficulty merging their personalities. What if she said the wrong thing? Worse, what if Dr. Phil disagreed with her advice?

*Relax. You're trained for this. You're an expert.*

*Except in my own relationships, where I'm the epitome of disaster.*

*Nobody knows that. As far as they're concerned, you married your Mr. Right.*

But what if the media attention from this appearance invited scrutiny of her marriage? What if someone figured it out? What if one of Bryan's relatives saw the show and leaked the truth?

Kate closed the closet door. She could only hope for the best. She'd already taken preventative measures. Maybe one more call to Bryan, asking him to check in with his family, wouldn't hurt.

But maybe that was just her wanting to talk to Bryan. She was suddenly tired, though it was only nine o'clock. She approached the nightstand, ready to set her alarm, when she noticed a box on the new nightstand Lucas had brought home.

The box was wrapped in pale pink paper with a white bow. She picked it up. "To Kate," it said on the tiny gift tag in Lucas's left-handed scrawl. She pried open the piece of tape, unwrapped the package, and pulled out a navy-blue velvet box.

The hinge creaked as she opened the lid. Inside, a delicate pair of earrings were nestled side by side. Elegant in their simplicity, they were the same silvery tone as her wedding band.

"Hope you don't mind." Lucas's voice startled her from the doorway. He looked boyishly shy, and she couldn't keep from smiling.

"What kind of woman minds getting jewelry?"

He shrugged, walking toward her. "You don't wear much jewelry. I just thought . . . Well, it's been a month today."

Their anniversary, such as it was. Lucas stopped at the foot of the bed. She watched a blush creep into his cheeks.

"It was very thoughtful. Actually, they're perfect for the *Dr. Phil* show."

What did the gift mean? Flowers was one thing, jewelry another.

Was Lucas trying to make their relationship appear real? Or was there more to the gesture? Her insides fluttered at the thought. She remembered the way he'd laid a kiss on her head. It had been sweet. It made her feel . . . protected.

She glanced at the box in her hand. "I'm sorry. I didn't—"

Lucas waved her off. "I didn't expect you to. I saw those in the window at Pageo's and thought of you."

He was making nothing of it. Maybe it didn't mean anything, but it had been a thoughtful gesture. Lucas had some irritating qualities, but he could be awfully sweet when he wanted to be. Carried away by the moment, Kate reached up and kissed him on the cheek. Her lips tingled against the roughness of his jaw.

When she pulled back, she saw something in Lucas's eyes and wondered if she'd crossed some invisible line. But then he rubbed the back of his neck and turned away. "You heading to bed?"

She closed the lid of the box, watching him go. "Yeah, I'm beat."

He turned as he pulled the door. "'Night,"

"Oh, I forgot to tell you I talked with your mom this morning. The subject of conflict came up and I asked her about her and your dad."

Lucas stilled, his hand on the knob. "What did she say?"

Kate sighed and rolled her eyes. "She thought I was asking her because we were having trouble. Like I wanted her advice on how to handle conflict."

Lucas chuckled. "That's rich."

Kate frowned at him. "It's not funny. She must think I'm a lousy counselor." *She's wondering what kind of idiot her son married.*

"Relax. She's just doing what moms do."

Well, then. How would Kate know that? In her experience moms didn't give advice and nurture. They went out and came back unexpectedly and left you wondering what would happen next.

"Anyway," she said. "I wanted to tell you I'd gotten the ball rolling, that's all." She sat on the bed. "Good night."

After Lucas pulled the door shut, Kate threw the wrapping paper in the trash and tucked the jewelry box inside the top nightstand drawer. She flipped off the lamp and crawled under the covers, but it was a long time before she drifted to sleep.

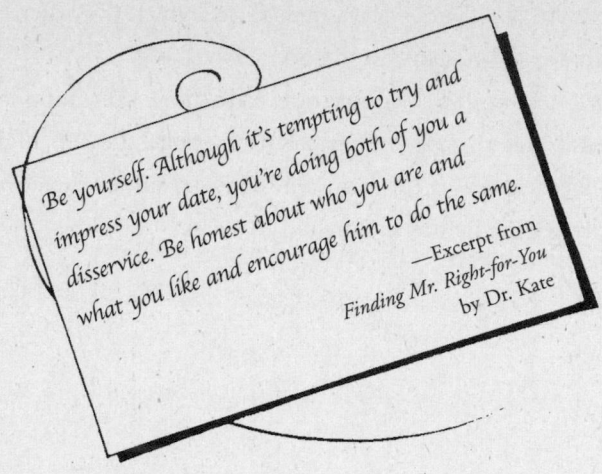

Be yourself. Although it's tempting to try and impress your date, you're doing both of you a disservice. Be honest about who you are and what you like and encourage him to do the same.

—Excerpt from
*Finding Mr. Right-for-You*
by Dr. Kate

# Chapter Fifteen

Kate stepped from the fog of the bathroom and toweled off her wet hair. She could smell bacon frying and hear it sizzling on the griddle. She'd come to expect Lucas's big breakfasts on Saturday and had decided it was a nice start to a weekend. As long as she stayed out of the kitchen while Lucas cooked and she didn't have to see the counters splotched with pancake batter or the cracked eggshells in a pile near the sink. If she faced the wall as she ate and didn't have to see the mess, she could almost put it from her mind.

Kate was shoving her towel into the bedroom hamper she'd bought when the phone rang. By the time she entered the kitchen, Lucas had answered.

"Who's calling?" he asked, setting the greasy spatula on the counter. "Just a minute." He handed her the phone, wearing an inscrutable expression.

"Who is it?" she mouthed

"Bryan." Lucas turned and stirred the pancake batter.

Kate's adrenaline spiked like she'd had three shots of espresso. Why was Bryan calling? She walked toward the back door and put the phone to her ear.

"Hello?" Her tone was cool and collected.

"Hi, it's me."

It rankled that he could still say that. *It's me.* Like they were still so close he needn't identify himself. Had he forgotten he'd dumped her for someone else? Kate stepped out the back door and closed it behind her, keeping Bo inside.

"Bryan. How are you?" There was nothing in her voice to make him think she actually cared to hear the answer.

"I'm good. Better than I've been in weeks."

"Wonderful. Is there something I can help you with?" Polite. Friendly, but not too friendly. It unnerved her that it was such a strain. Was it just barely over a month ago that he'd kissed her good night on the eve of their wedding day?

"Kate, I'm so sorry. It's killing me to hear you like this. Like we're strangers or business acquaintances."

Did he have any right to tell her about his pain?

"I called to say I was wrong," he said. "I know that now."

Kate stared toward the horizon and leaned against the square column that supported the roof.

"Things are over with Stephanie." He said it like he expected her to shoot off fireworks in celebration.

*Stephanie.* So that was her name. It was no one Kate knew. She was glad for that.

The pause was deafening. Emotions twisted in her like vines around a tree. She wasn't sure which was strongest.

"Kate, did you hear me?"

What did he want from her? Now that he'd dropped his other woman, was Kate supposed to fall in his arms again? "What am I supposed to say?"

"I know. I know," he said. "I—" Kate could hear the frustration in his voice. She imagined him running his hand through his blunt cut.

"I was a fool," he continued. "It was just like you said. It was nothing more than a fear of commitment. I was afraid and looking for an outlet, and Stephanie was convenient."

"Your outlet was costly."

*Costly* wasn't the word. It had changed her life, changed their future. It was a little late to realize he'd made a mistake. Did he think he could fix it so easily?

A seagull cried out overhead and swooped over the beach, soaring with wide wings. Kate wished she could leave all this behind her and soar over the landscape of her life as the bird did.

"I miss you, Kate."

The words, spoken softly, pried at the door of her heart. Kate closed her eyes. *I will not tell him I miss him.* He didn't deserve to hear it, and she wasn't even sure it was true. Her feelings for him were muddled, blurry, like the line between the ocean and sky. How could that be when she'd been so certain of her feelings for him only five weeks ago?

"I'm married, Bryan." It gave her no pleasure to say it. She'd heard the pain in Bryan's voice, and even though he'd hurt her terribly, she didn't wish to hurt him.

"I know." He swore. It was the first time Kate had heard him swear. Why had he called? He didn't know her marriage was temporary, though he must realize genuine feelings weren't involved. Did Bryan think she'd divorce Lucas the moment he returned?

"Who is he, Kate? Do you know what it's doing to me, imagining the two of you together?"

"Yeah, actually, I do," she snapped.

"I'm sorry. Of course you do." He sighed. "I don't know what I'm saying. I'm just—I'm just going crazy over here. My whole life has been so planned, all my ducks in a row, and now I just feel like it's all exploded in my face."

*Have you forgotten you're the one who lit the fuse?* She wanted to say it out loud, but what good would it do? What was done was done. She had to stay married. The media would have a heyday if she divorced Lucas and married Bryan. She shook the thought from her head. It was ludicrous to even entertain the idea.

"You don't love him, do you?"

Kate grabbed the hair at her nape and squeezed. To tell him yes would be a lie, but to tell him no felt like a betrayal to Lucas. She let the silence grow. She wanted to ask if he'd loved Stephanie, but what did it matter now? The other woman's journey with Bryan was over, and she had nothing but a foiled wedding as a souvenir.

A bolt of fear struck her thoughts. *What if Stephanie leaks the information to the media? What if she told them Bryan was supposed to be my husband and that I'm nothing but a fraud?*

"Bryan, how did things end with you and Stephanie?"

The pause seemed to last a lifetime. "What do you mean?"

"How did things end?" she asked sharply. "Did you break it off? Was she upset?" She grasped the phone tightly, wanting to wring the answer from it.

"I broke it off," Bryan said. "She was upset. Why, Kate?"

Kate descended the deck steps and crossed the sandy grass toward the shoreline. "What if she goes to the media and tells them everything?" She felt like swearing herself. She didn't know what kind of a person Stephanie was. Was she the vindictive sort?

"She wouldn't do that," Bryan said.

"How do you know?" She wanted proof. Or better yet, a reason Stephanie wouldn't want the news out that she'd broken up Dr. Kate's marriage. Maybe she detested being in the spotlight or had a career that would be damaged by the gossip.

"She's not like that. There would be no reason for her to do it."

"You said she was upset."

"Well, she was, but I think she'd—"

"You *think* or you know?" Kate kicked a hill of sand and took a breath.

"I'll call her if it'll make you feel better. I'll do whatever I have to do to protect you, I promise."

His tone was sincere, but the last promise Bryan had made ended with her at the altar saying "I do" to another man.

Lucas turned off the griddle and scooped the bacon onto a plate. It clanked as he set it too hard on the table. He opened the oven and removed the warming pancakes.

He had no idea how long Kate would be on the phone, but he was going to eat while it was hot. He scooted his chair back and sank into it. Bo, knowing better than to beg for food, settled on the rug beside him.

When Bryan had identified himself, Lucas had wanted to ask what business he had calling *his* home on a Saturday morning and asking to speak to his wife. He might have done it, if Kate hadn't been standing there with her wide eyes and tousled wet hair.

She'd gone outside for privacy, but he'd heard every word through the open window.

Lucas grabbed a piece of bacon and took a bite. He'd been relieved at Kate's cool tone even though he knew she was only guarding her heart.

When he heard her say, "I'm married, Bryan," he wondered what had prompted those words. Did Bryan want her back? Is that why he'd called?

The back door opened, and Kate entered. She set the phone in the cradle and joined him at the table. Her face revealed nothing. Was she wishing she'd never married him? Was she wishing it was Bryan at the breakfast table now?

Well, Bryan had left her for another woman. It was Lucas who'd cared enough to follow through. Lucas who'd stuck by her though all those publicity photos. Lucas who got up at the crack of dawn and fixed her eggs over easy, the way she liked them.

Kate picked up her fork, and the diamond on her finger glittered under the kitchen lights. Bryan's diamond. Lucas wanted to slide it off her finger and toss it into the ocean.

He took a drink of coffee and set the mug down hard. It clattered against the saucer and splattered on the table. Without a word he stood and retrieved a towel, wiping up the mess before settling in his chair.

"What's wrong?" Kate asked.

"Nothing." *My wife's ex-fiancé called my home and probably declared his love for her. What could be wrong?* He bit into his eggs.

"Well, something's wrong."

Lucas swallowed hard, trying to suppress words he shouldn't say.

"I don't appreciate your ex-fiancé calling here, is all." He applauded his calm tone. Across from him, he felt Kate still.

"I didn't think—I mean—" She cleared her throat. "It's not like this is a real—"

He looked at her, daring her to say it. Yeah, maybe it wasn't a real marriage in theory, but there were feelings involved. His. And he'd been hoping hers were a little involved. Had he been wrong?

"I just meant—"

"I know what you meant, Kate." Lucas stood and took his plate to the trash, dumping a half slice of bacon and the remainder of his sticky pancakes.

"Bryan was supposed to be my husband. Things ended very quickly and there was no time for closure—"

"I was there, remember?" He rinsed his plate in the sink, washing the yellowed yolk with the scrub brush.

"Of course you were."

She said it so quietly, he almost didn't hear over the running water.

"If you hadn't married me, I'd—I don't know what I would've done. I appreciate what you did. I hope you know that."

Did her voice shake on those last words?

Lucas had too many emotions storming through him. He was still angry, and yet, from her point of view, it wasn't justified. It couldn't be unless she knew how he felt, and it was too soon for Kate to learn that.

"What did he want, if you don't mind my asking?" He shut off the water and leaned on the sink ledge, keeping his back to her. His thumbs curled around the sink's corners.

"Of course not."

He heard her pick up her coffee cup and take a sip. It settled into the saucer with a quiet click.

"He had some unsettling news about the woman he was with. Apparently he broke it off with her and she's somewhat upset."

Lucas steeled himself at her words. What was to keep Kate from going back to him? Her career? Her book? Would she let those things stand in the way if she still loved Bryan?

"I'm concerned that she's going to leak the news to the media," Kate said. "If she's angry enough, it would be a one heck of a way to retaliate."

Lucas heard a scuffle on the deck. Bo? Then he remembered Bo was lying on the rug under the table. That meant . . .

*Oh, shoot!* He leaned forward and peered out the window far enough to see Jamie running from the house.

"Jamie," he called out the window, but she didn't stop. He rushed after her, opening the door and taking the steps in one leap. Had she heard everything they'd said? "Jamie, wait!"

He caught up with her on the grassy knoll and took hold of her arm.

She jerked her arm from his grip. "Let go of me!" Her chest heaved.

"What were you doing snooping outside my house?"

"I wasn't snooping. I came to talk to Kate and I heard you fighting." She crossed her arms.

"We weren't fighting."

"It's not my fault the window was open."

Lucas stuffed his hands in his shorts pockets and thought back to what Jamie might have heard. They'd said enough. "It's complicated, Jamie."

His sister glared at him. "You lied to us."

Lucas swallowed around the lump of pancakes that seemed to have congealed in his throat. He looked back at the house to where

Kate stood on the deck, one foot in front of the other, as if torn about whether to stay or come. He waved her back. It would be better to handle Jamie alone.

"I don't know how much you heard but—"

"I heard enough to know it's all a big lie."

"That's enough. It's not a lie. Kate was in a fix. Her career was on the line, and I stepped in to help her."

"How could you just pretend to love each other? We all thought she was part of our family, and now you're telling me it's fake."

Lucas turned toward the ocean. He remembered being out there with Kate the week before, remembered the feel of her in his arms when she'd been sick. There'd been nothing fake about that.

"I'm telling Mom and Dad the truth." Jamie turned to go.

Lucas grabbed her wrist. "Don't, Jamie." If their mom knew the marriage wasn't real, there would be no holding back the resentment. She'd scare Kate away for good.

His sister whirled around. "Why shouldn't I? You should've been honest to begin with instead of making us think your marriage was real."

"It *is* real."

"I'm not a baby, Lucas. I know your marriage is real on paper, but it's not real in here." She tapped her heart. "And that's the only thing that counts."

All those romance novels had gone to his sister's head. Sometimes reality couldn't live up to the happily-ever-afters in her books.

"Can you keep a secret?" Lucas asked.

Jamie stared at him, her green eyes squinting against the glare of the sun. She crossed her arms. "You know I don't like secrets."

She was growing up. He remembered a time when she'd collected secrets like seashells.

"This is personal. Like your feelings for Aaron. I'd never tell anyone about that."

He could see her acquiescence in the way she tucked in the corners of her mouth. "What is it?"

Lucas glanced over his shoulder toward the house. Kate had gone inside. "Kate loved Bryan." He rubbed the back of his neck. "She probably still loves him, for all I know. She married me because she was backed into a corner and I was her only way out."

Jamie's eyes softened, and her squared shoulders relaxed.

Lucas turned his face into the wind and let the salty breeze push his hair off his face. "But I had different reasons." Lucas met Jamie's gaze, then took his hand from his pocket and touched his heart. His eyes clung to Jamie's, and he saw hers glaze over.

"It's not a fake marriage." His voice deepened with emotion. "I love her. I'd lay down my life for her if necessary. Do you know how rare that kind of love is?"

Jamie blinked rapidly. "But she doesn't love you?"

Lucas gave her a half smile. "I chose to love her. Whatever she does with that is her decision."

Jamie sniffed. "That's so sad."

*Great, now she pities me.* "Hey, she's got to come around eventually, right?" He tapped her nose and struck a ridiculous pose. "I mean, what's not to like about this?"

Jamie pushed him, but she smiled around her tears.

"Are we okay now?" Lucas asked. He couldn't stand to have Jamie mad at him.

Jamie nodded.

"I can count on you to keep my secret?"

Jamie kicked his ankle with her flip-flop. "You know you can."

Lucas pulled her toward him and held her there, his hand on her head. He realized it felt good to admit how he felt about Kate. A relief to release it.

Then he heard Jamie's muffled voice. "And to think I was coming to *you* for love advice."

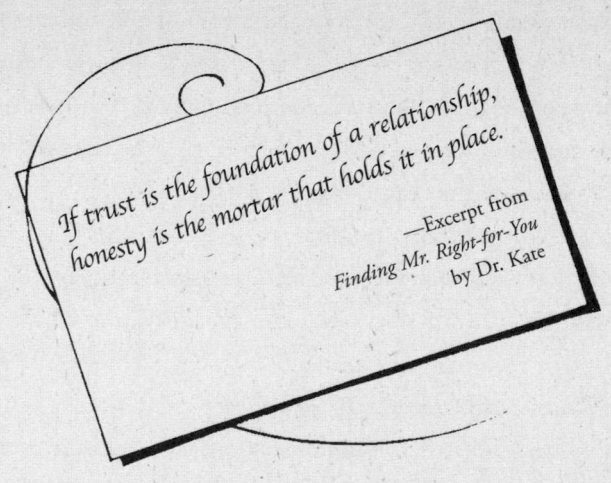

*If trust is the foundation of a relationship, honesty is the mortar that holds it in place.*

—Excerpt from
*Finding Mr. Right-for-You*
by Dr. Kate

# Chapter Sixteen

Kate clutched her hands in her lap, feeling her palms grow hot and sweaty. Dr. Phil's set looked exactly as it did on TV. She'd already been coached by Pam and Chloe, her publicist and her editor. Her agent, Ronald, had also met her at the studio for emotional support. But now she was on her own. When she'd left the green room, Dr. Phil had welcomed her graciously and congratulated her on her new book.

But now, as the cameras were ready to roll, Kate felt as if her nervous system was on overload. The newlyweds she was to advise sat on stage with Dr. Phil. The crew was placing mikes on their lapels and giving them last-minute instructions. Hope was a cute blonde with a pixie face and good taste in shoes. Ryan had dark hair, well trimmed, and repeatedly pushed his glasses up the bridge of his nose with his finger.

Kate was grateful to be on the first row of the audience rather than under the bright lights of the stage. Beside her was a child psychologist who was there to advise a family in crisis. She'd brought her husband, and they whispered back and forth. On Kate's other side were the parents of the couple Kate was to advise.

Kate straightened her suit coat, making sure the mike was well placed, then twisted the earrings Lucas had gotten her.

*Be still, Kate. It's not live, only tape. And they can edit if anything goes wrong.*

*Oh, please, don't let anything go wrong!*

She wished she had someone beside her to tell her everything was going to be okay. At that thought, Lucas's image flared in her mind like a Fourth of July firework. And just as quickly she reared back in surprise. *What is with me? I'm an independent woman.* She was accustomed to being on her own, and no one needed to tell her she didn't need a man to be happy. She'd been dispensing that advice for years.

But her thoughts returned to her last few moments with Lucas at the airport the day before. He'd managed to get her there on time and had insisted on walking her to the counter where she checked in. Then he walked her to security. Among the people being herded through security, Kate recognized Dahlia Stevens from the Chamber of Commerce, setting her bag and laptop in a gray tub. She waved at Kate and Lucas.

"Our first night apart," Lucas teased, setting her bag down.

"I'm not sure I'll be able to sleep without your snoring."

"I don't snore."

"Hah!" she said, and he grinned.

There was an awkward moment when they realized it was time to say good-bye. Kate was about to leave Lucas for the first time since their wedding. She was excited about the show, but also nervous. She wasn't used to hiding personal secrets and certainly not from the country at large. Now she would be on national TV, and what if something went wrong?

"You'll do great." Lucas seemed to read her thoughts. "Dr. Phil will probably make you a regular if you're not careful."

"I don't think I'm ready to move to Hollywood."

Lucas smiled. "Good."

Kate glanced at her watch. "I should get to my gate." She pulled her boarding pass and driver's license from her suit pocket.

"Have a safe flight." Lucas looked over her shoulder, and Kate knew he was conscious of Dahlia. He leaned forward and gave her a kiss. The gentleness of his touch tugged at her, even with the brevity of it. Would she ever get used to him kissing her? Wasn't it supposed to become old hat after a while?

Now, as Kate waited for the cameras to roll, she touched her lips, remembering the way they had tingled after the kiss.

*Do I have feelings for Lucas? Feelings that go beyond friendship?*

Before she could chase the thought, one of the crew gave the signal for taping to begin, and the show was underway. Her couple was up first, thankfully.

Dr Phil started. "Today we have Hope and Ryan. They've been married for eight months and are wondering if they're just too different to make it work. Come on, guys, you're supposed to be in the deliriously happy newlywed stage, so what gives?"

Hope twined her fingers with Ryan's. "The delirious stage lasted about two days for us."

"It was a whirlwind kind of courtship," Ryan said. "I guess we didn't know each other very well, didn't realize how different we were."

"How long did you all date?" Dr. Phil asked.

They looked at each other; then Hope cringed. "Five weeks."

The audience groaned.

"Five weeks!" Dr. Phil's voice rose. "You barely know how he takes his coffee in five weeks."

"I know, I know," Hope said. "It was impetuous, and we regret that we didn't wait longer. I guess I let the whole 'falling in love' thing go to my head. I mean, we are in love, and we want to make it work. But we're so different—we just aren't sure how to find a middle ground."

"Well, they say opposites attract," Dr. Phil said. "Tell us what your hot buttons are. What are the differences that drive you crazy?"

Hope and Ryan eyed each other again. "I guess our spending habits are one of the biggest issues," Hope admitted. "It's not like I go on spending sprees or anything, but I like to dress nicely, and Ryan was raised to be more tightfisted—

"Frugal," Ryan corrected. "I believe in a budget."

"And I think 'What's money for if you can't spend a little?'" Hope wrinkled her nose.

They went on to discuss their differing views on household duties, their differing social needs, and their differing recreational preferences.

"Well," Dr. Phil said. "We brought in reinforcements on this one. Dr. Kate, syndicated columnist and author of the newly released *Finding Mr. Right-for-You* is here to see if we can't help you two make this thing work out."

Kate smiled as the camera focused on her, and the audience applauded. She could feel prickles of heat singeing the skin under her arms.

"Dr. Kate has something else in common with you two—she's also a newlywed, so congratulations on that."

"Thank you." Kate smiled.

"Now, Dr. Kate," Dr. Phil said, "We know you advocate invest-ing the time and energy to make a solid match, but what about situ-ations like this? Are they too different to make it work?"

Kate felt a bolt of energy at the opportunity to help Hope and Ryan. How many times had she advised similar couples in her office? At least this couple hadn't waited until they had years of animosity between them.

"First of all," Kate began, "Congratulations on your marriage and on your willingness to seek help from the beginning. Every mar-riage is a merging of two personalities—sometimes more if there are children involved. When you're blending two sets of ideals and expectations, there's bound to be conflict. And when you're oppo-sites, there's a greater amount of conflict." *Boy, can I relate to that.*

"The key," she continued, "is to determine which areas need changing and find the middle ground. Pick your battles. Does it really matter that he balls up his socks before he throws them in the hamper? Probably not. Does it matter that you disagree on how much of your income is expendable? Definitely."

Kate swallowed, hoping nobody could tell how dry her mouth was. "Relationships are constantly negotiated," she added. "Opposites can make it work if they're both willing to find the middle ground. And both of you seem willing to make this work."

"We are," Hope said. "But every time we have discussions about our differences, we end up arguing."

Kate jumped in. "It's important to choose the right timing when you discuss your differing opinions. For instance, the arrival of the Visa bill isn't a good time to discuss Hope's spending habits. It's too late, and that leaves Ryan feeling stressed and out of control."

"Exactly," Ryan said. "I'm already angry that she's spent the money without regard for my budget."

Dr. Phil spoke up. "And, Hope, did you sit down with Ryan and work out this budget, or was it foisted upon you?"

Hope nodded. "Ryan did the budget on his own. There is no room for good shoes in that budget."

The audience laughed.

"A woman's got to have good shoes, Ryan," Dr. Phil said. "Rule number one."

He turned toward the camera. "You can read more about how to find a suitable mate in Dr. Kate's book *Finding Mr. Right-for-You.*" There was a close-up of her book cover, then Dr. Phil continued. "All right, next we have a blended family who can't seem to blend." He looked at Hope and Ryan. "And you thought blending two was tough! We'll be right back."

⌘

After the show, Kate slid into the black limo for her trip to the airport. In the back of the car, her nerves still jangled. It had been an exciting experience, and she felt giddy with energy. She'd already celebrated with Pam, Chloe, and Ronald in the green room, but now that she was away from the moment, she wanted to share it with a friend. Before she would have called Bryan, but who did she call now?

Anna? No, her former assistant was out of town with her new job.

Her dad? She considered it a moment, then took out her cell and dialed. It rang and rang before going over to voice mail, and she hung up.

She had to tell somebody. What good was exciting news if she had no one to share it with?

*Well, I know exactly who I could call.*

*Well, then, Kate, just do it.*

She dialed Lucas's shop, and when Ethan answered, she asked for Lucas. As she waited, she second-guessed herself. Would he find it odd that she'd phoned him when she'd see him at the airport in several hours? Why should he even care how the show had gone? It was her career, her book. In a matter of months, she'd be nothing to him but a name on the divorce papers.

*Shoot, why did I call him? Maybe I should hang up.* Kate pulled the phone from her ear.

"Hello?"

She put the phone back. "Hi, it's Kate."

"Hey!" He sounded happy to hear from her. "How'd it go?"

Kate relaxed a bit. He didn't seem confused by her call. "It went very well. Quick, but good."

"All your worries were for nothing. I knew you'd do great."

"Easy for you to say. You weren't the one on national TV."

He chuckled, and she realized she missed the warmth of his laugh. "That's why I make furniture and you give interviews."

She sighed, the excitement of the morning giving way to something calmer.

"Where are you now?"

"In the back of a limousine." The driver turned onto the freeway and accelerated.

"Aren't you special. How was the hotel?"

"Gorgeous, accommodating, and pristine. You could have eaten off the floors."

"Hope you didn't get too accustomed to that."

"Don't worry—I'm already anticipating the condition of the house."

He chuckled again, and Kate let a comfortable silence fall as she settled back into the leather seats.

"My flight's running on time. The question is, will you be?" she joked.

"Only time will tell," he retorted.

"Is that supposed to be a pun? It might help if you wore a watch, you know."

"What fun would that be?"

Kate chuckled. He was hopeless. "I guess I'll meet you outside baggage claim. Do you have my flight number?"

"Uh, let's see." She heard crackling, like he was holding the phone between his ear and shoulder. He was probably riffling through his cluttered wallet.

Some things never changed. "Here, let me give it to you again." Kate consulted her ticket and rattled off the flight number and arrival time.

When they hung up, Kate tucked the ticket into her suit coat and looked out the window, watching palm trees and tall buildings go by. In two weeks, the show would be broadcast, and the sales of her book, already good, from what Rosewood told her, might just skyrocket. Would it hit the *New York Times* bestseller list? She could only keep her fingers crossed. It couldn't hurt to have Dr. Phil announcing her title on the air.

But she couldn't quell the niggling fear that national attention would expose her to personal scrutiny. And now that she'd gone so public, what was to stop someone from digging around and finding out the truth? The answer was as close as Bryan and his family. Or, more likely, Stephanie.

Now that she was in the public eye, reporters would jump at the chance to smear her reputation. And, for the first time, she realized it wouldn't only be her reputation that got ruined. What would the exposure do to Lucas and his family? Jamie might already know the truth, but the rest of his family would feel betrayed, and Lucas would suffer the scrutiny and distrust of his own hometown.

*What am I doing?*

It felt as though she'd been asking herself that question every day for the past month. And she still didn't know the answer.

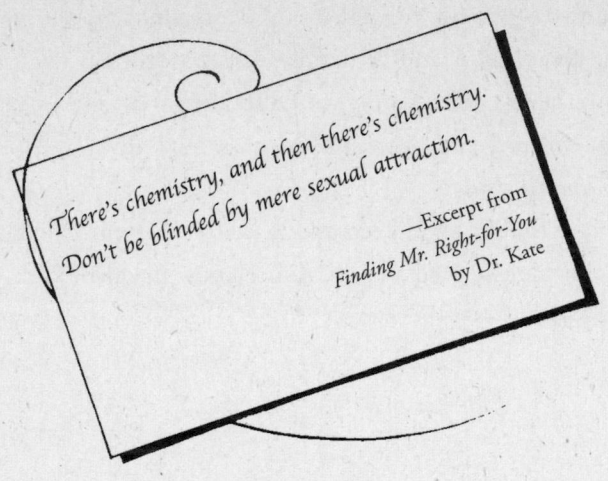

*There's chemistry, and then there's chemistry. Don't be blinded by mere sexual attraction.*

—Excerpt from
*Finding Mr. Right-for-You*
by Dr. Kate

# Chapter Seventeen

"Ready?" Kate heard Lucas call from the shop downstairs.

She saved her article and grabbed her purse. When she reached the bottom of the stairs, Lucas was waiting, keys in hand.

"What are you doing?" she asked.

"Taking you home to watch the show."

"Oh." The realization that he wanted to see it sent warmth through Kate. She avoided his gaze as she slid past. "Well, come on, then. It starts in fifteen."

After a quick trip home, Kate flipped on the TV, and Lucas made a pot of coffee. Kate's fingers fluttered like a ship's sails as she waited.

A tap sounded at the front door. Roy peeked around the edge.

"Hello! We're not late, are we?" He entered, followed by Susan, Brody, and Jamie.

"Oh, my goodness, you all came." Kate hadn't expected it to be a family affair.

"We wouldn't miss this for the world, would we, dear?" Roy said. "It's your national debut."

The group of them congregated on and around the sofa.

"Are you nervous?" Jamie asked.

"A little," Kate said. "Which is silly since it's taped."

"I'm sure you did fabulously," Roy said. "I'll bet your book is going to make that bestseller list yet. We have a real celebrity in the family!"

Kate glanced at Jamie, feeling awkward at the mention of family. Jamie withdrew a romance novel from her bag and propped it open on the arm of the couch.

"Coffee, anyone?" Lucas asked from the kitchen.

"Sure." Roy grabbed the remote and turned up the volume.

"Turn it down, Roy; that's too loud," Susan said.

Brody checked his watch. "You better hurry. Two minutes and counting."

Kate sank into the armchair.

"When is your segment on?" Brody asked.

"It's first—if they air it in the order they taped it."

Moments later, Lucas handed Kate and Roy their mugs, then retrieved his own cup and sat on the arm of Kate's chair. Bo settled on the rug beside Jamie and she scratched behind his ears.

"Hey, his icky yellow beard is gone."

Kate had donned rubber gloves the day before and scrubbed the mutt's chin. "I cleaned him up and put cornstarch in the fur under his mouth."

The corner of Lucas lips twitched. "Cornstarch?"

"It's amazing what you can learn when you Google something."

The *Dr. Phil* theme song began. "Be quiet; it's on." Roy increased the volume until Susan glared at him.

Jamie closed her book and leaned forward.

As they watched the opening, Kate's hands grew cold. Lucas's family's attention was rapt on the TV. She was the only reason they'd come. How easily they'd accepted her into their family, counting her as one of their own. Even Susan seemed to be giving her a chance. They couldn't be more supportive if it were Lucas on the show.

*I'm a horrible, horrible person.*

Dr. Phil introduced Kate, and her face appeared on screen.

"There you are," Jamie said.

"Shhhh!" Brody said.

The room got quiet as Dr. Phil mentioned her newlywed status. Kate felt her face heat, and Lucas set his hand on her shoulder. Kate sipped her coffee.

The segment continued, going exactly as Kate remembered. Her makeup, which had seemed too heavy on the day of the show, looked natural under the lights, and the stylist had done a nice job with her hair.

When Dr. Phil announced the title of her book and showed the cover, Lucas squeezed her shoulder. She'd hoped they wouldn't edit that out.

The segment ended and they broke for a commercial.

"Well done, Kate." Roy said.

"You did great," Jamie said. "How did you stay so calm? I wouldn't know what to say."

Brody elbowed her. "That'll be the day."

Jamie jostled him back.

"It's second nature by now," Kate said. "Though I was nervous since it was national TV."

"I couldn't tell," Roy said.

The phone rang, and Kate jumped up. "It's probably my publicist." She dashed to the kitchen and picked up. "Hello?"

"Hi, it's me."

Her stomach flopped. "Bryan," she said quietly, peering into the living room where Lucas's family continued their conversation. Lucas met her gaze, and she turned away, walking to the kitchen window.

"You were amazing, Kate," Bryan said. "I was so proud of you."

What right did he have to be proud? He didn't deserve to say those words. He hadn't coached her on what to say or driven her to the airport. *He didn't even show up for our wedding.*

Kate hadn't even thought of Bryan watching the show. She didn't think he'd even known it was airing today. Plus it was during work hours, and it wasn't like they were together anymore.

"You weren't even nervous," Bryan said. "And the way he plugged your book. I bet it'll take off now." He gave a familiar whistle. She'd forgotten that about Bryan—that little whistle he did to punctuate his excitement.

"That's the hope."

A long silence followed her words. Kate heard a ruckus in the living room and knew Lucas's family was leaving. Outside the window, the sea oats on the hill bowed against the breeze. Why had Bryan called again? Didn't he realize it was awkward for her?

"I miss you, Kate."

She gritted her teeth. "Stop it, Bryan."

"It's true. I miss the way you leave everything in tidy stacks, and the way you squint your eyes at me when I say something foolish. I miss the way you—"

"Stop it." He was getting to her, and she hated that. She rubbed her eyes. "You have to stop calling me here."

"Your cell was off."

"That's not what I mean. You can't just call me whenever you want now."

Kate heard footsteps behind her, heard the clatter of something being put in the sink. She turned and met Lucas's eyes. He knew it was Bryan; she could see that much in his expression. There was something in his eyes that tugged at her heartstrings. Hurt? Lucas looked away before she could pursue the thought.

". . . where we can talk in person," Bryan was saying.

What had she missed? He wanted to meet?

Lucas leaned against the sink, facing her, his palms braced on the ledge behind him. His stance said, *Talk all you want. I'm not going anywhere.* What did he expect her to do? Hang up on Bryan? *It's not my fault he called. I didn't ask him to.*

"What about it, Kate?"

What about what? She couldn't think straight.

"Or I could come there if that's easier. Whatever you want to do, but I want to see you. I need to be with you. Please." He grated out the word.

Lucas cocked a brow.

Kate's heart beat like a frightened bird's, and she wasn't sure why. She felt cornered. By both of them. She had to get out of here. Away from Lucas's strange looks, away from Bryan's hurt pleas.

"I can't talk right now."

"I'll call you back," he managed to get out before Kate hung up. She set the phone in the cradle. A step away, she could feel Lucas's tension.

"I'm going for a walk." Kate grabbed the doorknob leading to the beach.

"I want him to stop calling here." Lucas crossed his arms over his chest, his right bicep bulging over his left fist. He looked away.

"I'm a little tired of everyone telling me what they want right now." Kate pulled at the door.

Lucas put his hand against it. "He has no right calling my house."

"*Your* house? I thought I lived here too." Kate turned and was surprised to find Lucas so close, his arm extending past her.

"You know what I mean."

Did she really? Was he being possessive of the house or of her? Why did he care if Bryan called? Sometimes she thought she saw something in Lucas's eyes, but right now she thought it had nothing to do with her. It was about possession. Bryan and Lucas were like two wolves fighting over an animal carcass.

*And I'm tired of being caught in the middle.*

She jerked on the door, but he held it fast.

What was it with men and control? "Let me go." She pulled at the knob again. It didn't budge. "Lucas! Let me—"

"What if I don't want to?"

And just like that, time slowed.

Almost against her will she looked at him. And was caught by his eyes. They pulled her in, held her hostage. She stilled, her anger fading, replaced by something . . . more complicated . . . less welcome . . .

*"What if I don't want to?"* What did he mean? Suddenly desperate to understand, she searched his face and watched as his eyes darkened into shadowed whirlpools.

She forgot how to breathe.

"What if I want you to stay?" His gaze traveled the planes of her face and stopped at her lips.

"What . . ." He was so close she couldn't think. His thumb grazed her cheekbone, barely a touch, and yet it heated her skin. She shuddered and closed her eyes against the riptide tugging inside her. What was happening? This was Lucas, not Bryan. Lucas, who frustrated her with his lack of organization. Lucas, who annoyed her with his sluggishness.

*Lucas, who held you in his arms when you were seasick. Lucas, who stepped in and saved you when you were desperate.*

"Open your eyes, honey."

Her stomach tightened at the endearment. She was powerless against the emotion raging inside her. It felt wonderful and terrible and scary.

"Lucas." Nothing more than a whisper.

"Open your eyes," he said. "See what's right in front of you."

She obeyed his request. What was this spell he'd cast? She wanted to fall into the depths of his eyes and get lost. She wanted to touch his jaw and feel the roughness against her fingers.

But before she could follow the impulse, he closed the distance between them. And his lips touched hers, gentle and slow.

Without thought, Kate laid her palm against his face and heard his intake of breath before he deepened the kiss, pulling her closer, making her head spin. His movements were sure and slow, like everything else he did.

It wasn't even their first kiss. But the others hadn't been like this. There was no photographer snapping pictures, no public judging the validity of their vows, no family to convince.

It was just Lucas and Kate. All alone. Exploring feelings she hadn't known existed.

*No. That's not true.*

Maybe she had known, or maybe she'd been in denial. Maybe she'd been blinded by Bryan's rejection. But she was seeing things now. And feeling them. Things that she'd never felt before, not even with Bryan. The way Lucas made her forget everything except the feel of his lips. Made her want more. Made her need more.

*More.* She slid her hand into his hair, cupping his head, and arched closer. He was warm and strong. He smelled like cedar and musk. All man.

"Katie . . ." Lucas whispered against her lips.

She didn't think, just felt. The urgency pushed her on. *It's okay, Kate. You're married. Lucas is your husband.* She submitted to the thought, letting her emotions guide her.

*But . . . what happens when it ends?*

Against her will, the question rose from a deep and distant well of reason. Kate ignored it, let the feel of Lucas's body against hers drown everything out.

But the voice grew louder, more insistent.

*What'll happen when the year ends? Why are you becoming emotionally invested in a temporary relationship?*

And it had to be temporary. Muddled as her thoughts were, she hadn't lost all sense of reason. She and Lucas were too different— more dissimilar than her mom and dad had been, and look how that had ended. She of all people knew the odds against opposites making a marriage work.

*You have to stop. Now!*

Somehow mustering the strength, she pushed at Lucas's chest, separating them. Her chest heaved. She was beyond her target heart rate and she hadn't moved. Judging from Lucas's expression, he felt the same. A pink flush mottled his face. His eyes were glazed, his lips swollen. She was tempted to soothe them with her thumb.

*Stop it! You have to stop before this gets out of hand. You're too different.*

They might be different, but heavens to Betsy, the chemistry was there in spades. She had to escape before she lost her resolve.

She reached for the doorknob and pulled.

"Running, Kate?" The dare emerged, raspy and breathless.

She ignored it, pulling the door shut behind her and dashing toward the shoreline. Yes, she was running. And too afraid to say anything for fear it might reveal too much.

As if her actions hadn't already revealed far too much.

*Honesty begins within yourself.*

—Excerpt from
*Finding Mr. Right-for-You*
by Dr. Kate

# Chapter Eighteen

Lucas slammed his fist on the counter. He hadn't succeeded in opening Kate's eyes; he'd only succeeded in pushing her away. As he watched her scramble across the sandy grass toward the beach, he feared he'd scared her away for good.

He punched the counter again, then shook his throbbing hand. Bo nudged his leg with his wet nose. "Not now, boy."

Why had he moved so fast? He'd only meant to kiss her gently, to show her how he felt. But then her hand had wound into his hair, and she'd pressed herself against him.

His own hand now raked his hair. His timing couldn't have been worse. Fresh from a phone call from Bryan, she was probably thinking of him. She wasn't over Bryan; that much he knew.

*It's too soon to tell her how you feel.*

*But her response was so—*

*She was thinking about Bryan. Wishing it was him she'd married.*

Lucas left the kitchen and paced the length of the living room as if he could distance himself from the thought. But she wasn't Bryan's wife.

*She's my wife . . . Yeah. Temporarily. In name only.*

*You agreed to those terms, Luc, so stop your whining.*

Only he hadn't known it would be so hard. Hadn't known it would make him long for her more. Hadn't known it would hurt so much.

He sank into the recliner and let his head fall against the cushion. What was Kate thinking right now? Would she expect an apology when she returned?

Well, she wouldn't get it. He wasn't sorry, even if she had been thinking about her idiot ex-fiancé while he kissed her.

*All I did was lay my feelings out. Nothing to be ashamed of.*

So why was his gut strung tighter than a bowline knot?

⊸⊷

By the time Kate returned, the house was empty. Lucas's truck was gone, which meant he must've gone back to his shop. Relieved, but dreading the inevitable confrontation, Kate started dinner.

Her walk had helped clear her head. Obviously Lucas had feelings for her, and Kate admitted she'd grown fond of him as well.

*Fond? You were all over him, girl.*

She emptied a package of ground beef into the skillet, threw away the Styrofoam platter, and washed her hands. Okay, so maybe she had feelings for him. She had to remember the advice she dispensed in her book. "Once you realize a man is not well suited to you, it's imperative to end the relationship before you become emotionally invested."

Well, she couldn't end the marriage, but she could put the relationship back on track. They were friends. No—roommates. That was all. The sooner Lucas realized it, the sooner they could put this awkwardness behind them.

Bo sat by the back door and turned his big head toward her. She let him out and kept an eye on him through the window while she cooked. The smell of dinner soon drew him back.

The taco filling was hot and bubbly by the time she heard the front door open and click closed. Kate lowered the heat to a simmer and stirred the beef mixture as it sizzled. Would Lucas join her or would he grab a shower? She hated this indecision, this awkwardness. She didn't like walking on eggshells in her own home. She wanted to return to the way things were before.

When Lucas entered the kitchen, Kate gave the beef one last stir and turned. They might as well put this behind them.

Lucas removed a can of Coke from the fridge and popped the tab. He wouldn't even look at her. She wondered what he was thinking, what he was feeling. His expression revealed nothing.

"About earlier," Kate started, then wondered what to say next. Why hadn't she planned something? *Think!*

Lucas took a drink, then shook his head, a barely perceptible movement. "Not necessary."

He moved closer, and Kate pressed her back against the oven. The metal handle dug into her back. But Lucas reached into the cabinet instead. Shaken, Kate turned.

Lucas removed two plates and shut the cabinet door. "It was a mistake," he said as he stepped away.

Kate heard him setting the plates on the table. *A mistake?*

*Well, what did you expect him to say?*

She wasn't sure, but it wasn't this. Maybe she thought he'd confess he had feelings for her. But maybe he only missed Emily. Maybe he missed the intimacy of their marriage.

"Let's just forget it happened." His voice penetrated her thoughts.

*Let's just forget it happened? Forget the way you took my mouth, forget the way you touched me, forget the way you felt against me?* She wondered if that were possible. "Right."

Dinner consisted of tacos, avoided eye contact, and stilted conversation. When Susan dropped by and invited Kate on a walk, Kate readily agreed. Because despite her agreement with Lucas, she couldn't seem to eradicate the memory of the kiss.

⟡

Kate felt warm and cocooned as she stirred from sleep, only half-conscious. She kept her eyes closed, hoping to fall back asleep. The covers twisted around her legs in a snug knot, but a big pillow, snuggled into her stomach, warmed her.

She wondered about that because her pillow was under her head. Coming more fully awake, Kate opened her eyes. She could barely see by the soft morning light that filtered through the curtains. More important, her arms and face felt the softness of flesh against them and she knew it was no pillow she cuddled with. Her arm curved around Lucas's side and her body spooned into him, her face against his back. Her thighs pressed into the backs of his.

She started to jump away then stopped herself. Maybe he was asleep—completely unaware that she clung to him like a barnacle on a boat. A sudden move would wake him. If she disengaged slowly, he'd be none the wiser. *Oh, please, let him be asleep.*

She lay quietly listening to the sound of his breathing. He wasn't snoring, but that didn't mean he wasn't asleep. His respirations were deep, a good sign.

How had she ended up on his side anyway? Had she had some weird dream about their kiss? Where was her rolled-up quilt barrier? The way the covers tangled around her legs, she or Lucas must've had a fitful sleep.

*Okay, time to disengage.*

She carefully removed her hand from his stomach. Inch by inch, she lifted her arm until it had no contact with Lucas. Next she lifted her head, moving her face away from the heated hardness of his back.

*So far, so good.*

The only thing against him now was . . . well, the rest of her body. Her legs tingled with awareness.

*Stop that! Good grief, what has gotten into me?*

She eased her weight onto her elbow and held her breath as she moved away from him.

Lucas stirred and turned, settling on his back. Kate froze above him. His side pressed into her now and his face was inches away. Thankfully, his eyes remained closed. She lay still, hardly daring to breathe. Was her heartbeat shaking the entire bed?

She glanced at his clock. It was later than she'd thought. The alarm would sound in three minutes. She had to break away.

Kate scooted back, easing away from him. She'd moved only a few inches when she felt resistance. Her pajama top was caught. Lucas had rolled on top of it.

Gritting her teeth, she grasped the material and tugged slowly, watching Lucas's face for any sign of awareness. But it freed without incident, and she sighed quietly. Being careful to steady the bed, she used her feet and right elbow to support her weight and scooted her hips away.

When she reached her own side of the bed, she rolled to her back and let out a shaky breath. Her heart, beating more rapidly than could be accounted for, really was shaking the bed. Thank goodness Lucas had slept through it. There was no telling what he'd think if he knew she'd snuggled up to him like that.

"Next time you want to cuddle, just say so."

The voice from beside Kate startled her. Then the meaning of his words penetrated her mind. He still lay perfectly still, his breathing deep and even. *That jerk!* He'd been awake the whole time and let her suffer.

She yanked the pillow from under her head and swung it at him. But the only response she got was his insufferable laughter.

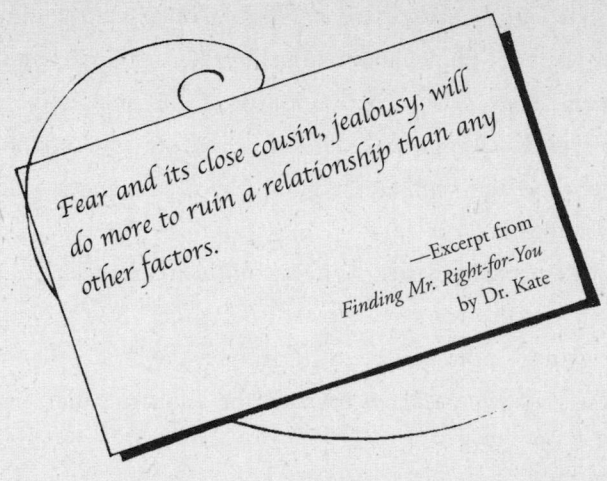

*Fear and its close cousin, jealousy, will do more to ruin a relationship than any other factors.*

—Excerpt from
*Finding Mr. Right-for-You*
by Dr. Kate

# Chapter Nineteen

The Wright house was buzzing with activity when Kate and Lucas arrived the next Saturday.

"Come in, kids!" Roy called from where he emptied ice cubes into glasses. He was about to say something else, but Susan turned on a noisy mixer and began running it through a pot of steaming potatoes. In the next room, the TV blared, but Jamie was curled into a fat armchair with a book.

Lucas and Kate greeted them; then Roy took Lucas into the garage to show him the new mower he'd bought. When Susan turned off the mixer, silence settled on the kitchen.

"Can I help with something?" Kate asked.

"No, thank you."

Kate searched for something to say. It was easier when they were walking; she didn't feel the need to fill the silence. For the hundredth time, she thought about addressing the issue of Susan and Kate's mom. Would it clear the air between them if she apologized on behalf of her mom? Would it open the door for Susan to confide in Kate about her marriage problems? Or would it just anger Susan that Lucas had told her?

She was formulating her thoughts on the matter when Lucas and his dad reentered. "You can borrow it anytime," Roy was saying to Lucas as he took a pitcher of tea from the fridge.

Oh well, it would have to wait for another time. "Is Brody around?" Kate asked.

"He's upstairs already," Roy said.

"I think I'll join him, if you don't need any help," Kate said.

Roy shooed her on, and Kate climbed the two flights, dreading the rooftop experience but wanting to catch up with Brody. They hadn't had an opportunity to discuss his majors since he dropped by her office.

She found Brody leaning on the widow's-walk railing, high above the landscape. He greeted her as she slipped into her chair against the chimney chase.

"Great day, huh?" he asked.

Kate forced her eyes from him. The blue of the sky melted into the expanse of ocean, its unending vastness interrupted only by the colorful dots of sails. The sun burned hot, and the breeze chopped at the water's surface. Kate's fists tightened around the chair's arm, its edges cutting into her palm.

"Beautiful." She tucked her feet under the chair. Why wasn't it getting easier to face her fear of heights? She'd thought she could overcome it if she only forced herself up here every week.

Her mind went back to the first time she'd felt the fear.

Ironically, it hadn't been her own life she'd feared for at the time. Her mom, belly filled with alcohol, had climbed out her bedroom window and onto the sloped roof of the porch. Kate had come home from a friend's house to find her teetering on the edge.

"Mom, don't move!" Kate ran upstairs, down the short, narrow hall, and into her mom's bedroom. The wooden sash was thrown open and the curtains fluttered in the night breeze.

"Mom, come here." Kate climbed out the window and took slow steps down the slope. Her mom's blouse rippled in the wind, and for a moment, Kate thought it would be enough to blow her right over the edge. She grabbed her mom's hand. "Come on, Momma."

Kate didn't know how frightened she'd been until they were safely inside the house. Only then did she realize her heart felt as though it was going to burst through her ribs.

Now, her heart pounded in remembrance. Ever since that day, heights had frightened her.

*This is not helping. I need to focus on something else.*

Brody shifted, drawing Kate's attention, and she remembered her purpose in coming. "I've been wondering about your career path. Have you given it more thought?"

Brody leaned his weight against the railing. Didn't he realize it could give way? If it did, he'd hurtle three floors to his death. Okay, maybe just a broken leg, but still. Kate's palms grew clammy; she felt dizzy at just the thought.

"It's all I think about," Brody said. "Other than girls, that is." He flashed a smile, revealing a dimple she hadn't noticed before.

Kate remembered the passion in his voice when he'd talked about tutoring his little friend. She had a suspicion education was his main interest. The question was, why had he changed majors? What was holding him back?

"When I look into the future," he said, "I can see myself teaching middle school. Maybe art or computers or even science. But—"

Kate waited for him to finish, although she had to look away; the mental image of the rail breaking loose was too much. She watched her oval thumbnail follow the square edge of the chair's arm.

"I don't know. I changed majors for a reason. I keep trying to remember why."

"You switched to art next, right?"

The wind tousled his hair, and he shook it from his eyes. "Yeah. Dumb move."

Kate shook her head. "We make decisions for a reason. Sometimes you just have to dig deep to find them."

She was beginning to think she understood Brody's reasons.

She leaned back, and her chair, its legs not quite even, rocked an inch. She stiffened, clutching the table's edge. Her breath caught in her throat, and prickles of adrenaline flared under her skin.

When she looked up, Brody was studying her. "What's wrong?"

Kate forced her fingers to loosen and crossed her legs. "The chair rocked back and I lost my balance."

Brody's head cocked. "You always sit with your back against the wall, and you never walk around up here." He pointed his finger at her. "You're afraid of heights, aren't you?"

Kate gave a wry laugh. "I'm not afraid of heights so much as I'm afraid of falling."

Brody sat at the table. "You should have said something. We could eat downstairs."

She shrugged. "I don't want to break tradition. Besides, I don't like letting fear rule my life. This little once-a-week trek is my way of telling my fear to take a hike."

Brody laughed, and as he did, a thought struck Kate. There was nothing like fear to change your course. How many people had she counseled whose fear of intimacy kept them from experiencing the very thing they desired?

She leaned back. "Maybe you're a little like me."

"What, me? Afraid of heights? No way. I've been parasailing lots of times and even hang gliding a couple times. Don't tell Mom and Dad. They'd freak."

Kate shook her head, sure she was onto something. "No. Afraid of falling." She watched him, waiting for him to connect the dots.

His head tipped back, his eyes narrowing. "You think I'm afraid of failing."

He was obviously offended, and Kate wondered if she'd over-stepped her boundaries. "Only you know the answer to that." She smiled to soften the words. "I'm just putting it out there."

It made sense. Maybe he'd only changed majors because he excelled at many things and couldn't make up his mind. But in light of his pas-sion for teaching, fear of failure made sense. He wouldn't be the first.

The sound of feet thumping up the stairs warned them they had company coming, and the topic was tabled for the day.

❧

Kate was eating alone at the Even Keel when her agent, Ronald, called with great news. *Glamour* magazine wanted to feature her in a monthly "Dear Dr. Kate" column. They'd seen her appearance on Dr. Phil and had been tracking her career. It had been between her and another syndicated columnist, and she was their first pick.

Kate paid her bill and rushed back to the shop, hoping Lucas was there, wanting to share her good news. She would have been eat-ing with him except he'd canceled because of an appointment.

But what Kate saw when she neared the shop pushed her good news from her mind and stopped her feet midstride. Someone behind her bumped her, treading on her good heels.

"Sorry," Kate mumbled as the tourist passed her with a glare, pulling a golden retriever on a leash. She shifted over, moving closer to the gift shop, out of the stream of traffic, her eyes returning to the scene that had stopped her.

Lucas helped a woman from a silver car. The woman unfolded herself from the compact vehicle, and Kate saw her long red, hair. Lucas shut the door and followed the woman into his shop.

It was the same woman Kate had seen him with the day Brody stopped by her office a month or so ago. Was she the reason Lucas had cancelled their lunch plans? Had he and Red had lunch together?

Something tightened deep in her stomach like a dishrag wrung hard.

*Don't be ridiculous. She's probably just a friend. Or a business acquaintance.*

From a distance, Kate watched Lucas hold the store's door for the woman. She turned and laughed at something he said, cocking her head.

Kate's lips pursed in reaction. She disliked the way the woman looked at Lucas. She disliked her own reaction to it more.

*It's not jealousy.* She looked away and watched the tourists and locals walking past her. What would people think if they saw Lucas and Red eating together? Especially if the woman was hanging on him like she had the first time Kate saw them together? He was married to her, Dr. Kate, and she couldn't have people thinking he was wining and dining another woman. As careful as they'd been to make the marriage appear legitimate, she couldn't believe he'd be so careless.

A passing dog bumped her thigh, and Kate straightened. She'd have to say something to him tonight.

*He'll think I'm jealous.*

*Not if you handle it carefully.*

Kate hitched her bag on her shoulder and set her feet in motion, her ire rising with each step. Didn't Lucas know she had a reputation to protect? Hadn't he given any thought to how it would appear, him gallivanting all over the island with another woman?

She composed her features as she entered the shop, the bell jangling against the glass door. Soft music greeted her, and the air-conditioning was welcome against her heated skin. But there was no sign of Lucas or the woman on the floor.

"Nice lunch, Kate?" Ethan called from behind the mahogany desk. He adjusted his wire-rimmed glasses.

"Sure." She hesitated on the first step. "Is Lucas around?"

"He's in the back." Ethan leaned over his papers.

Behind her, a customer entered the store, and Ethan stood.

Kate started up the stairs. "Thanks, I'll just . . . talk to him later."

*Why would he take Red to the back of the store?* There was nothing there but the pieces he was working on and a bunch of tools.

Her heels clicked up the wood steps. When she reached the top, she hung her bag on the coatrack and sat at her desk. Ethan hadn't acted as if anything was amiss. He would know if something was going on between Lucas and Red. Kate was letting her imagination run wild.

*Come on, Kate; get back to work.* She moved the computer mouse, stopping the screen saver, and the article she'd been working on before lunch appeared. She'd already condensed the letter and needed to formulate an answer for Never a Bride in Albany, whose letter smacked of desperation.

Kate wrote a reply then reread it, editing as she went. The second letter she'd chosen was already succinct, but she edited it down and typed it into the document as well, then formulated her answer. When she was finished with the article, she stood and stretched. Of their own volition, her feet carried her to the street window.

Below, in the parking slot in front of the store, was the silver car. Her heart sank. She checked her watch. It had been an hour. What were Lucas and that woman doing downstairs? What if . . . ?

What if Lucas had been dating Red before they got married? Was it possible he was seeing someone on the side? Was it possible he was in love with the woman?

A space inside her hollowed out.

*What do I care? Our marriage isn't real. We'll be divorced in less than ten months.*

But the memory of their kiss kicked to the surface of her thoughts.

*There is more than a contractual agreement between us.*

The confession filled the pit of her stomach with something both pleasant and disturbing. She was relieved to finally admit actual feelings for Lucas were growing like tenacious weeds in a carefully cultivated garden. But like those weeds, the feelings were undesired. They didn't belong; their presence was a hindrance.

Kate's gaze centered on the silver car, and she bit the tender flesh inside her mouth. What possible reason could the woman have for being down there so long? Were they still in the back? Maybe Kate could go down under some pretense.

But what reason could she have? Her mind was a blank screen. She could almost see a skinny cursor blinking on the white space, taunting her.

It would be suspicious if she went down. She never interrupted

Lucas while he worked, and the last thing she wanted was to give him the pleasure of thinking she was curious about Red. Or worse, jealous.

If only she could hear what they were saying. Then she would know if anything—

She remembered something. The vents. Kate walked across the room to her old apartment, the sound of her heels muffled by the rug. The noise from the workshop carried through the heating ducts into her old living room. She remembered all the nights listening to Lucas's sander through the vents. She'd contemplated throttling him some evenings when she wanted peace after a day of listening to people's problems.

She walked to the vent against the back wall, where she kicked off her heels and squatted down, listening. Were they still in the workshop or had they gone back into the store? On the balls of her stocking feet, she balanced with a hand on the wall and stilled.

There were voices, barely audible. She heard the deep tones of Lucas's voice, but couldn't make out the words. Was that a woman's voice she heard now? She couldn't be sure. Kate set her knees on the floor by the register and leaned down further, pressing her palms to the dusty floor. There was nothing now, just silence.

No, there it was, a woman's voice, too quiet to make out.

She needed to get closer. Maybe then she could hear what they were saying.

Kate glanced down at her suit, weighing the dirty wood floor against the notion of letting her curiosity go unsatisfied. Then, with a sigh, she lowered herself to the floor, lying flat on her stomach. The suit was bound for the cleaners now.

As she bent her head, her thick metal earring clanged on the vent's louvered cover and she rose up enough to remove it, then set her ear against the cool metal surface.

There was a screech, like the sound of a chair against the concrete floor. Lucas was saying something. She stilled.

". . . that's what I thought."

Red spoke again, but Kate couldn't make it out. *Speak up, woman!*

It was quiet again, and Kate didn't even dare to swallow in case she missed something.

"What do you . . ." The rest of Lucas's words were muffled, like he'd turned away. Kate heard a creak and knew he'd leaned against his old metal desk.

". . . like the way . . . very nice . . . ." Kate didn't like her tone, even muffled through the ductwork.

The sound of heels clicking on the floor reached Kate's ears. Was the woman walking toward Lucas? Away from him? She didn't hear his footsteps, though his sandals were soft soled.

Then there was nothing but quiet from below. The silence unnerved her. What were they doing down there? Her imagination filled the gap. She imagined Red approaching Lucas, placing her long, slender fingers along the side of his neck. Was he wrapping his arms around the woman even now? Was he kissing her the way he'd kissed Kate the week before?

Heat prickled the back of her neck.

*That's silly. If he were seeing someone else before he married me, he wouldn't have married me.*

*But that doesn't mean he isn't interested in the woman now.*

Maybe he'd met her after they married and was pursuing the relationship. Did Kate really have any rights to him? Any say in what he did in the privacy of his own workshop?

*He's married to me. Even if it is in name only, he owes me the respect of keeping his vows.*

She had kept hers, after all. It wasn't her fault that Bryan called sometimes.

She sighed. Though now that the cramped stiletto was on the other foot, she realized it was unfair to take Bryan's calls. Lucas had been angry last time Bryan called. *"He has no right to call my house,"* he'd said. Maybe it was just caveman tactics that inspired the words, but followed so closely by those other words—the ones she'd repeated in her mind ever since—his anger took on a different meaning.

*"What if I want you to stay?"*

Had he meant it the way she thought? Did Lucas want their marriage to be real?

*That's crazy.* Although the notion held more appeal than was healthy for two individuals so incompatible, Lucas had never given any other indication he considered the marriage binding. Except, well, the fact that he'd kissed her. And boy, had he kissed her. Her stomach fluttered now just thinking about it. Maybe he did want more.

*Yeah, Kate, that's why he's alone downstairs with that beautiful, leggy redhead.*

*And why is it so quiet down there?* Kate pressed her ear on the vent and listened.

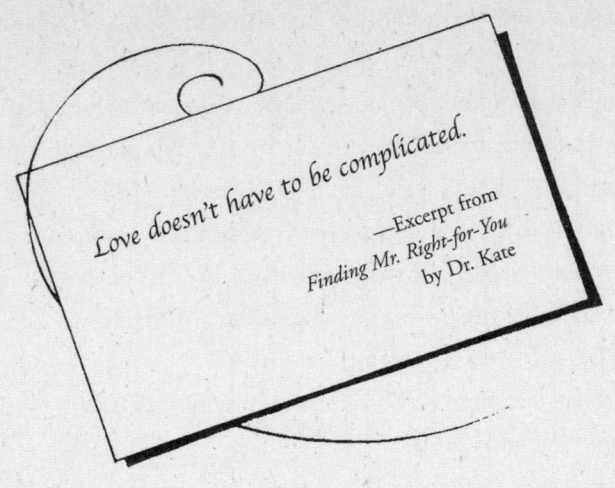

Love doesn't have to be complicated.

—Excerpt from
*Finding Mr. Right-for-You*
by Dr. Kate

# Chapter Twenty

"It shouldn't be too long." Lucas opened the door for Sydney. "I'll call you when it's finished."

"Feel free to call before then if you have any questions." Sydney's smile indicated a call would be welcome, questions or not.

With nothing more than a polite nod, Lucas let the door close and wiped his hands on his jeans. He appreciated the business—she was giving him plenty—but the woman had the subtlety of a shark in a fish pool. He had little respect for a woman who ignored a man's wedding band. Did she even care that he belonged to someone else?

*You're only a name on a wedding certificate, man.*

His eyes wandered up the staircase to Kate's office. Would she mind if he interrupted her work? He hated to admit it, but he'd missed having lunch with her. Missed the way she wiped her lips after every bite. Missed the way she separated the food on her plate so nothing touched.

Mostly, he missed listening to her talk about her work. At first glance, some might think Kate's career was self-serving. But if they heard her talk about people—heard the excitement in her voice when she helped someone—they'd know differently.

It was quiet upstairs, not even the clacking of her computer keys. Maybe she was taking a break. Lucas took the stairs, glad for the opportunity to shake the cloying cloud of Sydney's perfume.

When he reached the second floor, her office chair was empty. A colorful screensaver danced on the computer, indicating she hadn't been typing for some time. Strange—he knew she was there; her car was out front.

He was about to call for her when he saw movement at the back of the building, through her old apartment doorway. He walked the length of the rug—and stopped. Beyond the coffee table, Kate lay flat as a mat on the floor. Her head faced the wall, ear to the floor—or was that the vent? One hand clutched the hair at her nape, pulling her cream-colored suit coat up at the waist. Her pants hugged the curve of her derrière, and the tops of her feet skimmed the floor.

*What in the world? Why would she be lying over the—*
*Unless . . .*

His lips curved into a smile as the wonder of it washed over him, cool and refreshing.

Oh yeah. This was going to be good.

Lucas leaned against the door frame, crossing his arms, biding his time. Finally, when she didn't budge, he cleared his throat.

Kate jumped, turned toward him, letting loose of her hair. The air must have kicked on because a blast blew a strand across her face.

"Looking for something?" He almost felt sorry for her as she scrambled into a sitting position. But the look on her face was too comical, and the feelings her jealousy inspired, too heartening.

"Lucas. I was just—" She dusted her suit coat, working her flattened fingers down the length of her arm in short swipes. "My earring." She held out a circular piece of jewelry lying in her palm. "I was getting my earring."

Who was she kidding? She'd been lying flat on the floor, her ear against the register. She was caught. Nailed. Busted.

"Did it fall down the vent?" He held back a smile, barely.

Her cheeks bloomed with color as she attempted to put the earring in. Even across the room he could see her hand shaking. "Of course not. It just—" Kate tried again to poke the earring through the hole and failed. She gave up and looked at him like a butterfly caught in a net.

He raised his brows, waiting.

At that, her shoulders drew back, her chin tipped. "All right, all right," she snapped. "You made your point."

Lucas approached her, feeling sorry for her now that she knew she was caught. Still, there was that whole jealousy thing that tugged the corners of his mouth.

Kate set her earring on the coffee table and struggled to stand. When he extended his hand, she smacked it away, her eyes narrowing as she straightened. Her crisp white shirt had come loose from her waistband, and her hair was tousled like she'd just awakened. She smoothed it and tucked it behind her ears with quick hands.

"I saw you after lunch with that . . . woman," Kate said. "I was worried about how it might look to other people." She crossed her arms over her chest. "We have an image to maintain, and it's not proper for you to be gallivanting all over the island with someone else."

Her words were so ridiculous he didn't know where to begin. *"Gallivanting?"*

She looked him in the eye. "You know what I mean. People will notice when you're eating with another woman. It's a small island—"

"I didn't eat with Sydney." Was that really what was bugging Kate? What everyone else thought? The notion sucked some of the air from his sails.

"Well, whatever. It's not proper for you to be seen with someone like that." Her lips, free of artificial color, pressed together.

Was she only concerned about her reputation, or was she hiding her jealousy behind its mask? "Someone like what?" he asked, curious to hear her answer.

"Someone like—You know what I mean. She isn't exactly unattractive, and she's . . . clingy."

"Clingy?"

"Like socks out of the dryer," she retorted. She tilted her head. "You know exactly what I mean."

Lucas lost the tug-of-war with his smile. "You're jealous," he said.

Kate turned away, tucking in her shirt before grabbing the earring off the table and walking toward a mirror that hung over the armchair. "I'm concerned about my reputation." She took the back off the earring and put it in.

"And that's why you were spying through the vent?" It didn't wash. If she were concerned about gossip, she would confront him, not eavesdrop.

Her eyes met his in the mirror. "I'm just trying to protect my career."

He walked closer until he was behind her. "Is that what you're telling yourself?"

Her hands fell slowly to her sides. In the light of the window to the side of the mirror, her eyes brightened to a caramel color. He wanted to get lost in there. Better yet, he wanted to climb behind those eyes and see what was holding her back.

Did she love Bryan still? He reviewed their kiss for the hundredth time and felt his confidence climb. A woman didn't kiss a man like that when she was in love with someone else. Maybe she'd never been in love with Bryan.

All Lucas knew was she had some kind of feelings for him.

"Why are you so afraid to be honest with yourself?" he asked.

Kate stared back. "I'm not afraid."

Her bravado seemed to have shrunk two sizes. He wanted to reach out and wrap his arms around her, pull her against him as he had on the sailboat. But he had a feeling he didn't dare move or she'd run.

"Why can't you admit you're jealous? It's not a crime." He found the courage to open up. Someone had to. "When Bryan called last week, I was jealous."

Something in her face softened. Her lips parted to speak. Then, as if she thought better of it, they sealed again.

Why was it so hard to admit something was happening between them? They had almost ten more months together. Would it hurt to explore the feelings?

"There's something here, and you know it," he said.

She blinked, her eyes fastened on his for just a split second before she walked away. "Stop it, Lucas. Leave things as they are." She stopped behind the barrier of the sofa.

Heaven forbid she let her guard down. "All neat and tidy, you mean?"

"What's wrong with neat and tidy? Neat and tidy is simple and clear-cut, and nobody gets hurt."

"Is that what's got you worried?" Was she still nursing wounds Bryan had inflicted? Couldn't she see he'd never forsake her as Bryan had? He always wanted to be there for her. To protect her. To cherish her. To love her.

"Nobody likes to get hurt."

He held the image of her on their wedding night. Remembered the sound of her sobbing in that big empty bed. "I'm not the one who left you at the altar," he said gently.

Kate wrapped her arms around her stomach. "Look, it just—It just won't work between us. We're too different. *Completely* incompatible, for heaven's sake. I've seen what happens too many times."

Did she think feelings were planned? Scheduled and carried out like entries on her color-coded calendar? "There's never been another you and me. You can't compare us to some couple you counseled in your office."

"I don't have to look any further than my parents to strike a comparison."

Something in her tone alerted him. "What about your parents?"

"They argued constantly. Good grief, they were like hot and cold, hard and soft, and whatever other opposites you can think of. I can still close my eyes at night and hear their bickering."

It was starting to make sense now. Her passion for helping others find a compatible mate. Her parents had divorced, possibly damaging her greatly, and now she was out to save the world. "Is that why you do it?"

"Do what?"

"Counsel others. Help people find their soul mate."

She rolled her eyes. "Huh. I don't believe in soul mates. I believe in helping women find a compatible mate whose values and personality line up with hers."

"All neat and tidy."

"We can't all live a messy, jumbled life."

Is that the way she saw his life? Like a chaotic heap of garbage?

"It might not be pretty to look at, but I found love nonetheless."

It was out before he could stop it. His heart skipped a beat.

The look on Kate's face made him glad he'd risked it. The way her eyes widened ever so slightly before she looked down at her fingers curled around the sofa's cushion. Was it awe or joy he'd seen before she looked away?

"I didn't mean to disregard what you had with Emily. I'm sorry."

*Emily.* She thought he was talking about Emily. The disappointment was keen. Hadn't he shown her his feelings these weeks they'd had together? Even if he hadn't said them. Apparently, he'd been too subtle. Or she just didn't want to see the truth.

She was waiting for his response. "Don't worry about it," he said, feeling like a fool. She didn't want anything between them; she'd made that clear. Maybe he wasn't the kind of man she wanted. Maybe she was waiting to be with Bryan.

For the first time he wondered if he'd ever be able to change her mind.

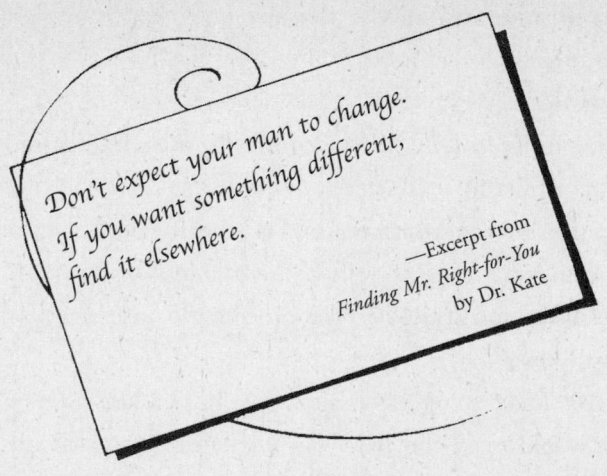

Don't expect your man to change.
If you want something different,
find it elsewhere.

—Excerpt from
*Finding Mr. Right-for-You*
by Dr. Kate

# Chapter Twenty-One

The phone on Kate's desk rang. She saved her column before answering.

"How's my favorite author?" Pam, Kate's publicist, greeted her.

"Pam! How are you?"

"Good, good. I wanted to update you on a few interviews I've scheduled. I e-mailed them to you a minute ago, but I have a last-minute opportunity, so I wanted to see if you were available. My contact from *Live with Lisa* called a few minutes ago, and they want to interview you tomorrow morning. They probably had a cancellation, and it's a fabulous opportunity for exposure on cable TV."

An interview on the popular program would be a boon. "That's great. Let me check my schedule." Kate pulled out her calendar. There were a couple appointments, but nothing that couldn't be rescheduled. She was almost finished with her column and her *Glamour* piece.

"I can do it."

"They intimated that Lucas would be welcome if he'd like to take part," Pam said.

Kate doubted he would but said she'd mention it to him and get back to Pam.

The discussion turned to the other radio interviews scheduled for several weeks out.

"Is *Mr. Right* doing okay saleswise?" Kate asked. Rosewood had hoped it would make the *New York Times* list, but so far it had only appeared deep on the *USA Today* list. She was afraid they were disappointed with sales, and this far out from the release, it wasn't likely to improve much, although an appearance on *Live with Lisa* wouldn't hurt.

"The book's fine. I know Chloe is eager for a new proposal."

"I'm working on an idea. Once I have it nailed down, I'll send it."

After Kate hung up, she closed her document and gathered her things. She had to get home and pack because her flight would leave that evening. Unless Lucas agreed to participate, they'd be apart another night, but what would it matter? It seemed as if they were on two different planets since their confrontation in her office nearly a month earlier.

⟨∾⟩

"You didn't have to take me, you know." She almost wished he hadn't, since he'd dawdled around for fifteen minutes—after she'd rushed to pack and stowed her suitcase in the car. Now she was arriving later than she'd planned.

Kate grabbed for her suitcase handle, but Lucas reached it first. They walked toward the airport.

"I don't mind."

Her heels clicked against the pavement. After hurrying with the packing, Kate felt as if she'd forgotten something. She mentally checked off the necessary items to assure herself.

After she'd gotten off the phone with Pam, she'd gone to Lucas's shop and told him about the interview.

"They'd like to have us both on, if you'd like to participate," Kate said.

He'd lowered a tool, his eyes widening. The cliché of deer in headlights came to mind.

"Don't think so," he said before picking up a rag and wiping down a chest of drawers with a honey-colored stain.

"Why not? It might be fun." And good for the public to see them together.

He gave the bureau one last swipe and stood back, looking it over. "Talking's not my thing." He set the cloth on the plywood table. "Words don't come easy to me, like they do you."

The more she thought about it, the more she wanted him there with her. Maybe getting off the island, away from the grind of life, would break the stalemate they'd had between them the past month. Ironically, she'd thought she'd wanted distance between them. But now that she had it, she was lonely.

"I'll fill in the gaps," Kate said. "You wouldn't have a thing to worry about."

"I can't."

Did he have work that couldn't be put off? Or maybe he just wanted a break from her.

"Look, something happened when I was a kid. I was supposed

to give a speech in front of my school. In a school assembly." He picked up the rag and twisted it in his stained fingers. "I froze. Forgot everything I was going to say." He wiped the top of the bureau again. "I haven't talked in front of an audience since."

Now, as he walked her to security, she imagined Lucas as a frightened little boy, paralyzed in front of his peers. He seemed so far removed from that little boy, so strong and capable. But she remembered his one request when he agreed to marry her: *"No interviews."* It must've been hard enough for him to be in the spotlight as he had. But he'd done it for her.

*And his parents,* she reminded herself.

As they approached the security officer, Kate remembered the first time he'd brought her here. Dahlia Stevens had been in line, and he'd kissed her good-bye. Today no one waited in security, and Kate noted the edge of disappointment that pricked her heart.

*What is wrong with you, Kate?*

*What's wrong? I want him to go with me. Want him to kiss me. That's what's wrong.*

Lucas handed Kate the overnight case before they reached the balding security officer. "Kate . . ."

She checked her watch before meeting his gaze.

He shifted his weight. "When you get back, we need to talk."

Something hardened in her stomach, gelling into a thick lump. She hated when people did that. Now, the whole time she was gone, she'd wonder what he wanted. The sudden fear that he wanted to end their arrangement left her speechless. What if he was tired of pretending? Tired of the awkward silence between them these last few weeks? She wanted to say she was sorry, but sorry for what?

"Is something wrong?" she asked instead.

Lucas waved her off. "Nothing to worry about." He looked at her as if studying her features. She'd only be gone one night. *What's going on?*

He reached out and rubbed her chin with his thumb.

Kate stilled at his touch, feeling the roughness of his thumb all the way to her toes.

"You had a little something right there," he said.

She remembered the globby grape jelly on toast she'd scarfed down on the way out the door and ran her finger over the spot, rubbing away the feeling his touch had left behind.

He scanned the area around them. Was he remembering Dahlia and wishing for an audience? The airport was quiet as a sepulchre tonight. *Where's the media when you need them?*

Kate wanted to run her fingers along the rough surface of his stubbly jaw. What would he think of that? Would he kiss her then, if she took the first step?

Lucas caught her staring. She was loath to leave him for a night. How had she gotten so accustomed to his company? She remembered how he'd irritated her when he was just her superintendent. How had he found a way through the cracks in her heart? How had she come to expect his presence, depend on it?

He cleared his throat and pocketed his hands. "Well. Have a safe trip."

Kate blinked and looked away, hiking the weighty bag on her shoulder. "Thanks."

When he walked away, Kate realized her feelings for Lucas were rising dangerously high, like floodwaters on the banks of an unprotected shore.

Three cups of coffee and Kate was finally awake. She sat opposite the interviewer, Lisa Evans. A mike had been placed inconspicuously on the collar of her red Donna Karan blazer. The makeup people had done a good job, but the foundation was heavy and felt like it was melting under the hot lights.

The producer gave last-minute instructions, but Kate had heard most of it before. She settled back in the chair and waited while they opened the show with news on the other side of the studio. A copy of *Mr. Right* was propped on the glass cube between them.

Lisa, in a robin's-egg blue suit, reviewed her notes, making no conversation. That was typical. Interviewers liked to save it for the show.

When it was time for their segment, they were cued, and Lisa straightened, smiling toward the camera.

"This morning we have syndicated dating-advice columnist and noted author Dr. Kate. Welcome."

Kate smiled. "Thank you for having me."

"I have to say I read your recent release, *Finding Mr. Right-for-You* and was riveted." Lisa's eyebrows inched up into her blonde bangs.

"Thanks, Lisa. There's a lot of interest lately in compatibility in dating and marriage."

"Which begs the question," Lisa said. "There are numerous Web sites and books on the subject. What makes yours different?"

"Good question. In my counseling with couples, I've found the key ingredient to a lasting relationship to be compatibility. So many times we women get our hearts way ahead of the game. In the book, I teach women to put their hearts on hold long enough to establish compatibility."

"Is that what you did with your Mr. Right?" Lisa tilted her head.

The personal question caught Kate off guard. "Of course. You really can't make a rational decision about someone's suitability when your emotions are clouding your judgment."

Lisa nodded. "We know how emotions can affect good judgment."

Lisa asked several more questions about the book; then they opened the line for callers.

"Stephanie from Boston, you're on the air." Lisa said.

"I have a question for Dr. Kate," the caller said.

"Go ahead." Lisa smiled, her berry lip gloss shimmering under the lights.

"I'd like to know why she married someone else when her real fiancé dumped her on their wedding day."

*What?* The malicious tone, the ugly words, sent a wave of fear through Kate. She smiled through it. *What was the caller's name?* Had Lisa said Stephanie?

"Dr. Kate?" Lisa asked, clearly confused. "I'm not sure what the caller's referring to."

"I'm not sure either . . ." *Hang up. Disconnect the caller.* Her eyes pleaded with Lisa.

"Her real fiancé was Bryan Montgomery," the voice on the line continued. "And he dumped her the morning of the wedding. I'm not sure where Dr. Kate found her fake groom, but the wedding was phony, and so is she."

*This isn't happening.* Kate's thoughts seized in a paralyzing spasm. She fought to control her expression. The camera was on her. What could she say? Her mind was a numb void. *Say something. Anything.*

"Dr. Kate?"

Her head buzzed with electrical activity, all of it sparking nothing.

No clever turn of phrase. No smooth transition of subject. The seconds stretched out like a long empty runway.

"My marriage is not fake." She forced a calm tone. "It's legal in every way." *Change the subject!* "The advice in my book comes from years of extensive counseling and research. I have a passion for helping women find suitable partners, and that's what this book is about."

The producer was cuing a commercial. Sure, just as soon as Kate had found her tongue.

But Lisa was ending the segment. When they were off the air, she reached over and placed her hand on Kate's. "I'm so sorry about that, Kate. I assure you it was as unexpected for me as it was for you."

Kate stood on shaking legs as someone disengaged her mike and battery pack. She had to get out of there. She wanted to run someplace far away and hide.

*Regret is a bitter friend.*

—Excerpt from
*Finding Mr. Right-for-You*
by Dr. Kate

# Chapter Twenty-Two

The same plump woman who'd escorted Kate around the studio since her arrival accompanied her to the green room, where Kate collected her things. Her mind spun, but she feigned a smile and followed the woman to the car that waited at the curb.

Once in the luxury vehicle, she told the driver she was going to the airport. He pulled away.

*What now? What should I do? Everyone knows.*

Rosewood was going to be turned on its head! She reached for her cell phone and turned it on. She'd missed three calls. Kate didn't stop to listen to the messages. She had to call Pam. They needed damage control. But how could they control damage that was already done? It was live TV, and every viewer watching this morning had heard she was a fraud.

She punched in Pam's cell number. The driver had a talk radio program on in front, so she could talk quietly without being overheard.

Pam picked up on the first ring. "Kate! That was just awful."

"It was Stephanie. The woman Bryan left me for." The shock was wearing thin, revealing a layer of anger beneath.

"I know. I saw the whole thing. This is not good. Not good at all."

"What are we going to do? Did Chloe see it?" Kate's editor might know about her marriage, but she would have to explain it to her boss, who didn't know. *Have I jeopardized Chloe's and Pam's jobs?*

"She called me after the segment. She's pretty upset," Pam said. "Listen, we need to figure out how to handle this. There's going to be a lot of media wanting an interview with you now."

"Sure, there will, but I can't do that, Pam." The idea of exposing herself to that kind of spectacle was unthinkable. *How can I defend myself when it's true?*

"You need to do whatever Paul says." Pam's tone chided, reminding Kate that Chloe's boss was in for a rude awakening. "It's the least you can do at this point."

Of course Pam was angry with her. Chloe would be too, and Kate didn't blame either of them. Rosewood would come off like frauds, same as Kate. Everyone who'd known the truth would pay a price.

*Lucas.* She closed her eyes and let her head fall against the firm leather headrest. He'd watched the interview; she was certain of that. What was he thinking now? Thank goodness he hadn't come along for the interview. But how would this affect him? How would it affect his family?

*What have I done?*

"This is bad, Kate. The media will make this into a huge scandal, and we'll have to fight our way through it."

It was a career-busting scandal. Who would want her advice now that she'd proven herself a hypocrite by marrying her complete opposite, a virtual stranger? It would kill sales on her book. And she could probably kiss the *Glamour* and syndicated columns good-bye. How could she face Rosewood after disappointing them so? How could she face her faithful readers?

"I suggest you call Chloe and offer to break the news to Paul. She probably won't let you, but—"

"I will. I'll do that. What else can I do?"

"Don't talk to anybody. You might be getting calls, or worse. Let us get a game plan together before you say anything publicly."

No need to worry about that. All she wanted to do was crawl into a hole and have someone fill it with dirt. "All right. Calling Chloe now."

"Good luck." The sarcastic tone wasn't lost on Kate.

She punched in her editor's cell number, seeing the calls she'd missed on the screen and thinking about Lucas again.

Chloe answered immediately. Her tone was basted in stress. "Kate." She swore. "I guess you know the spot this puts me in."

"I'm so sorry, Chloe. I'll take complete responsibility." And she should, as it was entirely her fault. "Let me call Paul and tell him. He needn't know you were involved."

Chloe raised her voice. "You don't think he's going to ask me if I knew? I'm not going to lie, Kate."

Kate rubbed her forehead. *Why did I do it? If I could only go back and do the day over.* She should have done the honest thing and admitted to the media that the engagement was broken. But how could she have done that at the release of her book? Rosewood would have paid the cost for her personal crisis.

They were paying now anyway. A higher price than before.

"I know. I know, Chloe. Tell me what I can do." She waited, sure Chloe was doing her deep yoga breaths. There weren't enough yoga classes in the world to help ease this kind of stress.

"Just give me time to think. I'll tell Paul when we get off the phone and get back with you. Just—just go home and hole up until you hear from me." She huffed. "You know this is going to be all over the news by tonight. The papers, the news—it's going to be everywhere."

Kate had been hoping it might quietly blow over, but she knew that kind of optimism was unjustified.

Chloe ended the call, and Kate thought again about calling Lucas. She decided to listen to the voice mails first.

The first two were Pam and Chloe. Lucas's was the third. She listened to the familiar deep tone, closing her eyes and wishing he were beside her in the car.

"Kate? Are you all right? I saw the interview." A long pause followed. "I'm just—Call me, okay?" There was another long pause, like he wanted to say something else, before the click came.

Kate exited voice mail. It wasn't lost on her that Lucas was the only one of her messages that sounded remotely sympathetic. He, who had more personally at stake than anyone.

She still had a while before they reached the airport. She checked her watch and punched in their home number. Lucas answered quickly.

"It's me," she said.

"Kate." He breathed her name like he'd been holding his breath waiting for her call. "Are you okay?"

"I'm fine." *So much for honesty.* "Well. Fine as I can be given that my whole career came crashing down around my feet this morning. On national television." Her throat stopped up and her eyes burned. *Not now. Buck up until you're home at least. You still have to face a two-*

*hour wait at the airport, and it won't help matters if you're seen crying in public.*

"It's gonna be okay." He was only trying to help—she knew that—but they were trite words. Trite and untrue.

"It's not going to be okay, Lucas. The jobs of my editor and publicist are in jeopardy because of me, Rosewood is going to drop me like a rotten apple, and my readers are going to turn on me. What's okay about that?"

Kate rubbed her temple, frustration choking further words.

"I'm sorry, honey."

Now she felt like a slug. It wasn't his fault. He was a victim in this nutty escapade—her short trip down Insanity Boulevard. He wasn't guilty of anything but trying to help her.

She sighed. "It's not your fault. It's all mine." She beat the back of her head against the seat. "How could I have done something so stupid? I don't do foolish, impetuous things, like marry a man last minute."

"You were backed into a corner. Give yourself a break, Katie. We'll get through this."

His soft tone broke her. Kate felt tears welling, and she blinked them away. She had to get off the phone before she lost it. She had a feeling once she did, she wasn't going to come up for air for a while. "I have to go. I'll talk to you when I get home, okay?"

By the time she hung up, they were nearly to the airport. She'd have to call her agent, Ronald, while she waited for her flight. And her dad.

Lucas's words echoed in her head. *"We'll get through this."* But there was no "we" now. No need for them to remain together. No reason for their marriage. Because come tonight, everyone would know their marriage—and Kate herself—was nothing but a fraud.

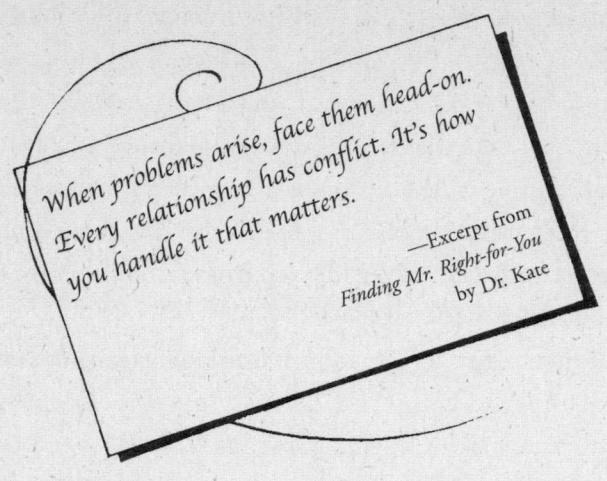

When problems arise, face them head-on. Every relationship has conflict. It's how you handle it that matters.

—Excerpt from
*Finding Mr. Right-for-You*
by Dr. Kate

# Chapter Twenty-Three

Lucas arrived at the airport, not merely on time, but early. He waited for Kate in a sling-back chair, his elbows propped on his knees. Their phone conversation haunted him. Her tone, so lost and broken, begged him to fix the mess. But there was no easy fix this time. The problem was too big, too overwhelming.

Guilt clung to him like grains of sand on wet skin. The marriage had been his idea. He'd practically talked her into it. He'd only been trying to help. He'd done it out of love, but look what happened. He'd hurt her instead.

When the time came for her flight's arrival, he watched for her. How would she react to him? How did this change their relationship? And he had no doubt it would change their relationship. Lucas regretted wasting the past month. He should have been winning Kate over, showing her his love. Instead he'd given her space.

Well, he was out of time now. Pretense had been the glue that held their marriage together and there was no need for it now.

*Kate has feelings for me. I know she does.* Maybe it was wishful thinking, but he was sure he'd caught her watching him lately with a certain look in her eyes. And there was no denying the passion of the kiss they'd shared or the jealousy in her eyes when he'd caught her spying on him and Sydney. Was it too much to hope that she might open her heart to him?

Kate appeared down the corridor, and he stood. She walked with her chin up, shoulders back. To anyone else she was the picture of a composed businesswoman in her stylish gray pantsuit. Her hair swung saucily with each step, and her eyes focused on a point straight ahead.

It was only then that he noticed another man walking toward Kate with a pad and pencil in hand. Lucas recognized him as Herb Owens, a reporter for the *Mirror*, and he made a beeline for Kate.

"Dr. Kate, I'm Herbert Owens from the *Mirror*. Would you like to make a comment concerning the allegations—"

"No comment." Kate's mouth pressed together as she looked away, quickening her steps.

Herb began walking toward her, then met Lucas's glare and slowed his steps.

Lucas knew when Kate saw him because her rigid features relaxed the slightest bit, her mouth decompressing, her eyes softening. The fact that his presence had that effect on her buoyed Lucas. He grabbed onto the notion, blew it up like an inflatable raft and took a ride on it.

*Get a grip*, he told himself. *She's probably just relieved to see a friendly face.* Who knew what she'd faced on the way home.

How should he greet her? They had an audience, but would she want him to keep up the charade? Was it a charade anymore? But as she neared, Lucas forgot about pretense. Kate's eyes looked weary, her face strained. He wanted to ease her worry, soothe it away with a touch.

Lucas took her bag, then set his palm alongside her face, making eye contact. He leaned close and pressed a kiss to her lips. His only thought was to comfort her.

She gripped his arm like it was a life preserver, returning the brief kiss.

When he pulled back, he draped his arm over her shoulder. "Let's get you home." He looked over her shoulder where Herb stood against the wall, watching.

By the time they reached the car, Kate had grown distant, remote. Did she think his kiss was for show? The ride to the house was quiet. Kate, her hands clutched together in her lap, her feet crossed at the ankles, seemed lost in thought. She stared out the window instead of facing him. Lucas felt her slipping away more each second.

"What can I do?" He asked, desperate to help, desperate to keep her.

There was a long pause, and he wondered if she'd heard him through the chaos of her own thoughts.

He braked at a stop sign, then accelerated. Was she shutting him out already? Hadn't they become more than just business partners? They'd shared a life these past three months. A life that meant everything to him.

"There's nothing we can do but wait," she said, still looking out the window where the glaring sun cut harsh shadows across the ground. "And hope the rest of the media won't hop on board and make it into the scandal of the year."

Even so, the news was out. Lucas didn't know much about publishing, only the little bit he'd gleaned from Kate, but it seemed her publisher wouldn't be interested in promoting her career after a scandal. Her readers wouldn't be too keen on her either. It didn't seem fair to crucify her for one decision. Bryan was the one who'd dumped this mess in her lap. Where was he now, when the chips were falling?

Lucas pulled into the drive and turned off the truck. When Kate didn't make a move to exit, he faced her, propping his knee on the cracked vinyl seat between them.

"We have to tell your family." Kate looked over the hill to where his parent's rooftop peeked above the sea oats.

"I already did." His dad had watched the segment. Lucas had gone over and told the rest of them in person.

Kate faced him. "I'm sorry I wasn't here. How did they respond?" Her forehead wrinkled, her eyes puppy-dog sad.

His mom had been angry at first, then seemed to realize she'd proven herself right. *"Kate's just like her mom, Lucas,"* she'd said. *"You're better off without her."* Of course, it was no surprise to Jamie, but Brody was hurt. His dad tried to be understanding, but Lucas could tell by the way he avoided Lucas's eyes that he was disappointed.

"My family will be fine," he said. "Don't worry about them."

A few quiet moments later, she exited the truck. Lucas followed her inside and set the bag in the bedroom. Bo, excited to see Kate, rubbed against her leg and shepherded her into the kitchen, where she started a pot of coffee.

"I feel like I've been run over by a city bus," Kate said.

Lucas pulled two mugs from the cabinet and the creamer from the fridge. "No wonder. What did the people at Rosewood say?"

Kate scooped grinds into the filter. "Right now they just want me to sit tight. I think a lot depends on how widespread this becomes."

Could they go on as if nothing happened? Would the readers who saw the interview conclude that it was an unfounded rumor? Apparently there was nothing they could do but wait and see. It had been so easy to step in and save Kate when her wedding plans had fallen apart. Now, all he could do was wait with her, and that was a notion that didn't set well.

※

Kate pulled her knees close, letting her toes dig through the hot surface of the sand to the cooler layer beneath. In the distance, the ferry horn sounded, announcing its arrival to the island. After stalling as long as she could, she'd called her dad and told him about the interview. She could hear his shock in the silence that drew out over the lines. It pulled her spirits even lower.

*"Oh boy, Kate,"* he'd said when he'd found words.

She'd never done anything so careless and never planned to again. How could someone who planned every facet of her life have taken this reckless road?

Once her dad had a moment to think, he begged her to come for a visit. *"Come to Maryland, just to get away for a while. You'll have time to think here. Time to plan your future. Maybe you can open an office in the city."* It was a tempting offer and one she'd give some thought to once she heard from Chloe.

After they'd returned from the airport, Lucas seemed to sense her need for space and had gone back to his shop. But now, as the sun seemed to still in the sky, Kate wished for a distraction.

She'd already finished her column and didn't want to be near the TV after watching it half the afternoon. Two cable news shows had mentioned the scandal, saying they were looking into the allegations. With a scorned woman like Stephanie on the loose, they wouldn't have to look far.

Her cell phone rang incessantly, but she didn't answer the calls.

Two reporters had had the nerve to show up on their doorstep, but she hadn't answered, and eventually they'd gone away.

She'd wait and see if the afternoon papers picked up the story. She imagined that's what Chloe was waiting for. Would the *Mirror* pick up the story? The thought of the locals knowing the truth was enough to put a lump in her throat. They knew her here not as Dr. Kate, but as a friend and neighbor. She ate and shopped and worked among these people. They would feel betrayed when they found out. And Lucas's family, natives of the island, would be center stage.

*My life is spinning out of control, and I'm helpless to stop it.* It was the same feeling she'd had as a child. Never knowing what to expect or what to feel because she had no control over it.

She pulled her legs closer, set her chin on her knees, and rocked in the sand.

⌘

Kate waited to hear from Chloe the rest of the day, but no call came. What was her editor waiting for? The morning papers? She slept restlessly that night. Beside her, Lucas seemed to sleep peacefully, his breaths deep and even in the darkened room.

She hadn't heard a peep from his family. Maybe Lucas had asked them to give her space. Maybe they were relieved she wasn't really part of the family. His mom was probably thrilled.

How were they treating Lucas? Were his dad and Brody angry at him for the deception?

Just when Kate thought it couldn't get any worse, she remembered his parents' marriage. She sighed, regret filling the hole in her gut. *I didn't do a thing to help—haven't kept my end of the bargain at all. Lucas married me for nothing—except all the grief he's getting.*

*It's not like Susan wanted your help.*

*Maybe not, but Lucas kept his part of the deal, and I let him down.*

*You didn't exactly have the twelve months you expected. You're not a miracle worker.*

*If only I'd had more time.*

Kate faced the wall, turning quietly so as not to disturb Lucas.

Why didn't Chloe call back? Were she and Paul and Pam deciding how to handle things, or was she so angry, she was making Kate suffer? Because that's exactly what Kate was doing: suffering. The waiting was killing her. She couldn't plan her next move until someone told her what to do.

Kate felt the bed shift as Lucas moved. Then she felt his arm settle around the curve of her waist, felt the warmth of his stomach against her back.

He pressed a kiss on the top of her head. Kate's heart sped. In his arms she felt safe and loved—cherished. Like her world wasn't a whirling top, spinning toward the edge of a table. She wanted to sink into his weight and let him be her shelter from the storm. But she was unaccustomed to counting on anyone other than herself. The very thought of sharing her burden made her anxious. *How do I know I can count on him? What if he fails me?*

And why was he holding her? *What is it he wants from me?*

She lay still, tense, waiting. He'd played his part of the game, met his end of the bargain. If anything, he should be angry with her too. Angry, like everyone else.

As moments passed and Lucas made no further move, Kate felt her body slowly sink into the hardness of his stomach. *Just for tonight. It doesn't mean I'm turning over control.* She closed her eyes again. Kate knew she shouldn't let herself find comfort in his arms, but she was too tired to fight the urge.

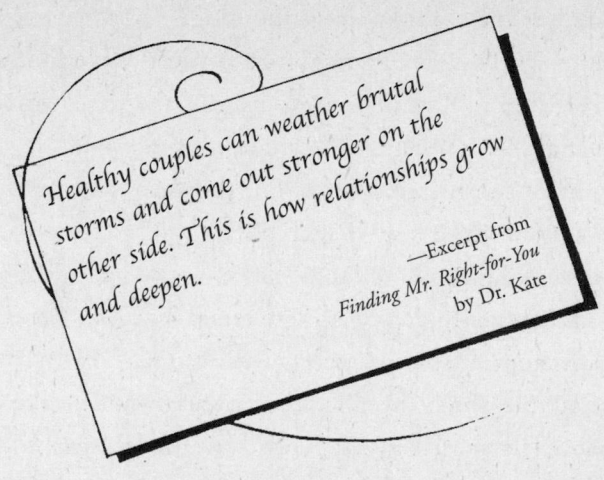

Healthy couples can weather brutal storms and come out stronger on the other side. This is how relationships grow and deepen.

—Excerpt from
*Finding Mr. Right-for-You*
by Dr. Kate

# Chapter Twenty-Four

The shrill of the phone pulled Kate from slumber. She stirred, orienting herself, then crawled across Lucas's empty side of the bed. The events of the day before crashed in on her like a tidal wave. *It must be Chloe.* She cleared her throat before answering.

A male voice greeted her. "Hi, kiddo. How are you holding up?" It was her agent.

She sat up in bed and looked at the clock. Seven forty-two. "Ronald. I'm doing as well as can be expected." Given that her career was on the line. She'd fallen asleep somewhere around three o'clock, when the rain had started, and had slept fitfully. Thunder cracked outside.

"I haven't heard from Chloe yet." Kate had told Ronald she'd call when she heard something. He must've thought she'd forgotten.

"Actually, Chloe called me this morning," he said.

If Chloe was using her agent as a go-between, her editor was distancing herself from Kate. Not a good sign. "You have bad news."

"I'm afraid so, Kate. It hit the papers this morning."

Her throat constricted. She rubbed the sleep from her eyes and braced herself for the news. "Which ones?"

"*New York Times, Washington Post, Chicago Tribune, LA Times.* The Associated Press picked it up. I'm afraid it's everywhere. Mainly in the entertainment section, from what I can see."

Entertainment. Like her life was a circus meant for the public's amusement. The worst had happened. *I'm a laughingstock. A fraud.* The letters from her disappointed readers would pour in. She'd disappointed so many people. The weight of it dragged her under the choppy water, and she fought for breath.

"Paul and Chloe scheduled a conference call with us at noon to discuss how to handle the media. They'll want your story in detail to determine if there's any way to spin this in a positive light."

"Of course." She didn't see how. For the life of her, Kate couldn't see how they could control the damage. It was all true. She was an expert on finding Mr. Right, and she'd impulsively entered a loveless marriage. A marriage with no real feelings.

*That's not true, Kate, and you know it.*

All right, maybe she did have feelings for Lucas now, but she didn't have them when they'd married.

"They'll call you on your home phone, and I'll be there too," Ronald said.

"What about my column? What about *Glamour*? Do you think—" She was afraid to pose the question, but she had to know. She pulled at a loose thread on the quilt and balled the string between her fingers.

"I wasn't going to say anything; you've got enough on your plate right now. But *Glamour* has asked you to step down for the time being. Maybe when this blows over . . ."

But even when it blew over, Kate knew the damage left behind would be irreparable. "I'm guessing the syndicated column is in jeopardy too?"

The silence on the other end spoke for itself.

Kate felt her throat closing, her eyes burning. *I can't believe this is happening. How have I fallen so far? So hard?* She was on the verge of losing control of her emotions. She cleared her throat again, hoping for a space to open up. "Listen, I've got to go. I'll talk to you at noon."

After they hung up, she set the phone on the nightstand. In the other room, she heard her cell phone ringing. She'd forgotten to turn it off. She couldn't talk to anyone. She wanted to pull the covers over her head and pretend none of this had happened.

But what good would that do?

*Come on, Kate. Buck up. Get out of bed and figure a way out of this hole you're in.*

That's what she would do. She had four and half hours to find a way to spin this to the good for Rosewood. Four and half hours to develop a plan.

Kate jumped out of bed, took a quick shower, then dressed. Realizing she detected the robust aroma of brewed coffee, she entered the kitchen, Bo on her heels. A note, scribbled on the back of the utilities bill sat beside the coffeepot.

KATE,
WENT OUT FOR A WHILE.
BE BACK SOON.
L

Where had he gone so early in the morning? It was pouring buckets outside. Maybe he really was having an affair with Red. Maybe he'd gone out to meet her. Maybe he realized the marriage was over now.

She'd no sooner finished the thought when she heard the door open. By the time Lucas appeared, she'd poured herself a mug of hot coffee and added cream.

"Morning." His voice was deep and groggy, a welcome sound. Even the stubble on his jawbone had grown on her.

"Morning," she replied. His navy T-shirt was plastered to his shoulders, and his hair was spiky-wet and tousled from the rain. Or maybe someone had run her hands through it.

She wasn't going to ask where he'd been. It really wasn't her business anyway.

"Don't suppose you heard from your editor," he said.

"My agent called. We have a conference call with the people from Rosewood at noon. The news has hit the press in a big way."

Kate realized this was bad for Lucas. It was his life they were talking about too. Everyone would wonder why he'd stepped in last minute, and he could hardly admit it was because of his parents' souring relationship. She'd put him in a tight spot.

"I saw the papers." He poured himself a cup of coffee and let Bo out the back door.

"Is that why you went out?" She didn't mean to ask.

"I was hoping to bring back good news." He tucked his hands in his pockets.

Kate pulled her laptop from her case and flipped it open. She still had—she checked her watch—almost four hours to come up with an idea. Something that would make the media back off or at least soften the blow.

"Do you have any of the papers?" Kate asked. "I need to see what I'm up against." She pushed the On button and tapped her fingers, waiting for it to boot.

"I left them in the truck." He shifted his weight. "What's the plan?"

Kate plugged her laptop into the outlet under the table. "My plan is to come up with a plan. I need some ideas for my publisher, some way of spinning this so they, at least, don't come off smelling like a pig."

Kate opened the word processor, and a blank document appeared on the screen.

"I'll be right back." Lucas left the room.

There wasn't much Kate could do until she knew what the media was saying. Maybe it was only hearsay, her word against Stephanie's. Though Kate hadn't exactly defended herself on TV. She'd only tried to change the subject. People would see right through that.

When Lucas returned, he carried a thick stack of damp newspapers. He set them beside the laptop and sat across from her. "Sure you want to do this?" His was the look of someone who'd already read the articles.

"Everyone else is going to know what they say; *I* may as well."

The kitchen light was off and the storm outside darkened the room, but there was enough light to read by. She'd start with the Nantucket paper. The *Inquirer* and *Mirror* had tried to call the day before, but she hadn't answered. The paper was already opened to the article. Kate unfolded it and read.

"Famous Local Advice Columnist Jilted at Altar"
In a TV interview on *Live with Lisa*, local resident and famous author Dr. Kate was accused by a call-in listener of marrying a stand-in groom. The caller, who identified herself as Stephanie from

Boston, claimed Dr. Kate's original fiancé, Bryan Montgomery, broke the engagement on the morning of their wedding. A marriage license bearing the names of Montgomery and Dr. Kate was found on record, substantiating the woman's claim. Neither Montgomery nor Dr. Kate could be reached for a comment.

Dr. Kate and local furniture maker Lucas Wright were wed on June 21, the same day as the release of Dr Kate's first book *Finding Mr. Right-for-You*. It is unclear how Wright came to be the stand-in groom.

"I should have tried to eradicate the evidence," Kate said. "I didn't think about the marriage license." Kate set the paper down and sighed. "I'm sorry they mentioned your name. I was hoping at least the local papers . . ." *Who am I kidding? It's not like everyone on the island doesn't already know Lucas is married to me. Now they just know it's a sham.*

"Which one has the Associated Press article?" She riffled through the papers.

Lucas pulled one from the stack and laid it open to the article.

Kate read the headline. "Dr. Kate's Mr. Wright is Mr. Wrong."

"Clever," Kate said, sarcasm oozing from a deeply wounded spot. The article read much like the local one; only the journalist had scored an interview with Stephanie. They cited the marriage certificate as well.

"This isn't good," Kate said, setting the paper down. "I didn't realize they'd find proof so quickly. I hope Pam hadn't planned to deny it, because there's no way I can do that now."

Kate glanced at her watch. She had to think. There must be a way to make this better. She shoved the papers to the other side of the table.

"Let's think this through," Lucas said. "Maybe we can come up with something if we put our heads together." He leaned on the tabletop, his bulky forearms planted squarely in front of him.

Kate didn't want to hurt his feelings, but she was done with depending on someone else for help. She worked better alone. "If you don't mind, I think I need to do this on my own. I need to focus, because I have less than four hours."

He shrugged and gave that half smile that charmed her. "We pulled off a wedding in barely under that."

She smiled wryly. "Seems to me that's what got us into this mess to begin with."

By the time the phone rang at noon, Kate had all her notes on the screen. Lucas was somewhere else in the house. She'd been lost in her own thoughts since he'd left the table four hours earlier, and she hadn't seen him since.

Kate answered the phone.

"Hello, Kate. It's Chloe. Pam, Paul, and Ronald are already on the line."

"Hi, everyone," Kate said.

Their greetings were less than enthusiastic. Hopefully, they'd agree to what Kate had come up with as the best approach.

Lucas entered the room and leaned against the doorway as she opened the conversation.

"Can I just say something first? I want to tell you how sincerely sorry I am for the trouble this is causing. It was never my intention to damage your businesses or careers, and I'm deeply sorry." Kate hoped her tone expressed the depth of her regret. "I'll do anything I can to help rectify this."

"Fair enough," Paul said. "The damage is done now, and we need to figure out how to proceed. Kate, if we could hear what happened, in your words, that might help."

Kate took a deep breath and told the story of her wedding morning: Bryan's phone call, Pam's news of the *Dr. Phil* show invitation, Lucas's offer.

Chloe stopped her there. "You said Lucas was only an acquaintance. Why did he offer to take Bryan's place?"

Kate stopped pacing, her eyes fastened on Lucas's. Could she tell them about Lucas's parents? She wasn't going to hang him out to dry again.

"I agreed to help him on a personal project. That part of the story really has no bearing on this."

"Tell us the rest of the story," Paul said.

Kate finished, explaining the temporary nature of the agreement. "I've done a lot of thinking this morning, and I think our best bet is for me to face up to what I've done publicly. I'm genuinely sorry, and I think once my readers see I was jilted at the altar and made a poor quick judgment, they'll be generous with their grace."

"Let's not overlook the fact," Ronald said, "that any publicity is good publicity. It's quite possible the scandal could increase Kate's sales. It's happened before with other books."

Kate stopped at the back window. Now that was the best news she'd heard in a while. Was it possible this might turn out well for her publisher?

"Keep in mind," Pam said, "that Kate's book is a self-help book, not a novel or a memoir. Her readers are willing to plunk down their money because they trust her advice. That trust has been broken. She might be seen as hypocritical since she advised her readers one direction and took an entirely different direction herself."

Kate jumped in. "That's why I should apologize, offer an explanation. I think my readers would sympathize with the fact that I was jilted at the altar. What woman wouldn't be confused and prone to bad judgment at that point?"

"The fact is, though," Paul said, "you aren't every woman. You are Dr. Kate, expert in love relationships. Your whole book is about finding a marriage partner for a lifelong relationship, and you've entered a loveless marriage on a one-year lease. I'm not going to sugarcoat it, Kate. The media sure isn't."

Kate felt heat flush her neck and cheeks. That was as close to a dressing down as she'd received since her dad scolded her for loaning out her Nikes when she was in fourth grade.

"We need time to digest this," Paul continued. "We'll get hold of you later today and let you know what we've decided. Until then, don't answer your phone."

By the time they disconnected, Kate felt wrung out. More waiting. *I'm tired of waiting. I want to do something.* She leaned against the windowsill. Outside, the landscape looked gray through the blanket of rain.

"How'd it go?" Lucas asked.

Kate shrugged. "They're going to decide how they want to handle it. They'll call back later today. I don't think they were too keen on my honesty plan."

Kate didn't think they were too keen on her either, and she didn't blame them.

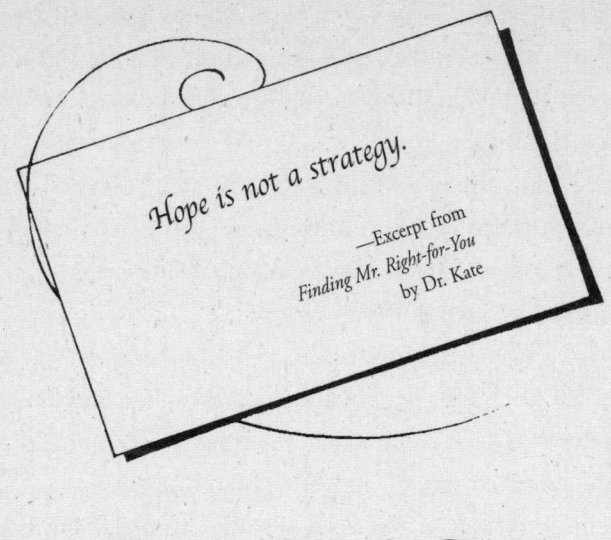

*Hope is not a strategy.*

—Excerpt from
*Finding Mr. Right-for-You*
by Dr. Kate

# Chapter Twenty-Five

Kate searched for ways to stay occupied as she awaited Paul's call. She filled the sink with soapy water and washed dishes. She wiped down the counters and table. When she was finished, she decided the linoleum needed a good scrubbing. Lucas worked on a design for an armoire while she cleaned.

Later, they had a quiet lunch of soup and sandwiches, then resumed working. The phone rang often, but the numbers were unfamiliar. She wished their number was unlisted. At least no one had shown up at the door today.

The storm raged on, rain tapping on the windows like a stranger with bad news. The sea oats bent in submission to the wind, and gulls floated high in the air, riding the gusts wherever it took them.

Lucas was stirring a pot of boiling pasta when the call came. Kate picked up.

"Kate," Ronald said. "I just heard from Paul."

"What did they decide?"

"They want you to avoid the press, kiddo. They're afraid you'll open yourself to all kinds of speculation. People will find out more than they already know, and from what they've heard, it's not good."

"They want me to do nothing?"

Lucas turned from the pot of spaghetti and studied her. As his eyebrows lifted, long lines formed across his forehead.

"Unfortunately, I agree, Kate. As much as I'd like to think this publicity will be advantageous, I think it's going to cause damage. And the more details the media gets, the longer this is going to brew. The best we can hope is that it'll blow over soon and be forgotten."

The thought of doing nothing was demoralizing. It wasn't in Kate to sit back and let things happen. She was a planner, a doer. She wanted to work this out; she wanted to fix it.

"If you're confronted by the press, Paul suggested you say, 'No comment' and keep moving. It would be prudent to tell your family and anyone who has details to avoid the press also."

Thunder cracked in the distance, and the rain pummeled the roof over the kitchen. "Paul asked about Bryan. I didn't see him quoted in any of the articles. They're hoping that's an indication he won't submit to an interview. They want you to confirm that."

"I'll call him," Kate said. Her voice sounded choked. The burden of her mistake weighted her. Her body felt heavy—too heavy for her trembling legs.

As she ended the phone call, her legs buckled, and she dropped on the wooden window ledge. "I have to call Bryan." She wasn't up for it, but that didn't matter. She dialed his home phone. It rang four times before the voice mail kicked on.

"Bryan, it's Kate." She ran her fingers through her hair. *What should I say?* "Can you call me when you get this? Listen, it's very important that you not talk to the press." *Unlike your skanky girlfriend.* Kate gritted her teeth. She needed Bryan to cooperate, and a snarky attitude wouldn't help. "Just call me."

She hung up. Lucas was looking at her with an expression she couldn't read and didn't have the brainpower to decipher. She dialed Bryan's cell and got voice mail again. She left a similar message and hung up.

"What did your agent say?" Lucas asked.

"They want me to stay quiet. Do nothing. Hope it blows over."

"You're not happy."

"I see where they're coming from. They might even be right; they've got more experience than I. It just makes me feel so—"

*Helpless. Useless. Like a sitting duck. Like a twelve-year-old girl waiting to see if her mom is Jekyll or Hyde that day.*

She walked away from the thought, into the bedroom, but it followed her there, like a persistent shadow. She didn't bother to flip on the lamp, though only remnants of daylight seeped through the curtains. Instead, in the darkness, she paced the short length of the room while rain pounded the roof, a surge of the storm's temper.

Lucas appeared in the doorway. He leaned against the doorjamb, watching her.

"I just—I hate this doing nothing." She whipped around, her hair slapping her on the cheek, and sank on the edge of the mattress. Would this be the way her career went down? With her forfeiting the match; not even putting up a fight?

Lucas approached Kate, aching to comfort her. "Maybe they're right," he said. "Maybe it'll blow over."

*And what will happen to us?* He wanted to know but couldn't ask. Not now, when she'd been bombarded by everyone else. Heavy clouds seemed to roll in, darkening the room.

"What if they're wrong? What if my readers think I'm a hypocrite?" Her eyes glazed over and she blinked rapidly. "Maybe I am a hypocrite."

He'd never seen her look so fragile, so vulnerable, not even on her wedding day. She looked broken, her always neat hair a disheveled mess, hanging in her face.

"Hey . . ." he said, smoothing the sides of her hair with both hands. He tucked it behind her ears the way she liked it. "Stop talking like that. It's going to be okay." He cupped her face between his palms. "We'll get through this."

A tear escaped, and he brushed it away with his thumb.

"Why did we ever plan my wedding around my book's release? It was stupid. I thought it was a brilliant idea, but it was just stupid. Look where all my planning has gotten me. My career is over, Lucas." Her voice wobbled. The tears chased each other rapid fire.

"Shhhh." He pulled her to him and caressed her hair, letting her cry. Her arms wrapped around his waist, her fingers clutching his T-shirt. She was falling apart, his composed Kate. He hadn't thought it possible.

A bucket of guilt poured down on him like the rain that deluged the ground outside. This was all his fault. He was the one who'd offered to stand in for Bryan. If not for him, Kate would have told the truth. Sure, it would have been hard. It may have ruined her book sales, but it wouldn't have wrecked her career.

"I'm sorry, Kate," he whispered into her hair. He'd thought he was saving her, but he'd ruined her instead. "It's my fault."

She sniveled. "No, it isn't." She shook her head against his chest. "It was my decision."

"It was *my idea*." His arms tightened around her as his thoughts went back to that morning when he'd seen her so shaken, seen her eyes deaden to the reality of her situation.

"I was just trying to—" *Save you. Love you.* His gut tightened.

She pulled away, looking up at him. "Stop it." One last tear trailed down her cheek. "You were only trying to help."

He brushed the tear away, dried her face with his thumbs. Her eyes were sad pools of regret, her lashes spiked with moisture. If only he could clean up the mess he'd made so easily. He had been trying to help that day, trying to wipe that look of despair from her face. He would have done anything to accomplish that.

And yet here was despair again, sevenfold.

"I would never hurt you," he whispered. Did she believe him? It was important that she did.

"I know." Her lips barely moved on the words. A tear trembled in the corner of her mouth. He swept it away, his thumb lingering over the plump curve of her lower lip.

Mercy, did she know how much he cared for her? How much he wanted her to be completely his? Did she know he'd do anything to protect her?

Did she know he loved her? The words hovered on the tip of his tongue, wavering, eager to escape, yet afraid of the consequences. What would she do if she knew? What would she say if she knew he'd loved her from the beginning?

Kate wanted to lose herself in Lucas's eyes, in those fathomless green depths. Something stirred in her. His words replayed in her head. *"I would never hurt you."*

She knew it was true. He would never have deserted her on her wedding day, like Bryan had. Lucas would stand by and defend her, protect her no matter what. Kate had never considered herself the kind of woman who yearned for a knight in shining armor, but just now the notion was appealing. And the look in his eyes was irresistible.

He was so close. She felt the warmth of him through his T-shirt. Kate turned her face into his hand and pressed a kiss against his calloused palm. He was a man's man, a hard worker. Loyal to the death. So many good things. She wanted all of them.

She kissed the curve of his jaw, feeling the coarseness of his stubble against her lips and relishing him for the man he was.

She heard his breath catch, and it emboldened her. With a hand against his face, she turned him toward her. Their lips met gently, and Kate soaked up his response. Her fingers tightened on the cotton material of his shirt.

Lucas pulled her closer, into the strength of his embrace. His stomach was hard against hers, his shoulders like solid rock. He was a sure foundation in a raging storm.

"Katie," he whispered.

The taste of her name on his lips, so desperate and devoted, was sweet and heady.

*I want him.*

*No, I need him.*

He deepened the kiss, and she responded in kind, drawing her fingers through his hair. Lucas leaned into her, pressing her back against the bed, the weight of him more welcome than a cool breeze on sun-scorched skin.

*What am I doing?* The thought had no more than formed than she pushed it down.

But it resurfaced with force. *Is this right? Do I love him?*

*He's your husband. You have every right.*

She latched onto the thought, clinging with everything in her. *He* is *my husband. He's mine.*

With the thought came complete surrender. She ran her hands along the plane of his back and returned his kiss with fervor.

"Katie," he said, his breath ragged. He pulled back, putting space she didn't want between them. His eyes were deep shadows of longing, a mirror of her own. "Are you sure, honey?"

Kate pulled him close, kissing his jaw and the corner of his lips before he claimed her mouth.

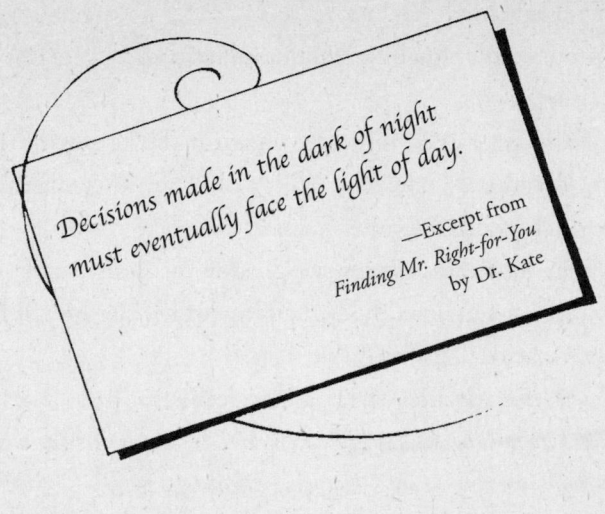

*Decisions made in the dark of night must eventually face the light of day.*

—Excerpt from
*Finding Mr. Right-for-You*
by Dr. Kate

# Chapter Twenty-Six

Morning light flooded through the windows, piercing Kate's aching eyes. She checked the clock and realized she'd slept late. Yesterday's shirt hung from the cone-shaped lamp shade.

The memory of the night before struck her like a rogue wave. She swiveled her head on her pillow and met Lucas's gaze.

"'Morning," he said. He lay on top of the covers in jeans and a T-shirt.

*How long has he been watching me?* Her own nakedness under the covers made her squirm. Kate clutched the quilt, pulling it to her shoulders, reality slamming into her hard. *What have I done? We didn't even use protection. What was I thinking?*

She was unaccustomed to waking with him in bed. Unaccustomed to what they'd done the night before. The two realities clashed, ushering in an awkward moment.

"You're still here."

He propped his elbow on the pillow, head in hand. "Just watching you sleep."

She could get lost in those eyes again if she let herself. But she shouldn't. Couldn't. What sense did it make? She looked away under the guise of checking the time.

Daylight had chased away the shadow of desire, exposing the irrationality of her actions the night before. She'd let herself become swept up in her feelings for Lucas.

And yes, she admitted she did have feelings. Strong ones.

*But he's all wrong for me. How could I forget that? Me, who wrote an entire book on the subject? Maybe I am a hypocrite.*

"Look at me, honey."

Her stomach tightened at the endearment, the same one he'd used just before they'd—

Kate turned her head. Lucas's cheek was pillow creased. She'd kissed that cheek the night before. Kissed those lips, run her hands over the sharp curve of his jaw. *Stop it!*

"What's going on behind those big brown eyes?" He brushed her hair from her cheek.

She flinched at his touch, wary of being swept into the tide pool of longing, and Lucas withdrew his hand, a frown pulling his mouth.

Kate needed time to think. Time to sort through her feelings. Time to get dressed, for heaven's sake. She pulled the quilt to her chin.

"I just need . . . a little time, Lucas. Everything's changing so quickly, I can't wrap my brain around it. I need time to figure things out."

The sparkle left his eyes. She wanted to say something that would light them again, but it wouldn't be fair to offer false hope.

"Right," he said.

She should say something. Something to soothe the hurt on his face, but nothing came to mind. Nothing honest. Not when her mind was a riot of confusion.

Lucas got up, the bed shaking in his wake. He cleared his throat. "I have errands to run anyway." At the foot of the bed, he slid on his sandals.

"I didn't mean for you to leave."

He walked toward the door without looking back. "It's okay."

Moments later she heard the door open and shut. His truck roared to life outside, and Bo entered the room, his paws clicking to a stop beside her.

What had she done? As if life needed to get more complicated. *What was I thinking last night?*

She'd been thinking with her heart, that's what. The way he'd touched her, like she was the most precious object in the world. Even now, she shivered in remembrance. She'd never felt so cherished, so . . .

Loved.

*Lucas doesn't love you. He was a man, wanting what a man wants.*

But it hadn't felt that way. Hadn't felt that way when she'd awakened and caught him watching her.

*Stop it, Kate. You need to think with your head, not your heart. Be smart. Listen to your own advice.*

Forcing herself to move, Kate got up and showered, dressing in her favorite jeans and her royal blue shirt. It was Sunday and she wondered if Lucas's family would welcome her to their family meal. Maybe she shouldn't go. But she had to face them eventually, even if only to apologize.

As she poured her coffee, she heard a car pull into the driveway. Her nerves immediately clanged, like the wind chimes on the back porch on a windy day. She didn't know what to say to Lucas yet. What they'd shared had been so intimate, and yet now, in the light of day, she knew it was a mistake. How could she tell him that?

*Maybe he's thinking the same thing.*

The thought disturbed her. Hurt her feelings—which was ludicrous considering she felt the same way. She couldn't even agree with herself.

Maybe a walk on the beach would clear her head. Through the kitchen window she saw the weather had calmed. It was no longer storming, just overcast and gloomy. The ocean was gray and choppy, its waves striking the shore with white foam fingers.

One thing she knew: she had to escape the island. There was no reason to prolong the marriage, and staying was too difficult emotionally. Obviously her feelings for Lucas had grown into something beyond her control. *If only we weren't so different. If only we weren't completely incompatible, we could make it*

Her heart ached for the chance to try.

But the memories of her parents' arguments, their vicious battles over every little thing, stopped her, even if her experience as a counselor didn't. She wasn't going to waste her life forcing a round peg into a square hole. She'd watched too many people try and fail. She'd watched her parents try and fail. That wasn't the life she wished on anyone.

A knock sounded at the front door.

Kate set down her mug and walked into the living room, peering through the window in the door. She prayed it wasn't another reporter coming to get the scoop on her private—

*No.*

Through the glass, the top of a head was visible, but she would've recognized that neatly clipped brown hair anywhere. She paused, gathering her thoughts a moment before she pulled open the door.

"Bryan." She hadn't seen him since the eve of their wedding day. He looked older. Tired. Wrinkles and creases covered his dress shirt and slacks, like he'd slept in them. "What are you doing here?"

"Kate." He heaved a sigh. Relief? "I've been trying to reach you."

She leaned against the door, keeping it partway closed. She'd expected to feel something if she saw him again. Longing, regret, anger. Something. The lack of emotion was a welcome surprise.

"I turned off my phone," she said. "But I guess you can understand why."

"I'm sorry I missed your call. So many reporters were trying to reach me that I turned mine off too. I just got your message when I got off the plane."

"What are you doing here?" Had he come thinking he could comfort her? Help her? Maybe he had a plan to make this disaster go away. He'd always been clever. And her own plan had failed.

"We need to talk," he said. "Can I come in?"

Kate looked across the street where two houses were visible from the front porch. It would be better than having Bryan seen on her doorstep. She opened the door wide and stepped back against the wall, giving him a wide berth.

Inside, she gestured him toward the sofa. She scanned the tiny, simple living room, seeing it through his eyes. It was a far cry from his contemporary city apartment. Bo appeared at his side, and Bryan inched away, but the dog only sniffed Bryan's shoe before following Kate to the recliner across the room.

"I'm sorry it got leaked." Bryan planted his elbows on his knees. "I'm sorry about the interview on TV. It must've been very uncomfortable for you."

*Uncomfortable is hardly the word.* "Your girlfriend must be having a field day."

"She's not my girlfriend. It was a big mistake. *She* was a big mistake."

Kate felt weary suddenly, like her bones might melt into the chair. "Let's not go through this again, Bryan. What's done is done. The main thing is that you can't talk to the press. You haven't, have you?"

"Of course not. I wouldn't do that to you."

He had some nerve acting as if he'd never hurt her. Kate stared him down until he looked away. "If anyone questions you, just say 'No comment,' okay?"

"Of course. I'll do whatever you want. I owe you that. I owe you so much more than that." His baby blue eyes shone under the lamplight. She'd once thought them beautiful, too pretty to be wasted on a man. Now they were a thin, cool sheet of ice, ready to crack under pressure.

"I know this is bad," Bryan said, "Our personal business all over the news, your career—jeopardized. I can't tell you how sorry I am, Kate."

His apology was sincere, his regret legitimate. Unfortunately it changed nothing.

But anger was futile. And even though he'd backed out of their wedding, it had been her decision to marry Lucas.

"What are you going to do now?" Bryan asked. "Can I help in any way?"

Kate shook her head. "I'm just going to hole up somewhere. My dad invited me to stay with him awhile, so I might do that. I need time for this to blow over, and time to rethink my career, if need be."

Two notches formed between Bryan's brows, and he shook his head as if to clear the cobwebs. "But what about—"

Kate realized her mistake too late. The public—and Bryan— didn't know the particulars of her and Lucas's arrangement. She'd never told Bryan the marriage wasn't a real one.

"Your marriage," he said. "It was just temporary? You're leaving him?" The hope in his voice was a warning siren.

A sick feeling worked its way into her middle, churning her stomach the way the wind churned the waves outside. "I'm going to visit my dad for a while, that's all."

His eyes narrowed. "It was temporary from the beginning, wasn't it? You never had feelings for him, never planned to stay married. It was just . . . a way out of the mess I put you in."

There was a certainty in his tone, and Kate knew she wasn't going to erase that. *He won't alert the media, so what harm is there if he knows?*

"Yes, it was temporary, all right?" she said. "But that's between you and me, and if you say one word to the press—"

Bryan extended his hands palm out. "I swear, I won't." He stood and crossed the rug, closing the space between them, dropping to his knees at her feet.

"Kate, do you know what this means to me?" He took her hands, pressing them between his own. The coolness of his palms, the shape of his fingers felt foreign against hers.

She pulled away. "It doesn't mean anything. It doesn't change anything."

"You need to get away. Come with me. We can stay at my place in Aspen. I'll take a leave of absence. You can figure out where to go from there."

Kate pressed her back into the cushion. "No, Bryan. It's over between us." She knew as the words left her mouth that she meant them now as she never had. There was nothing left, no feelings for him.

*Because they've been replaced by feelings for Lucas.* Kate shrugged the thought away.

"You don't mean that. Just think. We could move anywhere you want. You could open a counseling service like you did here. We could have a fresh start."

The thought of starting over was tempting compared to the months of uncertainty she faced, but she knew it was implausible. She was about to say so when the front door opened.

Somehow she'd missed the rattle of Lucas's truck arriving. He stopped on the threshold, his hand on the doorknob. His gaze darted between Kate and Bryan. She imagined the scene from Lucas's perspective and cringed.

---

Lucas's heart stuttered at the sight of Kate and Bryan. He'd thought the unfamiliar car might belong to some nosy reporter and charged up the porch steps ready to confront the jerk who'd had the nerve to show up on their doorstep.

But it wasn't some reporter who knelt on the floor at his wife's feet. It was her ex-fiancé. The look of shock on Kate's face at his entry would have been comical if it weren't plain hurtful.

His hands balls into fists. "What are you doing here, Montgomery?"

Bryan stood slowly, blocking Lucas's view of Kate as if to guard her. What a joke. It was Bryan she needed protection from.

"Knock off the doting husband charade. I know the truth."

Kate stood, and Lucas's eyes went to hers. He saw guilt there. And something else, before her gaze dropped to the floor. It was enough to shake his confidence.

Lucas took a step closer to Bryan, wanting to beat the smug expression off his face. "Get out of my house."

"Not without Kate."

"Stop it, Bryan," Kate said. "You should go." She grabbed his arm, but Bryan didn't budge. Kate's hand trembled.

"You heard her," Lucas said. "Get lost."

Bryan turned to Kate and touched her arm. Lucas wanted to grab him by the collar and haul him out the door. He ground his teeth together instead. Did Kate want to go with Bryan? Is that why she regretted the night before? She'd apparently told Bryan their marriage was a sham. *Why would she have done that unless—*

"Come with me, Kate," Bryan said. He added something else, too softly for Lucas to hear.

Kate shook his hand loose. "No."

Bryan whispered something. He took Kate's face in his hands.

Something red and hot spread through Lucas. He surged forward. "Get your hands off my wife." He grabbed Bryan's fancy shirt and shoved him toward the door. Lucas had five inches and forty pounds on him, and Bryan knew it.

Bryan caught his balance in front of the doorway, smoothing his sleeves, regaining his composure. He nailed Lucas with a glare. "She's not your wife, *friend.* She's just playing house with you."

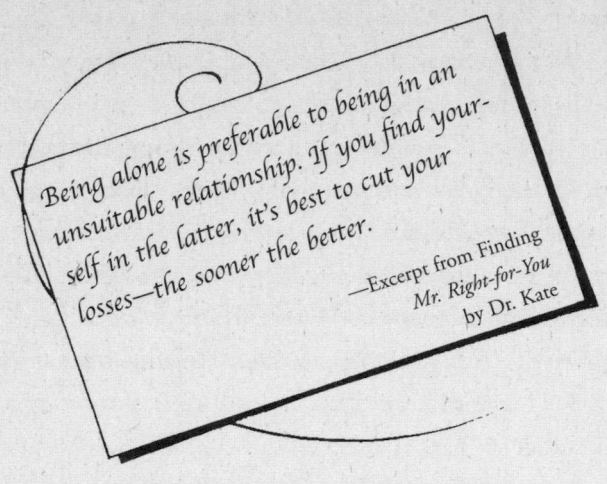

*Being alone is preferable to being in an unsuitable relationship. If you find yourself in the latter, it's best to cut your losses—the sooner the better.*

—Excerpt from Finding
Mr. Right-for-You
by Dr. Kate

# Chapter Twenty-Seven

If Bryan hadn't left on his own, Kate would have shoved him out the door after the way he'd spoken to Lucas. She wanted to soothe the hurt from Lucas's face with a well-placed kiss, but the anger lining his stubborn jaw stopped the thought as it materialized.

Lucas exited the room, leaving her to wonder what he was thinking. She heard him open a cabinet, remove something. The cabinet door slammed shut. Then she heard the pouring of coffee and the sound of the pot clanking back into its cubby.

Kate didn't know whether to follow him or not. Clearly they had a lot to discuss. He must be wondering what Bryan was doing there. He must be wondering what she was going to do.

Kate checked her watch. They were due at his parents' in an hour. *How will I face them? How can I tell these people who've become my family that I'm leaving?*

*How can I tell Lucas I'm leaving?* But then, he must know there was nothing holding her here now.

Except what had happened the night before.

Kate peered out the living room window. The wind wrestled with the leaves. They were already beginning to turn. Fall had arrived, and changes were in progress. The warm summer days were gone, and the cooler autumn days would usher in the frigid winter.

She'd never enjoyed winter on the island. With the winds blowing in off the ocean, it was impossible to keep a warm house. She mentally put another check in the pro column for visiting her dad in Maryland. There were many checks in the column already. Increasingly, she felt the need to escape. And soon.

Lucas's sandals shuffled to a stop somewhere behind her. His presence pulled her shoulder muscles tight, pushed the air from her lungs.

"Did you ask him to come?" Lucas said.

Kate pivoted. "No." She hated that he thought it. Did he think last night meant nothing? She wouldn't have slept with him if she were in love with Bryan. *Surely he knows that.*

Lucas took a sip of his coffee from the oversized Nantucket mug. It looked small in his hands.

Kate had to tell him what she'd decided, but getting the words out was harder than she imagined. *Strange, when I planned to leave him all along.* When he'd planned for her to leave all along. It shouldn't come as any surprise now that there was no point in her staying.

*Except for your feelings.*

She brushed the thought away, zooming in on the logical reasons that had added checks to her pro column.

"We need to talk," she said. It was a start. A slow one, maybe, but easing into it seemed kinder.

"Go ahead." He held the mug in front of him, a fragile barrier between them. His feet were braced as if for a blow.

She hated that she would deliver it. "I'm leaving the island." She measured his reaction and came away with nothing. "Now that the word is out about . . . our marriage, there's no reason for me to stay."

Kate chest pounded with the force of her heartbeats, walloping her ribs like a prizefighter. She waited for his response—and got nothing but silence.

"I need to get away." She filled the gap. "I'm too accessible here, anyway, to the press. I think if I go away somewhere, this will die down more quickly."

It occurred to her that she was leaving Lucas to deal with the press, with all the locals and their questioning glances. She was sorry for that, but staying wouldn't make it easier. People would talk even if she stayed.

She wished she could interpret his expression, but the light from the kitchen silhouetted him. She kept talking. "If there's nothing left of my career when this is over, maybe I can open another counseling service." She tried to sound upbeat, but the words fell flat. She imagined driving away, leaving Lucas behind. Never seeing him again. Her throat closed off.

"Are you going back to him?"

It took Kate a moment to realize what Lucas was asking. "No." She shook her head emphatically. "Bryan is—It's over between us." Hadn't Lucas heard her telling Bryan to leave?

"He doesn't seem to think so."

"I don't have feelings for him anymore. I wouldn't have—" *Slept with you if I did.* If she finished the thought, it would raise the subject she wanted to avoid.

"Wouldn't have . . . ?"

Her mind went back to the night before, returning like a dehydrated woman to a spring of fresh water. Kate knew she'd never wipe the moments from the slate of her memory. She crossed her arms, hugging her waist.

"I'm going to stay with my dad awhile," she said, avoiding his question. "In Maryland. Hopefully the scandal will fade quickly."

He walked toward her, and she tensed with each step. But he stopped an arm's length away. She could see his face now, lit by the light seeping through the window behind her.

"You could stay here . . ."

Did he know how tempting it was, with him looking at her that way? His eyes burning a path straight to her heart? It was the first time either of them had hinted at making the marriage permanent. It took courage for him to verbalize the idea that had floated between them for days. The night before, they'd silently brought the idea to life, but now that he said it aloud, it had a pull stronger than a riptide.

Kate tore her eyes away. *Be strong. Think with your head, not your heart. Think of your parents. Think of what you've learned from all your experience.*

"You know it wouldn't work, Lucas," She said. "And even if you don't know it, I do." She felt him watching her and wanted to run now, far away.

"What was last night?"

The edge of hurt in his voice broke her. No matter what, no matter that she was leaving, no matter that it was over, she wouldn't leave him thinking it meant nothing. She wouldn't cheapen something so special.

She was touching his face before she knew what she was doing. "Oh, Lucas. Last night was—it meant so much." The words jammed her throat. Her eyes burned.

He turned away, leaving her hand to fall on empty space.

Lucas walked away, putting space between them. Kate's touch had too much power. He would be lost if she touched him again. How could she leave if she felt anywhere near what he did? The thought of being without her ripped him in half, worse in some ways than Emily's death. That loss had been no one's choice, something that just happened. If Kate left him, it would be of her own choosing.

But maybe she didn't feel the way he did. He knew she had feelings, but maybe the depth of his love was . . . unrequited. Such a proper term for such a painful feeling.

"Lucas?" His name on her lips reminded him of the night before. She'd said his name over and over. Would he ever forget the sound of it? The heady way it made him feel to have her as his own?

He needed to change her mind. *If she would only give me a chance.* He faced her again, and now that he saw her watery eyes, he wanted to be close to her again, holding her. But he couldn't think with her in his arms.

"Stay here, Kate. There's something between us; won't you stay long enough to figure out what it is?"

She wet her lips and swallowed. "I told you about my parents—about their differences and how miserable they were. What I didn't tell you was how it ripped my mom apart when they divorced."

She looked out the window, and the daylight lit half her face. "Even though it was her choice, she couldn't be without him. She started drinking." Kate gave a wry smile. "Of course, I didn't understand it at the time. But I know now she was using the alcohol to escape reality. And the reality was, she couldn't live with my dad and she couldn't live without him. She was miserable either way. What kind of hope is there in that?"

"We're not your parents, Kate."

"We're *just like* my parents. Opposites in every way. I don't think I could've found someone less compatible. I should've followed my own advice and distanced myself before there were—feelings."

She made it sound so rational. Like you could tuck unwanted emotions in a box and toss them. "That's crazy," Lucas said. "Love isn't some item on a checklist."

Her fingers clutched the curtain, and she wouldn't look at him. He'd expected an argument. He'd expected her to rationalize why her way was best. He would find a counterargument to everything she said.

"I'll make reservations on the ferry as soon as I can," she said. "Possibly today. I'll have to send for my things."

Lucas felt like she'd punched him in the gut. She wasn't going to defend her decision? Wasn't going to give him a chance to convince her? He couldn't believe it was happening so quickly. Not after the night before, when he'd felt like a surfer riding the crest of a dream wave. Now he'd crashed headfirst into the rocks.

She checked her watch. "I want to talk to your family before I go. I owe them an apology."

It was his heart she'd broken, not his family's. *Say something. Say something to stop her before her plans set in her mind.* "You're in the middle of a crisis. Wait until things settle down. Don't make a rash decision." It was something she would say, something she could relate to.

Her eyes darkened with her frown. "It's not rash, Lucas. I planned to leave from the beginning, remember?"

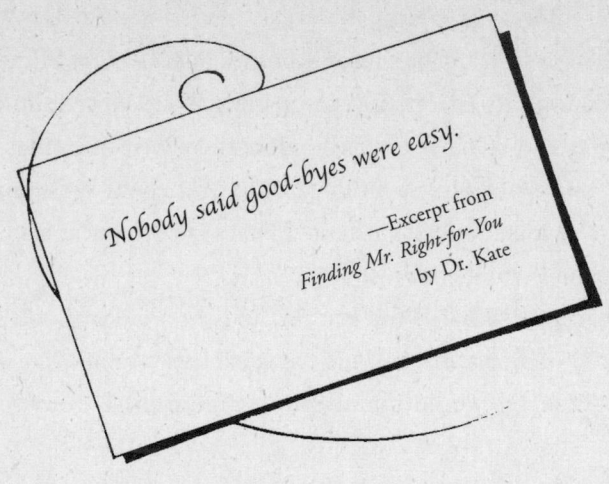

*Nobody said good-byes were easy.*

—Excerpt from
*Finding Mr. Right-for-You*
by Dr. Kate

# Chapter Twenty-Eight

Kate knocked on the Wrights' door, then clasped her shaking hands behind her back. Lucas had offered to accompany her, but she needed to face his family on her own. This was her fault, not his.

The door opened, and Susan's welcoming smile drooped. Kate watched the woman rise to her full height, watched her narrow chin notch upward. Regardless of how the woman responded, Kate was going to apologize to the family. Then she was going to have a heart-to-heart with Susan.

"Kate." Her name was a sour ball on the woman's tongue. "What are you doing here?"

"I came to talk to your family. Can I come in?"

Susan waffled in the doorway, clearly torn between opening the door wider and slamming it in Kate's face. Finally, she stepped back.

Kate followed Susan through the foyer and into the kitchen where Roy was putting a pan of dinner rolls into the oven. The smell of pot roast and garlic filled the air, and Kate's stomach growled in response. Jamie was on a stool at the kitchen island, a book propped open on the Formica counter. They both turned at her entry.

"Hi, Kate," Jamie said, a genuine smile on her face, and maybe a touch of pity in her eyes.

Roy shut the oven door and turned, offering her a nod and a reserved smile. Kate noticed his hands trembling for the first time and recognized it as a Parkinson's symptom. Guilt pricked her hard. As if the Wrights didn't have enough grief, she had made things worse.

"Is Brody around?" Kate asked. He was back from college for the weekend, and she hoped he hadn't left already.

"He went for a walk," Roy said. "Have a seat, Kate."

"No, thanks," Kate said. "I won't stay. I just wanted to tell you how sorry I am."

"I should think so," Susan said.

"Give her a chance." Roy pinned his wife with a look. "Go ahead, Kate."

*Where should I start?* There had been so much deception, and now the entire family was being publicly embarrassed. "I'm sure you're aware that my original fiancé backed out of the wedding on our wedding day. I can't begin to tell you how devastated I was. When Lucas offered to stand in, I thought it was crazy at first."

Kate tucked her hair behind her ears. "And then it began to seem like the only sane solution. With my book releasing the same day, I realized it would sink like an anchor if my wedding didn't go off as planned, and with all the media there to cover it—well, I guess I took the coward's way out."

Susan crossed her arms. Roy leaned his elbows on the island beside Jamie and studied Kate, the leathery lines around his eyes deepening.

"I never expected the truth to get leaked to the press. Lucas and I were going to divorce quietly after a year—we had it all planned. Obviously, everything's changed now."

Kate's throat was dry as desert sand. She wet her lips. "I take full responsibility, and I'm sorry for the embarrassment I've caused. I'm leaving the island this afternoon, but I wanted to let you know that you've become very special to me."

Jamie's eyes turned glassy and she blinked rapidly. Roy's face had softened, and Kate's own eyes burned. Even Susan seemed to lose some of her starch. That might change by the time Kate was finished.

Memories of the past few months flew through Kate's head at digital speed. The first time she'd met the Wrights, when she and Lucas had returned from their honeymoon. The time they'd come to watch her on *Dr. Phil.* All the walks with Susan. They were the family Kate never had, and she'd miss them. Even Susan.

Her throat thickened. "Thanks for opening your home to me. It was truly an honor to become part of your family, even if only for a little while."

Jamie jumped up and hugged her. "I'll miss you, Kate."

Kate returned the embrace. "Me too, Jamie. You're the sister I never had."

When they parted, Roy embraced her. "I wish you didn't have to go."

Kate wrapped her arms around his broad shoulders and spoke around her closed throat. "It's for the best. Thanks for all those home-cooked meals."

There was a moment of awkwardness as she faced Susan. "Can I have a word with you in private, Susan?" Kate asked.

Susan gave a short nod, her styled hair bouncing, and Kate followed her into the foyer. The woman turned to her and crossed her arms over her chest. The overhead light was harsh on the woman's face, making her appear older than her years.

Kate tempered her words with grace. "I wanted to talk to you about my mom."

Susan's jaw went slack; then she pressed her rosy lips together and looked away. "Lucas shouldn't have told you."

Kate shrugged. "I asked him why you didn't like me, and he felt he owed me an explanation."

"I don't want to talk about this with—"

"You don't have to say a word; just let me say my piece. Please." It was the last time Kate would see her anyway. The woman needed to hear the truth from someone, and if her own family wouldn't say it, Kate would.

"What my mom did was wrong. I don't know if she ever apologized, but it's too late for her to say it now, so I'll say it for her." Kate waited until Susan met her gaze. "I'm sorry. It was a terrible thing for a friend to do."

Kate wondered if it would help for Susan to know the misery her mom had gone on to endure. A failed marriage and a battle with alcoholism. Not to mention a premature death. Kate had dreamed of the kind of childhood Susan had provided her kids.

Kate could've sworn she saw a filmy glaze on Susan's eyes.

"I'm sure Roy regrets it as well," Kate continued. "And I hope somewhere along the way, he's found the words to tell you that."

"Saying you're sorry doesn't erase the pain," Susan choked out.

*Boy, can I relate to that.* How many times had Bryan apologized? "I know." She hoped Susan was remembering that Kate had her own heart broken not long ago. "But at some point you have to forgive the other person. It doesn't mean what he did was okay. It just means you're going to stop punishing him for it."

Susan stood to her full height, her jaws hollowing as she sucked in her pale cheeks.

Kate was treading where she was unwelcome, but the woman had held the mistake over her husband's head for over thirty years. Kate didn't know how Roy had endured it.

"Well, that's all I wanted to say," Kate said. She knew Susan hadn't wanted to hear it, especially not from her, but she hoped the woman took it to heart anyway.

Kate reached out and put her arms around Susan, feeling the stiffness of her shoulders, but embracing her regardless. "Thanks for all the walks, Susan. And for your hospitality."

She felt Susan's arms unfurl, felt her hands land on Kate's arms. It was enough.

Kate pulled back and smiled. "I'll try and catch Brody later. Will you let him know I'm looking for him?"

"Of course," Susan said.

Kate said good-bye one final time and left the house. Her feet took the uneven porch steps before she cut through the yard to the grassy knoll that separated their houses.

*This is the last time you'll see them. You'll never sit down to a meal on that insanely high rooftop or listen to Jamie and Brody tease one another again. It's over.*

Somehow, in a few short months, the Wrights had wiggled their way into her heart. And now she was leaving.

The crisp autumn air washed across her face, tugging at the short strands of her hair. She crossed her arms against the coolness and looked toward the ocean, the direction she'd soon go. A movement on the beach below caught her eye.

Brody threw something into the water, walking backwards, then turned toward his house. Kate changed directions, aiming her feet toward him.

When she reached the place where the long grass gave way to the sandy shore, Brody saw her. He stopped at the steps leading up from the beach, waiting for her approach. The wind pulled at his white T-shirt and tousled his blond curls.

"Hi," Kate said over the sound of the waves lapping the shoreline. "I was just at your house."

Brody nodded, his guarded smile reminding her of Roy's.

"I came to say I'm sorry," she said. "Sorry about deceiving your family. I never meant to hurt anyone, but I realize I have."

Brody dug his bare feet into the sand. "It wasn't right."

"I know," Kate said. "I'm not going to offer excuses." A seagull soared above the water and cried out—a lonely, high-pitched squeal. "I also came to tell your family good-bye."

Brody met her gaze, his eyes flinching for just a second. She watched the emotions dancing across his face. He'd never been good at hiding his feelings. "I didn't think you'd leave."

She shrugged, turning her face into the wind, letting her hair blow off her face. "Everyone knows the truth now. There's no reason for me to stay."

Brody studied her, his head cocked to the side. "Isn't there?"

His tone held a challenge, but she wouldn't take it. *There are things he doesn't know, doesn't understand. How can he?*

"How are things going this semester?" she said. "If you don't mind my asking."

The pause was so long, Kate thought he wasn't going to answer. When he finally did, she was relieved.

"You were right," he said. "About my being afraid to fail." He smiled and she saw a glimpse of the old Brody. "If you tell anyone that I'll have to come after you."

Kate held up her right hand, palm out. "I promise."

Brody sank onto the sandy wooden step, and Kate eased down beside him.

"Teaching is what I want to do," he said. "I think switching from major to major was a stall tactic because I was afraid I'd get out in the real world and fail. If you hadn't shown me that, I would have been a college student the rest of my life."

Kate breathed a laugh. "Nah, you would've figured it out."

"Yeah, when I was thirty and on my tenth major."

Kate was glad something positive had come from her time here, because everything else was a disaster.

Silence fell again. The seagull flapped its wings, flying away, growing smaller on the horizon.

"I'm still afraid," Brody said. "I guess that makes me a total wuss."

Kate traced a dry crevice in the step with her index finger. "It's fear that makes an act courageous, you know."

Brody drew in the sand with his big toe. "Huh. Never thought of it like that."

"You'll make a great teacher, Brody. I hope we can stay in contact." Kate huddled against the cool wind, tucking her knees close to her.

"Sure. There's always e-mail." He looked at Kate. "What about Lucas?"

Her heart wobbled at the mention of Lucas's name. "I suppose e-mail is out for him, huh? I guess we can keep in touch by phone."

"That's not what I mean."

He wasn't playing the part of Kate's brother-in-law now; he was a little brother watching out for big brother. She envied Lucas having a sibling that looked out for him.

"Lucas will be fine," Kate said. "It—it wasn't like that between us."

The words felt soiled coming out. It may have been true at one time, but not after the night before.

*It hasn't been true for weeks.*

"It's best that I leave." What would happen to her heart if she stayed? She'd already lost it to Lucas, and what hope did they have for a future together?

Brody nodded thoughtfully.

Kate let silence fill the space between them, let the sound of the surf rushing the shoreline fill the gap.

"Well," he said, "at least you won't have to fight your fear of heights anymore."

Kate smiled, remembering all the rooftop meals they'd shared. She elbowed Brody. "Fear of *falling*," she corrected.

Brody's expression changed, growing serious. "You know, a wise person once told me it's fear that makes an act courageous."

Kate's breath caught in her lungs as Brody held her captive with his pointed look. He knew. He knew she cared for Lucas. Thought she was a coward for running.

But sometimes, running was the courageous thing to do. At least, that's what she told herself.

❧

Lucas was gone by the time Kate returned home. She realized he must've gone to his parents' house while she was on the beach with Brody. Kate made reservations on that evening's car ferry and packed her belongings. Everything would fit in the car except her treadmill. She'd have to send for it and her things from the apartment when she found a place in Maryland.

For tonight, she'd take the ferry to Hyannis then drive as far as Wareham or New Bedford, then find a hotel. She called her dad and told him she was coming.

By late afternoon, she was wondering if she was going to have to track Lucas down. She had to leave soon if she wanted to make the ferry, but she owed him a good-bye at least.

Kate was packing her laptop and cord when she heard Lucas return. He opened the door, and his eyes landed on her suitcases. He paused for a moment before shutting the door.

Kate wrapped the recharging cord around the battery pack and stowed it in her bag with the laptop, then zipped it shut.

Lucas pocketed his keys and leaned against the sofa back. Rather than focus on him, she looked at the sofa itself. How many nights had they sat on that couch, disagreeing about what program they should watch? Kate had learned it was easier to read in the evenings because they could never settle on a show.

"When do you leave?" he asked.

Bo nudged Lucas's leg, but when he got no response, he crossed the room and settled on the rug with a loud sigh.

Kate checked her watch. She had to leave soon or take the risk of missing the ferry. "Now."

He was wearing the black T-shirt that stretched across his broad shoulders, and the faded jeans that made his legs look long and solid. *I'll miss him.* Kate didn't want to consider how much. She just needed to get out of there. She could deal with the feelings of loss later, when she was a safe distance away.

Lucas watched Kate hitch the leather strap on her shoulder and turn to him. The moment seemed surreal. It was happening so fast. Last night they'd been closer than ever, and tonight she was leaving.

He wanted to beg her to stay. He swallowed his pride and opened his mouth to do just that. Maybe he could find the words that would change her mind.

But what good would it do to beg? She had to want to stay. She had to want him. He could love her all he wanted, but it had to be her choice.

He closed his mouth, clamping his lips over the words.

"I'm not sure how to say good-bye," Kate said.

*Then don't. Stay. Stay with me forever.*

Kate tucked her silky hair behind her ears. He would miss that simple action.

"Regardless of how this turned out," she said, "I'm grateful for what you did. I've never had anyone go to so much trouble to save my skin." She tried to smile, but it wobbled on her lips.

It was no trouble. It had been his pleasure. He wished he could save her now, save her career from spiraling out of control. Save their marriage from falling apart.

"I'm sorry I wasn't able to help your parents," Kate said. "I hope they'll work things out."

*Tell her now. Tell her your parents are fine, that it was all a ruse to conceal the fact that you loved her from the beginning. Tell her you love her now and that if she stays, you'll spend every day proving it.*

But he had shown his love every day for the past three months. And still she was leaving.

"Say something." Her brown eyes, warm as melted chocolate, pleaded.

He tried to imagine sleeping in an empty bed, waking to a quiet house, making coffee for one again. The thought hollowed his stomach.

"Is there anything I can say to change your mind?" He would say it, whatever it was. *Do you know how much I love you? I'd give anything to call you my own.*

Kate looked away, clutching her purse strap. "It's for the best, Lucas. You'll see. It's hard right now, but later . . . later we'll know it was the right thing."

"Are you trying to convince me or yourself?"

She checked the time. Her eyes seemed to catch on her fingers. He watched her touch the wedding band he'd bought her, watched her slide it down her finger with the engagement ring. She closed the distance between them, pocketing the engagement ring, and held out the wedding band.

"Keep it," he said.

She shook her head. "I can't."

When he refused to take it, she sighed softly and set the band on the end table. Lucas wanted to snatch it up and force it back on her finger. She was his wife, even if only for a short while longer.

But what good would it do? He couldn't force her to wear his ring any more than he could force her to stay. *Any more than I can force her to love me.*

"I have to go."

Lucas straightened. *Have it your way, Kate.* "I'll drive you."

"You won't have any way back."

He opened the door and picked up her bags. "I'll take a cab." He carried her suitcases to her car.

"There'll be too many people there," she said, her voice sounding like it was being pushed through a sieve.

Lucas loaded her bags in the backseat, then faced Kate. Her eyes glistened like the surface of the ocean on a sunny day. She didn't want to say good-bye in front of an audience.

Neither did he. "All right." He opened the driver's side door for her.

"I'll file papers for the . . . divorce. And cover all the costs." A breeze blew, and dead leaves scuttled past their feet. There was a nip in the air that warned of winter's approach. "And I'll send for my treadmill," she said. "I think I got everything else."

*Including my heart.* Did she think she could run from these feelings? Did she think mere miles would separate her from his love?

Lucas studied her face, memorizing the way her eyes looked when she squinted against sun, the way her brows puckered when she frowned. He reached out and smoothed the hair the wind had ruffled, wanting to remember the feel of it between his fingers.

She closed her eyes on a sigh. "I hate good-byes."

He thought of Emily and how sudden her death had been. He'd always regretted that he hadn't kissed her that morning when he left for work. He was running late and only called good-bye on his way out the door.

Lucas took Kate's face in his palm, waiting for her to look at him. If she was going to leave him, she was going to do it with her eyes wide open.

He closed the space between them, pressing a soft kiss to her lips. Her hair smelled of lilacs, and her lips tasted like honey. He wanted to remember everything about her. He wanted to close his eyes at night and be able to summon the feel of her lips on his, the sound of her voice.

Kate pulled away. "Good-bye."

She refused to meet his gaze as she lowered herself into the car and put her keys in the ignition. Refused to look at him as she put the car in Reverse and backed out of the drive. He watched until her car disappeared over the slope in the road, knowing that all that awaited him was a house that would feel empty without her.

His feet felt heavy as he entered the house. Bo, seeming to sense his sadness, nudged his leg, tried to shepherd Lucas toward the couch. But Lucas didn't want to sit and think. Think about Kate leaving—getting further away by the minute.

The room seemed big. Kate had decluttered every corner of the house, leaving it spick-and-span, but now it felt bare. The treadmill was the only token of her existence, and it stood in the corner like a memorial.

He walked to the bedroom and stopped in the doorway. The spaces where her alarm clock and jewelry box had been were empty. He saw something on her nightstand and went closer. A small blue-velvet box. He opened it and looked at the earrings he'd given her for their first-month anniversary. It was as if she'd wanted to leave everything behind, to have no reminder of her time with him.

A scrap of paper on the clean hardwood floor caught his eye, and he retrieved it. It was a list of things she'd done in her preparation to leave. A laugh caught in his throat. Kate and her lists. Someday she would learn that life is what happens when you're busy making plans.

He threw the paper in the wastebasket and left the room. It felt as if the walls of the house were closing in on him. He realized for the first time that the house smelled like Kate. He wanted to get away from this place, occupy his mind with something else. If it weren't so late, he'd go sailing.

Bo barked from the back of the house. Lucas followed the sound to where the dog sat by the back door. Bo craned his massive head around, looking at him with inquisitive brown eyes.

"Wanna go for a walk, boy?"

Bo wagged his tail.

At least it would get Lucas out of the house.

They walked westward down the beach, Lucas occasionally tossing a piece of driftwood for Bo to fetch. The sun lowered in the sky, casting a pinkish hue over the beach. Bo trotted beside him, sometimes wading into the incoming surf or chasing a seagull that landed nearby. The dog had just returned from such a chase when Lucas heard it: the haunting sound of the ferry's horn in the distance.

He stopped, a catch in his breath, a stutter in his heart. The sound was the period at the end of a sentence, the whisper of goodbye from a lover, the clock striking midnight for Cinderella.

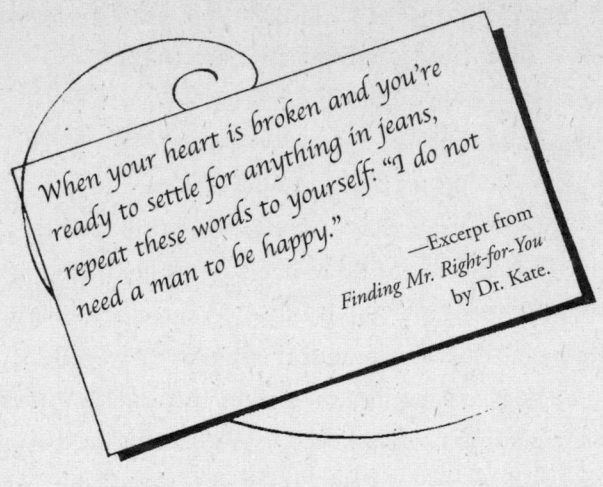

When your heart is broken and you're ready to settle for anything in jeans, repeat these words to yourself. "I do not need a man to be happy."

—Excerpt from *Finding Mr. Right-for-You* by Dr. Kate.

# Chapter Twenty-Nine

Kate opened the *Columbia Flier* on the picnic table and perused the apartment rentals section. The savory smell of grilled sirloin wafted by on the breeze. Her dad, draped in a red canvas apron, checked the meat, then closed the grill lid.

Kate noticed a new apartment listing and marked the ad with a yellow highlighter.

"See anything interesting?" Her dad sat across from her and brushed a red leaf from the wooden table with the side of his hand.

"There are a couple new ones I'll check on tomorrow. I'm still considering the one on Green Meadow Drive." Kate didn't want to overstay her welcome. She'd planned on staying at a hotel, but her dad had insisted she take his spare room. And she had to admit it had been a relief to hide away the past three weeks.

"How much longer on the steaks?" she asked.

"Oh, seven or eight minutes," he said.

"I'll put the salad together." Kate entered the house through the sliding door, careful not to fingerprint the glass. She found the head of lettuce and chopped it, then sliced a ripe tomato and placed the knife in the dishwasher.

Her cell rang as she was getting the dressing. Every time it rang, her thoughts turned to mush. She hadn't heard from Lucas since she left, but Jamie had e-mailed her twice.

*It's not Lucas, Kate. For heaven's sake. Get on with your life.*

Bryan had called the day she arrived in Columbia. She'd told him not to call again, and so far, he'd respected her wishes.

She pulled her cell from her purse's side pocket and answered.

"Kate. How are you?" Her agent's voice greeted her.

Kate squelched the inevitable disappointment. "Hi, Ronald. I'm okay. Getting settled in, looking for an apartment, avoiding the media. You know, the usual." It had been easier than she'd hoped to avoid the press since only a few people knew her whereabouts.

"Yeah, I've noticed," Ronald said. "It looks like they've run out of things to say about you."

"That's what we were hoping." A flurry of papers had covered the story initially, and several tabloids had joined the fray, but the scandal seemed to have died down already.

"That part's working for us." The caution in his tone warned of a negative flip side.

"What's wrong? Have you heard from Chloe or Paul?" Her editor had been quiet. In fact, Kate hadn't heard from Chloe since their conference call over three weeks earlier.

"I called her this morning just to check in," Ronald said. "I'm afraid sales have dropped off quite dramatically. She mentioned the ugly 'R' word."

"Returns?" It was every author's worst fear—that the stores would be unable to sell their stock of books and would return them to the publisher, unsold.

Kate set the plastic tongs in the salad bowl and faced the sliding door. "I don't understand. I've done what they asked. I've avoided the spotlight, and everything has died down. I thought that's what they wanted."

"Yeah, I know. I called Pam after I talked to Chloe to get her take. The public is impossible to predict. They'd been hoping that with no new information, the story would die and the public would forget it."

"But that hasn't happened?"

"Pam said it's too early to say for sure. But the numbers aren't looking good."

Kate ran her hand through her hair. All this for nothing? The public apparently believed the reports and had decided she was a fraud. They were voting with their dollars, and she'd lost.

"Is it too late to fix it?"

"If you mean going to the press with your side of the story, Pam didn't recommend it. She thinks coming this late, it would feel phony. The public would be suspicious of all the time you were quiet."

Kate slapped the counter. "I was quiet because they told me to be."

"I know, kiddo, I know."

Kate dragged her hand down her hair and anchored the ends in her fist, pulling until her scalp stung.

"I'm afraid there's more bad news."

Kate braced herself. "My column?" If she lost her syndicated column, what would she have left?

"I'm afraid so," Ronald said. "I'm sorry."

*Not my column.* She'd already lost *Glamour,* but the column had been her baby forever. It was how she'd become Dr. Kate. She'd helped thousands of readers, and now it was gone. She remembered all the hours she'd spent reading letters and formulating answers. She remembered all the letters she'd answered privately because column space prevented her from answering all of them, and some of the letters seemed too desperate to ignore.

"We'll get through this, kiddo. Let's give it more time. Maybe your book sales will pick up again."

Kate grasped onto hope. "Is that what Pam said?"

If anyone would know, it would be Pam. Her publicity experience allowed her to read the public better than anyone.

"No, she didn't say that. But you're too good at giving advice to be holed up in some office. It's your calling, your gift, and we can't give up just yet."

It felt like it was over. She could write all the articles and books she wanted, but if readers didn't trust her anymore, what did it matter?

Kate hung up and put the salad on the table as her dad entered with a plate of sizzling steaks. They served themselves and began to eat. Kate hardly tasted the food.

They were halfway through the meal before her dad spoke. "You're quiet." He speared a chunk of meat and put it in his mouth.

Kate told him about Ronald's phone call and the apparent effect the scandal had on her career. "It's not looking good, Dad." That was an understatement.

He set his knife and fork down. "Look, Kate. I realize it must be devastating and maybe even humiliating for your wedding fiasco to be public knowledge. But your goal has always been to help troubled relationships. Ever since you were a little girl, you were helping people solve problems. You don't need fame or notoriety or even a book contract to achieve that."

Kate swallowed the bite of salad. He was right. She had enjoyed helping couples in counseling. However, it was more logical to prevent the impossible relationships than it was to fix them. And no one sought counseling until there was a problem. That's why writing relationship books made sense.

But lately, Kate wondered if she knew anything about relationships at all. Everything that made sense in theory was more complicated in real-life application. Case in point: Lucas.

Her stomach clamped down on the food she'd eaten, and she pushed her plate away, the sirloin half-eaten. A week ago, she'd realized her night with Lucas hadn't resulted in a pregnancy. She'd expected profound relief. Instead she'd gone to her room and closed the door before having a good cry. What was wrong with her?

"What's really wrong, Kate?" Her dad's brown eyes were an antique reflection of her own.

"My career is falling apart. Isn't that reason enough to be depressed?"

Her dad sliced the steak with the serrated knife and placed it beside his plate. "Is that why you don't eat? Why you stare off into space for minutes at a time? Why your eyes are so sad all the time?"

Kate's head throbbed. She'd had a constant headache since she'd left Nantucket. Like her body was having withdrawal from the island. *Or from Lucas.* She stifled the thought.

She stood and carried her plate to the sink. "I'd rather not talk about it." She didn't even want to think about it, but her mind never cooperated. She tried to put it behind her, but her thoughts returned to the island, to Lucas, like waves to a shoreline.

"It's that Lucas, isn't it?"

Kate gave him a warning look. He'd never been one to pry, and she hoped he didn't start now.

"Don't look at me like that. You've been moping around here for—"

"I am not moping."

"—three weeks, and I may be a man, but I know lovesick when I see it."

Kate gave a wry laugh. "Lovesick?" She pulled the sprayer from the sink and ran water over her plate. "It was an arrangement, Daddy, remember? You were there. You read the papers."

Her dad's chair scraped the ceramic tile as he stood. "And I saw the look in that boy's eyes on your wedding day." He held out his plate.

Kate pulled it from his hands. "That's ridiculous."

"Is it?"

She sprayed the salad dressing and A1 Sauce off the plate while her father cleared the table. Her father had imagined what he'd seen on Lucas's face.

"Anyway," Kate said. "It could never have worked. We were different as day and night."

"Opposites attract, you know." He leaned around her to wet a dishrag and went to wipe down the oak table.

"It's not like that. We have nothing in common, Daddy, and I'm not going to spend the rest my life arguing like—" She stopped, realizing she was crossing a line. Who was she to criticize her parents' marriage?

"Like your mom and me?" Her dad finished the thought.

Kate loaded the two plates back to back in the dishwasher and shut the door. The crestfallen look on her dad's face exacerbated her regret. "I'm sorry. I shouldn't have said that."

He nodded slowly. "No, that's fair." He leaned against the kitchen counter across from her, bracing his hands against the ledge, reminding her of the way Lucas had stood so many times.

"I've always wondered how much you remembered," he said.

She remembered more than the yelling. She remembered the time her dad had dumped sacks of her mom's new clothes out the front door. She could still see the new dresses, tags still attached, strewn across the spring green lawn. "When two people are so different, conflict is inevitable," Kate said.

Her dad shook his head. "Your mother and I weren't so different."

"Oh, come on, Daddy. She was a spender; you were a saver. She was messy and disorganized; you were a neat freak. She wanted to go places; you wanted to stay home."

"Is that what you think? That our marriage fell apart because we were too different?" Her dad drew in a deep breath, exhaled, then straightened and walked toward the living room. "Come sit, Kate."

She followed her dad into the room and sat on the center of the sofa, opposite his recliner.

"Your mother and I had a good marriage in the beginning," he said. "But soon, we began to disagree about a lot of things. At the time, I thought I was right about everything. I thought it was smart to control the money the way I did. I told myself I was looking out for our best interests. And I thought the house had to be kept a certain way. Your mom liked things neat too, but my standards were high. Unfeasibly high."

"Mom was a clutter bug."

"Not initially. The things I did drove her crazy. The way the labels on food packages had to be turned facing front, the way the towels had to be folded in thirds and hung in the center of the towel rack, the way our lives had to run by the clock, down to the second. It all became too much for her."

"You weren't the problem, Daddy. It was her. I remember. She was a spendaholic. She used to go out and shop and buy new furniture, new clothes, when we didn't have the money—"

Her dad tilted his head and gave a sad smile. "Your mom never liked to shop. She didn't care about new clothes or new furniture. She did it because she was angry with me."

"Why?" Kate shook her head, trying to make sense of it. "Why would she be angry with you?"

"You know what OCD is?"

"Of course. Obsessive-compulsive disorder. I've counseled a couple clients who—" Kate stopped, letting it soak in. *OCD.* "You, Daddy?"

"I didn't know it at the time. Your mom was after me for years to go and get checked. She insisted something was wrong, but I thought she was being critical. As the years went by, she got angrier and angrier. I wanted the house impossibly neat, so she made sure it wasn't. I wanted to control the money, so she spent it. I wanted to be punctual, so she dawdled."

Her dad pinched the crease in his pants, mechanically, following it down the thigh. "I didn't see any of it at the time. Of course, her actions made me furious, and we had terrible arguments. Unfortunately, you heard a lot of them. It was a vicious cycle that would've been broken if I'd just been able to see that I had a problem."

How could all of Kate's assumptions about her parents' marriage have been wrong? So much of what she advised stemmed from what she thought she'd learned from her childhood.

"One day, when you were eight or nine," he said. "I walked by your bedroom and heard you playing. I stopped and listened. Barbie was screaming at Ken, and Ken was yelling at Barbie. You were holding them face-to-face, and as you were talking in your angry little-girl voice, your mouth was all screwed up, your brows drawn together. I realized you thought that's the way families behaved. You thought that was normal."

Kate had spent a lot of time playing with her Barbies. When you were an only child, you learned to make believe. "I don't remember that."

Her dad folded his hands across his stomach. "It was then that I began to wonder if your mother and I would be better off apart."

Kate had thought it was her mom's decision. She'd been angry with her mom for months. But even though she'd blamed her mom—the woman was her caretaker, the one who fixed her French toast in the morning and made sure her favorite jeans were washed—Kate couldn't conceive of leaving her home. Even when her mom started drinking.

"When did you find out about the OCD?" Kate asked.

"Not until years later. You were nearly in college by then. None of the women I had dated could tolerate my behavior for long, and I finally opened my mind to the possibility that it was me."

Kate wasn't naive. She knew it took two people to nurture a relationship and two people to ruin it. But how had she gotten things so twisted around? Her mom had never set her straight, had never said a bad thing to Kate about her dad, even after they divorced. Instead, her mother drowned her sorrow in alcohol.

"I'm sorry about how I handled my marriage to your mom, Kate. I'm sorry you didn't have a better childhood."

Kate's eyes stung. "I appreciate that, Daddy. I know it's hard to make a marriage work under the best circumstances."

"I did love your mom. You know that."

"I know." *Does he know Mom went to her grave loving him? Mourning him?* Sometimes it was better not to know.

"I'm not very good at this stuff," he said. "But I love you, too, you know." He squeezed his hands together so tight, the tips of his fingers whitened.

Kate didn't remember ever hearing those words from her father. She'd known he loved her, but hearing them was a balm to her aching heart.

"I love you too, Daddy."

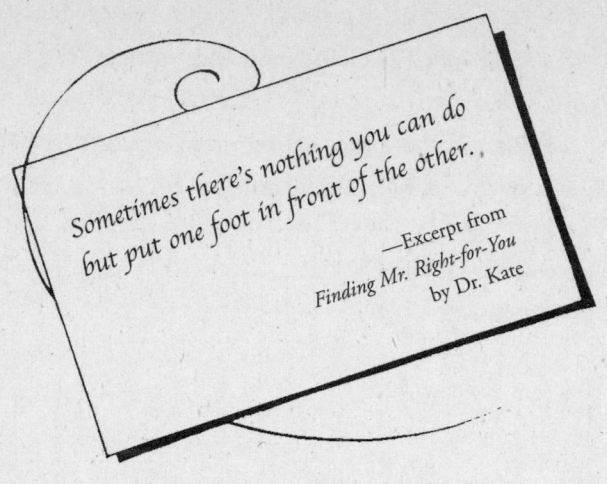

*Sometimes there's nothing you can do but put one foot in front of the other.*

—Excerpt from
*Finding Mr. Right-for-You*
by Dr. Kate

# Chapter Thirty

Lucas dipped the tack cloth in mineral spirits and wiped the sawdust from the oak pie safe. One more coat of polyurethane and it would be ready for Sydney. He was eager to be done with that job. The day before she'd come into the shop to check on his work, even though he'd told her it wouldn't be ready for two more days. She'd closed the distance between them and caressed the unfinished piece with her slender fingers as if it were a man's arm instead of a hunk of wood.

"Very nice, Lucas. You have a certain touch." She smiled slowly.

He put space between them, wiping his hands on the rag. He'd done everything he could to make it clear he wasn't interested. He tried to show professional courtesy without stepping one inch past that line. For the life of him, he couldn't see why she continued to pursue him when there were probably a dozen men who'd be willing to buy whatever she was selling.

The phone rang, and Ethan called him. "If you'll excuse me . . ."

"Well," Sydney said, "I'll check back in a couple days then."

Now Lucas ran the cloth along the edges of the cabinet doors, taking care to remove every speck of dust so it wouldn't mar the finish. There was only one woman he couldn't get from his mind, and it wasn't Sydney.

Lucas glanced at the calendar hanging cockeyed from a prong on the pegboard. October 21. Today would have been their four-month anniversary. If Kate were here, he might've bought her a bouquet of daisies and taken her to Cioppino's for lobster. Afterward, they would've gone home, and he'd have put on her favorite classical CD and kissed her on the corner of her lip, right where—

*Cut it out, Luc. You have got to move on.* How many times had he relived moments of their time together? Especially the last night.

He'd tried to stay busy. He worked well into the night until he was too tired to do anything but shower and fall into bed. It was easier that way. He was tired of pitying glances from friends and neighbors. He could imagine what they were thinking. *Poor Lucas. First he lost Emily; now he's lost Kate. Tsk, tsk, tsk.* But no one brought up Kate, as if the very mention of her name would shatter him.

Everyone wondered where she was, though, including the media, some of whom had come to the island, hoping for an interview. Was it any wonder he spent his days holed up in his shop? Even here, he hadn't escaped the phone calls. Ethan intercepted them, and at least now the calls were coming farther apart.

The story had quieted down the past couple weeks—a blessing for Kate, he was sure. He supposed her career would rebound since the scandal died so quickly. She'd probably have her next book on the shelves next year sometime, and her life would continue as it had before he'd entered it.

But Lucas couldn't imagine his life returning to normal. Even though the story had fizzled out, he still found himself avoiding people. Even his family—a fact that hadn't gone unnoticed.

*"We missed you at lunch Sunday,"* his mother had said when she dropped by the shop the previous week. Lucas noticed right away there was something different about her. She seemed less on edge. Happier, despite Lucas's withdrawal. Was his mom that happy to have Kate out of their lives?

Lucas didn't think she'd bought his excuse about being late on an order. His dad had come by later that week under the premise of borrowing his jigsaw, but Lucas had seen through that.

*"You're putting in a lot of hours lately,"* his dad said.

*"Business is good."* He wasn't fooling anyone, and he knew it.

*"You know, that Kate was something special."*

Lucas clamped down hard on his jaw. Was his dad trying to rub it in? Didn't he know Lucas knew it better than anyone?

*"She had a talk with your mom before she left,"* his dad said.

When had Kate had a chance to do that? Whatever she'd said must've worked a miracle. His dad said he was seeing a side of Susan he'd hadn't seen in years. She'd finally forgiven him for the mistake he'd made all those years ago. Lucas was happy for them.

Jamie visited him at the shop at least once a week and filled him in on her love life with Aaron. Brody kept bugging him to get an e-mail address so they could communicate more.

Lucas dipped the cloth in mineral spirits again and smoothed it over the drawer face a second time. He was nearly ready to apply the final coat of polyurethane when his shop door opened. Jamie entered, shutting the door. She turned and held up a copy of the *New York Times*.

"Did you see this?" Her chin jutted forward.

"See what?"

"The article about Kate." She extended the paper.

Lucas wiped the side panel of the pie safe, wiped the rim along the top, taking care to get into the crevices.

"*Luc.*" Jamie approached, her flip-flops shuffling on the cement floor.

"I'm not interested."

The newspaper smacked against her jeans-encased leg. "You are, too, and you know it."

He moved around the pie case and wiped down the other panel.

"She lost her syndicated column," Jamie said.

Lucas's hand paused over the rim, then continued. Why had Kate lost her column? The story had died down just as her publisher hoped it would. Had the scandal done irreparable damage? *How could they cancel her column when she'd worked so hard? She's Dr. Kate, for pity's sake.*

"You have to do something, Luc."

He shook his head. "Maybe Kate decided to focus on books instead of the column."

"That's not what the article says."

Lucas looked at the paper, torn between grabbing it and reading every detail he could find about her life without him, and burning the paper so he could spare himself the agony.

"I'm sure she's fine. The story faded quickly enough."

"Her book sales are in the toilet."

Lucas arched his brow. "Did the article say that too?"

Jamie hitched her pointed little chin up a notch. "I've been keeping track of her numbers on Amazon."

"What's that?" He wished he hadn't asked. His sister was drawing him in, and he only wanted to put it behind him. He wiped the top of the pie case even though it was already clean.

"Amazon—where people buy books online?" Her look said, *Duh.* "She used to be ranked, like, below two hundred, and now her book is nearly at two hundred thousand!"

Lucas gave up on the pie case and threw his rag on the bench. He hoped it wasn't true. Kate was too good at what she did to let it all go to waste. "I take it that's a bad thing."

"Terrible. I'm telling you, her career is falling apart. You have to do something."

"Me . . . What am I supposed to do?"

Jamie dropped the paper on the bench and crossed her arms, eyeing him. She tapped her foot, her glittery pink toenails rising and falling.

"You didn't tell her, did you." It wasn't a question so much as an accusation.

"Tell her what?"

"That you love her."

Lucas turned and wrapped the cord around the sander, then hung it on a prong. His sister had gotten too good at reading his thoughts. Maybe it was all those romances she devoured.

"Well," Jamie said, "I guess that answers my question."

Lucas pocketed his hands. "That's between me and Kate, munchkin."

"How can it be between you and Kate if she doesn't even know?"

Little squirt. She was getting too smart for her own britches.

"It might've made a difference if she'd known," Jamie said. "I know it's none of my business . . . but I want you to be happy. Besides, if you hadn't helped me with Aaron, we probably never would've gotten together."

"How's that going, anyway?"

"We're still going out, but stop trying to change the subject. Are you going to help Kate or not?"

Later that night Lucas lay wide eyed in bed. Jamie's question rang through his head. *"Are you going to help Kate or not?"* But what could he do when she was gone? He couldn't turn back time or make that Stephanie chick rescind the story.

The headline that had appeared in *USA Today* snagged in his mind. *"Dr. Kate in Loveless Marriage."* Two of the tabloids he'd picked up had an article that focused on their loveless marriage arrangement.

When he'd read it, he'd almost laughed. Little did they know, there had been plenty of love in the marriage. Unfortunately it was all his.

*Was it? Would she have given herself to me that last night if she didn't love me?* His chest tightened, aching at the thought. Maybe it was only wishful thinking.

*But what if it's true? What if Kate loves me? What if she only left because she's afraid?*

He remembered the articles about their loveless marriage and wondered if it would accomplish anything if her readers knew he'd loved her. *Still love her*, he corrected himself. Would it somehow redeem her in the public's eyes?

Even if it did, there was no way he could trust the media. They were sharks, out for their scoop and willing to trample anything that stood between them and their prey. Even if Lucas could somehow convey his feelings to the media, they would twist it and warp it and use it to hurt Kate.

Maybe he should call that publicity woman Kate worked with— Pam? Maybe he could bounce the idea off her without letting Kate know. Maybe then, if he did everything in his power to help her, he'd finally have peace.

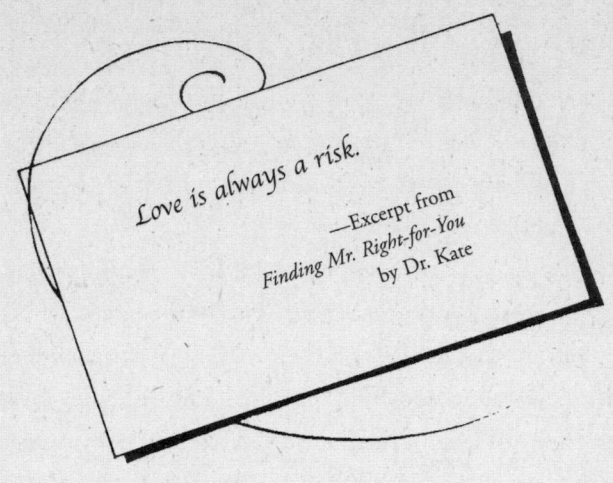

Love is always a risk.

—Excerpt from
*Finding Mr. Right-for-You*
by Dr. Kate

# Chapter Thirty-One

"I'm going to the grocery, Dad." Kate shut the dishwasher, latched it closed, and pushed the button to start it. It whirred into action.

In the living room, her dad turned on the TV to a Taco Bell commercial. He reached for his wallet. "Here, let me pay this time."

Kate waved him off. "I got it." She picked up her purse. It was the least she could do when he was letting her stay there until she found a place. She had a nice nest egg in her savings account. "I might run by that apartment on—"

"*Kate.*" Her dad turned up the TV's volume.

Kate followed his widened eyes to the screen. *Lucas.* Lucas was on TV. He wore a suit and tie. Her breath caught.

"—happened between Dr. Kate and her Mr. Right?"

The screen changed to show *NewsWire* correspondent Nancy Lopez. "Can you tell us how you came to be married to Dr. Kate?"

There was a quick clip of Lucas shrugging, a mischievous look on his face; then the camera cut to Nancy.

"Dr. Kate has been ridiculed for entering a marriage as if it were a business arrangement. Was it really a loveless marriage?"

The camera cut to Lucas. "Funny you should ask that." He gave his charming half grin.

The *NewsWire* logo appeared on the screen and a voiceover sounded. "Everyone wants to know why renowned columnist Dr. Kate married Mr. Wright, and *NewsWire* has the exclusive. Tune in tomorrow night at ten o'clock Eastern Standard Time."

Another commercial started and her dad turned down the volume. Kate sank onto the couch, numb. *I don't understand. Why did Lucas do it? Just when the scandal died down, he went and brought it to the surface again.*

"I can't believe it." She stood again and paced the room as anger fired through her veins, her heart beating double time. She was furious—and hurt. *Why is he doing this?*

"You should call him," her dad said. "Maybe there's a—"

Her cell rang. She pulled it from her purse, hoping it was Lucas, because she had a few things to say to him. Her hand shook as she answered.

"Kate, what's going on?" her friend Anna asked. "I just saw a promo for *NewsWire*—"

"I know. I saw it too."

"You didn't know about it?" She'd kept Anna up-to-date on everything through e-mail.

"No, I didn't know. I can't believe he's done this." Kate ran her hand through her hair.

"Just when everything was starting to die down," Anna said. "Why would he do it?"

"I don't know, but I'm going to find out. I'll call you back after I talk to him."

They hung up, and Kate looked at her dad. Her throat was tight, her head ached behind her eyes, and she wanted to hit something.

"Maybe there's an explanation," her dad said.

"Sure there is. About two hundred thousand of them." They'd probably paid him at least that for an exclusive. Did Lucas hope to expand his shop with the money? She'd never thought him ambitious, yet what other reason could he have?

She remembered how he'd turned down the opportunity to be interviewed on *Live with Lisa* alongside her. What had he said? *"Talking's not my thing. Words don't come easy to me, like they do you."* She remembered the sob story he'd told her about being paralyzed with fright in front of a school assembly. Apparently he could keep his composure if enough money was involved.

The betrayal hurt.

Kate dialed Lucas's number. He should be home by now, probably making a mess in the kitchen. *I hope he chokes on his dinner.*

"Maybe you should wait until you've calmed down." Her dad flipped off the TV.

The phone rang over to voice mail. The beep sounded. Kate tried to swallow the lump in her throat, but it was firmly lodged. "What are you doing, Lucas? I just saw the *NewsWire* promo. I can't believe—" Her voice wobbled, and she took a steadying breath. *I am not going to let him know he has me in tears.*

"I can't believe you'd do this. Call me." She disconnected the call.

She paced the room. She was a traveling earthquake, and Lucas was the epicenter.

"So, this is the guy you've been mooning over for weeks," her dad said. "He doesn't deserve you."

"He doesn't have me, Dad." Not now. Not after this. She couldn't stand the thought of him anymore.

*Come on, Kate. Feelings don't evaporate simply because you've been betrayed.* She knew it was true. All she had to do was remember Mrs. Hornsby and all the other victims of unfaithful spouses she'd counseled. But couldn't she just be mad without her internal therapist kicking in?

"Well, I suppose your career can't be damaged any more than it already was."

No, but Kate had hoped the public humiliation was over. She'd hoped to fade from the public eye and return to private counseling. The last thing she needed was to have the scandal revived. She'd thought if anyone would betray her to the media, it would've been Bryan.

She'd never thought for a minute Lucas would cave to the pressure.

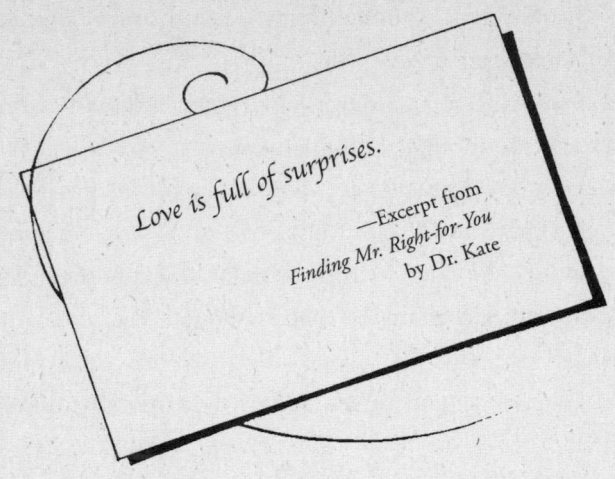

*Love is full of surprises.*

—Excerpt from
*Finding Mr. Right-for-You*
by Dr. Kate

# Chapter Thirty-Two

Kate tidied the kitchen, then straightened the seasonings on the wooden rack. Two more minutes. Each one passed like a turtle on Valium.

All day she'd tried to reach Lucas. When she called the shop, Ethan said he was out, yet he didn't answer at home. No one picked up at his parents' house, and her e-mails went unanswered. They were probably embarrassed by Lucas's betrayal. But maybe they'd been interviewed too. Maybe they were splitting the bounty and taking a trip to Europe to celebrate.

A dish towel fell to the floor and Kate kicked it, leaving it crumpled between the fridge and cabinet. No one from Rosewood had returned her calls either. She'd phoned Ronald first thing that morning, but he hadn't been able to reach Paul or Chloe. It seemed she had become persona non grata. They had to know about the exclusive. They were probably angry with her for letting it happen. *As if I had a choice.*

"Kate, it's coming on," her dad called from the living room.

Kate entered the room where her dad perched on the edge of the brown sofa, his elbows on his knees.

Kate sat beside him and hugged the chenille pillow to her stomach. A barrier for the coming sucker punch.

The *NewsWire* theme song played as the logo appeared. They showed previews of the upcoming segments, including the same preview she'd seen the night before. The first segment began, but it wasn't Lucas's.

When they cut to a commercial. Kate released her breath. "I hope it's not last."

Her dad crossed his legs at the knee. "It might be."

She'd waited all day, a nervous ball of energy. Why hadn't Lucas returned her calls? Why hadn't anyone returned them? Was he too ashamed to face her? *He should be.*

"Want some coffee?" Her dad asked. "I can put on a pot."

Kate shook her head. "I feel like I could run across water as it is."

When the show returned, they focused on the TV, but it was a segment about trans fats in restaurant food.

Kate wondered what questions they would ask Lucas. Would he tell them she'd cried herself to sleep on their honeymoon? Would he tell them his mom disliked her from the beginning because of whose daughter she was? Would he tell them about the special moments— the ones when they forgot their marriage was an arrangement?

Fear sucked the moisture from her mouth. Kate felt as if she stood on the gallows, with a thick rope at her neck, waiting for the floor to open. And there was nothing she could do but wait.

The segment ended and another commercial break ensued. It was half past the hour.

"Hang in there, Kate. Whatever comes, I'll be here for you." Her dad reached over and squeezed her cold hand.

"Thanks, Daddy." She couldn't sit anymore. She stood and walked to the patio door. Outside, darkness swallowed the yard and a sliver of moon peeked from behind a curtain of clouds. She kept remembering the last days with Lucas, the way he'd held her that night, pressing kisses to her forehead and chin, smoothing her hair from her face. She'd never felt more cared for, more cherished.

*And now he's airing our dirty laundry on national TV. It doesn't make sense.*

"It's back on," her dad said.

Kate returned to the living room, stopping behind the recliner. Evan Greggory began a segment about the sole survivor of a ferry accident overseas. They were saving Lucas's segment for last, which showed they viewed it as important. *They must've gotten some juicy material from Lucas.*

The ferry segment seemed to last forever. A long commercial break followed. Kate's heart rate tripled as she waited for the commercials to end. This was it. There was only twelve minutes remaining—only enough time for Lucas's story.

When the program returned, her dad cranked up the volume. The camera panned in on Nancy Lopez. "Welcome back to *NewsWire.*" She turned to a different camera. "She is the queen of relationships and the author of recent self-help book *Finding Mr. Right-for-You.*"

Nancy held up a copy of the book. "Dr. Kate's book was released with much media attention on her wedding day this summer, and it soared to the bestseller's list."

Kate nearly rolled her eyes. The book had barely made it to the bottom of the bestseller's list, achieving less than Rosewood had hoped.

Nancy continued. "But Dr. Kate's career recently turned upside down when it was revealed that her real fiancé, Bryan Montgomery, left her at the altar, and that Dr. Kate impulsively entered a loveless marriage arrangement with Nantucket native Lucas Wright as a last-ditch effort to save her book from certain death.

"Little is known about the terms of the arrangement or Dr. Kate's feelings on the matter, but *NewsWire* has gained an exclusive interview with the man who found himself at the altar with marriage expert Dr. Kate." Nancy smiled and turned as the camera cut to Lucas. "Welcome to the show, Mr. Wright."

Kate honed in on Lucas. He'd shaved, and his hair was combed neatly off his face as it had been at their wedding. He wore a dress shirt and tie she'd never seen. He thanked Nancy.

"Can you tell us how you knew Dr. Kate and for how long before the wedding?"

Lucas shifted subtly. He was uncomfortable. *Good.*

"Kate had been on the island for three years," Lucas began. "She was born there, but her family left when she was young. I didn't know her then. When she moved back, she wanted to open an office in town. She rented the space over my shop."

"Can you tell us what happened on the day of her wedding?"

He nodded slowly. "I was working in my shop that morning. Actually I was putting the finishing touches on the gazebo she'd asked me to make."

"For her wedding with Bryan Montgomery?"

"Yes. She'd hired me to build it months earlier. Kate came to the shop to check on it because I was supposed to have delivered it already. When she was there, she got a call from her fiancé."

"Mr. Montgomery?"

"Yes. I only heard her end of the conversation, but it was enough to tell me he wasn't going through with the wedding."

"What was Kate's state of mind after the phone call?"

Lucas tilted back, and he shook his head. "She was devastated. She was trembling." He gave a sad smile. "You'd have to know Kate to know how unlike herself she was after that phone call. She's the most calm, capable individual I've ever met. She's the kind of person you want during a crisis because she—She just takes care of things. But it was five hours before her wedding, and her groom just left her at the altar, and with the publicity surrounding the release of the book . . . who wouldn't panic?"

"How did you come to be part of the solution?" Nancy asked.

"It was my idea. I don't know where it came from. It was impulsive, and it seemed like the only solution at the time. She needed a groom, and I wanted to help her."

"That's some help. Why would you agree to step in and save her wedding?"

Lucas looked down at his lap and paused a moment. "The reason I gave Kate was that I needed her help on a personal project."

"But that wasn't the real reason, I take it," Nancy said.

"No."

"What?" Kate whispered, staring at the screen.

"We'll get back to that in a moment," Nancy continued. "What were the terms of the arrangement?"

Lucas's mouth tilted in a smile as if remembering the moment. "There had to be an escape clause. We agreed to remain married for a year."

"Was there a contract between you? Financial arrangements?"

"It wasn't like that. We knew each other well enough to trust one another. We kept our finances separate."

"And no money exchanged hands?"

A pink flushed climbed Lucas's neck. He looked like a bashful schoolboy. "She didn't pay me for the honor of being her husband, if that's what you mean."

Nancy's smile made it clear she was captivated by Lucas's charm.

"Can you define your relationship with Dr. Kate prior to the wedding? Were you lovers, friends . . ?"

Lucas ran his fingers between his neck and collar. "No, we weren't lovers. I guess you could say we were friends. We spent quite a bit of time together when I renovated her space into an office and apartment. She lived and worked above my shop, so we saw each other frequently." His smile tilted. "Kate probably would've said we were acquaintances. I think I got on her nerves a bit."

"You say that like you enjoyed it."

Lucas smiled. "Little bit."

Kate squeezed the cushion on the back of the recliner, unable to take her eyes off Lucas.

Nancy continued. "You've denied being paid to marry Dr. Kate, and you've hinted that the reason you gave her was false." The camera cut to Lucas's face while Nancy stated the question. "Why *did* you stand in as her groom?"

Lucas looked down at his lap, his smile faltering. He swallowed.

Kate wondered for a long moment if he was going to freeze as he had so long ago on a school gym stage. She found herself pulling for him, wanting to help him formulate an answer.

But then he spoke. "I wanted to help her. If you'd seen her after that phone call—she was panicked. Afraid. Hurt." Lucas shrugged. "I wanted to help."

"Why?" Nancy asked.

Kate leaned forward, her breath on hope's threshold.

He gave a sad little smile. As his head tilted down, his hair fell forward, partially covering his eyes. Then he looked back at Nancy. "I love her," he said in a throaty voice.

Kate sucked in her breath. She stared into his familiar face and felt an ache behind her eyes. *He loves me? He married me . . . because he loves me? But his parents' marriage—*

The camera stayed on Lucas even though he stopped talking. He was clearly uncomfortable, like he wanted to squirm right out of the starchy suit.

He filled the silence. "When I saw how upset she was, I wanted to fix it for her." He lifted one shoulder. "Maybe I was a little selfish too. Maybe I thought if she was mine for a year, she'd somehow fall in love with me too." He shifted, looking away. "I was trying to save her wedding. I guess it was wrong of me to take advantage. She was vulnerable. I came up with the idea and convinced her it was the only solution. If anyone's to blame, it's me."

He went blurry as Kate's eyes filled. She blinked, not wanting anything blocking her view of Lucas's face.

The camera cut to Nancy. "In reality, you were only married three months. What was it like?"

"Being married to Kate?" He smiled. "Great. Fun. Challenging."

"Challenging because . . . ?"

Lucas tugged at his suit coat. "Because I love her. Because I wanted the marriage to be real, and it wasn't." He paused, looking down again. "In three months she solved problems that have been in place for years. She's got this deep well of wisdom . . . I don't know where it comes from. If something's broken, she fixes it."

"Except your heart?"

The camera slowly closed in on Lucas's face. His jaw clenched, then loosened. "I'm not sure she knows she broke it."

Nancy smiled. "She does now. It's fairly common knowledge that Kate left the island shortly after the scandal erupted. Can you give us your thoughts on that?"

Lucas sucked in a breath and blew it out. He shifted.

Kate wanted to brush the hair out of his face, run her palm down his tense jawline and kiss away the frown on his lips.

"I didn't want her leave. I asked her to stay."

"But she didn't."

"No."

"Was she still in love with her former fiancé?" Nancy asked.

"I asked her that. She said she wasn't, and I believed her."

The camera cut to Nancy as she studied Lucas, a thoughtful expression on her face. "Why are you here today? What do you hope to accomplish?"

"I wanted to tell Kate's side of the story. I wanted to take responsibility for my part in it . . ." Lucas pulled at his tie.

The camera cut to Nancy. "Anything else?"

Lucas looked down, then met Nancy's eyes again. "I wanted to tell her what I was afraid to say before she left."

He swallowed, then looked at the camera, his eyes burning into Kate's. She locked onto his face, feeling as if he were right in front of her, right now.

Lucas's chin came up.

Kate watched his lips, waiting.

"I want to tell her I love her," he said.

Kate put her hand against her chest, squeezed the stiff material of her shirt.

Nancy paused for a full three seconds, letting the words sink in. "On national TV?"

He gave his crooked smile. "I guess I'm laying it all on the line. I love her. I have for a long time, and I always will." He looked down again.

"That's a lot of pressure for a girl," Nancy said.

Lucas shook his head. "Hope not. That wasn't my intention. Kate's entitled to make her own choices, to choose her own life. I just want her to have all the facts before she does."

Nancy said something that tied the story into a neat bow, then signed off. Kate's dad flipped off the TV. Without the light and noise of the TV, the room fell into darkness and silence. Her mind whirled faster than a carnival ride.

"Well." Her dad flipped on the lamp.

Kate's legs felt wooden as she rounded the recliner and sank into it. She was shaking, her hands and legs trembling uncontrollably. *He loves me. He's loved me from the beginning.*

She felt a sudden, inexorable need to talk to him. To see him.

"Do you love him, Kate?" Her dad's voice broke through her thoughts.

*Do I love him?* She remembered the way he held her on the sailboat when she was sick. Remembered the way he held her when the scandal broke. Remembered how treasured she felt when he looked at her, touched her.

"Yes," she whispered.

But they were so different. It was why she'd left. She didn't want to wind up like—

*My parents? Well, I've already discovered how wrong I was on that one.* It wasn't their differences that broke them apart but her dad's disorder.

But even with that understanding, her heart faltered in fear. *What am I afraid of? That I'm going to wind up alone and desperate like Mom?*

*But I can't control the future. I can't even control the present. I just have to make reasonable decisions and hope for the best. Look how meticulously I planned my engagement and wedding. And still, it all fell apart.*

Did her obsessive need to plan stem from a desperate desire for control?

Kate remembered the conversation she'd had with Brody that day on the widow's walk. *"I'm not afraid of heights so much as I'm afraid of falling,"* she'd said. Was that her problem? Why she'd nearly married a man she didn't love? Why she'd been in such a hurry to leave the man she did love? She was afraid of becoming her mom. Afraid of becoming like the hundreds of women she'd counseled.

Kate gave a wry laugh. Some psychotherapist she was. She was only now figuring out that she was avoiding love.

"You think you should call him?" her dad asked.

What should she do? She wanted to tell him she loved him. She wanted to say she was sorry for leaving. A shiver of fear snaked its way up her spine. What if it didn't work? What if he broke her heart?

*It's already been broken. Let him heal it.* Her advice to Brody came back to her: *"It's fear that makes an act courageous."* *Do I have the courage to love him back?*

Kate straightened. She did. She was ready to put it all on the line, like he had.

But she wanted to do it face-to-face. She wanted to touch him, feel the strength of his arms around her when she said the words.

"I have to go to him," she said firmly.

Her dad nodded.

She checked her watch. "I can be there by morning if I drive to Hyannis and take the ferry."

"And drive all night? Kate . . ."

"I have to see him." She had to tell him she loved him. She could take a flight, but then her car would be here. No, it was settled. She'd never be able to sleep anyway. She might as well spend the night closing the distance between them.

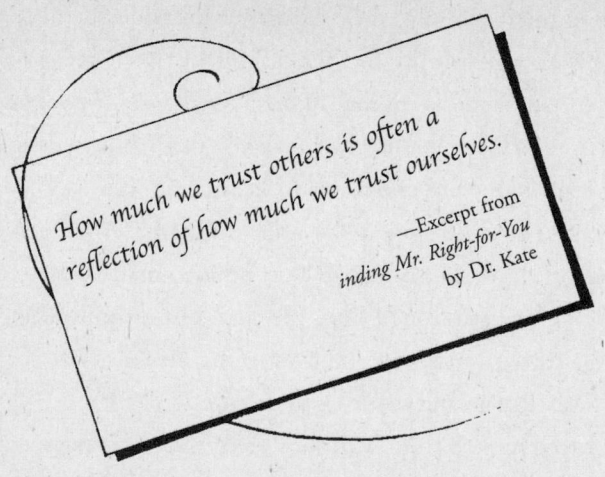

*How much we trust others is often a reflection of how much we trust ourselves.*

—Excerpt from
*inding Mr. Right-for-You*
by Dr. Kate

# Chapter Thirty-Three

She didn't call.

It was impossible to soothe the ache in his gut. Lucas rolled over and stared out the window, where dawn stretched, spreading gray across the midnight canvas. He pulled Kate's pillow close, inhaling. The scent of her was nearly gone—that subtle lilac scent that perfumed her hair.

He'd been pleased with the interview, relieved that the words had come when he needed them, relieved that he'd survived the interview without cracking under the pressure. After the show aired the night before, he waited, pacing the floor until Bo tired of his excess energy and curled up at the foot of the sofa.

When the phone had rung, his feet made quick work of the

distance to the kitchen, and he answered breathlessly, not caring if Kate knew he was waiting for her call.

But it had been his mom. *"Honey, I'm so sorry. I knew you loved her, but I guess I just didn't realize how much."* She apologized for treating Kate badly and asked if he'd heard from her.

He didn't give up hope until after midnight. And even though he turned off the lights and lay in bed, he still couldn't sleep. His ears strained to hear the phone's ring. He slept restlessly, awake as much as he was asleep, and now that morning had arrived, his hopes washed away like a sand castle at high tide.

He forced himself from bed, showered, and put on a pot of coffee, draining the first cup like it was medicine for his wounded spirit. When Bo picked up his tennis ball and carried it to the back door, he stood.

"Go for a walk, boy?"

He followed the dog outside, past the gazebo—a constant reminder of Kate and their wedding day. He crossed the beach and turned eastward, tossed the tennis ball into the surf, and watched Bo lumber after it.

Had Kate even watched the show? He knew from her voice mail that she'd been angry when she'd seen the preview. What if she hadn't watched it?

Worse, what if she had? What if she heard his proclamation of love and didn't feel the same way? What if he'd accomplished nothing other than publicly humiliating himself?

*I've done all I can. She knows how I feel now. The rest is up to her.*

Bo returned the ball, dropping it in the wet sand at Lucas's feet. Lucas picked it up and heaved it into the waves before stuffing his hands into his pockets. His fingers wrapped around cool metal. Kate's wedding band. He ran his thumb around the smooth surface. Its presence comforted him, like he carried a piece of her with him.

Bo turned in a circle, the tennis ball between his teeth, his paws dancing in the foamy sand. The sun glittered off the surface of the water like a million diamonds. When Lucas reached Bo, he tugged the wet ball from his jaws and threw it as far as he could down the shoreline, then followed Bo's footprints.

⟨∞⟩

Kate stepped off the ferry, her overnight case clutched in her hand. She'd left her car in Hyannis since there was no room on the ferry. Now as the crowd dissipated on the concrete dock, she wondered if she'd be able to get a cab.

She tugged the baseball cap low on her head to avoid recognition and pulled her sweater tighter against the nip in the air. The trees had fully turned, washing Nantucket down in vibrant hues of yellow and red.

Her phone pealed, and she moved to the side of the dock as she pulled her cell from her bag and checked the caller ID. It was Pam. Kate didn't want to talk business; she wanted to get to Lucas. She was so close.

But her publicity gal wouldn't call on a Saturday for nothing. Kate answered. "Hi, Pam. How are you?"

"Good. Great. Have you seen the papers?"

Kate had seen nothing all night but the yellow lines on the road. And she'd given little thought to her career or what others would be saying. "No, why?" Kate was almost afraid to know, but Pam didn't sound dismayed.

"It worked! Listen to this. 'Dr. Kate's counterfeit groom broke his silence on TV newsmagazine show *NewsWire* when he proclaimed his love for the well-known author and syndicated relationship columnist.' Blah, blah, blah—backstory and quotes from the interview.

Ah, here we go. 'It seems, even in the case of unpredictable disasters, Dr. Kate's own brand of relationship magic works like a charm. Even for herself.'"

Kate sank to the cement ledge overlooking the harbor. Through the phone, she heard the rattling of newspaper pages. "There are a dozen more just like it. And I caught it on several cable news programs this morning too. They keep running the portion of the interview where Lucas says"—she lowered her voice—"'I guess I'm laying it all on the line. I love her. I have for a long time, and I always will.' Oh, man, he has every woman in America fanning her face, Kate. I'll bet your book is flying off the shelves as we speak."

*I can't believe it. How have I gone from—*

Something Pam had said earlier popped into her mind. *"It worked."* The words had been buried beneath the good news, but now they surfaced like a piece of driftwood through the sand, uncovered by the relentless wind.

Kate interrupted Pam. "Wait. You said 'It worked.' What did you mean?"

The rustling of paper stopped. A seagull swooped down and landed in the harbor, bobbing on the waves beside a fat buoy.

"You haven't called him?" Pam's tone revealed shock.

Dread filled Kate, numbing her to the fingertips. "What's going on, Pam?" Her thoughts spun. Terrible thoughts that tortured her. "Was this just a ploy to fix my book sales?" She could choke on the acid that rose in her throat. Had Lucas only been pretending?

"No, sweetie, it's not like that."

"Then what is it like?" Her voice quavered.

Pam sighed loudly. "You should hear this from Lucas. Why didn't you call him?"

Kate suddenly felt like a fool for driving all night like this was some 911 emergency. "I wanted to talk to him in person." Her answer was feeble. Kate swallowed the acid and her pride. "I'm here now, on Nantucket."

"Oh, I am such a dolt!" Kate imagined Pam smacking her own forehead. "I've ruined everything. Go. Go talk to him. I'm hanging up now."

"No, wait. Pam!" A click, then a dial tone buzzed in Kate's ear. She jabbed the Off button and gulped three breaths of air, laden with salt and exhaust fumes. What was going on? Had Pam called Lucas and devised some scheme to get her book sales back on track? What if Lucas hadn't meant any of it? But why would he have put himself through it if he didn't love her?

*Uh, the money?*

She felt like a sailboat, pushed at the whimsy of the wind, and she'd just suffered a gust from an unexpected direction.

But this was the new Kate. The one who didn't have to plan every action. She was going to go with the flow. And right now, she needed to find Lucas, find out if he meant what he said.

Kate stood, hitching the bag on her shoulder, and turned toward town.

When she reached Main Street, she hailed a cab and gave him the address. Though she hadn't slept, the phone call and nervous energy at seeing Lucas again kept her alert.

*What will I say to him? Do I have the courage to face him? To put up my sails and let the wind take me where it may?*

Her muscles tightened until they cramped. She relaxed her hold on the leather handle of the overnight bag as Lucas's words returned to her: *"Love isn't some item on a checklist."*

Maybe sometimes you had to loosen your grip. But it was scary. It required trust and faith. Two things she ran short on.

*If there's anyone I can trust, it's Lucas.* Kate allowed herself that.

Reminded herself it was true. He'd never given her any reason to distrust him.

*"I love her. I have for a long time, and I always will."* She'd played his words over and over on the drive, drinking them up, soothing her troubled spirit with the promise. But now she wondered if he meant them.

A picture of her mom flashed in her mind. She was hunched over the kitchen table in her terry bathrobe, a bottle of scotch in her bony hand. A photo album was open on the table in front of her, and her hand smoothed over the glossy page as if she stroked the face in the photo. How many times had she seen her mother like that, dying one memory at a time?

Kate shook the thought. She wasn't her mother. And Lucas wasn't her father. It was like he'd said all along. She needed to stop analyzing and let herself love him. Let herself be loved, if he was willing. She couldn't think of anyone more trustworthy.

When the cab pulled in the drive, Kate withdrew some cash and paid the driver, then gathered her bag and exited the car. Lucas's old truck was in the drive. He'd surely heard the cab on the gravel, yet even after it pulled away, the front door remained closed.

Kate walked toward the house and up the steps, hesitating on the porch. Lifting her hand, she rapped on the wooden door, anticipating Bo's loud, gruff bark. But the only reply was the sound of the wind swishing through the trees. The small window in the door revealed only darkness. She knocked again. Maybe he was in the shower. It was still early for a Saturday, though Lucas was normally out and about by now.

She bit her lip, wondering if she should enter. Before she could dissuade herself, she twisted the knob and stepped inside.

"Lucas?" The rich aroma of brewed coffee permeated the house.

The bedroom was empty, the blankets a tangled heap at the foot of the bed. The bathroom was dark, and several crumpled towels littered the floor. She smiled.

"Lucas?" In the kitchen, his empty Nantucket mug sat on the table. The coffeemaker was still plugged in. He must've taken Bo for a walk.

Kate exited through the back, passing the gazebo, tracing the numerous footprints down the sandy path. The beach was empty except for a few gulls, plucking through the wet sand. Kate looked down the shoreline toward the Wrights' house. The beach was deserted as far as she could see.

She looked the other direction, and her eyes paused on two figures: a man and a dog.

*Lucas.*

Her feet carried her down the shoreline, her heart pumping in rhythm with her quick steps. Halfway there, Bo spotted her and lumbered toward her, but Lucas stared out across the ocean, oblivious to her appearance. Bo reached her side and barreled into her leg, tail wagging.

"Hi, boy." At least Bo was happy to see her again. It was Lucas she was unsure of.

Kate looked at Lucas in time to see him turn. He stilled, watching her approach. She closed the distance between them with long, eager strides. As she neared, she tried to read his expression, but the sun glinted over his shoulder, making it impossible to decipher.

She stopped a car's length away, suddenly uncertain. Would he welcome her home after she'd left so suddenly? He'd asked her to stay, but would he forgive her for leaving?

Fear left her mouth dry, sucked the words from her lips. It clawed at her throat and churned her thoughts like sand in the surf.

Her limbs felt as stiff as a ship's mast. Tears glazed her eyes, and she told herself it was the biting wind.

Then he moved, walking toward her, stopping just a touch away. "You came back," he said.

His eyes were just the way she remembered, warm and soft. Welcoming.

"I had to see you," she said.

"Why?"

All the words she'd planned in the car scattered like startled gulls. Pam's call had changed everything. She was no longer sure of anything, least of all, Lucas's feelings.

"I saw the interview." *Was it all a ruse, or did you mean it?*

"I was hoping you'd watch." He tilted his head. "Are you angry?"

He was remembering the voice mail she'd left. Her anger had drained away with his proclamation of love. "No." The wind kicked up, and she pulled her sweater tighter. She had to settle this before her heart jumped through her rib cage. "Pam called."

He tucked his hands in his pockets. "She told you, then?"

Suddenly, Kate realized it didn't matter why Lucas had done the interview or what plan Pam had been talking about. She'd come to tell Lucas how she felt, and she was going to do it.

"She didn't tell me anything." Kate gathered her courage and drew a shaky breath. "I realized something last night while I watched you on TV." *I love her. I have for a long time, and I always will.* "His words were a pedestal for her courage.

"What's that?"

Kate swallowed the fear and took a step closer. The wind ruffled his hair, and she smoothed it from his face, then trailed her fingertips down the rough plane of his jaw. "I love you."

She ignored the burning in her eyes and plunged forward, a sailboat into the wind. "I don't know when it started or how it happened. I only know that you captured my heart, and I don't want it back. I want to stay here forever. I want to wake up to your stubbly, scratchy face and lie next to you in bed, even if you snore loudly enough to peel the paint off the walls. I want to—

Lucas broke off her words with his kiss. Kate felt his fingers sliding into her hair, knocking her cap to the ground. She relished the tenderness in his touch, and as he claimed her, she gave herself fully to him.

When she finally pulled away, it was only to look him in the eyes. "Did you really—love me from the beginning?" She had to know if it was true. Had to see him face-to-face when he said it.

One corner of his lip drew up. "Yeah."

She let it soak in. "And that's why you took me as your bride?"

He cupped her chin. "The only reason."

Kate released her pent-up breath. It was true, then. Everything he'd said, everything that mattered, was true.

Lucas reached into his pocket and withdrew something. He took her hand and opened his palm.

"My wedding band," Kate said.

He looked her in the eye, pausing with the ring at the tip of her finger. "I love you, Kate Wright. There aren't enough miles on the earth to separate you from it. I want you to be mine." He squeezed her hand. "Fully mine." He looked at her, looked into her.

"I want that too." Kate said.

Lucas slid it in place. It was right where it belonged.

*I'm right where I belong.*

He placed a kiss on her mouth and wrapped his strong arms around her. She felt safe in his arms. Loved. Cherished.

"Forever this time?" he asked.

She snuggled into his chest, inhaling the familiar scent of him, all musky and woodsy. *Man, I missed that.* "Forever." She smiled at the taste of the word on her tongue. No temporary arrangement this time. No twelve-month escape clause. She wanted in, and she never wanted out again.

She fingered the wedding band with her thumb. "My finger has felt naked since I took it off."

Lucas lifted her hand and kissed it. "Too bad I didn't accept the money for the interview. Could've bought you one heck of a diamond."

Kate squeezed his hand. "I could put the other one back on."

"Don't you dare." Lucas gave her a mock glare before pulling her back in his arms. "Did Pam tell you I called her?" He asked against her hair.

"You called *her*?" Kate couldn't imagine why he'd do that.

"I told her I loved you and asked what I could do to save your career and—" Lucas swept Kate off her feet, as a wave rushed under their feet. He set her down up shore on the dry sand. "Didn't think you'd want your shoes wet."

Bo bumped Lucas's thigh, a slobbery tennis ball in his jaws. Lucas tossed the ball a long ways down the beach.

"What did Pam say?" Kate slipped her hands into Lucas's, savoring the security of his warm grip.

"She said women love a fairy-tale romance."

Kate laughed, joy bubbling inside for the first time in a long time. "And you love being the knight in shining armor."

His shoulders rose in a shrug and he gave her his crooked grin. "If the armored boot fits . . ."

Kate elbowed Lucas then fell in step beside him as they walked toward home.

Home.

The word had a nice ring to it, and she felt a smile lift her lips. It wouldn't matter where she was or what she was doing, home would always be wherever Lucas was.

# Acknowledgments

My deepest thanks go to all the people who had a hand in the making of this book. Thanks to my editor, Amanda Bostic, and the amazing team of creative, talented people in Thomas Nelson's fiction department. I'm truly honored and blessed to work with you. Thanks to Leslie Peterson for helping me polish the story. Thanks to my wonderful agent, Karen Solem, and my critique partner, Colleen Coble, who squeezed in my chapters while on her own tight deadline. Thanks to my writing buds, Kristin Billerbeck, Colleen Coble, and Diann Hunt: you bless my life in immeasurable ways!

A special thanks to my readers—you make it all worthwhile! I'd love to hear from you. E-mail me at denise@denisehunterbooks.com, or visit my Web site at www.DeniseHunterBooks.com.

# Reading Group Guide

1. Lucas's love for Kate is an allegory for Christ's love for us. In what ways are the timing and qualities of Lucas's love symbolic of Christ's love?

2. What are some of the ways Lucas saved Kate in the story? What was Kate's reaction to his saving her? How has Christ saved you? Have you ever responded in some of the ways that Kate did?

3. One thing Kate was apt to do is fix things on her own. In our culture, that's a popular reaction. Do you respond to crises in a similar way? Is that the best way to deal with problems?

4. One of the hardest things to do when trouble comes is wait. Kate had difficulty waiting when her publisher was trying to find a solution to the problem. Is it hard for you to wait on God? Psalm 46:10 says, "Be still, and know that I am God." How can that be applied to trying times? Psalm 27:14 says, "Wait for the LORD; be strong and take heart and wait for the LORD." What can we learn about patience from this verse?

5. When Kate made the choice to leave Lucas, he knew it was a decision Kate had to make for herself. How has God been patient in waiting for you to come to Him?

6. When Kate left Lucas, he said that a thousand miles couldn't separate her from his love. How is Christ's love like that?

7. Lucas laid it all on the line when he faced his biggest fear and publicly proclaimed his love for Kate. How has Christ proclaimed His love for you?

8. Even though Kate broke Lucas's heart by leaving and by fighting her relationship with him, he gladly welcomed her back. Have you ever pushed Christ away or run from His love? What does it feel like to know that no matter what you do, He will always welcome you home?

On the beautiful island of Nantucket,
salt and roses scent the air,
waves sparkle over hidden currents,
and a storm-tossed soul seeks safe harbor.

## AVAILABLE NOW

THOMAS NELSON
*Since 1798*

# An Excerpt from
## *Surrender Bay*

### Prologue

"Why'd you wait so long to turn on the flashlight last night?" Landon asked.

Even though evening shadows crawled over Landon's backyard, Samantha Owens could see his eyes searching hers. He hadn't said anything about her delay before now, but she could tell he'd been bothered all day because he didn't once tug her ponytail.

She lifted her body out of the waist-deep Nantucket water, flipping over to land on the pier with a sodden plop. The outdoor lamp lashed to the last post spotlighted her. Her bathing suit clung to her stomach, and she pulled at the fabric just to hear the sucking sound as it left her skin.

She looked over her shoulder and saw Landon's mom through the lit kitchen window, washing supper dishes. Mr. Reed appeared just then and pulled her against his chest. She laughed at something he said, then turned in his arms. Sam looked away.

Landon splashed through the water and hoisted himself onto the pier beside her. His arms had filled out over the summer, and he'd shot up a good two inches. Sam wasn't sure she liked him changing so much.

"Did you hear me?"

Landon bumped Sam's foot under the water, and she felt him

watching her. She shrugged as casually as she could. "I went to bed late. I got a book on the Red Sox. Did you know they used to be called the Boston Americans?" A breeze drifted over her wet skin, tightening it into gooseflesh.

"Your light wasn't on." Skepticism coated his words.

Changing the subject never worked with Landon. When would she learn? "I snuck in the bathroom to read. You know how Emmett is." Landon didn't know the half of it, but some things she'd never tell anyone. Not even Landon.

Sam lay back, resting her spine against the wooden planks. She closed her eyes and wished she could stay just like this all night, listening to the sound of crickets and the splash of water kissing the shoreline.

"I was worried."

His voice sounded older, deeper than she remembered. "You worry too much."

He shifted, and Sam opened her eyes. He was lying beside her, his body a plank-width away, his head turned toward her. The moonlight glimmered on his hair, and shadows settled between his drawn eyebrows. "Don't forget the flashlight again."

Sam didn't much like being told what to do, but something in the tone of his voice touched the deepest place in her as no one ever had. "I won't."

He held Sam's gaze as if testing her sincerity. After a moment, she crossed her eyes at him, watching his face blur into a double image.

"Weirdo," he said.

"Freak."

"Slime bucket."

"Geek."

A mosquito stung her neck, and she slapped at it. Her skin was already speckled with half a dozen bites, but they didn't bother her much. She was surprised Mrs. Reed hadn't come out yet with the can of Off!, but maybe she and Mr. Reed were too busy smooching in the kitchen.

Sam imagined the inside of her own house, just two doors down, and felt a shadow press its way into her soul. Her mom would be calling her in soon.

She turned to Landon, glad to see his face had softened. "Wanna have a sleepover at your house? We can decide what we want to put in our time capsule."

Landon glanced away, and Sam didn't recognize the look that passed over his face.

"We're getting too old for that."

*Well, la-di-da.* Maybe Landon thought turning thirteen had made him all grown up. Sam suddenly felt every day of their seven-month age gap. "Time capsules aren't just for kids, you know."

One corner of his mouth slid upward, but not quite enough to bunch up his cheek. He pulled himself upright and splashed back into the murky water. "I wasn't talking about the capsule."

She wanted to ask what he meant, but she could tell he didn't want her to by the way his head dipped low.

"Samantha!" Her mom's voice had an edge that said she'd been calling awhile.

"Coming!" Though Sam knew she should get up and go, her body lay against the boards as heavy as a ship anchor. She should have gotten out of the water hours ago so she wouldn't drip water across the kitchen floor. Too late now. At least Emmett wasn't home.

"I should go in too," Landon said, wading alongside the pier.

"The mosquitoes are bad tonight." He smacked at his arm.

Why couldn't she just stay at Landon's house? If he was so worried, why didn't he invite her over? He stopped at the shoreline, where the water licked at his feet.

"You'd better go."

He'd stand there until she left, he was just that stubborn.

Sam pulled her feet from the water and walked down the pier. They crossed paths in front of his parents' Adirondack chairs.

Landon turned and lifted his fingers. "Don't forget the flashlight."

"I won't." Her feet carried her across the Reeds' yard, then across Miss Biddle's. She knew by feel the moment she stepped into her own backyard. Emmett kept the grass clipped so short their lawn had turned wheat brown. It drove her mom crazy.

Sam entered the cottage through the back door, hoping she could sneak into her room and change into dry clothes before her mom saw how wet she was, but the squeak of the screen door gave her away.

"Samantha." Her mom's lips pinched together as she looked Sam over.

"Sorry, I forgot." Ribbons of water dripped from the edges of her swimsuit, carving rivers between goose bumps. They trickled over her ankles as she made a mad dash past her mom to her bedroom.

"I'll clean it up," she called.

"You bet you'll clean it up. I don't know why I bother cleaning around here."

Sam rummaged through her drawers, pushing aside the nightgowns her mom had bought, and pulled out her favorite long T-shirt and a stretchy pair of shorts.

A few minutes later, Sam entered the kitchen and took a towel from the drawer, then wiped up the mini puddles. The bones of her knees knocked against the wood floor as she crept along, swiping in wide arcs.

"Why do you wear that ratty old thing? You look like a boy, Samantha."

"It's comfortable." Sam slung her wet ponytail across her shoulder.

"You missed a spot." Her mom pointed toward the door.

Sam backtracked and dried the area. By the time she finished, her mom had left the kitchen, so Sam tossed the towel in the washer and returned to her room, shutting the door. The doorknob was the old-fashioned kind, cut glass with clear angles. She'd thought it beautiful when she was little. When the sunlight flooded the room and hit the glass, it splayed prisms of light across the wall.

Now she wished for a plain old metal doorknob, the kind with a lock.

Sam turned out the light and slipped under the quilt. Before she lay against the pillow, she reached into her bedside drawer and withdrew the flashlight. The switch flipped on with ease, and she set it on the wooden sill of the window. She turned on her side and tucked the covers under her chin.

She lay that way for a long time, hearing the sounds of her mom getting ready for bed. She knew it would be a while before Emmett came home, but still she listened for the sound of his car, for the crunch of gravel under his work boots. She listened until her ears were so full of silence it seemed they would burst.

Sometime later she startled awake to the sound of the front door opening. She heard her mom talking; then Emmett's voice rumbled through her closed door. "She didn't pull the weeds like I told her to." He cursed.

"Well, she can do it tomorrow." Her mom's voice was fading.

"How much did you lose tonight?"

The sound of their bedroom door clicking shut resonated in her ears.

"Get up."

Sam's arm stung with the sharp slap, and she shot up in bed. Dawn's light filtered through the window, gray and dim.

Emmett was already walking away. "Go pull the weeds like I told you yesterday. No breakfast until you're done."

"I already did." In her fog of sleep, the words slipped out.

He turned and hauled her out of bed, and her knees buckled as her feet hit the floor. Fully awake now, she realized it was Saturday and her mom was at work. "I'll do better."

He straightened, and she noticed tiny red veins lining the whites of his eyes. She looked at the rug beneath her feet. He released her burning arm.

When he left, she traded her long T-shirt for an old, faded one and set to work in the flower beds, pulling the weeds she'd missed the day before. The sun was nowhere to be seen, hiding behind a thick curtain of angry clouds. She'd emptied two bucketfuls and was back on her knees when Emmett opened the back door. The squawk of the hinges made her jump.

"Since you didn't do what you were told the first time, you can pull the dead blooms and trim the hedges too." With that, he disappeared into the house.

She sat back on her haunches and brushed the hair from her face with dirty fingers. She scanned the rows of lilies, and she pictured all the rose blooms in the front yard and the hedges lining the yard. With a sigh, she leaned forward and grabbed a dandelion, wrapping it around her hand and yanking hard. She tossed it, roots and all, in the bucket.

The rain started then, first a drop on her hand, then one on her cheek. Within a minute, a steady shower fell. She planted her knees in the dirt and began pulling wilted blooms from the lily plants. By the time she'd finished the first one, the dirt under her knees was mud, and her empty stomach twisted. She scooted toward the next plant and went back to work.

Sam didn't see Landon until he fell to his knees beside her. Wordlessly, he plucked a bloom and then another, tossing them in the bucket. When he finally looked at her, his hair hung in wet, dark strands over his eyes and a clump of dirt smudged his cheek, and Sam knew she looked no better.

His lips turned up on one side, and she couldn't stop her own smile.

They worked until the beds and hedges were done and their clothes were soaked clean through. Landon reheated the pancakes his dad had made that morning, then they watched TV with his younger brother, Bailey, until lunchtime. By then, the sun had come out again, and the threesome played all afternoon, passing a football and fishing off the end of the Reeds' pier.

At supper time, Landon headed inside, and Sam said she had to go in too. But when she got home, her mom and Emmett were gone, so she had a bowl of Lucky Charms and a handful of peanuts. When she saw Landon in his backyard again, she joined him, and they tossed his football until it was too dark to see.

Later, Landon stood at the water's edge, the cool water nipping at his toes, while she stood poised barefoot on the first plank of the pier like a 747 aimed at a runway. At the end, the light glowed against the black sky.

Even in the dimness, she saw his hard, flattened lips and knew they suppressed a reprimand, just as he knew a scolding would not stop her.

Sam smiled impishly at him, then darted forward, building speed in just a few long strides. At just the right spot, she sprang into a round-off and followed it with four back handsprings.

Her hands and feet alternately punched the boards, making a rhythmic *thud-thud, thud-thud.* She landed solidly in the spotlight four planks shy of the water. Nearly a record. She was no Mary Lou Retton or Julianne McNamara—she was too tall and big-boned to be nimble—but she didn't care so much about form.

She strode back toward Landon and stepped into the dark water, making sure to keep her clothes dry.

"I wish you wouldn't do that," Landon said before compressing his lips into a tight line again. His olive green eyes looked almost black in the nighttime shadows, and she could see the shimmering lights from the water reflected in them.

"I haven't fallen yet," Sam said as she worked her toes into the silty sand until the tops of her feet were covered.

"When you do, don't come crying to me."

Sam smirked at that because Landon knew she never cried, and if she ever did, he'd be the first one to scoop her up and sweep away her tears.

When the moon was high in the sky, Landon's mom called him in, so they said good night and Sam went home. She could hear the TV blaring in her mom and Emmett's room, so she crept into her bedroom and shut the door. After getting ready for bed, she lifted her window to invite the night breeze inside and set the flashlight on the sill.

Sam curled up on her side and closed her eyes. Sometime later, she heard her mom and Emmett talking on the back porch. She strained to hear them.

"The flower beds look nice," her mom said.

"Took the better part of the day."

Sam heard a rush of exhaled breath and envisioned the puff of cigarette smoke from her mom's mouth.

"What are our plans for tomorrow, baby?" Emmett asked.

Sam pictured her mom crossing her arms, shrugging him off.

Sam thought she must have missed her answer because there was such a long pause. Then she heard her mom's reply. "We don't have any."

There was a haunting tone in her mother's words that Sam hadn't heard before.

Their voices lowered to low mumbles she couldn't interpret, so Sam listened to the nocturnal orchestra outside her window. A loon called out over the buzz of the insects, and the water licked the shoreline. If she concentrated hard, she could hear Mom's boat knocking against the pier bumper. A breeze rattled the tree leaves and carried the sweet scent of salt-spray roses through the air. Her body began to relax. Her thoughts slowed and her breaths deepened.